DULCIE
GOES NATIVE

DULCIE
GOES NATIVE

Bad Housekeeping
(Volume 4)

Sue Limb

Published by Solidus
www.soliduspress.com

15 January 1994

Pack up Bonkbuster and post to publisher, though have my doubts whether semi-apocalyptic ending will prove acceptable, with heroine giving birth in garage in St Tropez. (Second Coming: girl called Nellie.) Come to think of it, I wonder by my troth who the hell was St Tropez? They do say Mary Magdalen retired to the South of France, confirming her status as the glamour queen of the Gospels. I, however, no longer have any wish to go there. I seem to recall a roll of film costing the best part of a tenner – and this was eight years ago.

An orgy of holiday speculation has seized Cranford Gardens. Elaine comes round bearing catalogues.

"Why don't we share a *gîte*?" she enquires sweetly. "Look, here's an old stone-built Provencal *mas*, surrounded by woods. 'Nightingales sing in the early summer'. Have you ever heard a nightingale, Dulcie?" Admit not, except on BBC sound effects record. "It's got its own little swimming pool, too. How lovely! We could lie by the pool while the men cook."

"What men?"

"Well, Tom, and your dear spouse."

"You think Tom should come too?"

"Why not?" Elaine ducks her head towards mine in a naughty and intimate way as the children are watching TV four feet away. "You never know, the old embers might burst into flame."

Deplore this possibility, and insist that if they did, I wouldn't hesitate to chuck them out of the back door on a shovel. Elaine looks disappointed. I think, sometimes, she's a bit of a bawd.

"Tom's still very sweet on you, you know," she whispers – unnecessarily, as children, when watching TV, are oblivious. I often think I could collapse and die in deafening technicolour next to them and remain unnoticed till the National Anthem or whatever they have at the end of TV these days. Have not watched TV till the bitter end for years.

1

Hours of motionless goggling can only safely be attempted by the young and fit.

Assure Elaine that Tom's sweetness and light is the problem and that, all things considered, I prefer the sour darkness that seems to hang around my spouse.

"Oh yes," agrees Elaine at once, "Gordon is a scream."

"Do you know," I confide, "he wants a dish." She is flummoxed. "A satellite dish," I elucidate. "So he can watch the cricket from the West Indies."

"I bet he'll peep at the porno while you're out," giggles Elaine.

"I bet I'll peep at it while he's out, too."

"Oh Dulcie! You're a scream!"

So we're two screams, apparently. It sounds like the beginning of a John Major proverb. As in 'We were two screams short of a Sunday afternoon in January'.

One of the brochures features a visit to Transylvania. Perhaps Spouse might fit in well there. Children clamour for Dracula and it's certainly cheaper than Eurodisney.

"Oh, but the food . . ." falters Elaine. "It might be a bit unhygienic, mightn't it? All beetroot soup and black bread . . ."

Secretly feel urge to experience the last beetroot soup and black bread before the continent disappears under a welter of Eurocoke and Eurochips. Indeed might be preferable to experience quaint local gutrot rather than non-specific Eurothritis.

Wonder if, within a decade, we will avoid holiday angst entirely by strapping on our virtual reality goggles and be transported to our respective idylls without ever leaving the sofa: Elaine to Majorca, Spouse to Sabina Park, self to a green lane in County Mayo, kids to Orlando.

Speaking of Orlando . . . perhaps holidays will be available in works of literature, with the hero or heroine of your choice. Confide this idea to Elaine (not an easy task) and suppose aloud that Spouse would choose to frolic in the Dorset fields with Tess. Children would, I fear, desire to plunge hock deep in the project known as Where's Wally? (In the Cabinet is the obvious answer.) Since I am now a bit too old to roll on the moss with Heathcliff (fibrositis etc.) will happily settle for picnic at Box Hill with Emma.

Suspect I would still get stung, all the same.

22 January

Whilst filling up with petrol, overhear strange conversation between two lorry drivers, or as they seem to be known nowadays, truckers.

"Trouble with 'im is, 'e ent got a shag in 'im."

"'Sright. A good shag 'd kill 'im, look."

"What about them other dirty bastards though eh? What!? Benders!"

"Ar. Might as well admit it, mightn't they? Might as well say if bum's on the menu I'll have some, John."

Assume that they must be discussing affairs of state, and am sufficiently distracted to buy a sack of coal, or perhaps coke.

On my return, Spouse stirs briefly from his deep hibernation and lights a real fire in the sitting room. Elaine and I watch him hold a sheet of newspaper across the fireplace to help it draw. I am reminded of the frozen backs and mottled legs of my childhood. Spouse places himself before fire and slowly acquires the demeanour of a boiled ham. I worry about stray sparks.

Repeat truckers' comments on PM's Back to Sickbags campaign.

"Don't you mean Back to Bastards?" Spouse corrects me (his favourite mode). Passing the bookcase on my way out to kitchen, I glimpse a book which, for a split second, seems to be called 'The Oxford Book of Bastards'. But alas, closer inspection reveals it to be *The Oxford Book of Ballads*. Pause and peruse for a moment.

"There should be a directory of Ministers' Sinister Offspring," suggests Spouse. "Called 'The Oxford Book of Bastards' Bastards'. Or 'Who's Whose'."

Elaine sighs, and smiles politely. I often think she wishes she could add three spoonsful of sugar to us and stir vigorously.

I take *The Oxford Book of Ballads* to the kitchen with me and discover that families were breaking up, indeed gleefully slicing each other up, seven centuries ago. 'And after ye breake, The Cruell Brothers; Lord Randall Fears He is

3

Poisoned; and Ladye Diana vowes to Lock Hirselfe up in a Tower for XX yeares.'

"Dulcie? It's Alice. We're in Sintra. Listen!" Hear distant, presumably Portuguese, cock crow. "Did you hear that? Isn't it wonderful?" Agree. Feel it is the middle-aged equivalent of those saucy sex-by-phone lines. Dial a cock, dial a lark, etc. "Why don't you join us? We've got this lovely old *Casa* for the next two months. It's warm enough to have lunch on the terrace. And there's a sour old cook. Saskia's bet me a tenner I can't make her smile before St Valentine's day. Do join us. Bring the kids and Gordon. Or better still, leave them behind."

Make note of her phone number with plangent sigh, promise to get back to her in a day or two, and attend to kettle's steaming tantrum.

Search for biscuits but only one stale Eccles cake left. No point in offering it for five to share so secretly wolf it down myself. Let them eat coke. Punished for this violation of family values by phone ringing again. Answer in irritable bark only to find it is my publisher Cleo Goldstone who has at last had time to read the completed MS of my bonkbuster. Cringe in confident expectation of brickbats, but . . .

"It's terrific, Dulcie. All it needs is a bit more Euro-sex in the second half. You know. The odd bonk on the Left Bank, a romeo or two in Rome. A couple of weeks' work. Can't you go off somewhere for a bit of peace and quiet, tell the family to get stuffed for a week or two? It'd do you *so much good*."

Ring off tingling with excitement at the thought of telling the family to get stuffed. Fate must have contrived that Cleo's phone call should have followed hot on the heels of Alice's. Experience deep urge to set up feminist *ménage à trois* in Southern Portugal. Living in Sintra. Particularly since Sintra was one of Byron's old haunts. Only problem: how to sell it to Spouse?

Suddenly notice desiccated old lemon in fruit bowl. Symbol perhaps of Spouse. But suggests also Lenten cuisine. Fly to cupboard: even we have egg, milk, flour. Whizz together and make delectable (well, by my standards) pile of pancakes. Carry into sitting room with fresh tea. Am welcomed with rapture especially by Elaine who clearly regards me as the embodiment of family values.

4

Little does she suspect it is to escape the cursed tentacles of family that I have so cunningly exerted myself.

29 January

In Rusbridge, we endure the rainy season. Have formed cunning plan to escape to Southern Portugal and stay with Alice and Saskia in their *Casa* in Sintra. Alice and Saskia are thrilled to find themselves in a place where most of the locals are Lisboans. Another gay emigré was William Beckford, who was forced to flee Britain in the 1790s because of a homosexual scandal. *Plus ça change.* Though in those days buggery was a hanging offence. Or do I mean vice versa? Being a frigid old bat I would much rather have an early night with P.D. James than indulge in either.

Am intrigued however by the thought of certain Portuguese Celtic tribes who, Strabo informs us in 20 BC, 'consulted prisoners' entrails without removing them'. (*The Rough Guide to Portugal.*) Early gynaecology, perhaps. Wonder if I shall ever have to have a hysterectomy.

"It's wonderful, Dulcie," Alice reported after hers. "Only don't let them cut you – make sure you have the sort where they pull it out through the vagina."

Although she said this several years ago, I still cannot think of it without getting hysterical. What I really need is a hysteriaectomy.

Banish all thoughts of gynaecology and menopause or, as Portuguese might have it, *Minhopaoz.* Instead, tiptoe through Sintra with my Rough Guide. Love the idea of a rough guide. "Right, you 'orrible lot, this 'ere's the bleedin' Moorish castle, ennit, eh?" etc. Secretly practise favourite bits from phrasebook such as *'Boa Tarde'*, which allegedly means Good Afternoon though I would much rather it meant The Snake is Late.

Only problem: getting around Spouse, unreasonably obstructive since my escape depends on his staying at home and looking after kids.

"Mrs Body'll help, and Tracey, and Elaine." I coax. Spouse

5

groans ungratefully. "And if I finish the rewrites we'll get the money due on delivery." Spouse sighs grudgingly.

"Oh well. I suppose if you must have seminars on the menopause, I'd rather you had them several hundred miles away."

Refuse to rise to this bait. Instead smile graciously. Anything so long as I can go to Portugal. Issue silent prayer to the gods to send a modest sign. Even Spouse would surely yield to angel in full heavenly rig bearing what used to be called a Madonna lily and insisting, "And lo, thy wife shall go south into another country, and thou shalt not complain, yea even though thou sufferest little children for three weeks, mate."

"But three weeks——" his moan is cut short by a strange but determined slither of dirty water which wriggles in under the back door as though it means business. Intrigued. Open back door: yard area awash, three inches deep. Drain has clearly seized up. Deluge running off back garden, which falls steeply down towards the house, something I insisted would present no difficulties whatsoever when I first fell in love with house. Performed similar acts of self-delusion vis-à-vis Spouse's laziness and Tom's naiveté.

"What do you expect me to do?" shrugs Spouse. "Build an Ark?" Children appear and delight in the novelty of paddling indoors.

"Mummy . . . ? Was Joan of Arc Noah's wife?"

"No . . . she was a French . . . sort of general thingie."

Suspect, if I had been Noah's wife, I should have put my foot down when it came to the two slugs. Spouse returns soaked from yard, and glares at me as if the weather is somehow a side effect of my malicious *Minhopaos*.

"Bloody drain's solid," he grunts. "Call Dyno-rod."

"Why don't we ask Tom first?" suggests Henry, and is encouraged to nip across the road and fetch him.

"I expect he'll be out," growls Spouse, torn between his habitual desire to heap scorn on Tom, and his present need to benefit from his skills.

Tom arrives immediately with rods, kneels in the mire, and scrabbles about arm-deep in our drain. Spouse retires to sitting room to avoid the ignominy of being only a spectator at this manly sport. I hover, congratulate, encourage, mop, and feel enormous relief that this particular flood does

6

not involve the sewer. Ten minutes later, Tom, stinking but triumphant, sits at our kitchen table and accepts the laurel wreath.

"I hear you're off to Portugal," he whispers with a wink. "I've always fancied Sintra . . ."

It's hard to refuse a man anything when he's just had his arm up your clogged-up sluice.

26 February

After living in Sintra for three weeks, I return to the arms of my family. Just hope it's not heavy shelling. Spouse opens with light sniper fire, supposing that Rusbridge looks grey after the lemon trees of Portugal. Will not mention lunch al fresco, or being gloriously buffeted by wind and sun on the ramparts of the Moorish castle. Oh how I love the Moors. They are so moorish.

Attempt to disarm him instead by announcing that Bonkbuster is finished (though this is a lie-ette) and emphasise the extent to which Alice and Saskia are currently obsessed with The Shining Woman Tarot. Do not reveal, however, that my Tarot card seems to be The Tower. ('She shouts with the thunder. She dances in fire. She grabs hold of the dirt. Signifying . . . revelation . . . overwhelming or ecstatic experience . . .')

One glance at the interior of 196 Cranford Gardens, however, convinces me that a good deal of dirt-grabbing will be necessary before there is any hope of ecstasy.

"Mummeee!" cries Harriet with a glint of devilment in her eye, "we've got satellite TV! And there are ladies on it showing off their rude bits!" Spouse blushes.

"It was only a German advert for Nivea," he sighs.

I am led back outdoors to admire the tasteful dark grey dish nestling in a gully above the porch. Pray that it is not visible from the road.

"It's only for the cricket," insists Spouse defensively. "We can send it back afterwards."

"Won't you miss the Nivea ads?"

"It's all unbelievably naff and boring," he drawls. "Thank

God we're not Germans, that's all I can say. In fact, thank God we're not foreigners."

"To the rest of the world," I inform him, "we are foreigners."

Flick through the endless new channels available to us, though convinced that they all must be inferior to our own dear Home Service. Am diverted by film starring Sean Connery speaking German without moving his lips. More channels reveal more German ventriloquism. It seems there is nothing the Germans have not dubbed. Wonder how they translate those classic old war films. "The Jerry blighter's bought it!" for instance. Come to think of it, wonder how you'd translate it into English.

Understand no German whatever despite having mysteriously acquired German O level. Recall I was always rather frightened and depressed by the black thorny appearance of the Gothic script. Wonder if my godmother's old copy of Goethe's *Faust* is still around. Ransack bookcase, locate and peruse. There seems to be a character in it called Lustiger Person. Nivea-ad addict, presumably.

Further in, discover character called Wagner. Wonder if he is any relation. Surprised to find him spouting a couplet I understand:

Ach Gott! die Kunst ist lang;
Und kurtz ist unser Leben.

This must be Goethe dubbing that old Latin tag '*Ars Longa Vita Brevis*', or 'Life's too short for *War and Peace*'. Well, Wagner should know. His *Ars* is certainly *Ars* and *Ars Longa* than anyone else's. Pleased by this brief moment of comprehension, but the subsequent couplet is obscure.

Mir wird, bei meinem kritischen Bestreben,
Doch oft um Kopf und Busen bang.

Do not like the sound of *Busen bang*. Suspect it may turn out to be Lustiger Personen Fodder of the Late Night variety.

"Well, well," marvels Spouse, bringing in the tea without being asked (but that will soon fall away, alas), "who would have dreamt that satellite TV would inspire you to reread Goethe in the original German?"

Amused at the thought of my rereading Goethe at all, let alone in the original German. After children have been safely heeled in for the night, restore Goethe to the bookcase for another three decades and settle down to finish *Pride and Prejudice* whilst Spouse watches sport against foreigners. Alice would say that sport only ferments pride and prejudice, and is a form of ritualised war. Quite restful that she is still in Sintra.

After stumps are drawn (always has a nasty dental sound, that) we flick through the channels in order to observe the Germans dishing the dirt. The Dish of the Day is a Valkyrie endowed with *Ars Longa, Busen* and *Bang* – but (a curiously touching human detail, this), a massive zit on her chin. Oh well. Don't mention the wart . . . Just pray they never get their hands on Blue Peter.

5 March

Deeply upset by death of Mark Hebden on *The Archers*. Can't help feeling it was all my fault. If only I hadn't found him so boring, perhaps it would never have happened. Still, be grateful for small mercies. At least it wasn't Joe Grundy. Come to think of it, Joe's a widower. Perhaps, in time, Shula will become Mrs Grundy.

Harriet's birthday arrives. She requests a canary. I make a secret trip to the pet shop. There is only one canary, left over from last season, and he is green. Cannot remember canaries being green in the past and wonder if perhaps he has gone off in some way. If indeed he is a he. I am assured he is.

"He used to sing quite a lot, but he's gone a bit quiet recently," admits the Petshop Boy. Perhaps he is depressed by *The Archers*. No doubt it is a mistake to buy a canary left over from last year. But on the other hand, he awakens my liberal instincts. In buying him I will be doing my bit for the less able bird.

But what about the Robin Redbreast in a Cage dilemma? Things behind bars have always upset me – except barmen of course. There's probably an Avian Wing of Animal Liberation

9

called Nesty International. So what if he is green? Green has resonance. We can call him Graham.

Hurriedly purchase him, together with largest possible cage, seed, grit, bath, ten new carpets, etc. etc.

Convinced he will die in the icy blast before I can stagger across the car park, but only mishap involves my dropping and treading on his bag of grit, which explodes. He is silent on the way home, but utters a faint squeak when placed on the kitchen table.

"What's that?" enquires Spouse. "Supper?"

Harriet informs me she will never speak to Daddy again but the canary is Ace. Assume for a while that this is to be his name but despite Spouse's suggestion of Wharf and my partiality for Gregory Peck, Harriet settles for Charlie.

Her birthday party is at Rusbridge Pool, which we have hired complete with inflatables, lifeguards, etc. Thank God I don't have to organise Pass the Parcel or sprain my wrist making sandwiches. The pool has a spectators' gallery where, afterwards, we can have The Tea (crisps, Coke, and cake).

Elaine-over-the-road, with that enthusiasm for children's parties which only the childless can muster, begs to be allowed to attend. Arrive to find all our little guests milling about in the lobby and creating a nuisance. Tell Spouse to marshal them, and, clutching my Nibbles, dash up into the humid embrace of the spectators' gallery.

Glasses steam up. Temperature must be close to ninety. Feel faint. Wonder if I was a canary in a previous existence. Throw off coat, cardigan and sweater, revealing torn old black T-shirt. As glasses clear, a ravishing vision appears before me. It is Elaine in what I believe is known as a playsuit: the sort of thing Edwardian gentlemen used to wear when swimming, picnicking, being painted by Rousseau, etc.

Spouse arrives carrying two large bottles of Cream Soda and two of Coke.

"Oh, Cream Soda!" cries Elaine in rapture. "We had that when I was a child! May I taste a little bit?"

She tastes it, and is transported back to Guildford in the Sixties. Spouse and I would need Tizer to get back to the Fifties.

Children splash about shrieking for an hour. Cannot believe I ever splashed about shrieking. Indeed, suspect I was never a child at all. Perhaps I am an alien, my extra-terrestrial parents having parasitised this body as a host. If this is so, I wish they had parasitised Elaine's. Watch her slinking and leaping about in her playsuit as if her bones are made of rubber.

After the racket of the swim comes the din of the party. The shrieking of children's voices expands into a band of pain that drifts inevitably down over my brows. Luckily I have brought the Solpadeine – the painkiller preferred by Robin Hood. Attempt to dissolve it in Cream Soda but it never stops fizzing. Rather like Elaine.

Return home covered with crisps, crumbs and glory to be welcomed by a sympathetic silence from the canary.

"I think," observes Spouse, "that you have managed to buy the only Trappist canary in the country."

Reply that if so, this is grounds for congratulation, not censure.

12 March

Cannot decide how to end Bonkbuster: with a bonk, a bust, or an er . . . Alice and Saskia insist that my heroine Fanny must be reunited with her mentor Gertrude Lillywhite and set up a Sapphic Salon in Salamanca. Elaine-over-the-road wants her to return to Scotland and marry dark brooding minister Dougal MacPravity.

"But I married him off to Mairi Thingummy," I object. "What's-his-name's sister."

"Well, Mairi can fall down a well or something," insists Elaine.

Harriet wants Fanny to become a mermaid. Spouse cares not how it ends as long as it ends and we can get the delivery cheque.

I would have liked apotheosis. Fanny gives birth to the Messiah: a girl, second time around. Of course there would be problems in people recognising the Messiah were he to be female, since all women perform miracles every day. Mothers of teenage children, for example, are skilled in raising the dead and feeding the five thousand.

Not sure I could turn water into wine, however. Not terribly adept at turning it into drinkable coffee. As for walking on water, I find it increasingly difficult even to walk on pavements. Publisher has vetoed second coming, anyway, so it'll have to be social realism. Seize pen, award Fanny a teaching job in Kirkcudbright and marry her off to a local librarian who looks like John Selwyn Gummer.

Then relent and rework librarian along lines of Tony Blair. Sit back and admire oeuvre. It is nearly two inches thick. A good idea, using that heavy quality paper. Sigh deeply and stroll to kitchen. Make celebratory cup of coffee and slump triumphally in chair. Huge feeling of relief slides off my shoulders like satin ball gown in Thirties movie. Place three lumps of sugar in cup as prize for reaching The End.

Tomorrow I will give up sugar, white bread, etc. But today I deserve a treat. I shall rest and indulge myself. I shall be lazy. Damn it! No teaspoon handy, or even biro, with which I have oft stirred things in the past. Teaspoons two yards away in drawer. Experience monstrous wave of indolence, and am tempted for a split second to stir my tea with my finger even though I know it would hurt quite a lot.

"Mummy! The bath tap's bunged up!"

"Get me a teaspoon, please, darling."

"But Mummy I must have a bath! I'm a mermaid and if I don't have a bath I'll dry up and die!"

Had noticed progressive malfunction of hot tap. It used to provide a splendid cascade but recently this has dwindled to a piddling widdle, and am not surprised to hear that now it has altogether ceased. Had hoped it might heal itself. Didn't want to ring Tom's company, somehow. He has been mysteriously silent recently. He threatened to turn up in Portugal during my recent sojourn there but mercifully refrained. What is he up to? Lift phone and dial Buddhist-Anarchist Plumbing Collective. Harriet produces object from her pocket.

"And Mummy! I've found this lovely earring of yours under your bed! Will you give me fifty pence as a reward?"

Examine earring. It is a small refined item consisting of pearls and gold.

"It's not mine," I sigh. "It must be Mrs Body's."

"Will she give me a reward?"

"No! What were you doing under my bed?"

"I was being a mermaid in a cave, but I banged my head."

Admire Mrs Body's taste in earrings.

I am promised a plumber in two days' time. Sigh in martyred way, and enquire as to Tom's whereabouts. He moved out of Elaine's place shortly after Christmas.

"Oh, he and Sabrina have gone to Goa," I am informed.

Egad! So he is back with his wife. More relieved than annoyed. So all's well with the world. Spouse comes in. Reach out and embrace his lower half. Not a bad old thing really. Harriet joins in and embraces us both, informing us that we are the best Mummy and Daddy in the world. Bask in this unusual harmony as usually we are various sorts of bastard.

Soon tiring of accord, Harriet runs off, and Spouse sits down looking wary.

"I'm afraid," he announces, "that I've got myself into a bit of a mess."

19 March

"What do you mean, you've got yourself into a mess?" Spouse's messes are usually financial, though he has accepted dinner invitations from disastrously boring colleagues in his time. Usually he looks defiant when in the wrong, but this time he has a strange half-apologetic air. Feel half-unnerved.

"Mummy!" Harriet rushes in. "You must come upstairs now!"

"Not now, darling. I'm talking to Daddy. In a minute."

"But . . ." Harriet writhes in agony and whispers in my ear, "I've pooed in my pants. Please help me clear it up. Please PLEASE!"

Sigh deeply and enquire whether she isn't a bit old for this sort of thing. Do not wish to blight her adult life with the sort of guts-and-lavatories angst that has blighted mine, but do not wish to go on performing nappy duties indefinitely.

"It's not my fault. I thought it was just a fart," the stricken whisper continues. Cannot help sympathising at the grotesque betrayals of nature, and beg Spouse to excuse us for a moment.

Harriet's bottom is soon restored to a sparkling state. She lies on the bathroom floor and asks me to give her a mirror so she can examine her private parts in detail.

"Oh my God, how GROSS!" she shrieks on beholding her fundament, then hurls the mirror aside and runs off, in a pathetic attempt to escape from her own arse.

Rescue mirror, managing not to look into it. Like Harriet's knickers, mirrors often seem to contain an unpleasant surprise these days. Wonder, as I go downstairs, what skeleton is about to be released from Spouse's cupboard. Although that particular image has acquired a horrible reality in recent weeks. Decide instead to concentrate on idea of spring: season when buried things burst into luxuriant and fragrant life.

"Why don't we postpone whatever it is till after the kids are in bed?" I suggest brightly, making the tea.

"No! I can't. I promised I'd tell you today. Before the sun goes down."

"Before the sun goes down?" I gasp, incredulous. "Promised who? Butch Cassidy?"

Spouse's half-hearted attempt at a smile falls off his face. Suddenly feel sick with foreboding and slump into chair. What is it? Cancer? Aids?

"It's Elaine," he pronounces in sudden burst. "She's got . . ."

"Got what?"

"She's got a bit of a thing about me, and I couldn't help getting, well – involved. I thought you'd have noticed."

Room rocks and darkens. Oh, not that. Surely not. Spare us. So familiar. So dreary. Such a cliché. Cannot speak. All the air knocked out of me by terrific wave of Stone Age fury and panic. Sudden desire to crush Elaine, and possibly also Spouse, with nearest boulder.

Notice that my hand is trembling. Put it in my pocket where I encounter the alien earring which Harriet found under my bed. Place it on the table. Earring – handkerchief – handkerchief – goats and monkeys! Long to fall down in fit, but *Petit Mal* not available, let alone *Grand Mal*, so instead stare at earring, condemned to continuing consciousness.

"This must be hers, then." Voice echoes in my skull.

"Ah yes. Sorry." Spouse swiftly pockets the earring. Somehow this gesture is terribly shocking. It presents me with a fait accompli: he will return it to her at their next meeting. Well, hell, why not now?

"I suppose you'd better go and tell her you've told me."

Spouse hesitates.

"Don't you want to – know any more?"

14

Not really. Only where, how, since when, why, how could you, how could she, when can I kill you both, would Thursday be convenient, etc.?

"Not just now."

Spouse scrambles to his feet with ill-concealed relief, then pauses, hesitates and, with a bizarre clumsiness, pats my shoulder.

"You're amazing," he murmurs. "I told her you wouldn't turn a hair. But then, you're an old hand at this sort of thing, aren't you?"

Thus he discreetly reminds me I am not entitled to outrage, because of Tom. So this is what it feels like from the other end. Wouldn't turn a hair, indeed. As he tiptoes eagerly away, every hair on my body withers in his wake. Off he goes. For him, the buried secret can now burst into luxuriant and fragrant life. For me, it's a case of Mind the Bones.

26 March

"Good God! I dreamt I was about to marry Geoffrey Boycott!"

"Well, you could do worse," yawns Spouse. "At least he could make it last all day."

What does Spouse mean by this? Is it an erotic quip? Or a warning that our marriage might not last all day? That he is about to pack his bags and join Elaine at number 193? I lie there frantically speculating beneath a mask of élan.

Since his recent bombshell, have gone into boggle over-drive. Many philosophical conundra have attained strange new resonances. For example, I now know why the chicken crossed the road. *Because bloody Elaine was waiting across there with her tender young cleavages and potages.*

The worst of it is, I've got nobody to confide in. I used to confide in Elaine. But she cannot face me at present. Besides, I can hardly confide to her the fact that I feel like killing her. Mustn't breathe a word to Mrs Body – her pity would feel like a dumper truck delivering a rockery. Twills next door would probably put their house on the market at the suspicion of any

15

more hanky-panky on this side of the privet. Tom, who might have mutated by now from ex-lover to sympathetic chum, is back in the matrimonial manacles.

As for the children, I recall when I was myself involved in a little extra-curricular activity, I felt more guilty towards them than Spouse. Absolute priority is to convince them that, whatever the situation, I am relentlessly delighted therewith. Poor, dear, sweet, defenceless darlings. I hear the manic thudding of their hooves. Here they come now.

"Mummee! It's the start of the holidays!"

"Ouch! Stop it! Get your knee out of my eye, you swine!"

Banish children to the TV room, and hope nothing depraved is available on satellite at 8.00 a.m. on Saturday mornings.

Spouse clears his throat portentously, at which every nerve in my body leaps into state of flight-or-fight readiness.

"We would like to go away for a couple of days, if you don't mind," he says, meekly. It is such a bizarre novelty to hear Spouse all meek. It disarms me, even though my blood runs cold at that strange *we*. We used to be him and me. He strokes my arm gingerly, as one might ingratiate one's self with an unreliable old Rottweiler.

"Of course!" I cry, relentlessly delighted. "As long as you're here for the Easter egg stuff."

"Of course!" grins Spouse, and leaps out of bed like a salmon. "We're thinking of going on Tuesday, Wednesday and Thursday."

Oh are you, you bastards, cries a voice inside me. Not a still, small voice, you understand: more a monstrous roar. *That's three days not a bleeding couple!*

"Ah yes," I chirrup with a delighted smile. "You can have a dirty mid-week."

Spouse laughs more than strictly necessary at this limp jest. "And of course, if you want to go away at all . . . ?" If I want to go away at all, it will be jolly convenient, because it leaves them together here – a cheaper option than the dirty mid-week. Spouse seems positively eager for me to go away, even though I have recently spent three weeks in Portugal. "After all, the Sintra trip was really a working holiday, wasn't it? You probably need a break."

One of the strangest things about the Brave New World we are exploring is that Spouse has started saying the things traditionally expressed by me. I used to have to bargain till I

16

was blue in the collar to get a couple of days' break, and now he can't wait to send me off round the world, preferably in a coracle.

"Well, I'll think about it," I sigh, and yawn and stretch as if I have just awoken from a deep and delicious sleep, instead of being tossed and turned all night in the greasy Wok of insomnia. He departs – only for the bathroom at present, in which he is spending more time these days.

Left to myself, I slump gratefully back into my comfy old gloom. This relentless delight is tiring. Feel brief pang of sympathy for the Royals. Their faces must ache from all that smiling. If only I was entitled to a bit of outrage I could be hurling thunderbolts. As it is, I have to keep a straight bat. But where is Geoffrey Boycott when I need him? In Trinidad. Wonder how long it would take me to weave myself a coracle.

2 April

Glad to get past April Fool's Day. Too much like everyday life. Spouse and Elaine spent mid-week in Weymouth. They sent me a postcard which included the observation that it was raining. Was this to comfort me with the thought that this might put a dampener on their brazen extra-marital romps?

Spouse looks sheepish, as I imagine do most husbands returning from their ram-raids. He agrees eagerly to buy Easter eggs and hide them in the garden on Saturday night, a ritual he would until recently have reviled as a synthetic transatlantic antic.

"Where can I buy them, then?"

Doesn't that just say it all. Inform him of the existence of shops.

"Where's Daddy going?"

"It's a secret!"

"Why can't we go too?"

"Because it's a secret for you – to do with Easter."

Nudge nudge, wink wink. Children begin to salivate horribly in anticipation of the feast. I too am getting hungry. Not

17

literally – hungry for facts. When did he and Elaine first indulge in dalliance? And where? And how? And do they ever talk about me? And what do they say? And how can they be so shameless? Waaaaah! At least I had shame! I slunk, I ducked, I weaved, I feinted, I stalked, I cringed, I blushed. I know I'm not entitled to outrage but I'm going to have some anyway.

"Mummy! Do you think the Easter Bunny's come, yet?"

"No, darling. It's still early. Go to sleep."

"But I want to catch him at it!"

Later Spouse tiptoes out among the daffodils with a torch, hiding the eggs. He bought the wrong sort, of course.

"Er – Dulcie – Do you think we might ask Elaine over to watch the kids looking for them in the morning?"

"Naaaaaow!"

A strange scarlet snarl leaps out of my mouth. We both recoil in alarm.

"OK, OK, it was just a thought. She very much wants to see you."

"I just want to be us. Just the family."

A squadron of pigs flies low over the roof. I have just identified myself with family values. Soon I shall be sewing skirts for the wanton parlour chairs and trousers for the Mars bars.

Easter Sunday dawns. The children rush out. Spouse and I follow, I in my slippers, lest I miss one magic moment of infantile rapaciousness.

"Oh, Mummy, he hasn't been! There aren't any anywhere!"

Spouse's idea of hiding an egg is to thrust it into a rocky crevice twelve feet high and cover over the hole with half a hundredweight of cement. What Harriet requires is a plump red cushion in the middle of the lawn, with a clutch of eggs, preferably Fabergé, nestling thereon. Spotlit.

Speaking of the lawn, its sap is rising, too. Soon it will need cutting. Perhaps they will plan to kill me with the lawnmower. Reassured by the knowledge that our old lawnmower couldn't even kill a blade of grass.

"I can see one from here . . . Up the other end . . ." I call helpfully, then turn on Spouse and hiss, *"How long's it been going on?"* He looks startled, as if he was entitled to avoid this question for ever.

"Well . . . you remember you went off to Aunt Kitty's funeral . . . ?"

"But that was last *May* for God's sake!"

Staggered and shocked by the antiquity of Spouse's amour.

"Mummee! I've found one! Under the flowerpot!"

Recall funeral. I went alone. Spouse could not attend because of distant lecture. Tracey Body could not babysit because of hay fever: Elaine stepped in to the breach . . . I was amazed, on my return next day, to find her still there, ironing in my own kitchen whilst Spouse watched the cricket. Recall her exact words: "This was my chance to play Mummies and Daddies till you came back."

"Oh *Christ!*" I scream suddenly. "This is worse than the *Archers!*"

"What's worse than the Archers, Mummy?"

"Life, darling."

"Are there any more hidden?"

"I don't know. You'll have to ask Daddy."

"*Daddy!*" Stricken face. "I thought it was the Easter Bunny!"

Whoops. Apocalypse.

9 April

"Mum? I don't mind the Easter Bunny not being real. About it being Daddy really. It's all right." Harriet gives me a serious look and departs for her brave new world. No Easter Bunny. No Tooth Fairy. And mention of Father Christmas is avoided. The gods are fled. Bite lip and resist strong urge to join RCs or even better, Muslims. Used to deplore the veil but these days would welcome one.

It is just as much a metaphysical fallacy that Daddy is the Easter Bunny, though. Cannot inform Harriet that the Easter Bunny has always been me, along with Father Christmas and the Tooth Fairy, and that Daddy only turned out this year in a mood of penitence for his extra-maritals. Still, if my daughter can be brave, so must I be. Modest hopes, only, now; go to bed hoping to sleep, for tomorrow I lunch with Elaine.

Awake to hear blackbird singin' in the dead of night . . . well, 5 a.m. to be exact. Glorious thread of sound. Fills the mind with pearly fields. Translucent airiness. Or is it a thrush?

That sings his song twice over, rather like John Major. Oh yes. Dawn chorus a good thing: good for the country, good for the unemployed, and good for Europe.

What's he actually saying though? The blackbird, I mean. 'Naff orf, eff orf aht of it you long-tailed gits, this is my tree, see? So Gertcha you riff-raff, chiff-chaff, stone-prats: up yours orioles!' Or so one assumes.

Have managed to endure ten minutes of insomnia without thinking of Spouse or Elaine-beyond-the-pail. Perhaps I shall have more time on my hands now he's got a bird. Perhaps I shall become an ornithologist. I should like to be conversant with the doves. Although it would be braver to confront modern life and attempt to understand the hearts and words of businessmen. I could become an entrepreneurologist.

On the whole would prefer blackbirds. What a misfortune for the thrush, to have a gynaecological complaint named after it. Or as Alice would say, what an honour. Alice! She must be back from Portugal by now. Must ring her and demand sympathy. But first, search vainly for another ten minutes' sleep.

Endure insane, frantic dream. The insomnia was more restful. I was suddenly responsible for rehearsing a town band, as well as trying to stuff live fish into a suitcase for a journey to Peasmarsh. Rise and take tea. Don't eat much these days.

Spouse drives children to the Rainge-Roughvers' for a day of genteel horsiness. Ring Alice and blurt out whole story.

". . . and we're having lunch today. At her place. It makes me squirm. At least when I was seeing Tom I had the decency to . . ."

"To lie and cheat? A different sort of decency, perhaps." Begin to hate Alice. "So he's got a bit on the side? So what? What do you expect after twenty years? He's just settling a score. You know. Knock for knock. Tit for tat."

"Tom was not tat!"

"Hang on, Saskia wants a word."

"Dulcie? Remember one thing! *Cling* to your *hate*!"

Ring off confused, but not as grateful as I had hoped.

Spouse returns, and we prepare for the excruciating trip over to the other side of Cranford Gardens, or as it may soon be renamed, the Rubicon.

Whatever she wears, Elaine will make me look crumpled

and fat. Wish I could become a Muslim in next five minutes. Seems a long way to cross road. This what it must be like to be old. Spouse rings her doorbell. Certain this is hypocrisy, and he must have a key. Door is flung open, and Elaine, radiant in coral silk, stammers, "Oh Dulcie – I don't know what to say!"

She flings her fragrant arms briefly around my neck, then retreats, quivering, to the depths of her vestibule. I am reminded for a split second of how much I like her, but remember Saskia's advice and cling to my hate.

Spouse removes his shoes. Elaine's is all beige wall-to-wall.

"Take your shoes off, Dulcie!" he reproves me in an embarrassed hiss, lest I offend the goddess. Obey. Socks are smelly and holey. I sit on the great cloudy sofa. Have they canoodled on this very cushion? If so, I hope I manage to fart into it later.

"But Dulcie!" cries Elaine, in a voice full of concern. "You're looking so thin!"

Ah, it's this new diet I'm on, you see. Diet of Can of Worms.

16 April

"You're being just marvellous about this, Dulcie!"

Elaine's doe-like eyes swim in admiration of my sang-froid at her theft of my husband. Must not lose temper. Must at all costs retain dignity. Indignation must remain double-wrapped for freshness so I can savour its full flavour later at my leisure. She and Spouse eye me warily. They are on tenterhooks. Now I have become the wronged woman, I am frightening. (What are tenterhooks, by the way? Something to do with boy scouts?)

Being frightening is a new sensation, and enjoyable in a macabre way. I'm a loose cannon. I could embarrass them horribly. I could rant. I could weep. I could tear my hair. I could wave my lily-white legs in the air. But instead I smile sweetly. Not too sweetly, though. Keep 'em guessing.

"Oh, why make a fuss?" Shrug in what I hope is elegant, perhaps Gallic way. *"C'est la vie. Che sara, sara. Auf wiedersehn, pet."*

The lovers look flummoxed at this cryptic Eurospeak. Am I sending them up? Am I reducing their grand amour to a mere peccadillo? I certainly hope so.

What a strange word peccadillo is. A cross between a pig and an armadillo -- which is what I have become, these days. I spend half my time rootling through my memories of recent months, desperately trying to sniff out suspect stratagems of theirs. The rest of the time I am growing armour.

"So you're quite happy, then?" enquires Spouse, trying not to make it sound too much like an order. *Quite happy?* My indignation stirs deep within its clingfilm. *Quite happy*!!? What does he mean by that? Can hardly believe he said it. Feel a curious sense that none of us is really speaking our own words, like Sinn Fein on the telly. A little bit of indignation escapes and surges up my gullet. I manage to trap it by my tonsils.

"So what exactly are you envisaging then?" I enquire snappishly. "A timeshare?"

Elaine does not know whether to laugh or not. Spouse frowns as if to warn me that levity is not appropriate when discussing their sacred love.

"All we want," he says briskly, "is to be civilised about it. If we want to spend a bit of time together, we don't want to lie to you."

"The last thing we want to do," implores Elaine, "is hurt you."

Well, exactly. The last thing. The first thing they want to do, and the second and the third, are all a lot more fun.

In other words, embrace your cuckoldhood with cheerfulness. Cuck off. That's an interesting word, cuckold. There isn't a female equivalent, of course, because it goes without saying that all women will be cuckolds anyway. Why is it such a pleasant, cosy word?

"My old cuckold's gone broody again," sighed Angostura, as a cloud passed briefly across the face of Mount Boutros-Ghali. "He's building a nest in the woodshed."

Is this the dawn of a new bonkbuster? I think not. I shall

write no more bonkbusters. I have been outbonked. Instead I think I shall embrace zoology. I shall read about peccaries and armadillos. I shall breed witolds. I shall study the spider who, to prevent marital incongruences, has the foresight to devour her mate.

"Oh, don't worry about hurting me!" I warble airily, trying to keep the sarcasm out of my voice. "Have your fun. Life's too short. Get stuck in. Be my guest. Who cares?" They watch me suspiciously. Am I about to pull a Kalashnikov out of my knickers and mow them down, all over the beige wall-to-wall? Indeed, why didn't I think of it earlier?

"Oh Dulcie, you are being a brick," sighs Elaine.

No, dear. If I was a brick I'd have hurtled through your plate glass long ago.

Lunch is attempted. I cannot face her dainty crêpes, though Spouse wolfs down several and assures her they are delicious. I have never made crêpes for him and now it is too late. Thank God. Suddenly announce I must go. They look startled. When I stand up they actually flinch. But now I am a cuckoldess I can behave badly. Transparent objections are made to my departure, but I insist. Can't bear the sight of them trying not to ogle and pet.

Walk out. Pass own house, though not sure why. Eventually realise I am going shopping, i.e. about to commune with the Almighty.

23 April

Miserable women console themselves with shopping. Although am I miserable? It suggests too constant, too drizzling a state of mind. I am April embodied, sweeping from fury to despair to a strange kind of exhilaration. For the first time in my life, I do not have to feel guilty. Spouse is the guilty party. His is the guilt. But his is also the party.

Every third weekend he frolics with his mistress in quaint hostelries tucked away in the wolds or wilds. He also spends Tuesday and Thursday evenings at her house. To me he has become strangely polite and conciliatory. O brave new world that hath such creatures in it.

I have not evolved, however. I am stuck down in the primal slime with the kids in Woolworths.

"Mummee! Look at that Asian Sindy! Isn't she beautiful?"

Harriet has cleverly engineered a multi-racial slant to her greed. Admit that the Asian Sindy is preferable to the all-American sort.

"Can I have her then? Instead of my next birthday present?"

Her next birthday is in March 1995. Thus recklessly she pawns her future for gratification now. What, I wonder, will 1995 bring? Will their father have decamped altogether?

"I don't mind him being away," declared Henry last Thursday evening with a savage grin. "Because Mum lets us do things."

For some reason this speech rang on and on in my mind for hours like a dreadful bell warning mariners of rocks up ahead in the fog.

And here we are hurtling towards more rocks in Woolworths. Sensing Harriet might achieve a Sindy, Henry salivates over a cassette.

"After all," Harriet reminds me politely but firmly, "you just bought yourself that monkey."

Ah yes. Touché. They have just watched me buy myself a small wooden statue of Hanuman the Monkey God in the multi-ethnic emporium up the road. Hanuman is slightly larger and even more Asian than the Asian Sindy.

"Oh, all right then. But only to celebrate -- er er Shakespeare's birthday."

Children squeal with triumph. Several other women shopping with children dart me contemptuous glances as if I have let the side down.

Leave Woolworths as quickly as possible and drive straight home before more madness can envelop us. Well at least it was an Asian doll and an Indian god and a cassette, not a video nasty.

"No more treats till the summer holidays!" I cry severely.

"Oh, no, of course not, Mummy!" they carol hypocritically.

Whilst placing Hanuman on the shelf above my desk, wonder if he was carved in an Indian sweatshop and if Alice will nag me about it. Even though the canary was hatched in

24

Swindon, Alice rebuked me as if I'd personally netted him in the rainforests.

Home alone with kids whilst Spouse cavorts in quaint and no doubt expensive inn. Vow next time I fall in love it will be with somebody rich. Although have never felt less like falling in love. Wish I were a hermaphrodite so I could cut out the middle man.

Experience sudden urge to be in the rainforests. Borrow book I gave to Henry for Christmas, which he has steadfastly ignored. Suspect that Henry is temperamentally on the side of the loggers and the parrot-trappers. Gaze reverently up at Hanuman, the god of cleverness. Request he will so direct my fingers that I shall select a page where I will find divine guidance to help in my present dilemma. Open book and am instantly surrounded by snakes.

'Moth Caterpillar, Costa Rica. This harmless caterpillar convincingly mimics an extremely poisonous viper with the underside of its body . . . Parrot Snake, Costa Rica. A supreme bluffer, the Parrot Snake is not venomous, but its vivid colouration and threatening posture, with mouth gaping wide, imply to predators that it is.'

There you are then. I am nothing if not a harmless caterpillar. Not sure I could convincingly mimic a poisonous viper with my underside, though. However, could easily mimic a mouldy rice pudding which might have similar deterrent effect. At nine o'clock, however, when the children pester me indignantly to let them stay up, I shall conjure up vivid colouration and a threatening posture with my mouth gaping wide. Thanks, Hanuman.

Practice snake-like gape in bathroom mirror and dislocate jaw. Never mind. These things take time. I shall coil myself up in a dark corner and one day soon I shall shed my scarred old skin and emerge dangerous and gleaming.

30 April

Waiting outside Harriet's school in hangdog mope. Dogged by despair since Spouse surrendered to the youthful charms of Elaine-over-the-road. True, the zip had long gone out of our sex life. We had become more robotic than erotic. And I admit it – Spouse had attempted several times over the last few months to rekindle the dying embers, without much response on my part. In that sense I don't really want him any more. But nobody else is going to have him either. Hangdog in the manger.

A mum whose name I can't quite remember approaches me. Smile broadly to disguise amnesia. Smile feels odd. Must be out of practice.

"Isn't it outrageous about the shortfall?" she demands.

Hesitate. I've never been entirely at ease with the word 'shortfall'. Prefer nightfall, waterfall and pratfall. Shortfall reeks of economics, at the merest hint of which my brain has always toddled off to its basket. Wonder if her remark has local or cosmic application.

"How much exactly is it?" I enquire cautiously, fishing for a clue and anxious to avoid pratfall.

"He thinks he'll be £3,000 short," she sighs. Aha. There is a shortfall but there is also a he. "John says we're just whingeing about having to pay twice." Wish there were not so many Johns about. If she'd said Leonardo or Curtly we'd know where we were. Make all-purpose sympathy-in-endurance noise: a sort of click and sigh suggestive of old boiler switching itself off, which to be honest is what's really taking place. "But the fact is," she continues relentlessly, "why should we? Although I know we'd all sacrifice the shirts off our backs for our kids."

Kids? Ah. This is the best clue so far. It's something to do with the school.

"But asking the PTFA to stump up for books and blackboards when we've already paid for it once in our taxes, well, it's so manipulative, isn't it? They know we will, because when it comes to our kids we're all vulnerable."

It's the budget! It's the school budget she's on about! Did she say three thousand quid short? Three *thousand*? A flood of indignation rushes through my ducts, quite fluently as that's one thing I have had a lot of practice at recently. Try to conceal the fact that I have only just cottoned on to what she is talking about.

"Well, what can we do?" I enquire eagerly, remembering the exhilarating Seventies when at a demo I courageously threw an empty paper bag at a policeman. Oh yes! The powers that be didn't get away with much in those days.

"There's a meeting next week," she pounces. "I'm going to go, I don't normally but I feel it's really getting ridiculous." She throws this down as a sort of challenge. I realise I must go too or it will seem that I am unaware how ridiculous it has become. Goodness knows I am uninformed about most important issues in the universe but on the subject of the ridiculous I am red-hot.

A bell rings and our children rush out into what, in a decent country, would be the sunshine. Sod education – I'd vote for anybody who'd tow the British Isles a few hundred miles south and drop anchor somewhere off the coast of North Africa. But no. Not sod education. Here they come, Harriet's little face lighting up, as would any tyrant's at the sight of her slave. The future foams and fusses around us in a tide. Their faces lifted up for kisses. Not long till addle-escence so make the most of this sweet breath.

How dare the powers that be refuse to pay for kids' books? My political idealism has slumbered silently for years like a millionaire's head in a Californian freezer, but now its eyelids flicker and its hoary locks snake about with indignation. We, the children of the Fifties, drank our school milk out of bottles with solid cardboard tops, sat at desks made of solid wood and read solid books. If we cannot now summon up a bit of solidarity, there is no hope for us. For the sake of Aneurin Bevan we must stand up and be counted. If there's anyone out there who can still count.

On the way home, suddenly realise I have not thought about Spouse and Elaine for at least ten minutes. Have instead enjoyed alternate waves of political outrage and Fifties nostalgia. Most refreshing. In the back seat, Harriet moodily tears her way through a bag of crisps.

"Why do children have to suffer, Mummy? It's all God's fault. I think I hate him sometimes." She is miffed that she can't be King Rat in the school play.

Prepare to defend God, but after a couple of moments' reflection decide perhaps it's more than my job's worth.

7 May

I have heartburn. A rod of pain rises from my guts to my gullet. My breath stinks, and deep within I smoulder. I am Dame Etna.

"It was ace at Elaine's, Mum! She made a yummy chocolate cake!"

Having stolen my husband, she is now after my kids. No, no no, ignore that. I never said it. I never even thought it. Natural she should want to see them sometimes. Elaine a delightful woman fond of children. Not her fault she can bake. It's her forte. We all have our fortes. It's just that, compared to her fortes, mine are so very piano.

"But, Mummy, why didn't you come? Elaine said she wanted you to come. Daddy said he wanted you to come. So why didn't you?"

How come I'm the one who has to answer the difficult questions, dammit?

"I just had a little bit of work to do, darling."

"Work! I hate your work! You'd rather work than be with us! I wish you were like Elaine!"

"Yes, you'd like that, wouldn't you? Well, I'm sorry I'm not young and pretty, I'm sorry I'm not a cake-making Sindy doll, but God made me a hideous old bat, so you're stuck with me, so there!"

Deeply ashamed of this eruption. Henry goes pale and leaves the room to bottle up a few emotions. He's putting down a cellar of male neurosis. Harriet bursts into tears.

"Don't you dare call yourself a hideous old bat! You're not! And I don't wish you were young and pretty! I like you as you are!"

Spouse's key turns in lock. He sent the children home ten minutes early to give himself time for a tender goodbye. Oh yes. I know his little game. I've been there. I've done that. I know how it feels. Lucky bastards.

Sweep Harriet off her feet into overpowering hug. Spouse must not see her in tears in case he thinks I've been rocking the boat. Rocking it? I've been painting the keel with pitch. On my back, like Michelangelo.

"Tell you what, darling. We'll make a cake! Just you and me!"

"What, now? Oh, ace, Mum, brill, thank you, thank you, oh whoopee!" Spouse enters, and enquires of his daughter the cause of her elation.

"Mum's going to make a cake just like Elaine!"

Spouse looks astonished and amused. Resist the temptation to relieve my feelings by making jokes about tarts, or possibly by killing him, and manage to confine myself to enigmatic smile. Haul huge old mixing bowl out of back of cupboard, remove three dead flies, blow dust off cookery book and commence. After five minutes of creaming butter and sugar together, however, my right arm drops off. Agony! How does Elaine manage with her thin little brown arms? No. Better not to think of Elaine's arms.

Harriet, tiring of cake-making once it appears to entail hard work, disappears upstairs and I am left alone to wrestle with flour, eggs, etc. Greaseproof paper is so old it has gone yellow and cracked like the Mappa Mundi. Astonished and indignant cake tin is wrenched from its graceful retirement, filled with unpromising slop, and thrust into oven. Takes hours to clear up the mess, too, when I could've been making the most of my education and reading Baudelaire.

Whilst cake is baking, throw all children's old clothes into plastic sack for developing countries. Clear desk also. Will take paper for recycling. Wash alcoholic dregs of jam, honey, lemon curd, etc., out of several jars, and rinse out seventeen old bottles. Phone rings. Spouse leaps to answer it in case it is the adored one. After all he has been absent for a whole harrowing half-hour. He used to be too important to answer the phone but now he jumps to it as if from an ejector seat to spare her the mortification of having to ask me if she may speak to him.

"It's for you!"

Time was when such a call would summon up the blood, etc., but nowadays it is only Alice. She cross-questions me urgently on the progress of Spouse's amour but as I know Spouse and children can hear every word, am heroically non-committal and increasingly annoyed with Alice for persisting. Plucked from this futile failure of communication by the smell of burning.

"Oh my CAKE!"

"Your *what*?"

Hurtle to kitchen but find that cake has gone black on top. Try and turn it out too soon, tearing it in tender places. Try

29

to slice off the burnt bit but knife slips and cuts my thumb. Cake is now ragged, burnt and blood-stained. Weep, curse, gnash teeth, etc. Hurl cake out of back door, frightening the birds. Harriet appears at my side looking concerned.

"Mummy," she whispers urgently, "I think I can smell burning."

15 May

Rusbridge Gazette invites me to contribute to a series in which local writers are asked to describe their favourite church. My favourite church is actually Blythburgh in Norfolk, but fear the *Gazette* will consider this is a church too far, and hastily develop an enthusiasm for St Mary's, Lower Sodbury. Rather bored with all the old saints. Except of course St Protase and St Gervase of Little Plumstead, a fond memory of my wanderings in East Anglia. If they were alive now they'd be running an antiques shop in the Cotswolds.

New saints ought to include Brian Lara. He flashes his bat like a Renaissance prince his sword. And his demeanour! So modest, so courteous, such grace! He is a *parfait gentil* knight. Indeed the knighthood is a foregone conclusion. But my money's on St Brian too. Or at least Brian the Blessed – except I think we've already got one of those.

Spouse announces he is off again – a seminar in Oxford. No, he insists, it really is a seminar, and Elaine will not feature. But alas it means he can't deal with the children, a necessary precondition for my being able to inspect St Mary's in peace. Discover I don't like Spouse just going to seminars. Prefer him to have dirty weekends as he is infinitely more helpful when guilty.

Ask Mrs Body to collect Harriet and take her home from school, which means I can be driving serenely through the countryside or idling in an extasie upon some crumbling tomb. Can also visit Tesco's on the way back, and perhaps recycling centre (formerly the Tip), before meeting Henry off the coach. He has been on a field trip with his school in the Somerset Levels. Observing the last dollop of peat, perhaps.

Drive off with sense of treat, though irritated by the rattling in the back of the bottles-for-recycling. St Mary's a joy, and so as usual is Pevsner's lingo: 'Cusped and sub-cusped entrance arch, hood-mould on big busts with fleurons on the arch . . . a putto standing by, and pointing to, an urn . . .' Admire angel resembling Brian Lara.

Not sure if this is the sort of thing the readers of the *Rusbridge Gazette* would relish, however, so mentally substitute instead anecdote about how I once skived off from school in order to rub brasses with Paul Partridge. I wonder what happened to him. He had a fine baritone voice and a face like a putto. I bet if I'd married him, he'd never have dallied with Elaine-over-the-road. Idle in nostalgic haze on crumbling tomb. Clock strikes the hour in sleepy way. The murmuring of innumerable . . . wait! Five o'clock! Heck!

Run to car. Engage first gear with horrible grinding sound, and hurtle off, wounding the peaceful air of St Mary's. In theory an hour more than enough to get back to Rusbridge, but oh, the roadworks! Rusbridge High Street resembles the Grand Canyon. Two-mile tailbacks or as they used to say on the wireless, traffic jams. Arrive behind cement lorry and wish had taken motorway after all. Although even on motorway don't like overtaking if there's anything coming in the opposite direction. Tempted to overtake, but sensibly resist. Henry would prefer mother late, hot and embarrassed to mother dead. Although not so confident about Harriet.

Stuck in Rusbridge jam. Minutes race by. Ten past six. Twenty past. Endure ghastly hallucination of Henry waiting bravely, alone, with irritated teacher long after the others have all gone. Eventually arrive at school to face worse scenario: no one there at all. Henry abducted! Not sure what to do so sit in car and bite nails.

Teacher appears. Cringe, expecting six of the best or at the very least, an order mark.

"Sorry, Mrs Domum, didn't you get the message? The coach has broken down in Bridgwater."

"Oh, thank God!" I cry – mysteriously, perhaps. Don't care that son is marooned in Somerset. All that matters is that I should not be in the wrong. Assure teacher I am delighted at having to come back in 1½ hours. Time for Tesco's after all. They are now selling art books as well as things to eat. Buy book on Van Gogh and foreign strawberries.

31

Return to school to discover more delay. Eight p.m., now, at the earliest. Sit in car, read Van Gogh, eat strawberries. Am just thinking how unexpectedly enjoyable this is when I realise with a guilty lurch that I have entirely forgotten to ring and inform Mrs Body of the situation. Drive off to find a phone, but someone is using it, and by the time I get back to school Henry is waiting, bravely, alone, with the irritated teacher, long after the others have all gone. Oh well. If it's got your name on it . . .

21 May

We spend more time apart these days. When it's my turn with the kids he rushes off to his mistress. When it's his turn with the kids I do things like go to the Tip. Driving to the Tip is not very inspiring at the best of times. Begin to feel that of all the surplus objects in the car, I am the least recyclable.

"This is not the end of anything, Dulcie," Saskia informed me sternly during one of her intense bouts of telephone counselling. "This is the beginning of the best bit of your life."

Bottles and cans and rags and bones. Rattle rattle, stink stink. Not a very promising situation in which to be born again. On the way to the Tip I notice a sign saying 'To the Sale'. For some reason this reminds me that 'Sale' is the French for 'Dirty'. The filth of commerce. To the Dirty. Rattle rattle, stink. Here I come.

When I arrive at the Tip, discover that recycling has become so specialised that my humble rubbish hardly qualifies for any bin. 'Newspapers Only' shrieks one sign. 'Cardboard' insists another. 'No Metal' is the stern commandment here, 'No Plastic' there. Gaze at my rubbish in perplexity. Most of it seems to be knitted together in incompatible conjuctions of metal and wood and plastic to the point where they can never be put asunder. Divorce is easier for us biodegradables.

No bins for surplus wives, however. There should be one: a little cabin with a picket fence around it and a few hens pecking about. And the sign would say 'Has-bins only'.

Drive back still encumbered by half my debris. Mortifying

to find that not only myself but my rubbish is ineligible. See 'To the Sale' sign again, and following sudden urge, turn down country road. Soon find myself in grounds of big old house with marquee on lawn, in which an auctioneer's voice can be heard rattling away like a machine-gun. Venture timidly towards it as the hammer falls.

"Lot 160!" he sets off again, almost without drawing breath. "A Georgian silver snuffer tray of waisted form with gadroon borders . . ." Marvel at Antiquespeak. Gadroons! A fine old Georgian oath. Halfway between Gadzooks and Doubloons. Watch for a while. Seems to be a lot of money about. Not many of these punters on social security.

Become convinced that a fine old Georgian profile standing nearby belongs to the philosopher Roger Scruton. Spouse spoke to him once at an academic thing years ago, in the good old days when I hovered in the background. Scrutinise Scruton but he looks inscrutable, which would probably have been the case even if he was really Scruton. This is obscurely satisfying, but too obscurely to be satisfyingly satisfying. Fear this is the nearest I shall ever come to philosphy, and it won't do.

"Come on, ladies and gentlemen! Thirty pounds for a Victorian harmonium by Mason and Hamlin . . . ? Twenty . . . ? Twenty pounds only . . . ?"

Feel sudden surge of pity for lonely unwanted harmonium and stick up hand. Auctioneer seizes on me like a hungry osprey diving on a fish.

"Twenty pounds at the back, thank you, madam . . . a maiden bid."

Blush in maidenly way, and as nobody else can be per-suaded to join the bidding, unseen and unknown harmonium is knocked down to me at £20 plus 10 per cent plus VAT. Harmony is not wanted these days.

I have bought the heaviest and most worthless object in the sale, but I do not care. Recall previous boyfriend in Cambridge who had a dear little harmonium and we all used to gather round it and sing 'The Lost Chord'. Lost boys. Lost days. Melancholy thoughts in this strange white tent. It is the Marquee de Sad.

Make arrangements to transfer harmonium to 196 Cranford Gardens, where it is met by outraged Spouse.

"What the hell have you gone and done now?" he demands.

"Just trying to introduce a little harmony into the house," I smile sweetly. The children are delighted and wild to play it, but I insist I shall christen it myself with 'The Lost Chord'.

Sit down and pedal but the harmonium utters only a dreadful gasp. Harmony's death rattle. The Trappist canary watches in silent sympathy. Spouse grins, enjoying the long-forgotten taste of superiority.

"Only you could go to the Tip and come back with more rubbish than you left with," he sneers. Tempted to inform him that I would rather spend the rest of my days with this broken harmonium than him, but following the example of the harmonium, I preserve a graceful silence. Although Harriet is bawling too loudly for it to be fully appreciated.

28 May

"Mrs Domum? I've come to examine your organ."

Francis Flute, the bellows-mender, is alive and well and living in Swindon. Determined that my silent old harmonium shall sing once more, and to this end have ransacked Yellow Pages for an organ builder and repairer. Yellow Pages yielded, incidentally, many diverting moments en route, none more so than the cryptic entry: 'Boring: See ENGINEERS'. How very true.

The organ-mender is a streamlined fellow, with crinkly hair smoothed back like that of a Battle of Britain pilot. I thought all men with crinkly smoothed-back hair had gone but here is one on my doorstep. And he's a fast worker. Seconds after saying hello he is lying on the carpet with his arm thrust deep into my organ.

A moment later he leaps up, unscrews a panel at the front, and exposes rows of reeds like little teeth. He pulls one out, puts it to his lips and blows softly, producing a thin but musical note. He then smacks his lips appreciatively at the taste of antiquity and pronounces it delicious. Wonder for a split second whether I should fall in love with him but decide it would be a safer bet to fall in love with the harmonium.

He informs me it is in original condition, never been touched since 1876, and an MOT will cost about three hundred pounds.

At this moment Spouse, who has been eavesdropping by the door, suggests it might be kinder in the long run to have it put down. Quietly advise Francis Flute to ignore this and assure him I have funds of my own. Oh yes. Have just received royalty cheque for *Birches*. Not very much but enough to mend the harmonium and elope with it afterwards to – well, to the Forest of Dean, perhaps.

It is Tuesday: Spouse soon departs for his evening over the road. He seems rather quiet on his return. Wonder if he has experienced The First Cloud. Hope so. But perhaps it is only guilt and foreboding. Perhaps Elaine has demanded an elopement and he can't bring himself to tell me. Elope a funny word. Sounds like the way a rabbit moves.

Exhausted by the effort of being nonchalant in the most trying circumstances, I go to bed early and close my eyes with a short thanksgiving that the children don't seem to wake in the night these days. Two minutes later, am roused from honeyed slumber by Spouse.

"You're not really going to waste your money on mending that clapped-out old organ, are you?" he sneers.

"Why not? It's my money. I can spend it on whatever I like."

"But it's not as if you can even play it properly. And for three hundred quid you could get an electronic keyboard for the kids – with all the stops and the rhythm options and everything."

"My old organ has stops! It's got Vox Humana and Vox Celeste – which at least have got a bit of poetry about them, unlike that synthetic rubbish. And if you're so keen on buying the kids a keyboard, you could buy them one yourself. It'd only cost the equivalent of two of your precious weekends with Elaine."

"But why repair an old organ that you're never going to play, when you could give yourself a really nice holiday in, say, Sardinia?"

"Leave off! I don't want to go off on holiday just so you and Elaine can play Mummies and Daddies. Alone in Sardinia? I'd probably be kidnapped by bandits. But of course you'd love that, wouldn't you?"

"There's no need to be hysterical. I just think it's madness to repair that ludicrous old wind instrument when anyone with any sense would get rid of it. And of course you shouldn't go to Sardinia on your own. You could go with Alice and What's-her-name."

"Don't pretend you can't remember Saskia's name. And stop trying to pack me off. I live here – inconvenient though it may be for you – and I'm going to bloody stay, so there."

"Don't be so effing stupid, woman." I flounce out of bed. All this unaccustomed rowing has stimulated my bladder. "Where the hell are you going now? There's no need to storm off in a huff."

"I'm not storming off in a huff. I'm going to the lavatory."

Storm off in a huff, but the effect is spoiled by a rogue fart which I had hoped to contain. Sit on loo for a long time, pondering the discovery that I, too, am a ludicrous old wind instrument that he wants to get rid of.

Determined not to replace the harmonium with streamlined young electronic job, however. My clapped-out old organ is much more, well, organic.

4 June

"Bubby! Stop pickig your dose!"

The whole family is nasally challenged. The children's noses will run and run. Spouse is too grand for a bunged-up nose, so he has 'inflamed sinuses'. Mine is like a speech by Churchill. Blood, toil, sweat, tears – I've had the lot. Thighbone of Broxbourne man? Fossilised dinosaur turd? It's appeared in my handkerchief.

The body is like a pyramid – connected to the outside world by a series of passages. And in my case, shaped like a pyramid too, from aircraft-carrier arse to pea brain. Vow never again to take my bodily passages for granted. Maddened by suffocation, by night I toss and turn, and by day recklessly pick, even in public. Thank God I'm not a Test cricketer, or by now I'd have done it on TV.

Strange, the things one cannot do in public. Oh lucky dogs, lifting their legs in the streets in perfect felicity. Mind you, the upper classes enjoy more doggy freedom and confidence in this respect than us middle-class prudes. If you grow up in a semi you're constantly aware that you can be overheard by the neighbours. I know a chap who used to pee kneeling down so the drumming couldn't be heard in the flat below. But the toffs, inheriting rolling acres, burp, fart, pick and pee with swagger and abandon. Their problem is making themselves heard at all – even indoors, at the other end of the mile-long dining table. Let us bray.

How would I have managed as a Sloane, I wonder? The black velvet Alice band would not have suited me. I do not look my best with the hair swept back. Now my brow has come to resemble the Rosetta stone, I look my best in a balaclava. Who would I have married? A Hooray Henry? Henry Worth-Matravers. He'd be a Lloyd's name and we'd have lost a fortune. We'd commit a stylish double suicide – he'd shoot himself in the library, I'd throw myself in the lake. With the water shortage, though, I expect it'd be only two inches deep, and I'd really hurt myself.

What is behind this train of thought? Public school. Spouse is an ex-public schoolboy. But he went to a decent, modest Scottish version, not the whole hog. In September he is planning to send Henry to the decent, modest public school down the road – St Archibald's. This is an ongoing saga. I don't mention it much. In response to Family Money Left for the Purpose, Henry was fished out of Rusbridge primary some years ago and plopped into the chic little prep school recommended by the Rainge-Roughvers. I watch, silent, trying not to feel too appalled.

Harriet stayed on at Rusbridge Primary and has become a lout. Spouse never suggested fishing her out, but then she is only a girl. Not that I want her fished out. I just want him to want it for her if he wants it for him. Children are engrossed by *Crystal Maze*, so march to study.

"I'm not at all happy about Henry going to St Archie's."

Spouse squints at me as if I am talking Farsi.

"What?"

"This public school crap. Do we have to?"

"Dad left the money . . ."

"But that's no bloody reason at *all*!"

"What is this? P.M.T.?"

"No, it bloody isn't! It's just what I feel. I've never liked it. This country stinks. Buy a better education. Buy better health. The poor are always with us but you can step over them so don't worry."

Spouse sighs, smiles, and pats me on the head.

"I know the Labour party have seemed a bit glamorous recently, but there's no need to get carried away. You'll feel better after the election."

"You bast—"

Further indignation is prevented by a torrent of blood bursting from my nose. Spouse sighs as if nasal bleeding is another tiresome form of female incontinence, but accompanies me to the kitchen where I hold my nose over the sink whilst he puts the kettle on – a gracious concession.

"I just dod't see the poidt of it," I persevere. "You dod't really wadt your sod to turd idto a toffee-dosed twit, do you?"

"Toffee-nosed?" smiles the supercilious one. "You're a fine one to talk."

Have to admit that I would prefer Earl Grey to British Workman's tea. Spouse offers Eccles cake. "That should be prole enough for you." Silly ass. He really knows how to get up my nose.

11 June

"Look at my back," demands Spouse emerging from the shower. "Can you see any blisters there? An inflamed area?" He is terrified of being necrotised. Assure him there is only the usual red patch he gets in the shower. No blisters – yet. He hurls himself into bed and pummels the pillows. "Oh well. If you hear a munching noise in the night, it'll probably be that bug having a go at my arse."

It's the Age of Anxiety, all right. I'm biting my nails again, right down to the quick. I expect that's where the bug'll get in. If it isn't in already. Apart from the bug, and other, perhaps more stylish forms of sudden death, there's the usual wars and famines, there's the arms trade, the drugs racket, the row with Spouse about Henry's school, the phone call from Alice and Saskia in Bath ("The Department of Transport are complete vandals, Dulcie! Get down here immediately! We've just seen Bel Mooney!").

Then there's the Labour Party Leadership. Spouse is for

the amiable thug as he's 'The Real Thing'. I'm reconciled to Little Boy Blue, though I have a thwarted longing for the Garden Gnome, the only one with real sex appeal in my opinion. But what the Labour Party really needs is the third great Antichrist called something like Brodde (according to Nostradamus) who's due to appear any minute and finish the whole debacle of human civilisation off quickly.

If all that wasn't enough to guarantee insomnia, there's also the possibility that Spouse will run away across the road to live with Elaine, taking the children with him. Or even worse, leaving them with me. But I realise that is an event completely beyond my power to control. I must do the sensible thing and concentrate on identifying Brodde, the Third Great Antichrist, instead. I could save the world from his reign of terror by inviting him to supper.

One of my recent culinary efforts had Henry and Harriet puking in unison. The sight had a strangely industrial quality, like peasants scything in rows or slaves hoeing in gangs. I must stop this or I'll have a bad dream. Concentrate on Brodde. It sounds like a Scandinavian breakfast cereal . . . And another thing, apart from the anxiety about the school budget being £3,000 short, there was the letter that came recently from Harriet's teacher announcing a trip to Stonehenge.

"Mrs Curtis?" I enquired sweetly of the headmistress (there is the rumour that she's the Third Antichrist but she's changed her name and sex to avert suspicion -- though it didn't work for Thatcher). "This coach that's going to take Class Four to Stonehenge – has it got seatbelts?"

A strange sigh wafted down the wire – or whatever Telecom wafts things down these days.

"Well, to be honest, it doesn't, and we have absolutely no control over that," she admitted, sounding rather wan for an Antichrist.

By tomorrow I have to decide whether Harriet will be allowed to visit Stonehenge with the rest of Class 4. Shall I withhold consent as a brave gesture? Toss, turn. Spouse emits a horrible racking snore. Kick him on the spine, but not too hard in case it crumbles into dust. However, if he is going to disintegrate it might be fortuitous if he were to do so before abandoning us, changing his will, or even – horrid thought – begetting a second, more charming family with Elaine.

Toss, turn. Nose still blocked. Lie on hands in a futile

attempt to avoid picking nose. Suddenly arrive in a large house on a Tuscan hillside. House has no floors. Find myself upstairs, balancing on rotting beam. Abyss beneath. Glimpse window. Inch towards it: possible escape. Look out and see horrible grinning face of demon who seizes me by the wrists and pulls me out of window. Brodde? Or – more likely – Harriet?

Awake with huge twitch. Am lying on my crossed wrists, still hurting from the demon's grip. Liberate hands, which have become large, numb and wooden like butter pats. They start to tingle and burn. Any minute now they'll be necrotising. Damp shreds of the dream still unpleasantly festoon my brain. Have to fight off suspicion that my darling daughter may be the Third Antichrist.

Wish I was in Tuscany, though enjoying slightly more satisfactory accommodation.

It is 2 a.m. Creep downstairs and consume three pieces of hot buttered toast. Oh, all right then. She can go to Stonehenge. I bet one of those damned Sarsens will topple over and squash her, though.

18 June

Spouse takes children to school, then enters my study and stands there looking indecisive. Try to conceal the fact that I am sitting there looking indecisive.

"How's your work going?"

Now *what the hell does he mean by that*? Shuffle a few papers importantly about and assure him I am about to start brand-new epic, though aware had privately forsworn any more historical fiction. Still – can't seem to write anything else which is publishable.

"So where's this next book going to be set?" he half-sits on the windowsill.

Realise with a horrid lurch that this token interest in my work and welfare must be the preamble to some horrid fait accompli which he is poised to reveal. Is he going to move in with Elaine? Is she pregnant?

"Er . . . well, I dreamt about Tuscany the other day."

"Perfect!" pounces Spouse. "That's what you need: sunshine, grapes, olives, campaniles and stuff. You always used to love all that."

Have to admit this is true, but very wary. Sense he is about to pack me off there.

"You ought to go out there this summer for a couple of weeks, have a rest, do a bit of background research."

Odd that such an attractive prospect can feel so much like a trap.

"What are you thinking of doing, then?"

He flinches slightly, and falls into deep shiftiness.

"Oh, I don't mind staying at home and looking after the kids."

"With Elaine."

"Well – not *all* the time."

Well of course, the poor girl's got to get a few hours sleep now and then.

"Wouldn't you like to come to Tuscany with me, then?"

Horrible split-second of hesitation before the mock-enthusiastic: "Of course! I'd like nothing better! But what about the kids?"

"Elaine can look after them on her own if she's so keen."

"Don't be silly. I mean, you can't take kids to Tuscany. They'd ruin it. You wouldn't be able to concentrate on anything."

True, but somehow treacherous.

"You and Elaine thinking of bunking off somewhere together?"

"Well – perhaps. But you organise your Italian trip first."

Spouse looks longingly at the Sunday travel supplements strewn across my floor, as if desperate to ring requesting brochures for me immediately.

"And then what?"

"Well, we'll fit in with you."

I am not, it seems, part of the We any more. Not so much the Royal We as the Disloyal We. Enquire if We have any idea where We might be going.

"Oh – well – we, er, we quite fancy the Seychelles."

What! Spouse, on a tropical beach? Suppress incredulity and fury and manifest instead a synthetic indifference.

"Isn't that rather far away? Who's paying? Her ex-husband?"

41

"Well, strangely enough – yes."

The errant Marc has, apparently, come up with a post-divorce settlement of staggering generosity. Well, by our standards. He's in business, of course. So that's it. Swanning off to the Sodding Seychelles. Traditional honeymoon island. Staring into each other's Pina Coladas as the sun sets behind a sweaty palm. Strange to see Spouse embarking on a series of manoeuvres which will be Not Quite Him. Is he remembering our stay in Siena in Le Tre Donzelle? Is he already secretly wishing he could be peering at Daddi's frescoes with me rather than swatting the mosquitoes with her? Er . . . no.

"So you see," he continues, relieved now he's revealed his Seychelles to me, "since Elaine's paying for our holiday we can afford something special for you. A sort of Enchanted April – only without the April. And if you want company, I'm sure Alice and Saskia would jump at the chance."

The Enchanted April has suddenly become The Irritable August.

"What about the kids?"

Spouse looks startled. Evidently has not realised the children might like a holiday too.

"Oh, we can take them to Centerparcs for a couple of days. There's that new one opening at Longleat."

Bankruptcy beckons. All we need now is for the canary to decide he'd like a holiday by himself this year: a week in Tenerife, no doubt.

25 June

The Rainge-Roughvers fly to Australia for a family wedding, leaving their guinea pigs, Alec and Edward, in our care. Alec is brown with red eyes; Edward is black all over. I'm normally not too keen on rodents, but these two look reassuringly blunt: like a couple of oven gloves with legs.

"What is the point of guinea pigs?" asks Spouse. The guinea pigs stare at him, also silently baffled. Perhaps they are thinking the same thing. I hate the fact that they have to live in a cage. Though the thought of free-range guinea pigs is even worse.

"Didn't the Victorians eat them?" ponders Spouse. "They'd just fit nicely into one of those pitta bread things."

"Don't say that, Daddy!" screams Harriet. "Mummy – can I take them upstairs and play with them on my bedroom floor, please?"

"Their pee is only like Lemonade," Henry reassures me helpfully. "And their poo is like All Bran and we'll clear up every bit."

Agree wearily, and children depart with whoops, carrying apprehensive guinea pigs.

"Our subscription to Amnesty International has lapsed," I inform Spouse. He shrugs. "And our membership of Gloucestershire."

"I don't think I'll be watching much cricket this year."

For some reason this announcement strikes fear into my heart.

Why won't he? It's obvious. Elaine. She did accompany us to a match last year, and seemed in extraordinarily high spirits, but I now realise it wasn't the cricket – it was the fact that she was secretly in love with Spouse. The bastards! No wonder I got a headache. I remember her placing her cool hand on my brow on the way home. Was she praying that a nice quick stroke would carry me off, leaving her free to move into 196 Cranford Gardens, and endear herself to Henry and Harriet by producing two cute little half-siblings for them to pet and torture?

Emerge from this horrid hallucination to find that Spouse is majestically veiled by the *Independent*, like Everest behind a cloud. I bet he never hides from Elaine behind a newspaper. I expect that damned gazing and fondling goes on all the time. In fact, the stern fortification of his lifestyle here may well have evolved to keep me out of his sight. Feel an overpowering need to escape into the garden, or as it is known nowadays, go down the docks.

The nettles are doing well, too. Nearly the end of June and I haven't even stuck the odd tomato plant in a Gro-Bag. Trip over a hidden brick and fall onto a slug. Suppress cry of horror. Recall Harriet's Buddhist advice: "They can't *help* being slugs, Mummy". Feel I am becoming a slug myself: repulsive and vulnerable.

Oh, why didn't I run away with Tom when I had the chance? We could be plumbing in Tuscany by now. Henry and Harriet would be bilingual. And Spouse would have consoled himself with Elaine so it would all have ended happily for everybody. It was my duty to run away with Tom. Now he's shackled to the frightful Stalinist Sabrina, and I've ended up down among the bricks and nettles. Perhaps there's a message there. Perhaps I should stop being such a brick and start behaving like a nettle.

Pace up and down garden like caged -- well, caged, middle-aged, guinea pig. Tormented by the revelation that Spouse does not wish to renew his joint subscriptions with me. I am being phased out. The nuclear family is being decommissioned. He's watching me carefully through the bars of my cage, seeing what he can get away with. There was a soupçon of sensitivity at first: the hint of apology, gratitude for my being such a brick.

Now they're an institution. Every other weekend, every Tuesday and Thursday, and now this holiday in the Seychelles. I suppose we tell the children that Daddy's gone to America for a conference again, and hope they don't notice when he and Elaine reappear simultaneously with matching sunburn and (one hopes) insect bites and mild dysentery.

"Mummy! Look at Alec!" I can tell by the guinea pigs' reproachful stare that some outrage has been perpetrated. "We've put a bit of that Body Shop mango oil on their fur to make it shine and smell nice."

They smell like a brothel. Horror! Will the poor creatures try to groom it off, and poison themselves? Should we wash them, and if so, would it be better to hang them out to dry or use the tumble drier? Remember recent debate about whether or not Body Shop products were tested on animals. Well, they sure as hell have been, now.

2 July

"It's only a matter of time." Spouse stares moodily into the distance. Alarm bells jangle. What's coming now? An announcement of his imminent departure for a new life with Elaine?

"What's only a matter of time?"

"Before rabies arrives down the tunnel."

You'd think the bloke would have reasons enough to be cheerful. Beautiful young woman across the road madly in love with him. Heroic old wife keeping stiff upper lip. Two lovely children – well, two children, anyway. Cricket season. Tennis girls to ogle on the telly. Long Vac already in full swing. Prospect of a holiday in the Seychelles paid for by his girlfriend's ex-husband. What more does the blighter want? All this and he still finds something to moan about. Spouse could out-jib Job.

Me, I'm cheerful. Life in ruins. Husband deep in extra-maritals. Children ghastly. Summer hols looming. Stuck with book. Ex-lover married off to brawny stonemason. Seventeen new grey hairs this morning. But what am I up to? I'm planting a rose. Roses round the door before it's too late. I found an intriguing old climbing rose in an out-of-the-way plant nursery. It's called Sombreuil. All right, the name's a bit sombre, but I looked it up in a book which said it was one of the treasures of the past. I need a few of them to shore up against the bankruptcies of the future.

Watched by the children, I dig a hole. Sombreuil waits, watered, in its container. A bucketful of muck, and a packet of bonemeal, stand by. Mr Twill provided these – he encourages me. Spouse dislikes my fitful interest in the garden, clearly thinking 'Tis Pity She's a Horticulturalist.

"It could be a pond, Mummy! We could have a pond instead!"

Ignore this suggestion. If we had a pond by the front door I know I would throw myself into it. Spouse appears flourishing a newspaper.

"It says here that people who eat Black Pudding are twice as likely to get Mad Cow Disease." He has gone rather pale. Evidently haunted by the memory of past haggises. He waits for reassurance, but I can't be bothered these days.

Send the children away as I remember reading somewhere that bonemeal can be bad for you. Unless you are a rose. Scatter it around the roots of Sombreuil. Fill in and tread lightly. Experience strange but pleasurable sensation. A hortigasm perhaps. Then recall something else about bonemeal. Someone – probably a Eurobeefophobe – said we mustn't feed it to cattle because of the risk of BSE. But

45

– horried qualm quite blots out gardener's delight – plants eat bonemeal. What implications does this revelation have for vegetarians? Stare aghast at Sombreuil. Is it going to get Mad Rose Disease?

O Rose Thou Art Sick. What could you get from being pricked by a mad rose? The Cow may be Mad but the Rose is Madder. Wait. I am now hopelessly confused between Rabies and BSE. I expect confusion is the first symptom of one of them. Sit down on the doorstep and wait for head to clear. Perform modest mental exercise – try to recall all the Eurowords for Rabies. *La Rage. La Rabbia.* I don't suppose you could get a rabid rabbit, could you? Unless it had nibbled grass that had been nobbled with bonemeal. I can think of the odd rabid rabbi, though.

Feel hungry, but dare not eat anything. Eating used to be a joy, but now it has become a dangerous chore. We are all manacled to the Food Chain Gang.

"Mummee! Do you want a Nerd?"

Accept gratefully. Nerds, for the uninitiated, are small but delicious sweets resembling fluorescent pink morsels of canary-dung but made entirely, I suspect, from chemicals. Hope so anyway. Munch away gloomily till remember that I am supposed to be being cheerful.

In my young day the sweets used to be called things like Love Hearts. Now it's Nerds. And the other day on children's TV I saw a new toy advertised – a plastic bucket that vomits balls all over the carpet. Perhaps it is too late for roses round the door. We have, as a species, seriously goofed and can only wait on our doorsteps for Nature's various revenges to sweep down and devour us. Rabies, Mad Cow Disease, AIDS, Black Spot, the flesh-eating bug . . . take your pick.

The Mad Dog Rose is in bloom. Me, I'm hoping for a long slow mildew.

9 July

Right then. Hence loathed Melancholy. Count blessings: children healthy, roses blooming, Spouse only involved with one other woman. And even if they're going off to the Seychelles he's said I can have a few days in Italy on my own. Giddy with desire, I rifle through old guidebook to Urbino. 'The tourist today is pursued by the passiflon to get round quickly.' How true! I have often been pursued by the passiflon, especially in Italy, though I guess I am now antique enough not to have to worry. Long to gaze anew at the pale solemnity of Piero della Francesca, who painted Duke Frederic (1444–1482) and his wife ('two ethereal figures against a background of boundless lands, gradually fading in the distant sky').

Close book, close eyes, and conjure up in anticipation that ancient, that mysterious, that shadowy, that twinkling landscape. Reverie suddenly shattered by arrival of Spouse from school run.

"We're in serious financial schtuck," he announces severely. Wait patiently for more information. It's all those dirty weekends of his, of course. It's not cheap, two nights at The Toad and Eartrumpet at Mellstock Parva with intimate candlelit gourmet dinner (purloins of tender ewe-lamb marinated in Olde Scrumpy, with Dorset Knobs and old Vinny to follow, then coffee and the After Eights).

Spouse is still attracted to Thomas Hardy despite all my warnings. If it comes to Kiss me Hardy, give me Francoise any day. Get involved with Old Tom at your peril. One minute you're arrayed in the habiliments of a goddess, the next you're blind, mad or drowned. Mind you, teenagers lap it up. They like that sort of thing. And Spouse is, it appears, some kind of arrested teenager.

But Dorset's expensive these days. All the same I gape in disbelief as the horrid depths of our penury are revealed. We are apparently flat, stony broke. I falter. The landscape of Piero dims suddenly as if a gigantic cloud has passed across the sun.

"So it's a good job we hadn't booked your Italian jaunt."

What? A good job? And jaunt? How dare he? My hackles leap up smoking like pop-tarts from the toaster.

Usually my worst problem is working out how much anger I'm entitled to. This time I don't care. I embrace my rage joyfully. It costs nothing and it doesn't make you fat. Why should I sacrifice my one piddling little treat, just because he's got us into the red through a whole series of sybaritic bed and breakfasts with his scarlet woman?

47

"So you'll cancel your Seychelles trip as well?"

"Ah . . . well . . ." he looks shifty. "After all, Elaine's paying for that. And it is already booked."

"Cancel it. You're bound to spend a fortune in everyday expenses. She's bound to have cancellation insurance."

He hesitates nervously and, I swear, looks across at the sitting room window i.e. in the general direction of Elaine's house across the road.

"I don't think that's really on . . . she's made all the arrangements . . ."

In a flash I realise that he is afraid of her. He dare not postpone their holiday. I am torn between pity and contempt. Hate my own vices in others. I am myself all too easily cowed. Just wish he wasn't. I never cowed him, for God's sake. Why should this cow cow him? "It's only a temporary cash-flow problem," he falters. "You can have your Tuscan holiday in the autumn. You know you hate the heat anyway."

"But it's not a *holiday*!" I howl, hastily transforming my idyll into a stern quest. "It's a research trip! For my next novel! I've got to immerse myself in the Quattrocento!"

Spouse thinks with furious speed. It's very stressful for him, of course, having to juggle a terrifying and sexually demanding mistress and a hideous old wife transfixed with indignation. I hope he's finding it really tiring.

"Why don't you go to Cambridge for a week?" he crows in sudden revelation. "Stay in a college guest room . . . spend all day in the Library . . . no domestic distractions . . . do all the research you want."

Reluctant though I am to acknowledge any of his ideas as good, this one has a certain charm. Mind you, to escape domestic duties I would gladly spend a week in a drainage pipe. Ring up my old college and am offered a room for less than fifteen quid a night. Even we can afford that. And O the owls . . . the towers . . . the river . . . the place where I lost my – er, chord.

So. I still have something to look forward to. Although at my age it's only nostalgia.

16 July

About to whizz off to Cambridge. Spouse wears martyr's slight frown even though we both know he will be helped by the lovely Elaine.

"Mummy! I don't want you to go! I hate Cambridge!"

"I don't want to go either, darling!" I lie passionately. "But I've got to do some background reading for my next book."

"What's background?"

"Daddy will explain – I must just pack my last few bits of paper. Don't forget I'm going to bring you both back a *lovely treat*." Escape to study, grab all loose pieces of paper and thrust into old leather briefcase, trying not to notice that an ancient bag of boiled sweets has gone critical in the bottom. I'll sort it out when I get to Cambridge. I'll sort everything out when I get to Cambridge. Mind, body, soul.

Running the gauntlet of family pique, praying no one will abort my departure by being sique, I leap into the old Volvo and head east.

Diverted en route by the idea of Marston Moretaine Safari Park. Out of Africa and no mistake. Heading Out of Bedfordshire on the A45, I realise that I am really going home to mother -- i.e. taking my bruised and battered Alma back to Mater. Have only seen Cambridge once in almost twenty years, though have oft dreamed I was sitting Finals again and awoken screaming.

Familiar place names appear, at which the heart gives a small nostalgic flop, like a tired toad. I'm saving up the huge leaps for later. Caxton Gibbet! But altered. Caxton Gibbet Chinese Restaurant. Faintly disturbing somehow.

But something faintly reassuring about Caxton Gibbet Recovery Service. Reminds one of *The Beggars' Opera.* 'Cutpurses Cut Down and Counselled.' So if I am reduced to suicidal despair by thoughts of Spouse's infidelity, I won't have to swing alone for long.

More names ring out in my memory: Pampisford, Prickwillow, Whittlesford and Wicken, Trumpington and Toft. Have packed Pevsner, of course. ('Arch with zigzag, three-dimensional zigzag, and billet.')

Arrive at old college and gain access to billet, although alas without zigzags. Small and pleasantly austere Guest Room with view of gardens, where later I hope owls will sing. Smile patronisingly at group of young people rehearsing *Othello* below my window. 'A plague o'hanging thyself!' How true.

Unpack, and become uneasily aware that at home I have a desk to work on and a separate table to eat at and whole different rooms to do my sitting, washing and sleeping in. Here it's a challenge to sit in the armchair without one's chin arriving inconveniently in the washbasin and one's feet in the wardrobe. No matter! As Russell remarked with such asperity: what is mind? No matter! What is matter? Never mind. These few days are dedicated to mind.

Mind won't mind about the cramped conditions. They offer the chance of reducing my daily habits to a Zen simplicity. Smile benignly and empty old briefcase onto desk, melted boiled sweets and all. But what is this?

'PACK HOLIDAY '94' shrieks a piece of paper. I have brought away with me a horrid reminder of the maternal duties awaiting me on my return: kit list for Harriet's Brownie Camp, provided by Brown Owl or perhaps Barney. 'Flannel with loop; small towel with loop . . .' Realise, with sinking feeling, that none of our washing apparatus is yet looped. 'Tea towel -- named if possible.' None of ours are named, but I suppose "I name this tea towel Yasser" shouldn't take long. 'Plate, bowl, mug, knife, fork, spoon -- marked for ident., in a named bag.' Named cutlery, for God's sake? 'Sleeping bag, 2 extra blankets, pillow and pillowcase -- Please make into a bedroll and cover with named plastic bag.' Eyes glaze over. Tempted to make myself into a bedroll and cover with named plastic bag. 'Hairslides—' Wait a minute -- *hairslides*? Don't they mean toenails? Eyebrows? Named scabs? Owl, owl owl, owl owl!

Toss aside paper. What hopes for scholarship with this relentless treadmill of parental duty hanging over me? When the day began, names were a delight. Now a torment. Wish I had named Harriet Zigzag like that All Blacks rugby player. Then I could just chalk a Z on all her stuff like they used to do in Customs back in the good old days when we had Customs. Perhaps I shall hang myself after all. Or – much better idea – change my name and flee to a new life in Bottisham.

23 July

The Cheltenham Festival: cricket, not music. Gloucestershire v. Yorkshire. We usually go – last year we took Elaine, whose crazy high spirits, I now realise, were because she was newly in love with Spouse.

"If I borrowed Henry's Walkman," muses Spouse, "I could watch Gloucestershire and listen to the Test match at the same time."

Like making love to me whilst thinking of Michelle Pfeiffer, I enquire? He flinches. But at least I didn't say thinking of Elaine. I bet he doesn't think of Michelle Pfeiffer whilst making love to Elaine. Not yet. I give it a year.

"Or you thinking of the whole West Indies cricket team?" enquires Spouse, recovering.

Touché. I did try to fantasise about the New Zealanders, honest, but I found I had to think about the West Indians at the same time. I wonder whether these South Africans will prove a bit more dynamic. Funny names. Wetsujts. Broejken Bloed-Vessels. Goen wij je Klappers.

"Do you mind if Elaine comes to Cheltenham with us again?"

What, *again*? It's no coincidence that Elaine rhymes with again. Steady on, now, I tell myself. Don't lose your rag. Dignity at all costs.

"Oh, do take her, by all means," I cry airily. "I've got a prior engagement, I'm afraid."

"What prior engagement?"

"Oh, nothing that would interest you. Off you go to the cricket. Enjoy yourselves."

In other words, silly mid-off!

They do. The children have been summoned to a fraitfly jolly bearbecue and kemping on grarse at the Rainge-Roughvers'. So I am free to enjoy my prior engagement – with the sofa. Lie on it in luxurious silence for five minutes before bothering to switch on the TV. Watch Test Match, but cannot help longing nostalgically for Malcolm Marshall, Desmond Haynes, Brian Johnston, John Arlott . . . well, let's be honest, W.G.Grace. Realise with sickening thud that I am now old enough to be the mother of a test cricketer, indeed, have been for some time.

Cannot escape feeling that the world now belongs to the

young. My time is past and I don't care much, either. I cannot master grunge. Pass me my Zimmer. Lulled by Richie Benaud (my teenage idol – now the Wizened of Oz) I drift off to sleep and dream of houses with rotting floorboards, as usual.

Awake with a horrid twitch, slop to fridge in search of oral gratification and realise that my most urgent prior engagement is with Tesco's. Hurtle thither and seize trolley – a sort of trainer Zimmer frame for the middle-aged. Roll up and down aisles, trying to remember what I need. Pop-tarts and sandwich spread for Harriet. ("Ugh!" cries Henry. "It looks like a pot of sick!") Coke and Scampi'n'lemon flavour Spud Stix for Henry. Stilton'n'Bath Olivers'n'Earl Grey for Spouse. And for me, fresh pasta, crusty u-bake-it French bread, huge suppurating slab of Brie, several bins of Fromage Frais, and lorryload of profiteroles.

Wonder if perhaps I am developing an eating disorder. In shock when Spouse revealed his extra-maritals, I went off my grub and lost two stone. Now I fancy a blow-out. Cringe slightly on being told it all comes to £64, but offer plastic and pray. Spouse will probably spend twice that on posh lunch within tent. Wonder if they will stop for quickie on the way back. Spouse prudish and idle, but for the lovely Elaine he'd perform in a lay-by. Perhaps even on the hard shoulder – which is what he'll get from me when he arrives home.

Still, mustn't begrudge him his little pleasures when I have just performed the shopping equivalent of the Ode to Joy. Could not resist also purchasing Duchy of Cornwall organic oatcakes – i.e. supporting Prince Charles's oats. If we must have a king, at least let's have one who's an anxious idealistic adulterer like the rest of us, who buy decaffeinated diet Coke in a futile attempt to postpone death.

At least won't have to shop again for a fortnight. Arrive home to find message from Alice on the answering machine: "Hi, Dulcie! We thought we'd drop in on you for a few days arriving for lunch tomorrow if that's OK. Saskia's on a new diet for her warts: no wheat, no corn, no dairy produce, no citrus fruits, no chocolate. I'm still a Vegan. Otherwise everything as per usual. See yah!"

Oh well. They can wash down the patriarchal adulterous oatcakes with decaffeinated diet Coke. Sometimes I think life would be simpler as a hyena. A lot more laughs, too.

30 July

August looms worse than any month save December. August looms like a fat lady in a sweat-stained flower-sprigged frock. Come to think of it, Great Aunt Elspeth is part of the reason August looms. But before that we have Alice and Saskia. And then Spouse will be away with Elaine. Just thinking about it all makes me feel totally Augusted.

Alice and Saskia however insist they are radiant, restored, never better. Although I notice they still scatter fag-ash all over the kitchen table and leave me to do the washing up.

"It's since we went on this course, Dulcie. You should try it. Soul Retrieval."

"Mummee! Where are the Pop-tarts?"

All gone down your gullet, darling. Like my soul. *Soul Retrieval*? You'd need colonic irrigation to recover any fragments of mine.

"We've got a much more stress-free lifestyle, now," beams Saskia, half-prone across the kitchen table, her dreadlocks in the butter. "We're going to Madeira to witness our Ch'i and connect with energy."

"I hate to see you weltering in so much domestic dross, Dulcie," sighs Alice. "Especially when these middle years should be serene, full of sharing and self-affirmation."

"Mum!" Henry hovers urgently at my elbow. "I'm worried about the comet. The one that's going to hit the earth when I'm seventy. It could completely destroy the earth."

Recall the mood of fierce protectiveness that enveloped me when Henry was a new baby. Then, I would have seen off any threatening comets with an old tennis racket, no trouble. Now, it's Can I Survive Sunday afternoon?

"Let's go to see the open gardens in East Moulder," I plead. "It says they do teas at The Nobbetts."

"Will there be chocolate cake?" demands Harriet.

"How the hell do I know?"

"There's no need to shout Mummy! I was only asking!"

Before we depart I go to the bathroom and secretly swallow

a migraine pill – the sort that gives you a raging thirst forty minutes later. Never mind, by then we shall be at The Nobbetts and having spent ten seconds admiring their Physostegias I shall collapse into the nearest deckchair for an hour.

Drive towards East Moulder, enduring Alice and Saskia's relentless diatribe about peace, love, serenity and caring. Privately reassure my throbbing head that one day soon I shall put it somewhere nice and quiet – the oven, for instance.

"Mummee! We're hungry! We want chocolate cake!"

"Yes, and I'm thirsty, but I'm not complaining about it."

"But Dulcie, we should complain more. These negative stresses have to be outed. Then your soul would have a chance to start the healing."

Never mind my soul. What I'm worried about is my tongue. And where the hell has East Moulder gone? Has a comet perhaps quietly removed it from the face of the earth? We're already terribly late, owing to Alice and Saskia's habit of lounging about after lunch and my perverse inclination to wash the dishes – alone. Will we reach East Moulder before my tongue turns to a scorched shard of india rubber?

But here it is! Park in sweltering field, enquire where is The Nobbetts, am told On Other Side of Village, ignore other open gardens and sprint thither. On arrival discover Tea's Off, sorry, the advert got it wrong, they couldn't possibly cope. There is however a craft stall selling kits for little girls to knot themselves a friendship bracelet, and for little boys to test their soil. Instant covetous clamour: give in and hope Alice and Saskia won't notice I'm placating Mammon again.

Too proud to ask for glass of water, so hurtle back to car. Ignore children wailing for chocolate cake in my wake, and Alice and Saskia ranting about harmony, and drive like bat out of hell back home.

"MUMMY! Dammit! My friendship bracelet has got knotted!"

"Mum! Can we stop here for a minute so I can test the soil?"

Cannot reply as tongue has turned to chamois and soul has been pulverised by comet. Arrive home and stick tongue under tap for five minutes.

"Saskia and I are just going up to meditate," Alice places serene and caring hand on my shoulder. "We'll be down for tea."

"Mummy! Please will you get rid of the knots so I can make Alice and Saskia friendship bracelets?"

"Mum! Will you help me test the soil?"

Soil? Lead me to it and just watch me disappear down one of the cracks.

6 August

"Can't you use the American Express Card a bit more?" complains Spouse, scrutinising his mail. "We haven't earned enough air miles so far to pay for a game of hopscotch."

"I thought we were broke."

"I'm not saying spend more money, I'm just saying when you have to spend money, use American Express."

He only wants air miles so he can take Elaine off to exotic locations, I bet. Next week it's the Seychelles. He'll have to pack his own suitcase this time. If he can remember how.

"Mummy! I don't want to be horrible or anything, but I'd like to run into the Houses of Parliament and stick a knife into John Major's guts." How ugly political indoctrination is. Especially when it's your very own. "I love Tony Blair, Daddy," she goes on. "Because Mummy says his is the nearest thing to a pink party and pink is my favourite colour." Yes, he appeals to the Bambini. My Little Tony. The Care Blairs.

"I don't agree with John Major but that's no reason to stick a knife in his guts, darling. We can vote him out in the next election."

"Ah, but *can* we?" enquires Spouse, with heavy satirical emphasis. "And for a shy woodland creature, Bambi seems to say sod all about your precious environment."

"*My* precious environment? Where the hell do you live, then?"

However, it's true that the sexy new Labour party hasn't remotely established its Green credentials. Although I'm sure that in Islington they're all devoted bottle-bankers, there is such a thing as the wrong sort of growth. All the same, I seem to sniff the promised land. All those lovely nursery schools, buses, retraining schemes for redundant hospital managers . . .

Open fridge. Nothing within except the wrong sort of growth. Perhaps in the new Labour Jerusalem there'll be house-to-house delivery of Tuscan olive bread and radiccio by a charming lesbian in a horse and cart.

"Which would you rather do? Childcare or shopping?"

"Oh, leave the kids here with me," Spouse is glued to TV Sport.

In the circumstances 'childcare' is a euphemism for 'coma'. Never mind. At least they're safer indoors than out on the streets – until the Scarlet Milennium, when all streets will be paved with seisal.

Decide on Waitrose instead of Tesco's for once. 'Waitrose' rather apt: having to wait for the Parliament of the Rose. Come over hot by the Delicatessen. First hot flush? Or symptom of Utopic pregnancy? Warn myself sternly that I must save up panic attacks till I really need one.

At checkout, annoyed to discover that Waitrose do not accept American Express. Present VISA instead. Reliable old VISA. You may not get airmiles but at least you get by. Assistant frowns at electronic clicks.

"I'm afraid the transaction has been refused, Madam." Panic and shame clothe me in crimson. Skint. The cardinal sin. Splutter that we put loadsamoney in only last week – which is true, but I expect they all say that. People behind me in queue sigh audibly. Rip guts out of handbag, but no chequebook, and purse only contains £9.34. Express horror, outrage, incredulity, and abject apology, leave shopping and hurtle out.

Halfway home realise car is about to run out of petrol. Just in time, spy filling station (Gas'n'Go) and, since the VISA doesn't work, am relieved to see the magic logo American Express. Still hot and shaking, fill up and present AMEX card.

"Sorry, love, this one's expired."

AMEX old and invalid: suddenly suspicious – scrutinise VISA card and discover it is not valid till next month. Plastic yesterday and plastic tomorrow, but never plastic today. Proprieter of Gas'n'Go accepts £9.34 cash and an I.O.U. for the petrol because he likes my face. Wonder if he is available for marriage.

"You've got to live in the present, love," he urges me, pointing out that my credit cards betray a consciousness both yearning for the past and panting for the future.

"The trouble is," I complain, "the present is so awful."
"Couldn't agree more. Bring back Maggie I say."
Nod spuriously and creep off home. Do not inform Spouse
of my adventure as suspect it does not redound to my credit.
Instead clean out fridge in anticipation of new milennium and
inform family that we are entering new age of austerity.
Wonder if Tony Blair can do that trick with the loaves
and fishes.

13 August

Spouse is in the Seychelles with his lovely bronzed young
mistress. Heroically I lie to his children that Daddy is 'at
a conference in America'. Their greedy eyes light up at
the thought of state-of-the-art Sindies and Game Boys he
might bring back. Alas, I suspect Daddy is surrounded only
by palm-thatched bonking couches. Was it the Seychelles or
the Maldives which were likely to be submerged as the polar
ice-caps melt? Torn between my ecological duty and a desire
to apply blowtorch to Antarctica.
"I know Mummy! Can we go over and see Elaine? She might
give us a Tropical Whopper: she's got some in her fridge."
"I think she's gone to see her mother this weekend, darling."
Listen: I'm not a brick, I'm a brickworks – no, I'm the entire
Campo at Siena. God how I wish I was there.
Uneasily aware that by misplacing but one letter a brick can
deftly become a birck. Although I know berk is not spelled
birck I wonder if it is a message from the great philologer
in the sky. Why doesn't Michael Buerk change his name to
Berkeley? And what is the origin of berk and Buerk? Wonder
if I should take the children to Berkeley Castle, but fear it is
too near Berkeley Nuclear Power Station, being dismantled
and therefore probably more dangerous than ever. Oh why did
mankind ever start tampering with dirt at all?
Exhausted by the thought of taking the children to Berkeley
Castle, although I remember that the skull was a great hit.
Grateful that they are slumped in front of TV, though unnerved

by recent reports that the rays from a TV screen can cause cancer. When Henry is not goggling at the TV he is symbiotically linked to his computer. Oh why did humankind have to invent artificial intelligence? Wasn't our own natural intelligence bad enough? Notice that in the absence of Spouse I am becoming a philosopher. Admire myself in pose of solitary sage, though would prefer to be in Siena with Michael Buerk.

Phone rings. Socrates did not have to put up with this. Answer in irritated bark.

"Air hellair Dulcie it's Lydia Rainge-Roughver."

After exchanging civilities, she invites Henry and Harriet to come orf with them to a friend's hice in Blairgowrie. Tairdebly short notice but Julian and Emma would be apslootleh thrilled.

Agree immediately. Blairgowrie? Cannot possibly refuse to let children visit somewhere so ecumenical. Although I know one mustn't look a gift horse in the mouth, consult map to see if Blairgowrie is near a nuclear reprocessing plant. Apparently not – though a coastal strip to the south looks as if it might be ripe for heavy industry. Coastal strip is apparently called the Arse of Gowrie. Briefly diverted by this, remembering that Gowrie was – or is – something to do with the Arse Council. Then discover I have map-read badly as usual and it is not Arse but Carse.

Grab the Greenpeace book *Coastline: Britain's Threatened Heritage* to see if the Carse of Gowrie is fit for my little darlings' toes to twinkle upon. Book laments the proliferation upon the Firth of Forth of nuclear power stations, paper mills, cement and linoleum works, oil refineries and rig construction works, but acknowledges that the Carse of Gowrie is 'less industrialised' though 'not much purer'.

Rush upstairs and throw childrens' clothes into bags. Well, it did say less industrialised. Besides, they probably won't go to the Carse at all. Suddenly dawns on me that August in Scotland means shooting birds. No doubt Henry will be offered his first gun, and Harriet will have her first nervous breakdown. The slaughter of defenceless and harmless fowl bred for the purpose has always disgusted me, but children need to be able to make up their own minds on the subject. Especially as it means they're off my hands for a week.

Inform them of this sudden delightful expedition, at which Henry cries "Hurrah" but Harriet whispers, "Mummy – I hate Emma Rainge-Roughver. And their dogs stink. But I think

I love Julian a bit." Well then, I pounce, here's the perfect opportunity to find out.

Lydia collects them in her new Discovery. Belt them firmly into the back seats, suppressing shiver of foreboding as usual at the thought of the hundreds of miles of motorway they will be exposed to, and wave them off. Then go back into house. Front door shuts with curiously hollow bang. I am alone. Put kettle on, and enjoy that first solitary frisson: the unmistakable thump and rustle of the axeman hiding upstairs.

20 August

Home alone at last. Open back door and admire wind blowing through nettles for a while. Quality time. The barbarians have fled.

"Mrs Domum!" Bernard Twill next door pops up over the fence at me, flourishing a marrow big enough to feature in the old May-Day parades in Moscow. "Or would you prefer a yellow one?"

Insist that green stripes are my favourite, so very Regency. Express gratitude, enquire after Audrey's piles, and escape indoors as soon as decent. Blissful solitude will have to be enjoyed indoors, unless I drive off to a remote beauty spot. But somehow the phrase remote beauty spot makes one think of murder. Perhaps a Cotswold tea shop? Drop finger at random upon map of Gloucestershire. Lower Slaughter.

Think perhaps an afternoon on the sofa might be safer. One does not wish to ignore messages from the gods. Browsing through the *Radio Times* I come upon the horoscopes. Frighteningly accurate, as usual. For more detail, one can dial-a-seer. Now, this is exactly the sort of project which thrives in the absence of a spouse. Rush to phone and am greeted with a robust "Hello Virgo!" from male mystic voice.

"You must be wondering just what's wrong with you at the moment," he begins. Inspired. But then, I wonder that regularly. However, sage insists, this is a time for contemplation, not self-flagellation. What a nice man. How true. Replace receiver with frisson of guilt: thank God nobody knows I've just done that. Wait! Stop! That's self-flagellation for a start. Ring your soothsayer with pride. Alice would say it was no more bizarre than going to church.

Hungry. Wander, in self-indulgent floating motion, to kitchen, which offers a pound of Sturmers and the marrow. Hurl marrow into cupboard under stairs. Return to sofa and eat three Sturmers whilst reading *Marie Claire* – the thinking woman's filth – then yawn, stretch, luxuriate, etc., as recommended by astrologer. Wonder if Tony Blair believes in an afterlife. Wonder if I do.

Stare at the ceiling. Wonder if any of my ancestors are floating up there, admiring my Sturmers and wishing I would switch on the TV. You're never alone with superstition. By mid-evening, the shades begin to gather. Hastily draw curtains and double-lock doors. Sofa is beginning to pall so decide on that exquisite middle-aged treat: early to bed.

Halfway upstairs am smitten by cramps in the belly. The Sturmers strike back. Collapse into bed fully-dressed and groan. Serve me right for being so greedy and lazy. I should have stuffed the marrow. No, stuff the marrow, I'm flagellating again.

Wrenched from blessed slumber by horrid flash of lightning and clap of thunder. Terrified of death by thunderstorm, though at least it would be quick. Can one be struck indoors? Wonder if the bedframe is metal. Suddenly realise am still dressed and trouser zip is metal. Rip off jeans with almost adulterous alacrity. Would be horrible to be zapped in the zip. Flash – BANG! Cringe under covers and whimper. This is God punishing me for ringing astrologer. Well, he did warn us he was a jealous God. FLASH CRASH! Wonder if it would be safer under the stairs. Wonder if house has a lightning conductor – something I only ever think about during storms.

Flash-Bang – BANG! Palpable extra bang downstairs. Seize phone. Phone dead. Dead! The storm has killed my phone! Flash-BANG! Run to loo. Vaguely remember electricity and water don't mix so pee as quickly as possible then, wrapping myself in duvet, run downstairs, shut myself in cupboard under stairs and thrust fingers in my ears. Uncomfortable – sexually harassed by broom and marrow – but at least cannot see flashes. As my eyes get used to the dark, however, I can make out a large packet of Flash right under my nose. Ha ha, God, nice one.

Then realise in a flash I am sitting on the electricity meter. Leap up as if scalded, scuttle back upstairs and hide under Harriet's bed as the frame is wooden. Last flagellating thought: can't die yet, Lord, I haven't done the washing-up. And I'm sorry I said ringing a soothsayer was no more bizarre than going to church. Will go to church assiduously if spared. And will forgive my Spouse, Thy representative here on earth, everything if he'll only come back.

. . . A lull. By Jove! I think the old flasher has wandered off to another part of the park. Lie low under Harriet's bed for a while, though. Had enough quality time for the present. Bring back the barbarians.

3 September

Spouse returns from Seychelles in sombre mood. Perhaps life on tropical beach with deeply-tanned mistress began to pall. Perhaps he found himself wishing she could discuss cricket or remember the Goon Show, or make jokes about Hurd and Bottomley. Perhaps he began to wish he was on holiday with somebody a bit more like George Eliot than Kim Basinger. Although my resemblance to George Eliot is merely physical. And come to think of it, George Eliot's husband threw himself into the Grand Canal.

Spouse does remember to ask How Things Are. As chief Thing, I have to inform him that in his absence the house was struck by lightning and the answering machine killed. I am the answering machine now.

"We had a hell of a storm in the Seychelles, too. Terrifying."

My modest self-effacing English thunderstorms cannot compare with his big tropical ones. I bet Elaine was terrified. I bet she found refuge in his manly embrace. Recall Spouse's reaction last time we shared a marital thunderstorm: "Get off! Don't touch me in case you're struck by lightning!"

Children mob their Papa with greedy anticipation. What have you brought us, what have you brought us Daddy?

"The only thing I've brought back," he warns them with

beetling brows, "is a bloody awful cold, so keep your distance."

Strangely glad to have him back, though. Something to be said for the nuclear family -- even if, as in a pride of lions, the women do all the work. The way he roars at the cubs and cuffs them now and then is useful, I admit. Didn't like the thunder on my own. Or the dark.

Spouse very quiet for two days. Says he has jet lag. Spends all daylight hours asleep and most of night on the phone to Elaine, who has gone to see her mother. On the third day his cold arrives in my throat, gift-wrapped in barbed wire, and just in time to accompany us to Centerparcs Longleat. Within hours my voice has completely disappeared. Strange, having your vox popped. Oh well. I've always wanted to be enigmatic. Now's my chance.

"They should let the lions loose in the Subtropical Swimming Paradise," observes Spouse as we settle into our executive villa with jacuzzi en suite. "They could clear up the kids on remand." Laryngitis gives me an excuse to ignore this kind of thing.

Children rush off to hire bikes, and with a sudden surge of assertiveness I suggest in silent croak that as Spouse has just enjoyed a holiday in the Seychelles and two days in bed, perhaps he would like to unpack whilst I lie in the jacuzzi and peruse the list of pleasures offered by the place.

"What?"

Climb into the jacuzzi anyway. An odd but pleasant sensation – like sharing the bath with whole shoals of fragrant baby farts. Peruse booklet and feel faint at the thought of Aerobics, Rollerskating and Racket Ball. Enquire of Spouse What is *Pétanque*? But alas he has switched on the executive TV and my plaintive whisper is drowned.

In fact, I could be completely drowned and he'd be none the wiser. I bet if it was Elaine in this jacuzzi he'd be lingering in the doorway and ogling her effervescence. Must raise spirits. Family holiday and all that. Attempt to sing in the bath, but can only achieve mime. Too croaky for Karaoke.

Children return with bikes, express ecstasy, and urge us to accompany them to Subtropical Swimming Paradise. Haul myself out of jacuzzi, get dried and dress, in order to get wet again family-style three hundred yards away. Spouse strangely co-operative -- suppose he wants to show off his tan.

Under glass dome, happy families frolic in water. Spouse and I bask at cafe table. Spouse manages not to make any comparisons with the Seychelles, for which I am grateful. Children rush up, drip all over us like wet dogs, shout It's brilliant! and rush off again. They're old enough now to leave us alone a bit, bless their little hearts. Rather pleasant sitting here. Alice would sneer, but can't help feeling Centerparcs is very much in the spirit of Ancient Rome.

"The thing is," Spouse turns to me with sudden awkward emphasis, "Elaine wants me to go and live with her."

Luckily, there's no answer to that. Except perhaps bring on the lions.

10 September

Alice rings enquiring how I am. Have to admit I'm in a jam. What sort? Gooseberry, I suppose since Spouse has been ordered by his mistress, the lovely Elaine, to go off and live with her.

"Good God!" shrieks Alice, "Men just defy belief! I hope you said bugger off and good riddance."

"Er no, actually. I suggested a timeshare."

"You what?"

"Friday to Monday with Elaine: Tuesday to Friday with us."

Silence: Alice evidently flabbergasted.

"I'm sorry, but I find that utterly sordid. With me it's passion or nothing. I've only got one thing to say to you, Dulcie: *kill!*"

"But what about the kids?"

"Oh yes . . . Er . . ."

The silence of a woman so undefiled by child-rearing, she'd forgotten I'd got any. With her it's passion or nothing. With me it's Just Wait Till Your Father Gets Home. Spouse's most vital function, as far as I'm concerned, is to glower down through the clouds and hurl the occasional thunderbolt.

"Mummeee! Aunt Elspeth's taxi is outside!" Children rush in, putting an end to civilised life as we know it, accompanied by Spouse looking tired now to save time later. I wonder if he's planning to break the news to his puritanical aunt, too? A strange smile leaps unbidden to my lips. Sense there might be treats in store. Feel half-strengthened by Spouse's threat to half-depart. Perhaps I am experiencing some divine transition from sinner to martyr.

"Och, Dulcie, you're so *thin*, dear! You've been overdoing it again." As if overdoing it were some kind of perverse self-indulgence on my part. "My word, Gordon, you're looking well! He looks ten years younger, doesn't he, Dulcie? What's your secret, my boy?" What indeed.

The children endure her embraces, hoping for presents. We steer her into the sitting room where she disgorges a tartan propelling pencil for Henry (received with resignation) and hideous white nylon fur hamster in kilt for Harriet (received with rapture).

"Oh, she's lovely Auntie! I'm going to call her Sharon! Can I take her and show her to Elaine, Mummy?" Harriet leaps up and is already at the door.

"Certainly not! We're going to have tea with Auntie first."

"Who's Elaine, dear?"

"The lady across the road."

"Och, yes, I remember: Mummy's little friend."

"Daddy's as well!" cries Harriet, putting her foot not just in it but halfway down her throat. Elspeth cocks an eyebrow: Spouse actually blushes. I swoop serenely to the rescue.

"Elaine is everybody's friend. Now relax Elspeth, I expect you'd like some tea and scones."

Escape to kitchen, leaving Spouse enquiring urgently about Elspeth's grandchildren, without mentioning them by name in case he gets it wrong.

Arrange WI scones and raspberry jam on silver salver (wedding present from Great Aunt, and only ever used when she visits) and return to sitting room, where I am pleased to see Spouse looking guilt-edged.

"Oh, Mum! Sharon's ear's come off! Never mind. I'll call her Nelson instead after that man who cut his ear off."

"A scone, Elspeth? Get up off the floor, Harriet."

"OOOOOOWWWWW! Something's bloody stung me, Mummy!"

Somehow in getting up Harriet has brushed against and angered a comatose wasp, which drones off round the room.

At the sound of her screams, something inside me snaps as they say in pulp fiction, and seizing the local newspaper I pursue the venomous beast, thrashing and thrashing and thrashing, and then when it falls, stamping and stamping and grinding until it is deader than a wasp has ever been. Look up to find family staring at me in alarm, even Harriet's screams suspended for an instant.

"That's made me feel a lot better," I beam. Spouse has gone pale. Perhaps he thinks it might be him next. Perhaps indeed it might. How dare he drone about for years and finally settle only to administer sudden horrid shock and leave us stinging and screaming? Alice was right. Flushed with bloodlust – wonderful feeling. Beats martyrdom any day.

24 September

The swallows have flown south, and The Aunt north. The sun has turned his back on us and every day tilts further towards the dark. To cap these seasonal modulations, today Spouse has moved into Elaine's – and I'm the one who has to tell the children.

"I'm not much good at that sort of thing," he observed this morning, stuffing two clean pairs of underpants into his briefcase. "You're so good with people, you'll do a much better job of it."

Oh yes, I'm good with people. I'm effing brilliant. I do a particularly good Epoux Infidèle Rôti au Coulis de Goolies. Followed by Tarte Minceur.

"I see," I sneer. "Wasn't it lucky I was so much better at shopping, cooking, washing, ironing and all that crap as well?"

Annoyed by my inability to preserve an indifferent Garbo-esque iciness.

"Oh, come on," he sighs, hesitating over which socks to offer the hospitality of Elaine's fragrant drawers. "Mrs Body does the ironing anyway."

"I bet it's dead cushy at Elaine's." My rampant resentment will not be stopped. "I bet you won't so much as have to stack a plate, there."

"That just shows how little you know about it," remarks Spouse airily, and makes for the door.

"Well, you wouldn't expect me to know much about my husband's intimate domestic habits with his mistress, would you?" I shout, suddenly blinded by tears of fury.

"I know you must be tempted to give me an almighty bollocking," he pauses graciously by the front door. "and of course I deserve it. But I know you'll hang on in there for the kids' sake. Think of it as getting a lazy bastard out of your hair."

He goes, horribly liberated by his acceptance of his own bastardhood. I could've been the one walking out. Didn't Tom urge me to run off to Tuscany? And I refused, for the sake of the kids. Looked at objectively, you've got to admit I'm a bloody saint, but unlike Spouse, I can't accept myself for a minute. Perhaps that's the definition of a saint.

Cry furiously into the carpet for a while. Afterwards, recall that Tom was willing to elope, kids and all, but I declined because I was beginning to find him irritating. Better to be irritated in Tuscany than reviled in Rusbridge. Better to be a bastard than a saint, too.

Put on what I hope will be consoling music. Bob Dylan. 'You've been down to the bottom with a bad man, babe: now you're back where you belong.' But where's *that*, Bob? Realise that I shall be able to listen to Bob Dylan all evening if I like. Spouse despised everything after Monteverdi. But why am I thinking of him in the past tense? He's still alive, dammit. Probably listening to Mantovani with beatific smile on his face.

Depart to pick up children. Henry is safely installed at St Archie's and is beginning to wilt at the excesses of public-school sport and discipline. Our bank account wilts at the bills. £70 for a child's blazer! But that is Spouse's problem. If he wants to waste perfectly good money on turning his son into a bottled-up little prig, fine. Actually Henry is pretty much a bottled-up little prig already. So it's even more a waste of money.

Whereas his little sister is turning into a lager lout. Whilst we are ingesting our dinosaur burgers, I listen to the weather forecast.

"There will be showers at first with rain later."

"What bollocks!" cries Harriet. "If there's going to be

showers, that's rain as well, isn't it? So why don't they say rain and rain?"

"Or even just rain?" Henry is inclining to the terse. His upper lip is visibly stiffening. However am I going to tell him his Dad has gone across the road to live with his mistress? Put a note under his door?

"Harriet! You shouldn't use swear words – especially when you don't know what they mean."

"I know what bollocks are!" she shouts indignantly. "Sharon says her brother's got hair growing on his."

Alas, I cannot say "Wait till your father gets home" as he won't be back for three days. Sigh and make myself a cup of Red Zinger tea, although feel about as far from red and zinging as I have ever been.

Henry goes upstairs to do his homework without being asked. Whatever is wrong with that boy? Harriet digs in for a bout of goggling. This, I sense, is the worst possible moment to break the momentous news.

"Daddy has gone to live with Elaine," I burst out.

"Oh, brilliant. That means I can stay up and watch *Red Dwarf*."

1 October

"Mummy, why has Daddy gone to live with Elaine?"

They said nothing at first: swallowed it whole without comment. Admittedly they were watching TV at the time, so probably wouldn't have turned a hair if I had informed them that Daddy had metamorphosed into a pink inflatable pig and gone soaring up to the ceiling. Which, let's face it, would have been much more reasonable behaviour.

We are in the supermarket, in itself quite enough of an ordeal without having to discuss paternal adultery.

"Well," I whisper, "they love each other."

"What?" Harriet still quite deaf. Henry walks away fast. Whisper more loudly. "Ugh! They don't kiss and have sex and things do they?"

"Sssssh!"

"Why shhhh? When you told us about sex you said it was nothing to be ashamed of!"

"Yes, but . . . there might be some people here who might not want to hear all about our private affairs."

Henry for a start: up ahead, studying the cereals with a furious frown and pretending he doesn't know us. I'm pretending I don't know us too.

"But you and Daddy still love each other don't you?"

"Yes, of course we do."

"Well I think it's horrible of Elaine to steal our Daddy."

"You like Elaine, darling. We all like her."

"Don't you mind, then?"

Important for the children not to feel their mother is suffering.

"Of course I don't mind, darling! It gives me lots more time with you." Dazzling, deceitful smile.

"Hey, Mum! Can we have popcorn?"

"Oh, all right."

You can have cereal that plays 'God Save the Queen' if it'll help. Easily see how a lone mother might feel so guilty about her broken marriage that she'd spoil her children rotten in a futile attempt to compensate. Luckily with my kids it's a case of, Here's two I spoiled earlier.

Spouse hasn't gone altogether: he returns for weekends. I am only half-left. No indignant quivers. Only demisemiquavers. Return from shopping and beg children to help unpack it but they have already hurtled off to kneel at the feet of the TV and offer it their souls.

Sink into kitchen chair and open junk mail from this morning. Surely it will offer somebody or something worse off than myself. Ah! Today it's Endangered British Mammals, not counting the Royal Family. 'The dormouse and many bats are clinging on by their toenails . . .' Know the feeling. But wait! Aren't bats meant to cling on by their toenails? Silly philological quibble. Perhaps solitude will turn me into a quibbler.

Have to face the fact that I am metamorphosing into something else. No longer really somebody's wife. Wives not endangered British Mammals, however: cut the old ones down and new ones spring up, just like – well I was going to say roses but let's settle for nettles. And the young ones' sting is far worse, as I trust Spouse will soon find out.

68

Uneasily aware that Elaine may eventually insist on a baby, despite extensive exposure to Spouse's existing offspring. However will he pay for it all? Will he receive the attentions of the Child Support Agency? Wish, not for the first time, that I could write a best-selling bonkbuster instead of my usual tame historical forays. History isn't sexy, it seems, only shopping and power. Must attempt to shake off my fascination with dead people. Or perhaps dig 'em up and force 'em out to the shops.

Emma kicked off her mock-snakeskin Emilio sling-backs and collapsed onto the state-of-the-art anti-rhinitis organic feather Futon.

"Emporio Armani was madness," she called, hearing the jacuzzi bubbling beyond the open door of William's en suite. "But I got a fabulous bustier with finials and putti at Versace. Shall I model it for you, honey?"

"Sure. But come here a minute first – I want you to meet my friend Horatio." ..

Horatio? Emma hauled herself off the Futon and waddled into the Ambassadorial bathroom. I must book another Liposuction, she thought, catching her hip on the doorframe. There was her husband's distinguished grey head, rising from the foaming waters of the jacuzzi like a crocodile. And get this! The guy with him was wearing an eyepatch.

"Hey," grinned Emma, "cool attitude, dude. Where'd you get that eyepatch? Do they do one with rhine-stones?"

8 October

"Mummy! To cheer us up for Daddy going to live with Elaine -- can we have a cat?"

"No! I'm the one who'd have to look after it, buy its food, deflea it, clear up its messes." Exactly as with Daddy, come to think of it. "Besides, Daddy hasn't gone to live with Elaine all the time – he comes back here for weekends."

"But I waaaaant a cat!" Harriet's yowl of cupidity reminds me that it is time for Henry to do his violin practice.

St Archie's is a musical school. For reasons not entirely clear to me, a defenceless violin has been delivered up to Henry and someone called Mr Powell is encouraging him, at some expense, to make noises upon it. Not sure if mastering 'Air on a G-string' will add to Henry's career prospects. Except as a Chippendale.

"But Mum! I'm reading my comic!"

Who would not rather read *MAD* Super Special Gross-Outs 2 than experience violin practice? Me, for a start. Secretly peruse *MAD* whilst urging Henry to grapple more elastically with his G-string. His performance is so wooden, I just hope it came from sustainably managed plantations. *MAD* is full of jokes about vomiting and nose-picking. Wonder if I should censor it, but uneasily aware that I have recently picked my nose rather more often than desirable. Well, when you're an abandoned wife, you have to develop new hobbies to fill the empty hours. Does Elaine pick her nose? Has Spouse started to pick his in her presence, yet?

"Very good, Henry! Just one more time, with a bit more oomf."

Having exhausted *MAD*, I stick my nose in an old copy of *The Times* – 'Saturday Rendezvous'. The Top People's Lainely Hawts Column. Wonder what 'gsoh' is, apart from anagram of gosh. Decide it must stand for ghastly state of health. Then there's n/s. No Syphilis? Naturist/Socialist? New Shoes? We are deep in economic recession, after all. Ah! No strings, of course. Realise with a plangent twang, that mine have all frayed to the very last strand.

Henry's last encore breaks down halfway through. His shoulders droop. He hates his violin. If he were a scruffy Irish urchin who'd had a go on his Grandad's fiddle on the warm doorstep of a Galway pub, in June, with th' smell o'th'roses on th'air . . . Must pull myself together and stop wishing we were more picturesque. We are white suburban middle-class Anglo-Saxons and we must grin and bear it.

"Oh all right, darling, that's enough. Put it away now." Relief transforms Henry's face, upon which the first pustules of puberty are already a-quiver. Perhaps the cello would suit him better, as all too soon he will become preoccupied by what's going on between his legs. Or better yet, the Saxophone.

There's something so . . . well, stringy about strings. Henry runs off to the TV leaving me alone with the Lonely Hearts ads. 'Virginia Charles: the exclusive introduction agency for people of quality and integrity'. Well, you can't say they didn't warn you. 'Are you childfree, solvent, active, slim, artistic?' No, I'm lumbered, skint, idle, fat and clumsy.

'Windsor wench seeks warrior . . .' Avert my gaze from advert at the thought of our dear Windsor wench being driven to the lonely hearts column. Turn over paper and discover piece about the novelist Susan Hill's horticultural ambitions. 'In 30 years, I aim to create a garden which will be as good as Hidcote, but different,' says Ms Hill. Goodness me, whatever next? Heaven and earth in 4½ days?

Only jealous. Glare at my solitary windowbox, in which three stunted marigolds are starving in a gale. Queen Susan is a blooming landscape gardener made, and I am barren stock. She made her fortune with a sequel to *Rebecca*. Wonder if I could pull the same stunt.

Fortinbras: Take up the bodies: such a sight as this
Becomes the field, but here shows much amiss.
Go, bid the soldiers shoot.
Enter Jewish Grandmother, running
Grandmother: Stop! Wait! Give him some chicken soup!

Not sure if the idea of warmed-up Hamlet has legs, somehow. It'll have to be a millionaire. Or oblivion. To be honest, a good night's sleep would be a start. White suburban middle-class matron, no strings, no brass, too much wind, seeks concussion.

15 October

"You're not still using tampons are you, Dulcie?" Alice on the phone again being supportive. Feel a brief pang of longing for purdah, from which veiling mystery I could watch the world without intrusive questions about the state of my nostrils, let alone the Netherlands.

I do not wish to think about adhesive panty liners more often than absolutely necessary. Despite all the tasteful soft-focus ads on the telly, we all know the cruel fact: once in your knickers the bastards turn upside down and adhere to the hairs on your arse. The botty-ripper.

"Any signs of the menopause yet?" enquires Alice eagerly. Inform her airily that I am much too busy to notice. Hurt, she terminates the conversation abruptly saying she is off to St Kitts. Wonder idly if this is a form of rhyming slang. If so, hope that Alice's attack is particularly severe.

Further excursions into Caribbean rhyming slang hampered by the fact that most Caribbean islands are pronounced perversely: S'n Loosha for St Lucia, Nevis as in penis not devil, Grenada as in hand grenade not Granardour, and Dominica as in the execrable Eurovision hit of long ago, Domineeeka eeeka eeeka, not the Dominican order. There is another Caribbean country, the Dominican Republic, that inclines to the latter.

I think I probably incline to the latter these days. In fact I'd probably recline to the latter if I could clear a bit of space on the floor. It sounds restful. You know where you are with the latter. Better by far than anticipation. Was that another Eurovision noise? No, I'm thinking of 'Congratulations'. Or was it Congratulation, singular? Sung by Cliff Richard, singular singer. A born Singleton. A brother for Valerie.

Close eyes, lie back and construct a production of *Twelfth Night* with Valerie Singleton as Viola and Cliff Richard as her long-lost brother Sebastian. Who would Count Orsino be? Recall in my undergraduate days I used to imagine myself as Viola with the current heart-throb don as Orsino. Nowadays, despite the semi-departure of Spouse and the evident aching void in my life, it's as much as I can do to dredge up a flicker of attraction for anyone, let alone identify a heart-throb. Although Nick Clark and Paul Allen on Radio 4 both have rather sexy voices.

Open eyes and determine to do something constructive in the hour left before the school run. Resolve to attack the archive of children's drawings gathering dust on the top of the wardrobe. Pull down tottering lasagne of paper and card, and cover myself with dead spiders, etc. When the dust clears, vow to be tough this time and only keep the very best.

Henry's drawings revolve around machinery designed for fast travel or murder: fantasies of escape from suffocating mother, no doubt. The nearest he comes to human form is vampires and skeletons. But heart melts at the sight of Harriet's infantile effort of years ago: jolly people with faces like hopeful balloons. Recognise human race. Nowadays she draws pert Sindies embracing clean-cut Kens.

Ah! A self-portrait, complete with slogan laboriously scrawled in spiderish, staggering letters: ARIET WONTIN DADA CRINE. What does this mean? Looks like extract from menu of Chinese Restaurant. Then notice big tears sliding down Ariet's face. Of course! 'Harriet wanting Dada: crying.' Tears burst from my own eyes at this poignant relic. Crush it to my breast, sobbing. Transfixed with need to meet and embrace children, leap up and hurtle downstairs.

Drive through prism of tears to school; park tempestuously on pavement, glared at by old lady; jump out and apologise to her, spoiling her indignation. Children emerge from school. Harriet is walking beside boy and saying something like Cool Dude. Ah, but I know that underneath the cheap sophistication she is really wontin Dada crine.

Seize her and kiss raspingly. She hurls me off, and in the car informs me icily, "Never kiss me again at school Mummy. I'm in the top class now and it was GROSS!"

Wait in the car outside St Archie's as Henry has sternly informed me I am not to embarrass the tarmac by setting my ghastly foot thereon.

Oh well. Eagerly anticipate Paul Allen's resonant insights on Kaleidoscope but they are blotted out by childish babble. That'll teach me to anticipate anything these days, let alone eagerly. Daren't even look forward to the menopause. Ain't life an upside-down panty liner. What country friends is this? This is Delirium, lady.

22 October

Awake from bizarre dream. A tabloid headline screamed 'Tony Blair as you've never seen him before! Stark naked and fully-frontal!' Of course I grabbed a copy and gawped, astonished. He had *two willies*. Two. Side by side, like a two-pin plug. What does this mean? If Spouse was here I'd wake him up and ask him. Which perhaps is another reason why he left.

If only I'd been born in ancient times I could have been a Sybil. I could've had a lovely cave, very ecological, super view of the Aegean, barbecued red snapper washed down with plenty of Ouzo every night, and they'd all come and see me with bags of gold and ask me to tell them my dreams. And then they'd go back and say, "Great news, master: she dreamt you had two willies, that's two elections in the bag as it were."

Perhaps the dream means that Tony Blair is now the nearest thing we've got to Royalty. I wonder, if I had ever dreamt of Margaret Thatcher, how many willies she would have had? A dress covered with willies perhaps, rather like the portrait of Elizabeth I's dress covered with eyes – a style successfully aped in our own times by Dame Edna.

Drift into uneasy sleep in which I realise that Margaret Thatcher is a reincarnation of Elizabeth I. Imperious, more macho than most men, surrounded by handsome advisers . . . Both had close confidants called Cecil . . . And then there's Norman Tebbit, the Earl of Essex . . . And Robert, or Roberts, an important name . . .

"Mummy! It's half past eight!"

Hurtle out of bed, kick bottle of mineral water all over slippers, throw half-dressed children into back of car with crisps to eat on the way and perform school run wearing coat over pyjamas. Thank God it's winter.

Spouse arrives for his dutiful family weekend on Friday afternoon, and throws himself into what used to be his dear old chair with undisguised exhaustion. I make no comment. He closes his eyes and groans. Oh, all right then, if I must.

"Getting to you, is it? This double life?"

One reptilian eye opens. He does not like my acid tone.

"You should know: you've done your fair share of it with Tom."

"I only ever spent two nights with him." Try for martyrdom: my adultery was a lot more self-denying and dutiful than yours, mate. But Spouse abruptly moves goalposts.

"Sensible woman." Another groan. I don't know why he is being so petulant about being adored. I was adored, once.

74

It was all right. "The trouble is, she's talking about having a baby now." Spouse winces and farts loudly into his chair. "Thank God I can do that here."

"Oh, you can always come back across the road and fart at us, any time you like," I assure him sweetly. "We'll be grateful for any little attentions."

"For God's sake pack it in. I'm tired."

It's the thought of that awful new baby. Poor Spouse, having to go through that hideous baby-and-toddler stage all over again, just as he thought he'd reduced his childcare obligations to the odd weekend watching TV. Hee hee. The news revives my financial qualms, however. Observe that the best-selling bonkbuster is rapidly becoming a necessity.

"Oh, no. Go for the big time. Royal revelations."

"By the way," I rise gracefully and move off towards my study, "I had a dream that Tony Blair had two willies. What does it mean?"

"Poor sod," sighs Spouse. "I know how it feels. I'm thinking of having mine cut off and replaced with one of those bronze taps shaped like a duck . . . I suppose I've got to make the tea?" I nod. He drags himself penitentially out of the chair.

Rush to study. This time it's serious. Seize felt-tip pen; left uncapped, it has gone faint and whiskery. Seize pencil. It breaks. Only the ballpoint has the balls to get to grips with my treasonable secrets.

I was Prince Charles's intimate associate at Cambridge, back in the sexy Sixties. I was smuggled up to his rooms at New Court after dark, on a foggy November night. He was only a hesitant pink-cheeked youth then, but bold nonetheless. Suddenly I was in his arms – then he placed me between his legs, and soon we were making beautiful music together.

Expect someone has already bought an option on the cello's memoirs, though.

Suddenly surprised by shaft of pity for poor neglected John Major enduring this blare of Blair. I expect he'd be grateful if I dreamt he had even one willy. Must have Welsh Rarebit for supper.

29 October

Agent Penelope rings to express the hope that I am safely launched on new bonkbuster and sailing serenely towards the high seas of hyperbole. Have to admit I have endured several false starts and am distracted by personal problems. Penelope invites me to tell all over lunch in Town. Treat yourself, she urges. London. Just the sound of it makes me feel tired. Like something heavy falling downstairs.

Tired of London, tired of life . . . maybe the heavy thing falling downstairs should be me. It worked for Amy Robsart. But at least her rival was the Queen of England. Wouldn't mind so much if Spouse had become the Buckingham Phallus. No problem about accommodating the kids either.

Although in a sudden rush of stepmotherliness, Elaine has installed bunk beds in her spare room. Hope I can trust them to spill Coke over her flawless cream carpets. If I ever buy floor-covering again, it will be all swirling browns: marmite, mud, coffee, tea, blood and toil and tears and sweat. The Elizabethans had the right idea. Strew rushes about and muck out twice a week. Farthingale also a good thing: hid body and kept men at arm's length.

What to wear? Wardrobe taunts me with evidence of past poses: the hippy, the vamp, the Edwardian governess. Only the tomboy remains feasible, though my sole clean pair of trousers bulge up in the front drawing attention to belly. Don jumper long enough to hide belly, then veil whole ensemble in cheap imitation Burberry, which I've hardly ever worn as it's the wrong colour: putty. Well, why not? I am behaving like putty at the moment. Obligingly holding it all together.

Look forward to train journey, but notice with dismay that now even Intercity's buffet brown paper bags are adorned with puzzles and adverts. Oh, for the taciturn brown paper of my youth – the saturnine plimsoll – the silent vest. A string bag! Very laconic.

On arrival in London, find myself in Selfridges. Enjoy long overdue attack of selfridgeness. Buy underwear, scent, pair of leggings the colour of horse manure and sweatshirt the colour of cowpats, all for me, me, me. Why should the kids have all the treats? He left me, too, dammit.

Take bus along Oxford Street. Smoking used to be compulsory upstairs, but now it is forbidden. A stern notice threatens a £1,000 fine. Progress, of course, but somehow it only makes me feel more disoriented. London is a different planet nowadays. Roadworks below. They are enlarging the pavements, perhaps to make room for more advertisements.

Arrayed in my new shades of muck, I meet Penelope for lunch and reveal that Spouse has left me up shit creek without a paddle. Her face buckles, a tidal wave of aghast sympathy knocks over my fragile props of self-control, and I weep bitterly into my Gazpacho.

"I know it'll be good for me," I snivel, "I'm sure my work will benefit – in the end. But at the moment – well – she wants a baaaAAAby!" Penelope assures me I am not even to think about work until I feel like it and offers me her house in the Dordogne if it might help. But the thought of a week in the Dordogne by myself is unbearably lonely.

"What happened to that lovely young plumber of yours?" enquires Penelope, as we prepare to part. Inform her that Tom is safely married to a stonemason. We agree one must never offend a woman with her own hammer and chisel and access to Portland stone.

Drive home from the station listening to Mozart's *Requiem*, suiting my sombre mood. Stop for petrol. Am filling venerable Volvo when man comes up to me, leans in very close and says, "I hope you don't mind my asking your advice but I've only had it for a couple of weeks and I'm wondering if it'll be too long to fit in the car wash." He indicates another Volvo, drawn up next to mine. "So far," he goes on, "I've only given it hand jobs and I haven't achieved a very satisfying result."

Assure him that his Volvo will fit in the car wash, but before going in he must retract his aerial. Wonder if a woman too obviously lonely and up shit creek attracts peculiar and rather unwelcome addresses.

Home horribly empty and silent. Wish I had asked Tracey to babysit here so I could rush upstairs and kiss the children as they slept. Only way to kiss them, nowadays. Awake, they escape crying "Ugh, Gross!" They, too, are moving inexorably away. Search for bottle of plonk in fridge, but find only Elderflower Pressé which has gone flat. Manage to get drunk on it nonetheless. Don't trust myself on the stairs so go to sleep on the hearthrug. Not so far to fall.

5 November

The bonfires are piled high, but where are the ministers that should grace them? It's a solitary sparkler for me this year. Spouse is permitted a break from the treadmill of exhausting weekends here in front of the TV. It is not enough for the lovely Elaine to enjoy his weekday embraces. She has cunningly won A Romantic Weekend *à Deux* at The Shaggy Old Bear Inn, tucked away in the wolds near Coombe Parva.

And I have won a romantic weekend *à une*, because the children have been invited to fireworks parties. Henry is to go to Julian's and Harriet is staying the night with Shelley.

"Has Shelley got any brothers or sisters?" I enquire.

"Oh yes, she's got a brother Tarquin. He's twelve. He's lush."

"Oh well," I sigh. "At least it sounds impeccably literary."

"Oh Mum! You're brain dead!"

Thus are the treasures of a literary education reviled by the ignorant infantry.

Uneasily aware that I must put my literary education to work immediately. This solitude will be a heaven-sent opportunity to get the next bonkbuster launched. But first one must prepare for the overnighting. Yes, it has turned into a verb, as so often happens these days. Or perhaps overnighting is a Gerund.

('"Anyone for tennis?" enquired Gerund meekly, admiring the syrupy shine of Cecil's Marcel waves as he bent over the wireless.')

Wait, that's wrong. Pre-war wirelesses weren't things you bent over. 'Cowered in the shadow of the wireless' would be more like it. Don't think I am quite up to Thirties Gay Melodrama, somehow.

Ask children seventeen times to pack their night things, clean clothes for the morrow, etc., but they are glued to the telly. Wonder whether to throw a tantrum but decide instead to pack everything myself. Less wearing. As I pack, remember with fondness Eddie Waring. If I'd married him I could have had a child called Terribly Waring. Terry for short. Perhaps Harriet was right about the brain death.

Deliver children, express gratitude and admiration, and hide secret fear that something unfortunate may occur with a banger. Drive home through a dusk already threaded by the hopeful arcs of rockets: like optimism, royalty, marriage, etc., dying at the zenith and falling away in cinders and ashes. Stride purposefully up path. The Muse awaits. I'll just have a quick cup of tea first.

The setting sun swam like a plum in brandy behind the mountains of Darjeeling. Earl Grey stirred in his hammock. He heard a light footstep, the faintest tinkle of an ankle bracelet. She was coming: bringing some ambrosial treat, no doubt, to whet his appetite for the twilight hour, when they always retreated behind the mosquito nets and—

"Sahib," Rose Pouchong's face was less radiant, less intimate than usual. "There is a visitor."

A crumpled, sweat-stained man stumbled into Earl Grey's view: a person of grovelling manner who had clearly never enjoyed the benefits of a public school education. He approached the hammock, writhing and bobbing and extending a horny hand.

"My Lord, pleased to meet you," he whined, with the horrible twang of Hendon. "My name is P.G. Tips."

This will never do. Kitchen a distraction. Stride to study.

Then mesmerised by speculation at the thought of a night with Shelley. Avocado terrine and a suicide attempt at 3 a.m., presumably. Wouldn't fancy a night with Byron either. Not in the mood for it. Wordsworth worse: like going to church. But Keats! Claret and cricket. Uneasily aware that am now old enough to be Keats's mother.

Feel hungry, return to kitchen and find avocado. Salivating, seize vinegar bottle, but avocado has gone black. All around me, in this avocado-black night, my countrymen gorge themselves on parkin, toffee apples, hot dogs and cup-a-soups but my destiny is a limp Rice Krispie.

'Aceto Balsamico looked out of his palace window. The sun was setting over Modena in a miasma of red pesto. How dull Modena was! Aceto longed to travel, to explore the remote city whose musical name rang in his imagination like bells: Manchester.'

Abandon novello, switch out lights and watch the dying arcs of rockets, alone. Not bad actually. No child-noise. Only the deafening babble of my own brain.

12 November

I've got such a bad case of writer's block, I feel like laying my head down on it and imploring the man with the axe to be quick. Perhaps I've writ myself to a standstill. Perhaps that's all I've got in me. Penelope my agent says Relax, if you've got to live through this separation business first, so be it. But O! The penury. Spouse now supports two households.

"Can't you do some A level coaching again?" he suggests, warily. "Before they abolish it."

"But kids are so clever these days. I'm frightened of them. And I haven't read any proper books for ages. I'd have to read it all again. And what if I didn't understand it?"

Spouse sighs. I know I'm being irritating. Actually, being irritating is letting him off lightly. There are women in my position who would have relieved him of his manhood while he slept and cast it into the microwave. But my soul is not of Greek dimensions. I'm terribly, terribly reasonable at heart. No wonder I can't write bodice-rippers. If anybody ever ventured to rip my bodice, I'd offer them every assistance, nail-scissors, whatever.

But nobody is ever going to rip my bodice again. This is a big relief, let me tell you. I am content to ripen and rot alone, like a forgotten apple in an attic. Well, not entirely alone. There's always the pips.

"Mummy! Can we have some popcorn in the microwave?"

Cannot conquer my vague fears of radioactive leaks. How

long should you leave the door shut after it has stopped pinging? Have lost the explanatory leaflet. Wish Tony Benn had said something helpful about it in his diaries.

"All right." Get up, with wince of pain. Have done so much fruitless striding up and down in my study recently, have developed Byronic limp. Wince my way to kitchen and switch on microwave.

"We can do it, Mummy! Let me!"

Helplessly watch as children fight over who is to gain maximum exposure to radiation. Henry must be streets ahead anyway because of his computer. What is radiation anyway? And what are electro-magnetic fields? Stare out of window and detect, through rain, menacing wires crossing sky. Only telephone wires, though. Harmless. I hope. I am a stranger to science as well as passion.

Getting old. Too late for pastures new. Sit down heavily on kitchen chair and allow Harriet to give me a good hairdressing whilst we wait for the popcorn. ('Never comb your hair in the kitchen' – another edict I am incapable of enforcing.)

"Oh Mummy! You've gone all grey!"

Spouse puts his head round the door.

"I'd better be off, then." Interesting choice of words. *I'd better* suggests he will get into trouble if he does not, that the departure is reluctant. This is what passes for good manners round here these days.

"Daddy! Look! Mummy's hair is going grey."

"Well, none of us is getting any younger."

"But Mummy's still pretty, isn't she?"

"Oh yes." Spouse winces at Harriet's desperate attempts to arbitrate. Own heartstrings give audible twang, but luckily all sounds of passion are obliterated by the loud pinging of the microwave.

Popcorn distracts children whilst their father escapes to Elaine's more magnetic fields. Children devour the stuff, whilst I scan their faces anxiously for signs of suppressed grief. Passion is a bit like radiation, really: invisible but deadly. We build ourselves lead-lined hearts to keep it in. And the waste remains, the waste remains and kills.

"Mummy! Where did you first meet Daddy?"

"In Grantchester Meadows."

"What, in a field? Was he handsome?"

"Yes. And funny."

Absolutely killing. The killing fields. Find myself writing on back of envelope:

It wasn't love at first sight. "Hi," said Tim Whossname from King's. "Dulcie, this is Gordon Domum." The newcomer had long black hair and was scowling. What a bad-tempered swine he looks, I thought. But I liked a challenge: I usually fell for dead homosexuals. OK, he wasn't *that* interesting. But he shot me a look of withering scorn, and I'd just read Anna Karenina and falling in love with a flashy bastard seemed to be what was required of one. Literature's got a lot to answer for. I hope my daughter sticks to electro-magnetic fields.

19 November

Ring agent to report I have recovered from writer's block and am now filling whole exercise books with How I Met Spouse – the True Story.

"But that's therapy, right?" says Penelope. "I mean, you can't want anybody to print it."

"No, of course not."

Heart does sink, rather, at the cruel truth that all this literary activity is of absolutely no financial use whatever. Penelope expresses great delight that I am now firing on all cylinders, as she puts it, and rings off urging me to keep up the good work and give myself lots of treats.

Suddenly the house is very quiet. Suspect I am not firing on many cylinders after all. Today is Friday, and the children are being collected from school and entertained till Sunday by Spouse and Elaine. So there will be no noisy servitude to distract me. I have a whole day to get through – and a whole night, and another day. Smile grimly at the recollection that this would have been a great treat, a year ago.

Decide to give myself a real treat and have a bath. Warm waters: back to the womb. Wonder what I should do with the rest of the day. Beseech gods to send me a sign. Can't just lie in the bath – Bath! A day in Bath! Why not? I was supposed to treat myself to a day in London but it ended in tears. Lurch from bath, dry myself, dress with eccentricity but who cares? In Bath all are eccentric. Drive joyfully thither. Mozart on car radio. Sun comes out. Feel a thousand times better.

Upon arrival, park in Podium (where the Romans used to park) and sally forth for treats. Enter Monsoon and am ravished by ensemble in bottle-green silk. Try it on, but am distracted by sudden proliferation of grey hairs. Have not looked in mirror for weeks. Return bottle green suit to assistant and run out to seek hairdresser. Find same, and am offered chestnut rinse which will blot out grey. From bottle green to bottle brown. Emerge one hour later transformed from the eyebrows up. Well, it's a start.

Return to Podium. A bit of parking time left. Wander through precinct and am tempted to enter Chinese restaurant serving exquisite lunch to clientele, many solitary. A table for one my destiny now, so must practice. Order chicken satay and a vegetable dish created by Buddhist monks. Look at watch. Plenty of time. Only 1.15. Parking runs out at 2.15.

Jasmine tea delicious. Monks' vegetable dish delicious. Manage to eat with chopsticks without too much humiliation. Devour several squares of what looks like foam underlay and suspect it is tofu. Not bad. Must tell Alice. She will be pleased with me. Sip more tea. Not so bad being alone. Bath a lovely place. Must come and live here when old i.e. next year.

Look at watch. Still plenty of time. Still only 1.15. – Wait! Can't be right! Closer inspection reveals watch glass has fallen off and watch has stopped. O cursed spite. Summon waiter, who reveals it is already 2.15. Clearly remember warning signs in car park about fines.

Bill arrives. Open purse. Only a tenner left! Go hot, go cold. Luckily bill only £8-ish so leave tenner and run. But where next? Car park or bank? Dread being stuck in car park with machine – or even, God knows, human being demanding fifteen quid fine and no quids in purse. Run to bank and insert card in cashpoint. Moment's horrid pause. Queue gathering behind me, watching. Hideous message on screen: REFER TO BANK.

Refer to Bank? Can't! No time! Hurtle to car park and insert parking card in machine. It demands only £1.80 in payment. No fine even though I am fifteen minutes late. Redemption! But O horror redoubled! No small change either. Not even

£1.80. Only £1.62. Fumble, fumble. Queue forming behind of people anxious to kill me. Cancel own transaction and let them pass. Searching handbag for suicide pill, find crumpled fiver I wiped my nose on last week.

Insert card again. This time it demands £5. Machine's patience exhausted. Shove fiver in slot. Fiver regurgitated. Press button marked 'For assistance'. Disembodied voice enquires whether I am inserting the fiver correctly as directed with the Queen's head uppermost and up against the blue line. Try again. Success! Can now escape. Barrier will rise. Don't manage to stop blushing, however, till we are past Chipping Sodbury.

On my return, ring Alice, who detects an edge of insanity in my account of myself, and says menacingly: "Right! That's it! You've had enough, poor love. I'll collect you next Friday. Send the kids to Gordon for a week. Be packed and ready by six o'clock."

At last. Someone else taking responsibility for me. So relieved, and so grateful, fall into deep and blessed sleep for first time for months.

3 December

"Right, Dulcie," says Alice as we part at Gatwick after our week in Sorrento, "get back home and kick male ass, OK?"

I nod obediently, as befits one whose holiday was paid for. Although I wonder sometimes if it isn't a little ungrateful of Alice to be such a man-hater when it was inheriting her Pa's fortune which led to her jet-setting lifestyle. Promise to kick like mule, embrace and depart.

The Gatwick Express is half-empty, understandably. Who would want to come here at this time of year? Or indeed, ever? Wonder if we sold 196 Cranford Gardens whether my half would be enough for a little flat in Ravello. Or even the smart bit of Naples, Vomero. Odd name for an elegant suburb, since it appears to mean 'I am going to be sick.' I suppose this dates from Roman times, when you feasted to a standstill, puked, then began again. "Institutionalised bulimia," remarked Alice. "Di was born in the wrong milennium."

Bulimia was an executive affectation, presumably. Hence Vomero. 'I'm going to be chic'. Impatient to embrace children again, though their hugs are but grudgingly yielded these days. If I transplanted them to Italy, they'd soon adopt those courtly kisses. Harriet could grow up elegant on a Vespa. Henry could join the Mafia – it'd be just what he's always wanted. The fly in the ointment would be Spouse, of course. Presumably he'd want to exercise his paternal right to hide from them behind a newspaper on a regular basis. And that Elaine would egg him on. Sometimes I think she loves his kids more than he does.

Suppose I ran off with them to Italy – he'd have to disguise himself as a middle-aged woman and apply for a job as domestic help, just to get a glimpse of them. I like the idea of Spouse struggling with vacuum cleaners and saucepans whilst entangled with corset, bra and the Italian language. The opportunity for *Mrs Doubtfire* to be a focus for housewives' revenge was sadly missed. The wife was the dupe. In my version she recognises him on the first day and has him scrubbing the loo with an old toothbrush and sanitising the light bulbs.

Sigh. All I have left of my holiday is my memories. Stare morosely out of the window. Luckily England is invisible, triple-wrapped in fog, rain and darkness. Dig out guidebook for last forlorn smile. 'Positano is in a very suggestive situation in the middle of a small gulf.' Wish I could say the same. Well, you could say I'm in the middle of a very big gulf, but it lacks Positano's picturesque charm, somehow.

Met at the station by Spouse and kids, who throw themselves around me, possibly hoping for presents.

"Daddy! Kiss Mummy!" demands Harriet. Meekly we obey. He looks tired. Should feel triumphant but somehow cannot find it in my heart. Not sure I shall be kicking male ass much. Already feel guilty despite the certainty that had I not had a holiday, I would now be having a nervous breakdown all over them, like Vesuvius. Perhaps that's where Vomero got its name.

"If I ever write a best-seller," I inform him after the kids have gone to bed, thoroughly disappointed by their exquisite Italian wallets, "I'm going to buy a little place in Sorrento."

"Ah, the Gracie Fields syndrome," he sneers. Old habits die hard. "Without the star quality."

"But the light!" I insist. "It's so dark up this end of the world. I think I suffer from this Seasonal Depression thing: S.A.D."

"Try sitting under a lightbulb," he suggests. "It's cheaper."

Deftly I produce a lace tablecloth from my bag.

"I got this for Elaine," I smile.

Now he feels really bad. Actually I got it for Aunt Elspeth, but never mind. Aunt Elspeth's the sort of person that still thinks Italy is dirty, so it's a waste of time giving her Sorrentine lace. She'd probably think it had cholera in it like that parcel that carried the plague to Eyam. Besides, I can't wrong-foot Spouse so usefully via his aunt. It's his mistress that's the business. "And I think it would be best if she came and spent Christmas with us, don't you?"

Spouse goggles at me. He is speechless and suspicious at my serene magnanimity. Sometimes kissing ass can offer a subtler revenge than kicking it.

Elaine is so bowled over by my tablecloth and offer of Christmas that she offers to cook the turkey, leaving me free to enjoy the children. Suspect that will be even harder work, however. If only Spouse were an Italian he'd have a stylish three mistresses, not a measly one.

10 December

"Mummy! Some people in our school don't believe in Father Christmas!"

Somehow Harriet still clings to the hope that an overweight bearded traveller will force his way into our house in the middle of the night. Odd, as she is nine, already a cool dude impatient for lipstick, high heels and marriage to Meatloaf. To me her belief in Santa is a sacred relic of childhood, something to protect against the horrible searchlight of Spouse's scepticism. Although the weather's so gloomy at the moment, any form of enlightenment would be a help.

Less than two weeks to the shortest day. I'd be happier dancing round oaks and tossing mistletoe about on 22 December, but Christmas is bearing down on me. Or rather, I'm bearing down on it. It's like a communal birth, these days. The labour pains build up – mine are coming along every ten minutes already – the anguish, the desire for gas'n'air, the conviction that there will be something wrong with our Christmas, that there will be something missing. "Will it have all its little silver balls and chocolate fingers?" we agonize, and fantasise about a general anaesthetic.

But anaesthesia comes afterwards. The strange dead fag end of the year. Shops shut for days on end. I shall petition John Major, waving my Shopper's Charter at him. I don't want to go shopping, I just want the shops to be open so it doesn't feel as if nuclear war is about to break out: the whole country shell-shocked, wrapped in numbness. Still, as 28 December limps to its close, I shall peer into the twilight and announce that the days are drawing out again.

"Kelly says her parents filled her stocking – she saw them do it – but Father Christmas could've asked them to, couldn't he?"

I am spared further interrogation by the arrival of Audrey from next door. Although by the look in her eye I could be in for a different sort of grilling. We are in the age of awkward questions, grown-ups and all. She and Bernard must have noticed that Spouse spends more time over the road at Elaine's than would be needed to help her unjam a seized-up stopcock.

"I just thought I'd pop round and ask what you think the children would like for Christmas," Audrey whispers, as Harriet runs out. Insist that she mustn't, really, too kind, etc. But eventually I agree to the idea of book tokens as they do not require much wrapping. Audrey gift-wraps things with such rugged ferocity, she could halve Group 4's escape rate single-handed. But at the moment her wrist is in plaster.

"I slipped on one of Hamish's little poopsies, dear, it was whilst you were away. I was carrying the laundry basket – couldn't see where I was going. And Bernard couldn't drive me to the hospital because his eyesight's not what it used to be." Express annoyance that I was absent when so sorely needed, but am assured that my Spouse volunteered with alacrity. "Luckily that nice friend of yours was there to look after the children," Audrey's eyes acquire a hawk-like glint. "The girl from across the road."

"Oh, you mean Gordon's fancy woman," I smile blithely. Three weeks ago my chin would have wobbled at this confession, but I am fortified by my trip to Italy. I have eaten swordfish and it has put lead in my pencil.

"Oh no, dear," gasps Audrey, "Surely not. You're joking."

"Never more serious," I assure her. "I only have a timeshare in Gordon now: weekends. On Mondays he goes back to Elaine."

Audrey's eyes turn to gobstoppers. Any minute they might burst from her head and go bouncing around the room. Harriet runs in.

"Mummy! How does Father Christmas get down the chimney? Is our chimney big enough?"

Assure her that our chimney is nice and wide and Edwardian, though I concede that the jar of dried Honesty in the hearth will have to be moved.

"Oh, your Honesty is absolutely lovely!" cries Audrey.

Harriet leafs through *Marie Claire* and Audrey asks, in sepulchral whisper, what the children make of it all. Assure her they take it all in their stride these days. Audrey gazes admiringly at me. Lovely old Honesty indeed. Beats guilt any day. Give me a truth, I'll tell it.

Harriet sidles up, still holding *Marie Claire*, and whispers anxiously that we must forgive her but she desperately needs to whisper.

"Mummy! How does the man actually Get It In?"

17 December

My private life is flawless. They do say virtue is its own reward. I always thought it was a sort of consolation prize, but if I compare my radiant state of self-righteousness now I am the wronged woman, to the torture of being the guilty party back in the good old days with Tom . . . Distracted from the admiration of my own virtue by memories of Tom's youthful form, wild curls, hot mouth, etc. Have not heard from him for months. Since he was concreted into matrimony by the Stalinist sculptor Sabrina, he has understandably fallen silent.

A cold chill runs up my spine. A spook? Tom, astrally travelling, conjured by my nostalgia? Astral travel unlikely at 7.30 p.m. on a Thursday, I fear. Henry comes in, looking aggrieved, though not as aggrieved as he'll look when the full awfulness of his parents' behaviour dawns on him.

"Mum the heating's gone off and we're freezing."

Enter Futility Room with foreboding, to discover boiler is on Lockout: red light and refusal to function. Phone manufacturer, but am granted only answerphone. Help at 7.30 p.m. even more unlikely than astral travel. But I shall not panic. Fortified by virtue, I shall attempt also technical virtuosity. Find explanatory leaflet (in itself a triumph of ingenuity and persistence) and peruse.

'The oil storage tank must be installed in accordance with BS799: Part 5. The tank should be arranged with a slope of 1 in 24 away from the outlet valve with a sludge cock at its lower end.'

Realise leaflet was designed to assist initial installation by specialist, not amateurish poking-about by mere Arts graduate.

Ring Spouse, but there is no answer. Peer across road. Lights all off at Elaine's. Either they are out to dinner or At It. Suddenly my radiant self-righteousness starts to seep away, and a swamp of self-pity encroaches. Wish I, too, was equipped with a sludge cock. Somehow this reminds me that I have not yet embarked upon my Neapolitan bonkbuster.

"Mummee! I'm cooooold!"

Piteous bleatings. Heartless Spouse frolics with hot totty whilst his children perish of hypothermia across road. Heat saucepan of beans up to violent bubbling level. Children burn mouths and revile me. Suddenly realise there is half a bag of coal in the garage, left over from last Christmas. Remove vase of dried flowers from grate and initiate conflagration.

"Oh Mummy! It's lovely! Can we roast chestnuts?"

Yes, we have no chestnuts. Hopefully chuck on a few spuds instead and instruct children to stare into the flames and seek inspiration. Immediately excuse myself, run to study and address myself to the waiting word processor.

"I have rented the Villa Portillo for six months, Cynthia," Gerald informed her. "In Ravello. Though it's rather precipitous, I think you will find it a pretty spot." A strange shadow fell across Cynthia's soul. She laid aside her cello . . .

Suddenly the top few lines of script seem to stretch upwards as if my flawless prose is being stolen by aliens. Then wreaths of smoke appear -- smoke? From a word processor? Medieval and inappropriate, surely? Switch off and watch helplessly as my word processor dies before my eyes. Thank God I was in the room when it happened. Otherwise, my darlings -- who are even now downstairs with an open fire, unchaperoned -- is this a sign? Unusual smell of burning beyond old coal, spuds and word processor. Hurtle downstairs and find the little darlings burning crisp packets.

"Look Mummy, they shrivel up!"

"Mum! Can we sleep in our sleeping bags in front of the fire?"

"Certainly not!"

Urgent knock at front door. What now? Disasters always come in threes -- I bet the chimney's on fire. Throw open door and there, for the first time in aeons, stands Tom, clutching enormous bunch of lilies.

"I came as soon as I heard."

"Heard what?"

"You mean he hasn't told you?"

"Told me what?"

"Elaine's pregnant."

A rather typical late twentieth century Annunciation, one feels. Sorry, dear, you're not all that highly favoured any more: you're husband's going to have a baby with somebody else. Try to think what the Virgin Mary would do in this situation. Or failing that, the Queen Mother.

"Come in," I sigh. "I think there's a bottle of gin somewhere."

Well, he is a plumber. And the boiler's on lockout. Let's deal with the real disasters first.

24 December

For once, Christmas is under control, perhaps because miserable women console themselves with catalogues. I'm not so very miserable now the worst has happened. Ha ha! Serve them bloody well right.

Oh, I'm cheerful now. But I was pretty miserable back in the autumn when I was ordering all those presents from the catalogues. I've had enough of Nepalese waistcoats. This year I went Hi-Tech with the Science Museum. Though I'm not quite sure what Great Aunt Elspeth will make of her Illuminated Pocket Microscope Zooms to 100x magnification. Just hope she will not train it on my complexion or scalp. My conscience is, however, clear, for what will probably be the only time in my life.

And also Christmas is painless. When you're trying to conceal from the children that their father has impregnated the woman across the road, you hardly even notice Christmas. You just sail through it. I heartily recommend it. Elaine had promised to come and cook the turkey for us, but she's too busy cooking Spouse's goose. Serve him right for goosing his cook. Never mind. Serenely I strain the gravy. After the straining of credulity that's going on here, the gravy's a picnic.

"Mummy! Can I wear my skeleton pyjamas all day?"

"Oh all right."

"Oh goody! I'm going into the cupboard under the stairs to look at my bones glowing."

"So we'll have a skeleton in the cupboard," observes Spouse, unwisely, given his recent activities.

"And a bun in the oven," I grin, with terrible triumph. Haplessly he struggles with the slithering parsnips. I am entitled to my triumph, he knows.

"What bun?" asks Henry, always alert at the possibility of unexpected food. "I thought it was just the turkey."

"It's only a saying," I inform him. "Clear that puzzle away and lay the blasted table!"

Henry obliges, grumpily. The walls and turrets of Camelot were just beginning to soar skywards as promised in the Science Museum catalogue. It's the vertical 3-D jigsaw puzzle. The brainteaser. Make sure it's just your brain that gets teased, son. Keep your body under wraps. Otherwise you could go the way of your silly old Dad and end up an elderly multipatriarch.

Still, 3-D guilt is making him awfully helpful on the domestic front. I'm not so narked about the actual pregnancy, just the fact that he didn't have the bottle to tell me himself. I had to find out from Tom, who, I now realise, is a bit of a stirrer on the quiet. He turned up and told me Spouse had been putting it about, as Lord Byron used to call it, without himself having the bottle even to stay on afterwards to console me. Not much bottle about in general these days. Never mind. Sod 'em all. I'll show 'em who's got bottle.

Mind you, I didn't have much bottle after Tom left. Why do they call it breaking the news when it's the recipient who is shattered? Ah well, I concluded when I'd wailed myself dry and, as luck would have it, found a nice cold bottle of Sancerre in the fridge. Ah well, now I can stop hoping that he will tire of Elaine's mere beauty, flawless cuisine and domestic order and return for ever to the stinking chaos over which I preside, ancient Yahoo beldame in trainers. Stopping hoping is a bit of a liberation.

Now I can choose the next big adventure of my life. Shall I let myself go and slide effortlessly into the likeness of a Vietnamese pot-bellied pig? Shall I become eccentric and walk round Rusbridge with a bucket on my head, shouting out quotations from Dylan Thomas? The possibilities are intoxicating.

After dinner Harriet is graciously granted charades. A pity Elaine isn't here so my children can appreciate how much better at charades I would be, but life's like that. And charades come but once a year, but beauty and cookery are a daily accomplishment. Harriet needs terrific clues to get her through.

"Hamlet Prince of . . . ? Hamlet Prince of . . . ?"

"Wales?" By Jove, I think she might have something there. It's also a possible new role for me. An alternative to the Vietnamese pot-bellied pig. There's a sensitive man who prefers grannies to bimbos: lonely, misunderstood, not allowed to Vote Labour. I could console him with my Goon Show impressions. On the other hand, it would mean more compulsory Scotland.

"So you'll be off to Kirkwhinnie next week, I suppose? To inform your aunt of the interesting state of affairs?" Spouse

92

goes green. This situation is not without its picturesque appeal. And we are past the darkest day. All I've got to do now is seduce Prince Charles or write a best-seller. Should be a pushover.

It's good stuff that Sancerre.

7 January 1995

Alas! My new year's resolutions are sicklied o'er with the pale cast of thought. I was going to put my foot down in several directions at once – but alas, only spiders can do that. If only I had been a spider. Moreover, I could have eaten Spouse once he had assisted in the production of Henry and Harriet, thus preventing his defection to a younger, more attractive spider.

"Mummy! There's something I don't understand about our Nativity set." Harriet is packing it away, reluctantly as the kings and shepherds have been partying with the Sindies. "Look! There's no Joseph."

This had also bothered me. We have two shepherds and three kings, but no faithful craftsperson with beard and sandals.

"I expect he's gone over the road to see Elaine." Harriet roars with laughter: I smile limply. The laughter fades.

"When's Daddy coming back?"

"Er – tomorrow, I think."

"Why can't we all live together in a great big house?" Unanswered, Harriet ponders other moral enigmas. "Why wasn't Jesus a girl?"

"Yes! Why not, indeed?"

"Or he might at least have had a sister! Called Sharon!"

"How about – er – Susie?" It's nearly an anagram of Jesus after all. Wonder if the course of human history might have been changed if it had been Susie Christ our Lady. But no. Women perform miracles every day: Susie's wouldn't have been noticed.

"Mum! I'm hungry!" Henry appears, looking aggrieved after a session with his computer. I recognise the Spousean scowl.

"You're old enough to get your own snacks now, Henry." My New Year's Resolutions stir and growl in their basket.

"Yes!" cries Harriet. "Don't treat Mummy like a slave! Go and make your own bloody sandwich!"

"You're just a pathetic little—"

"Stop!" I roar. "Silence, or nobody will get any popcorn!"

There may be a moral enigma here: that I distract them from their loutish yelling by offering a treat. That which we call moral enigma, by any other name would smell of maternal inadequacy. It has to be popcorn, actually: I'm clean out of loaves and fishes.

Popcorn is something they can fix themselves, too, whilst I creep up to the attic. Increasingly, these days, I seem to gravitate upwards – if that is not a physical enigma. Why? To feel closer to Susie? A search for a higher dimension in my life?

I pick up a very old Swiss travel brochure. Fifteen days at the Hotel Steinbock, Lauterbrunnen, for £43. Mind you, the air fare's extra: flight to Zurich, tourist class, one pound eight shillings and sixpence. Oh, how I love that sixpence, jolly little sixpence, I've got sixpence to last me all my life . . . Call me old-fashioned, but the single currency's all right by me as long as it's sixpence.

Deeply depressed, however, by this evidence of galloping inflation. A sort of loaves and fishes miracle in reverse: the creation not of plenty but penury. Tempted to torture myself once more by reading Spouse's old love letters (both of them) but decide to return to my maternal duties before Time's Winged Chariot whirls Henry and Harriet into a world where there is no kind Mama to make boiled egg and soldiers and a flight to Zurich costs £2,000.

"Darlings! Shall I make you boiled egg and soldiers?"

"Ugh! Yukky!"

Well perhaps they're right. Perhaps the dipping of the soldiers is a more bloody symbol than I had thought. Ye gods!

"Mummy . . ." Harriet approaches me guiltily. "Don't be cross, but I've cut all my Sindies' hair off."

Astonishing! The erstwhile vacuous bimbos are all now as alert and cropped as John MacVicar. Ready for action. This must be an example to me. A sign from Susie. Seize and embrace my daughter, who is puzzled by this new evidence of maternal enigma, but accepts my caresses with resignation. She thought she had sinned, but she is rewarded. Perhaps there are miracles after all.

94

14 January

Right. 1995 is the year of Assertion. I'm going to have it out with everybody. March to Henry's room and throw open door. He cringes palely, crouching at his computer.

"Turn that thing off and do your homework this instant!" He scowls and picks up his schoolbag. Satisfied, I withdraw.

This was an easy victory, though. Henry would do anything to avoid an emotional scene – even obey me. What's more, he knows that if he doesn't do his homework, the masters at St Archie's will humiliate him in front of the whole class. Harriet is a whole different ball game.

"Harriet! Put those dirty clothes in the laundry basket! And pick up all those animals off the floor."

"In a minute."

"Not in a minute – NOW!!"

My monstrous roar appears to have ruptured my larynx. Retire to the bathroom and gargle. Harriet runs in.

"Mummy! What's that horrible noise?"

"Have you picked up those animals yet?"

"Not yet. In a minute. What was that noise?"

"It was only me gargling. GO AND DO IT NOW!"

"I was only TRYING TO HELP!" she screams. "I thought you were DYING OR SOMETHING! I was only trying to SAVE YOUR LIFE and ALL YOU CAN DO IS SHOUT AT ME!" She storms off.

I watch helplessly. One shout and my voice is wrecked. I suppose I could follow her and whisper commandingly. Perhaps not. She'd think I was being conciliatory. And knowing me, I probably would be.

Next, Spouse. He is watching the highlights, or perhaps the lowlights, of the cricket in Australia.

"Right," I announce firmly, "Can we discuss the childcare arrangements, please? Since you started spending half the week with Elaine, the kids have ended up on my hands all the time."

Spouse's mouth opens in amazement and outrage that I

should dare to intrude with such a remark so soon after the New Ball. Never mind the New Ball, try the New Broom. Feel my Bristles.

"I help at weekends. And they're always coming over to have lunch or tea with us." Us, you notice, is no longer us. It is him'n'her. "And besides, you had your week in Sorrento."

"Listen, mate, if you don't pull your socks up I'll dump the kids at Elaine's and BUGGER OFF THERE FOR GOOD!"

Henry enters, paler than ever. I hope he has not overheard my last speech, which was a curious stylistic mish-mash of lorry driver and prep school headmaster. I can only assert myself in male jargon.

"Mum," Henry murmurs, "can I have a word with you, please?"

In the privacy of the hall Henry confides that he cannot get his poo out; he fears his bowels have set like concrete.

"I had two apples and three bowls of bran flakes this morning," he whispers, "but it's no good." Poor little bunged-up, bottled-up darling! "Don't tell Dad," he pleads. Spouse is in any case oblivious to all save Swing. I'll swing for him one day.

Drive to chemist, who recommends a micro-enema. Looks like a very short tube of toothpaste with a long nozzle. As I go home, rehearse dilemma. On the Continent they cheerfully stick things up themselves all the time but here you can't get within six yards of your child's anus without the social workers arriving on your doorstep.

Lock myself in the bathroom with Henry, show him the bum-squirter and ask if he would like to do it himself.

"Oh no, you do it, Mum, please!"

I perform the necessary act. It is ludicrously easy and painless.

"It didn't hurt a bit," Henry manages a weak, brave smile. "In fact I quite enjoyed it, Mum."

Trying to ignore this last remark, I leave him to await developments, go downstairs and feed Harriet a huge heap of baked beans. Henry appears twenty minutes later looking relieved.

"I think I'll get on with my homework now, Mum," he says with a curt nod. In the old days it would be Thank you Mummy and a cuddle.

Suddenly Harriet leaps up, flings her arms round me and

cries, "I'm so sorry I was rude, Mummy, you're the best Mummy in the world." Gratified at this evidence of psychic intuition and tender-heartedness in my daughter. "And Daddy is the best Daddy."

Well. The jury's still out on that one.

21 January

Desperate post-Christmas penury. Penury sounds like an ailment of the male urinary system. Feels like it too, I should think. I know a bank where the wild manager blows, And threatens us our Classic Joint Account to close, Quite overcanopied with Direct Debits, with Standing Orders but sod all Credits; There sleeps our overdraft some time o'the day, Lull'd in those vaults with interest to pay.

Once again we have an overdraft of more than three thousand. One thousand is only human, two thousand is stylish, but three thousand begins to look like carelessness. Only one person can help me with penury: Penelope. She is my agent, after all. Why hasn't she got me a multi-million contract with Megagalactic Books to write the blockbuster of the Nineties? No, forget the book, let's go straight into screenplay. The Remains of Mrs Funeral Pulp. I think it's got legs.

If only I were Martin Amis. Or even John or Hardy. Thomas Hardy Amis. Didn't he write The Return of the Lapel? Decide to ring Penelope and plead for more contracts, but am sternly informed by Tracey that Penelope is out to lunch – a sacred duty in the metropolitan literary scene. Make myself a Salt'n'Vinegar crisp sandwich, and eat it standing up at the sink, farting cheerfully in my solitude. Those London literary gourmets don't know what they're missing.

To postpone the onset of work, I wander through the cricket pages. It's taken a lot of sheer hard graft to fancy any of the Australian team, but I'm beginning to get the hang of it. Mark Taylor, for instance. He's got a big arse, and his eyes are too close together. What more could one possibly want in a man?

One never fancies the England team, of course. That would

be somehow incestuous. One enjoys them on the level of fairytale. Gooch and Atherton going out to bat are The Walrus and The Carpenter. Tufnell is The Artful Dodger. Russell is Flowerpot Man. Gatting is – oh heck! Almost two o'clock. Run upstairs and address myself to the word processor.

Actually it's a smart new one since the old one went up in smoke. It cost more than a holiday in the Seychelles, which is another reason for the penury, but it's got a beautiful blue screen and functions to take you from the cradle to the grave (Font to Exit). Menopausal marriage breaking up? You don't need counselling. The PC offers Help, Search, Switch, Bold, Flush, Underline, Block, Move, Merge, Save and Cancel. Oh, and Reveal Codes.

'The sun rose over the Murrumbigee' – well, why not? Why must blockbusters be Eurocentric? Why not the glorious brashness of Down Under? I'm sure there is a Murrumbigee. I remember reading about it back in the days when I fancied Richie Benaud. It was easier to fancy Australians in those days. It was easier to fancy anybody. I suspect it's the hormones. Like my bank balance, I am withering on the vine.

Never mind. There's always fiction.

Alice Springs Through the Looking Glass . . . .Alice stirred in her hammock. The sudden wild yell of the Kookaburra shattered her dreams. For a moment, it had seemed she was back in England, the judge looking severely down on her as he pronounced the dreadful word. Transportation. Then her eyes opened and she saw, beyond the open door of the shack, fierce sunlight slanting through the gum tree.

Er. Fear that if I go on much longer I shall be up one. All that's left in my Australian armoury now is Koalas and Kangaroos. Perhaps Alice was a mistake. I fear this diversion will not lead to Big Bucks. This one does not have legs.

Spouse knocks on my door. He has started to knock. A dreadful courtesy. This is what my PC would call a Revealing Code. My heart knocks at the ominous sound. "Come in," I cry. He looks furtive.

"I just thought I'd mention it," he says, with a good deal of bold flush and shift. "I've applied for a job in London."

Somehow this simple sentence fells me. It is the last straw.

My head falls forward onto my keyboard. I look up, eventually, and find I have written SYD%^F98*jf$"scjk%df^*ibn. I like it, especially the bit at the beginning about Syd, but I'm not sure it has legs. Spouse certainly has legs, however, and I've got a distinct feeling he's about to use them.

28 January

"Mummy! What's a git?"

They've been watching those Harry Enfield videos again. Fifteen and over. Oh dear. Still, all the rude bits go over their heads. They go over mine, too. I have no idea what a git is, either.

"I don't know. Ask Daddy."

"How can I? He's at Elaine's."

Come to think of it, I might be beginning to understand what a git is. Matrimonially I'm certainly getting an inkling of gititude.

"Hey! Look at those tits!" Henry is staring out of the window.

"Whose?" Harriet, lewd as ever.

"They're Blue Tits and Great Tits on the bird table, you stupid git!" Henry is displaying the deep misogyny of his kind, trembling on the brink of adolescence. Zithood. Wonder what else today has to offer. Raisin Splitz at the Ritz? Nitz?

Must not give up hope of ever finding out what git means. Am expanding my vocabulary all the time. Thanks to John Sessions's recent appearance on *Midweek*, I now cherish the word gobshite. Sounds a bit like a bird. The gobshites would nest all along the estuary.

"Mum! There's a nuthatch!"

The nuthatch always hangs upside down, perhaps to prepare itself for matrimonial betrayal. So it can tell its friends that its world has been turned right way up. But no. A male nuthatch would never abandon the brood only half-fledged to set up roost with a saucy little tit from the next tree.

Flick idly through a women's magazine, and am arrested by a photo of Naomi Campbell with her tits apparently hanging upwards. How does she manage it? Did they photograph her upside down? If I hung upside down my jowls would slither down to my temples making me look rather like a male orang-utan. But I'm hanged if I'm going to hang myself, for him or anyone else.

"Mummy! When's Daddy coming?"

"Tomorrow."

"When are we going to Elaine's?"

"Er – Wednesday."

It's very simple. Half of the time that he's with her, they're with him, and half of the time that they're with me, he's with us. Which leaves Fridays. Why in the world did we evolve a seven-day week? It's a nightmare for those of us who only have a timeshare in a husband. Friday's a maverick. Wild. Friday's up for grabs.

Elaine usually grabs him, mainly because she wants him more than I do. I only want him to impose chores on and sulk at.

"Mum! Can we have peanut butter sandwiches?"

But I don't sulk so often as I did. I got a bit bored with it. And something has happened to me. A secret delight has stolen over me. It's called Wednesdays and Thursdays. On Wednesdays and Thursdays they're with him at Elaine's. And I am Home Alone. Oh joy! Bliss! I've changed Mrs Body's day so she never comes on Wednesdays now. So I can 'work undisturbed'. Well, it is hard work sometimes. Watching the cricket. ('Support England's Cricket Team – Help the Aged.')

Poor Spouse. He lurches from one demanding household to the other and never enjoys any silence or space. And before the end of the year there'll be a baby bawling at him over there. I feel almost sorry for him sometimes.

Give up the unequal struggle to unscrew the new jar of peanut butter, nip across the road and ring doorbell. Elaine opens the door, looking apprehensive. Am I going to kill her at last? With a jar of peanut butter? A giant crunch for all abandoned wifekind?

"Could Gordon just unscrew this for me, please?"

She steps aside and reveals Spouse on his hands and knees – *shampooing the hall carpet*! He meets my eye with a sort of secret shared hysteria.

"I forgot to take my shoes off," he explains, daring me to

100

comment. A burning arrow of murder shoots through my guts. He never shampooed the carpet for me, the gutless git. I am rapidly soothed, however, by a wave of relief. Nobody's ever going to order me to shampoo the carpet. Thank God it wasn't me who ran off with Elaine.

25 February

"Mummy! Could you ever get half a million pounds for a book, like Martin Anus did?"

Explain, with regret, that the name in question is the rather less picturesque Amis and that Anus is something altogether different.

"What does Anus mean, then?"

"Your bottom."

"Which exact bit of your bottom?"

Isn't it typical that at the very moment when his children reach the age of indelicate interrogation, Spouse should evaporate, leaving me not only to struggle with the unmentionables, but also to do a convincing PR job on his flight.

"Daddy's not actually going to marry Elaine, is he?"

"Oh, I shouldn't think so." Yawn, to demonstrate supreme relaxation and well-being. And perhaps also to demonstrate half-term.

"But you wouldn't mind if he married her, would you?"

Assure her there is absolutely no need for panic, a phrase which, when used by governments, could be roughly translated as Run Like Hell. Harriet endlessly redefines the marital situation, trying to make sure that nobody is suffering. How like me. Whereas Henry confines himself to an occasional "Is Dad coming today?" on days when he knows darn well he isn't, and then looks martyred and resentful when I say no. How like his father.

Yawn again. It's not just the physical and psychical exhaustion, it's the lack of sleep. Why is it that things seem to go bump in the night far more often when you're on your own?

Try to prepare for bed in cheerful mood by watching *Fawlty Towers*. How much worse things would be were I also trying to run a small hotel. The thought of the general public having a perfect right to march into my abode and demand domestic comforts is the ultimate horror. Though if you had hotel guests they could help brain the burglars.

No sooner am I in bed than a sudden loud PING! catapults me upright. Not downstairs – right here in the bedroom. What was that? Wait, heart thumping. PING! Shrill, even deafening. Don't panic. Nobody ever died of a ping. Not yet. I could be the first. But my babies must survive unpinged to breed in the twenty-first century.

Suddenly realise PINGs are coming from the smoke alarm on the ceiling. Endure stupid pang of fear that house is on fire even though I can see perfectly well that it isn't. Then a rare shaft of rationality suggests that the battery is about to run out and the pings are a warning.

Clearly I must deactivate the thing if I am to enjoy any sleep at all. The ceiling is high, though, and the only ladder downstairs and outdoors, where things moan and slither at this hour. Anything would be better than having to go downstairs again, even climbing up on top of the wardrobe, naked – which alas seems unavoidable. Cursing Spouse anew, I lean out timidly from my dizzy perch, like a worm-eaten, middle-aged figurehead, and manage to wrench open the thing and claw its batteries out, at which the pings mercifully cease.

Then BANG! Leap up in panic and strike head on ceiling. Only a car backfiring. Sudden rustle on landing. Freeze. Henry creeps in.

"Mum!" he whispers, approaching the rumpled bed. "Did you hear a shot?" I see him blanch as he registers the empty bed. He thinks his Dad has shot me out in the street.

"It's all right, 'darling. I'm up here. It was only a car backfiring." Henry's expression, on seeing me naked and aloft, suggests it might have been preferable if Spouse had shot me after all. "Just de-activating this thing," I grin, to demonstrate supreme relaxation and well-being. "It was pinging. The battery's running down."

"But what if the house catches on fire?"

"I promise you it won't."

Henry goes back to bed to wait, gloomily, for the conflagration, leaving me with the renewed conviction that it is all my fault: the defection of Spouse, the malfunction of the smoke alarm, the fire of London, the Potato Famine, the Black Death: all, all.

Exhausted by my five minutes aloft. Wonder how Simon of the Desert managed – he who sat atop a pillar for years. And did the pillar enjoy en-suite facilities? One cannot help wondering. Count blessings before falling into an uneasy slumber. Found a dusty old biro on top of the wardrobe. Alway useful. Also am not John Major. Poor sod. For him things also go bump in the day.

4 March

Terrifying bright disc appears in sky for a split second: population cowers. Unidentified Shining Object.

"I think I'll get them curtains into the wash seein' as it's a good day for dryin', dear." Mrs Body climbs up on the bedroom chair, whilst I hover anxiously nearby, the more quickly to ring 999. I am too shy to warn her that the chair is but a frail antique, and that I hesitate even to throw my cotton cable-knits on it lest their great weight will prove too much. The little chair shudders under her fifteen stone, but amazingly survives. I expect it will disintegrate next time a gnat lands on it.

Left to myself, I would never think of washing curtains from one decade to the next. I don't want them taken down. I want more put up, especially to veil the garden path. Bernard and Audrey next door are unbearably nice to me now I'm a tragic abandoned wife. Though Bernard still chats to Spouse for ages about how effectively he would cane the football hooligans and he never says anything about caning errant husbands.

I wonder if the little old chair bearing up under the great weight of Mrs Body is A Sign. My toggles are trying to tell me something, that's for sure. Why do anoraks have horrible gathered hems held together with toggles in the first place? In fact, why anoraks? They're a bit like marriage, really – hideous, dreary, shapeless and cosy. I attempt to get out of the car: a toggle winds itself round the gearstick. I try to walk through a door: a toggle leaps into the crack and holds me back. A Sign about clinging to the past? And if so, to cling or not to cling?

Why do I long for more and more Antiques Roadshows with their quaint eighteenth century clocks and sad Edwardian bears? Because the past can't rear up and bite me? On Thursday night I discover that Harriet, too, is cultivating antiquity.

"Don't pick your nose when I'm trying to kiss you goodnight," I complain. But she persists.

"Sorry, Mum, but it's a nice crusty one," and whipping it out, she sticks it to the wall.

"Good God!" I cry. "There's a whole archive of the things!"

"Oh yes," says Harriet airily. "I think I'll leave them to my grandchildren. I can't bear to throw them away. You wouldn't like it if you were a bogey."

This is certainly A Sign. I am a bogey up the nose of time and I sense that any minute I may be picked and flicked away into the abyss awaiting all Old Wives. Meditate gloomily thereon for twenty-four hours.

"Hello!" Spouse disturbs my reverie. He is arriving home for the weekend, so it must be Friday. Home is the Hunter, Home from the Woman across the Road, and looking more guilty than ever. "Where are the kids?" he asks furtively.

"Watching TV. Where else?" Begin to feel nervous.

"Look, it's unbelievable really, but -- I've got that job."

"What! In London?"

"Yes, but – well, yes. I never thought I had a chance."

He offers this as a sort of apology. He never thought he had a chance, so it's their fault for choosing him, quite against all his hopes.

Suppose congratulations are in order. However, he'll have to make do with resentment and indignation.

"So you'll commute, or what?"

"I think I'll get a little flat in, er Paddington or Ealing or somewhere."

"What do you mean, I? You mean, on your own?"

"Well, not completely."

"With Elaine, you mean."

"Well . . . probably."

Probably! Hah!! I bet her coffee table is already inches deep in Estate Agents' blurbs. I bet her house is already on the market.

"So what about us?"

"There's no need to take that tone. I'll see as much of you and the kids as ever. Almost."

Oh, Mrs Body, why are the curtains not here when I need to drag them down about my hapless head? Or – far better idea – strangle Spouse with them. Instead I walk ceremoniously over to the kitchen drawer and get out the scissors. Spouse flinches and goes pale. With magnetising theatricality (I hope) I seize my anorak, raise both toggles into the fitful sunlight, snip the bastards off and hurl them into the bin. *Finità la Commedia.*

11 March

So that's it. Curtains. Spouse goes to London and builds a little love nest there with Elaine. The For Sale sign is already up in her front garden. Luckily he had the sense to shack up with a woman of property. Her ex-hubby, the mysterious Marc, has disappeared into Switzerland and is now so rich that he's said she can keep the proceeds from the sale of the house.

"So can I keep ours, too, then?" I enquire sweetly. Spouse stifles a spasm of indignation. He knows he is not entitled to any at the moment. It's my one little luxury.

"Well, I certainly wouldn't dream of putting it on the market, as long as you want to go on living here. Even though I'm still paying the lion's share of the mortgage."

The lion's share, indeed. Worm-eaten old donkey, more like.

"But if I should want to move – sell it – I can keep all the proceeds, can I? Like Elaine can keep hers?"

"Oh yes. Very disingenuous. I'm a starving academic, for God's sake, not a frigging gnome of Zurich."

Wonder if the manufacturers of erotic automata have yet explored the potential of the frigging gnome. Wonder also why nobody ever says ingenuous. Disingenuous only exists in the negative, like Disprin and Disney and Disaster. Wonder if, loosened from the obligation to provide rational discourse with a partner, my brain's hawser will slip gently from its bulwark, letting me drift off onto a sea of senility. Hope so.

Wonder also why, when I kicked over the traces all those years ago, I could not have chosen a merchant banker instead of a starving young plumber. Also why I could not have eloped with him to the Bahamas leaving Spouse holding the babies. Of course I know the answer – because, by some cunning contrivance of nature, the babies, though objects of loathing and terror to the rest of the population, are unaccountably delectable to their mum. The thing I find really incomprehensible and unforgivable about Spouse's departure is not that he can leave me – what rational chap would not – but that he can leave his children.

"Mum! I don't want a party this year I want to See a Show!" Harriet's birthday. Wearily accede to idea of a weekend in London and *Grease*. Henry is billeted on Spouse and Elaine and let's hope he does the decent thing and wets the bed. Harriet and I are soon ensconced in The Edward Lear Hotel, which is adorned with pictures of The Old Person from Norwich, etc. Lear apparently lived here when he wrote 'The Owl and the Pussycat' – that shocking tale of ill-suited elopement. Oh owl, owl, owl owl owl!

The Dominion is full of families, watching with embarrassment as the tale of teenage lust unfurls. ("Mum! What does *horny* mean?") I contrive a quaint pair of earplugs out of loo paper, close my eyes, and imagine I am on a touring holiday in the Peak District. Harriet turns to me after every number and whispers. "It's the most wonnerful film I've ever seen!"

"It's not a film," I reply, in vain. The concept of theatre seems alien to the young imagination. They can't grasp the possibility of a reality that's not virtual.

Afterwards we dodge the dossers in the Oxford Street doorways. Harriet enquires what these people are doing. Explain the concept of sleeping rough.

"Aren't they *lucky*!" she breathes. Fear my explanation must have lacked all political vigour. Dossers exchange pleasantries.

"Mum! What's an arse-bandit?"

"I don't know."

"I love London! It's ace! I wish I lived here!"

"Well," I pounce, "as it happens, Daddy's got a job here so you'll be spending a lot more time here in the future."

"Oh, but we're not selling our house in Rusbridge are we?"

Assure her I shall be keeping the home fires burning. What a brick I am. Back chez Lear, I while away the midnight hour making myself cups of Earl Grey. Is that what John Major will be called when he gets his peerage?

The trouble with 'The Owl and the Pussycat' is that it doesn't mention Mrs Owl and the Owlets, left in the nest with half their growing still to do. Weary myself with the thought that I alone will have to hunt and decapitate all the necessary voles, etc. Or perhaps I should hunt and decapitate Elaine. Cheered up by this thought, I fall into a charmèd sleep.

18 March

Dream that I am on a bus in Romania, and an old man sitting behind me urinates down the back of my neck. When Alice rings to enquire how I am, I ask her to interpret this message from the unconscious.

"It's probably a compliment in Romania."

Inform her that I may be a despised and rejected older wife, but if that's all I can hope for nowadays in terms of gallantry they can keep it.

"You're not stuck with any aspect of your life," Alice informs me. "Take a sideways leap – domestically, sexually, professionally."

She rings off. I take a sideways leap and bang my head on the door jamb.

"Oh buggerbuggerbuggerbuggerbugger!"

Hop around kitchen nursing bruised temple, wearing unbecoming rictus of middle-aged anguish. Henry observes me from the door, with rather less rapture than David Attenborough would bestow on a dung-beetle.

"Is it time for us to go across to Elaine's yet?" he enquires hopefully. How the poor child longs for domestic order, female beauty and good cookery. I wouldn't mind a bit myself. Perhaps I shall take up Alice's hint and sound out the gay scene.

Pack children off to Spouse and Elaine's, first. It's going to be a lot more crucial if they leave something behind when he and Elaine move to Ealing. Elaine of Ealing. It has a certain twang. Wonder if I should set my next bonkbuster there. Or perhaps Romania. Bonkbuster has been horribly stalled for months. Fear I may be bonkrupt professionally as well as personally. Wonder for ten minutes whether to spin a yarn about Zoster the gypsy violinist who lives in the mountains near Split with his flashing-eyed sister Zovira. Think on the whole would prefer Ealing.

Stop work and eat packet of hazelnuts. Then two apples. Then handful of dried apricots. At least I am bingeing sensibly these days. Was inclining disastrously to the oven chip and frozen pizza. But now it's nuts, fruit, baked spuds and beans. Boring but worthy. "More f—ing nuts?" I sigh. It's the F-word Plan Diet.

Look around kitchen, imploring Juno, goddess of Older Abandoned Wives, to Send me a Sign about what to do with my life. Suddenly the Persil packet speaks to me: OUTSTANDING RESULTS ACROSS THE WASH. Thank you, Juno! Seize road map, find The Wash and across it, Boston Spa, interesting old town I have always wanted to visit, and several attractively-named villages. Wrangle, Old Leake, Friskney Eaudyke. Obvious arena for happy retirement. One could become a Senior Wrangler. Incontinence wouldn't be a problem in Old Leake, and on sunny days one might become quite Friskney. Notice however proliferation of dykes. Hilldyke, Skeldyke, and Quadring Eaudyke. Not sure I am quite ready yet to please Alice by plunging therein.

No F-ing nuts left, so drive into Rusbridge to perform most sacred national ritual: shopping. Distracted, on way along High Street, by Estate Agents' displays. Perhaps Boston Spa is a Spa too Fa. Notice, with thrill, that delapidated old Georgian rectory I have always admired is for sale at knock-down price. Am about to go in and ask for details when am disturbed by horrid attack of farting. First one so loud and vile I walk on up the street so nobody will think it was me. Stop outside newsagents and to my horror discover fart has followed me.

Open coat, in relaxed and casual manner, and silently urge fart to do the decent thing. Depart, O Fart. Whizz off and destroy a bit of the ozone, can't you? No sooner has the air cleared, however, than another intestinal spasm strikes me and I am forced to walk the whole length of the High Street, trumpeting away like the 1812 overture. Fear I am becoming a serial farter. F-ing nuts!

Return to Estate Agents and acquire blurb on noble Georgian ruin. Grade II with star listing. 'Ashlar. Hipped . . . bull-nosed sills . . . bolection-moulded surround . . . pulvinated frieze . . .

rail and dado ramped to newels and muntins . . .' Wonder for a moment if I am back in Romania. Alas, fine old house has been subject to damp penetration and needs the loving care of a very rich person. As indeed do I.

Perhaps I could take a sideways leap by advertising in the Lonely Hearts Column. Or in my case, the Lonely Old Farts Column.

Neglected gem, thought to date from Georgian period (i.e. before 1953), having many character features, with flagged imagination, double-glazed eyes, shuttered sensibility, seeks sympathetic renovator (preferably, though not inevitably, male) with deep pocket. Must like children or perhaps wild animals. Incontinent Romanian pensioners need not apply.

25 March

"Beat him at his own game," says Alice down the phone. "He's got a job? He's moving away? *You* get a job. *You* move away. Further away."

"Further . . . than Ealing?" I falter. "And who'd want me?"

"Listen – in some parts of the world, they'd *kill* for you."

Alice is calling from St Lucia, where she spends the winters. A picture flashes into my mind of a cool schoolroom-on-a-beach, where I explain the mysteries of *The Tempest* to Caribbean adolescents, and they explain the mysteries of life to me.

"I would do anything, mind you," I warm to the idea. "Even teach at secondary level."

"Oh come on, Dulcie," Alice groans, "things aren't *that* bad." She tells me about a cartoon she saw of Bill Clinton saying *"Ich bin ein Beginner"*, then rings off promising action.

Me too. I need L-plates to indicate my status in the post-marital limbo. The Ordnance Survey has not been here. There are no maps. Morosely chewing the last Rice-no-longer-Krispies, I loiter by the bookcase looking for clues. Attracted as usual by the Rough Guides.

"Come on, you lazy old gits, you 'orrible lot, only three more peaks! Don't talk to me about blisters, mate, I've 'ad 'em up to 'ere." Pick up Rough Guide to Ireland and open at random.

CONG lies on a narrow spit of land that divides Lough Mask from Lough Corrib . . . the site of the ruined Cong Abbey, which was founded in 1128 for the Augustinians by Turlough O'Connor, King of Ireland.

And presumably also King Cong.

Somehow this reminds me of Tom. Didn't he once court me in a gorilla suit? The Mask of Cong. Since Spouse has semi-left me I have heard nothing from Tom. Not even a semi-postcard. He must know the score. He was quite thick with Elaine. But not a sausage. The silence is quite deafening. The absence of him pounding his way up the front path is dazzling. I know he's now married to the fierce Sabrina, but a brief, regretful postcard was surely my due. 'Sorry to hear about your troubles. Oh! That I could carry you off to Tuscany. But alas, Sabrina is even now brandishing her chisel.'

Must stop composing letters my men should have written, and start instead composing the novel I should have written. But first, The Truth Fairy from St Lucia has spoken. I have been a doormat for too long. Run upstairs and throw all Spouse's clothes, old letters, cassettes, etc. into open cardboard cartons. Place on Elaine's doorstep. A sudden squall blows pieces of paper all over Elaine's twee conifers.

A promising beginning. I know they are out – they have taken the kids to see *The Mask*. By the time they get back, his socks should be soaked and his archive nicely dispersed. Doorstep publishing. Return home and admire myself in the bathroom mirror. Beat breast and utter ape-like yell. Can feel myself changing from Fay Wray to King Cong. Converting all my songs of woe to Aaaaaeeeeeaaaaaeeeeaaaaaah!

What next? To Waitrose, where the bread department has become terribly United Nations. Select what I believe is known in France as a Big Bastard, return to car park and devour it sitting in car. I am going to eat Bastard till I live and breathe bastard. Mouth absolutely full, and stock of saliva

110

dangerously low, when suddenly – o my prophetic soul! – I see Tom walking towards my car.

Freeze. Has he seen me? Not yet. Pray he does not. Even if my mouth were not grotesquely full, I would be praying he did not see me. But he does. And at the moment he sees me, he flinches in a way that's a dead give-away, and I know for sure that if he had seen me early enough he would have pretended he hadn't seen me. As it is, he cannot but come alongside. I wind the window down.

"Hi, Dulcie. God, I mean, I feel incredibly guilty, y'know? Like, I should have rung you weeks ago, well months actually, only it's been madness at work, right? And well, you know how it is, but I mean, God! How could he do such a thing? I mean, for God's sake, how?"

Perplexed for a moment at the necessity for utterance. Bread in mouth approximately size of cricket ball. In the end, decide to do the decent thing.

Propel half-masticated ball of bread violently out of mouth and onto immaculate Waitrose tarmac an inch from his right trainer.

"Just like that!" I grin. "Well, lovely to see you, Tom, but I must go."

Start car, reach out and pinch his bottom, and drive off, badly. But not quite badly enough to run over his toes. Still, I'm only a beginner. There's no discouragement Can make me once relent My first avowed intent To Be a Bastard.

1 April

"Mum! Come!"

We do not like this summons. We do not care for peremptory rhyme. We would prefer blank verse. Blank cheques would also be welcome. Now that Spouse has more or less gone off to found his second empire, genetically speaking, we are broke. But Alice is going to find me a job. Secretly I hope for Archive Assistant, St Lucia. Till then it's domestic enslavement.

The Mayday Call comes from the bathroom. Enter with foreboding. Harriet is seated on the Imperial throne, looking guilty. The bath is full of water and the Sindies and Ken are engaging in an 18–30 holiday therein.

"Mum – I've pooed in the bath."

"Oh yeah? April Fool to you too."

"No really, *really*, Mum. I'm everso sorry. I was in the bath and I couldn't get out in time. It's only a little bit."

A little bit goes a long way, though, doesn't it? Examine water more closely and detect faecal contamination. Plunge arm into water, pull out plug, rescue and resuscitate Sindies, slosh out offending matter, scald bath with boiling water and scrub with Ecover Cream Cleaner for People Who Care About a Clean Environment and Crap in the Bath.

"Oh Mum! You're brilliant!"

"What would you do if you crapped in the bath at Elaine's?"

"Oh God! That would be awful! What a good job I crapped in the bath here instead!"

Inform her she will be spending the weekend across the road. She curses. Harriet prefers weekends here because I let her stay up to watch *Casualty*. I don't let myself watch *Casualty*, though. I haven't got Harriet's strong stomach. So unyoung and so tender.

Elaine and Spouse spent the week in London, house-hunting. At 10 a.m. I hear Spouse's key in the front door (when will he tactfully give up that symbolic little convenience, I wonder?) and prepare to receive moaning. He leaves me for a beautiful younger woman with money, heart and style – you'd think he'd have the grace to gloat a little. But no. What I get is whinges. Perhaps he thinks it's more tactful to whinge. Perhaps he thinks that what I want is evidence of his unhappiness. Perhaps he's right.

Something resembling Spouse enters the kitchen. It is clothed from head to foot in what can only be described as a dropdead elegant taupe suit.

"What the hell are you wearing? What is this? April Fool?"

"Er – Armani."

"*Armani*!! You!?"

"Elaine . . ."

Say no more. I offer him a cup of tea but he dare not accept in case he spills some on his Armani. Emporio Armani. Emporio for Emperors. Cannot stop staring. Suffer an acute attack of Emperor's new clothes. It is not Spouse any more, but a synthetic imposter.

"Well, I have to admit it makes you look thinner."

"I am thinner," snaps Spouse. "I haven't eaten any bloody butter for four months. Nor cheese. Nor bacon."

"Put you on a diet, has she?"

"It's done me the world of good," he sighs, and runs his fingers through what remains of his hair.

She'll be having a go at that, next. She'll be getting him thatched, like a Dorset cottage. Doesn't the silly chit realise Spouse is paunchy, balding, and wears crumpled old corduroys hoping it will make him look like Jonathan Miller?

Henry enters with a bucket of dirty water, having washed the car for £2. Wish son and heir would trip and deposit contents of bucket on Armani. Although dirty water also taupe.

"I don't know how you can let her buy you an Italian suit," I shake my head. "Not when there's good old British shell-suits about. Designer Imperialism, that's what it is. I came, I saw, I designed."

"Mummy! What's Imperialism?"

Deliver concise history of Imperial history.

"If I lived a hundred years ago," vows Harriet, "and I thought I'd been a bit Imperialist, I'd punch myself in the face!"

Good. That's laid down the liberalism against which she can rebel in a few years' time.

Later, seeing them all off across the road, I bend down to kiss her goodbye.

"I'll give you a fiver if you can crap in Elaine's bath," I whisper. Her eyes kindle with the acquisitiveness which fuels empires.

"How much if I crap in her bed?"

8 April

Right. Must find job. Seize and peruse Creative, Media, Sales and Marketing Appointments page. After all, I am in some senses a writer. I must be able to understand the ads, at least. So: 'Time Based Media Technician . . . Customer Satisfaction Officer . . . Project Control Assistant . . .' Napoleon was wrong, you know. We aren't a nation of shopkeepers. I tried to sell a couple of those sag-bags a few years ago. Ended up giving them away to a student because I felt sorry for him.

Now: trawl through the smaller ads. 'Are you energetic, enthusiastic, physically fit . . . do you have a good social manner, enjoy food and wine, arts and architecture . . . Can you cook, drive, map-read and speak two of the following languages to a conversational level: Italian, French, Spanish, Portuguese?' Wait a minute. Isn't this a Bob Dylan song? Well, if not, it should be. Portuguese, for God's sake. I don't even understand English any more. Time Based Media Technician, for instance. If that's English, give me Bantu.

Throw newspaper to floor and wonder what will become of me. Perhaps I could get a job in Woolworth's. They've got much more helpful tills, now. They tell you what the change should be. But would I need to know about Customer Satisfaction? Project Control? Satisfaction and Control are not my area of expertise, to be honest. Come to think of it, I haven't applied for a job since Bob Dylan was at full groan.

Perhaps I could become a songwriter? Cheer up: eyes brighten. A job you can do lying on your very own sofa, without being energetic, enthusiastic, physically fit or having to map-read in Portuguese.

Don't ask me, baby, I got no Project Control
Customer Satisfaction left a deep void in my soul
Can you cook, sew and map-read, fry eggs and make flowers grow?
Saw her walk in the breeze, she said something in Portuguese
To a guy I thought I used to know . . .

Brilliant, eh? How much do you think I'd get for it down in Whatsit Street?

"Mum! Here's the post!"

Another bundle of stuff from Plumb's Mail Order. What they fail to understand is that once people have been through the harrowing business of buying chair covers they would rather not think about the subject again for several years. Harriet tears it open, though: she is a junk-mail junkie.

"Look Mum! Dining chair covers! Can we have some? Table protectors! Sleeve Protectors! Fully waterproof Rose Scented

Mattress Protector! Isn't it nice of them to send it us? Can I have one?"

"No! What I want is a cover to protect me from junk mail."

"It's not junk mail! There's a lovely picture of a hedgehog and a squirrel! It's sweet! Don't be horrible!"

She runs off, clutching her beloved picture of the rose-scented mattress protector. A child of her time. A customer longing to be satisfied.

And here comes her brother, looking anxious, already accomplished in Project Control.

"Mum . . . ? Could I clean the car for you every day instead of every week? Then I'd have an extra fourteen pounds a week instead of two, on top of my pocket money, and now it's summer nearly, I can mow the lawn for you, especially now Dad's not here much, and if you would give me, say three pounds for mowing the lawn and I mowed it twice a week that would be an extra six, so I could earn twenty pounds a week from you, and if I did something at Dad's too I could probably save about a hundred pounds a month, and I could get a ZRX COMP CF5.2000 with Mega Flik by October." (I'm not entirely sure about the technical details, here.)

"Go away!" I cry. "I haven't got any money! Ask your father!" I pull the sofa cushions over my head, wishing they were rose-scented mattresses. Plumbs have really missed a marketing opportunity. A rose-scented, soundproof, ex-wife cosy: washable, offers protection against ex-Spouse, children's demands and tantrums, slings and arrows. And junk mail.

Suddenly realise I have not yet boldly gone and shopped and the cupboard is once again bare. Science has failed us here. Why can't Scotty beam us up our weekly order from Waitrose and have it materialise on the right shelves in the fridge? Go and shop. Return to find children watching programme about shopping.

"Alice rang," calls Henry. "She said she'd found you a job or something."

"She rang from – St Lucia?" Heart skips a beat. Could this be it? Sod Customer Satisfaction and Project Control. *Baywatch*, here I come.

15 April

April is the cruellest month. The sun seems to shine -- you rush out in a T-shirt -- a wind coming straight off the Urals slices your kidneys to ribbons. Oh, to be in St Lucia now that April's there. Alice has apparently found me a job, and though I haven't managed to talk to her myself yet and ascertain any of the details (will try again at five o'clock -- lunchtime in the Caribbean) I cannot help hoping I shall spend the January of 1996 under a palm tree.

And imagine the divine moment when I can inform Spouse that though he will dine at Ealing Town, I shall dine at . . . flummoxed by my total ignorance of Caribbean towns, though I suspect they are mostly called Bridgetown, Georgetown and Kingstown in memory of Nigel Hawthorne. I do know, however, that St Lucia is the one with those sharp mountains that look like Madonna lying down. The Pitons. Harriet is developing pitons, too, though she is hardly weaned herself.

"But you're only ten, darling! I didn't have breasts when I was ten."

"You don't have any now, either." Cruel but true. She admires herself moodily. "The left one's called Rory because it looks like Rory Bremner's nose."

Thank God Henry regards his adolescence as private. He has started locking himself in his room. Loud rap music discreetly veils whatever he's getting up to in there. Keeping it under raps. Still, I suppose it means he'll get on well with the kids on St Lucia. Speak their language and, I hope, translate for me.

Stare out at the rain and wonder what it would be like to spend a whole winter without a single shiver. Uneasily aware I have not yet hidden the Easter Eggs. Though the children are bursting into puberty, they still require the garden to be full of Easter Eggs on Sunday morning. Wonder for a while about Jesus. Why are there no genre paintings called The Puberty of Jesus? He had an absent father, too. Is Joseph the patron saint of stepfathers? Did Jesus ever, in a fit of adolescent pique, cry Why should I tidy my room? You're not my real Dad anyway!

Was the tomb really empty? How extraordinary that all this should be happening to me at Easter. 196 Rusbridge Gardens has started to feel a bit like a tomb sometimes.

And was St Lucia a mate of his? Was she something to do with light? Isn't there a festival called St Lucia in Sweden where girls walk around with lighted candles on their heads? I suppose adolescents are driven to acts of ludicrous danger in a cold climate. Feel deep pity for anyone living even further north than the UK. Begin to suspect that on St Lucia I shall get religion.

"Mum! I've cleaned the car!"

Henry enters, puts down dirty bucket and waits for his £2.

And that's another thing. I don't expect we'll need cars in St Lucia. I expect we'll walk everywhere, except up the Pitons. You'd need crampons to walk up the Pitons. In fact, we probably won't need to walk anywhere at all. We'll probably just sit right there under the palm tree and wait for the whatsits to drop. The children will ripen and so will I. I'm into a second adolescence, that's for sure. Some like it hot and that's what it's going to be.

Phone rings. Fly to it. Person enquires whether I might be interested in having my windows double glazed as their rep is in the area.

"No thanks!" I cry ecstatically. "I'm going to St Lucia!"

No draughts there. Even single glazing unnecessary. Lose myself in sweltering daydreams till the phone rings again.

"Hi, Dulcie, it's Alice. I've got you a job."

"Yes, Henry told me. What is it? Where is it? When do I start?"

"Well, listen, the thing is, it's nothing much. I mean, don't get excited. And I hope you don't mind but I had to forge you a CV. I invented a few more books that are out of print."

"That's all right! You're brilliant, Alice! Tell me more!"

"Well, it's only a writer-in-residence thing, so the money's practically invisible. But you don't have to do much either. Only teach creative writing a couple of times a week."

"Fine! Fine! Who cares about the money? It's the escape that I need! And anyway, my electricity bills aren't going to be much, are they?" A puzzled silence from Alice's end. "I mean, in the Caribbean."

"It isn't in the Caribbean, Dulcie. It's MacMurdie College, Big Jaw, Canada."

117

22 April

Inform Spouse that I have been offered a Writer in Residence post at MacMurdie College, Big Jaw, Canada, to commence immediately – well, at the beginning of May. Spouse's own jaw drops at the news.

"Someone must have died," is his only congratulation. In other words, they must be desperate. Further enquiries confirm the accuracy of his intuitions. Someone has indeed died. MacMurdie College had been looking forward to drinking in the aperçus of a writer of romantic fiction called Emerald Wilde, but Miss Wilde, perhaps at the thought of spending some time in Big Jaw, threw herself off a rock in Montana. So it's me, folks.

It's for a term in the first instance, plus summer school. Perhaps also the autumn. Alice is not sure. She fixed the whole thing up for me. I gather one of her best buddies is the Head of Modern Fiction Studies at MacMurdie: a fierce and feisty feminist called Sara O'Hara. I have to make myself fierce and feisty in two weeks.

"Oh, and I should start eating a lot of Marmite sandwiches," suggests Alice. "It keeps the mosquitoes at bay."

Debate with Spouse about what to do with the children. He insists it will do them the world of good: they'll learn French, develop huge muscles and frighten the mosquitoes. When he goes to America, you notice, he leaves the children behind; when I go to Canada, I have to drag them along with me. Not that I mind. I'd rather be irritated by their vile presence than tortured with nostalgic longing for them.

"Oh, Canada!" cries Harriet. "Cool! Where is it?"

"It's part of America," Henry informs her. "Mum do they have the World Series there?"

Not entirely sure what the World Series is. Am already comforting myself with the thought of the World Service. Annoyed that I shall miss the West Indies Tour of England, but am against blood sports in any case.

Sara O'Hara rings to tell me how delighted they all are that I am coming. She pronounces right as raid. I flannel, flustered at the thought that Alice invented my CV and has not yet managed to send me a copy. Sara O'Hara, however, seems determined to be thrilled with me, no matter how much of an under-achiever I am.

"Raid . . . raid . . . raid!" she agrees with everything I say. This is a novel, and not altogether unpleasant, experience.

Wonder if it will be hot or cold. Pack all my clothes to be on the safe side, then unpack and discard 90 per cent as uncool in both senses.

"I don't like to think of you bein' in Canada, dear," Mrs Body is almost in tears. Feel guilty qualm at the disappearance of her cleaning money. Suggest facetiously she might care to commute to Big Jaw and clean for me there. "Oh no bless you dear I couldn't stand all them wolves and bears." Wonder aloud if there are many such, and discover that my ignorance of Canada is total. Can only remember wolves, bears, Gen. Wolfe and Pierre Thingy. And the nice fat man on the advert. Oh well. An engaging mystery.

Inform Spouse it will be his job to look after, and perhaps let out, 196 Cranford Gardens. He looks furious.

"I've got enough on my plate as it is."

"Well, I'm afraid it's just going to have to be a case of My Plate Runneth Over."

"You're totally irresponsible."

"Oh yes? And were you totally irresponsible when you waltzed off to bloody America for a whole year leaving me with the kids, the house, the lot? Oh no. That was an important career move. Well, this is an important career move for me, mate."

Spouse snorts.

"Don't you snort at me! Or you'll find the kids on your doorstep on the 1st of May!"

Harriet runs in.

"You're arguing about us! Stop it!"

"Not really, darling. It's just that we both want to see you."

"Poor Daddy," she puts her arms around his neck with a sentimental sigh. "He's going to have to do without us."

"Never mind," says Spouse stiffly. "You can come over in the summer holidays or something."

"And besides," I beam, "Elaine will have had the baby by then – a little half-brother or sister for you. Now won't that be nice?"

Spouse goes green. It's always been my favourite colour.

29 April

Since I announced my imminent departure for Canada as Writer in Residence at MacMurdie College, Spouse has developed a reproachful, spaniel-like stare. He moons around the kitchen picking splinters out of the table and flicking them onto the floor.

"Why do you have to do this? What are you trying to prove?"

"To prove I can get along without you very well."

"Whatever for?"

"Because, though it may have escaped your notice, you have left the bosom of this family, moved in with the woman across the road and impregnated her."

A delectable silence. I am ironing my cotton shirts. I want to be crisp and crackling when I emerge into the pearly Canadian light at Big Jaw.

"So it's just to spite me."

"No, Gordon. It's to get the hell out of here. To have a bit of fun. And if it annoys you a bit into the bargain, so much the better."

He sighs, and sticks splinters into his brow. Crucifixion fantasy.

"As a matter of fact, Dulcie," he sighs, "it's only since I moved in with Elaine that I've realised how . . ." He sighs again. He cannot find the words. But his doggy stare clearly implies how whossname I am. But the great thing is, I don't care how whossname he has realised I am. I don't care! I don't care! I shall wave my lilywhite legs in the air!

"I expect some lucky Canadian bastard will snap you up."

"I am not going to be snapped. Listen, mate, I haven't escaped from your jaws in order to hurl myself down some other thankless gullet."

"Perhaps when you come back . . ." More mournful gazing.

"When I come back – if I decide to come back – you will have a baby to look after. Not to mention the hapless mother, poor girl."

Feel genuine pity for Elaine. She is going to be stuck with Spouse and baby, a deadly cocktail which I have drained to the dregs.

I am beginning to think kindly of Canada. There is something cheerful and wholesome about the sound of it. Best of all, it wants me.

"The only problem," I confess to Alice on the phone, later, "is that I'm afraid they aren't going to find me very interesting at Big Jaw."

"That's not what you should be worrying about, Dulcie," she replies darkly. "Quite the contrary, in fact."

Not quite sure what she means by this, but too exhilarated to pursue things said darkly. Not haunted by the dark any more. Light is breaking out, not just in the Northern Hemisphere. Light and lightness. I can feel myself floating up to the ceiling. Spouse slinks darkly about me, fathoms below, like a cur that has been kicked. Feel almost sorry for him for a moment until I remember that he deceived and betrayed me to the hilt and deserves not pity but perhaps an extra parting kick. One for the road.

He drives us to Heathrow, into the dawn, for an early flight.

"This light!" he groans, "I think it's going to give me a migraine."

"I'll drive, then," I say briskly. "Stop at the next Services."

He manages, though – so martyredly, I expect stigmata to burst from his palms at any moment. At Heathrow we have the second of many breakfasts and watch him gloomily wash down his headache pills.

"Cheer up," I grin. "Think of lovely Elaine waiting at home to soothe your fevered brow."

"And the lovely baby!" cries Harriet. "Although I'm a bit sad really that you two separated, I'm everso glad in one way because Elaine's going to have a wonderful baby! Can I babysit for you in the summer holidays, Daddy?"

He supposes she can. Henry returns from a brief trawl through the airport shops and asks if he may buy a hand-held computer gambling game.

Eventually the moment of parting arrives. Spouse gazes at me, eyes thick with torment. Decide not to kick and bestow instead peck.

"Cheer up, old chap," I smile. "There's always faxes."

121

He nods dumbly. Harriet wails but only for a split second. Henry is silent.

Then he is gone. We board, find our seats and are charmed to be by the window. The great plane breaks through the clouds into miraculous light. Sigh no more, ladies, sigh no more. Men were deceivers ever.

"Henry!" cries Harriet. "Did you feel your ears pop then?"

"No. Only my bottom."

Then sigh not so, but let them go, and be you blithe and bonny, converting all your songs of woe, to Hey Nonny Nonny.

18 November

We will draw a veil over Canada. Especially Eric. Whilst I was over there I developed hot flushes, night sweats and irritability. Well, you would, wouldn't you? I suppose I am sailing gracefully towards the big M. Unless MacDonalds has annexed that initial. No more buns in the oven. Since the buns I have managed to produce spent their transatlantic idyll being hot and cross, perhaps it's just as well.

I wonder about HRT. Sinister initials, somehow. Could it lead to HRT TRBL? BRST CNCR? 's OBVS GDS a MN.

Spouse, however, reproduces himself with abandon. Still deep in jet lag, I am summoned across the road whilst Henry and Harriet are at school to admire the great baby. Or rather, the great baby's great baby. Elaine could only manage a 9lb boy, who now, at four months, dozes in his Moses basket like a prize marrow at a harvest festival. Express admiration and conceal fleeting witchy impulse to bestow some supernatural disfigurement upon him. Although since the poor child already resembles Clive James, perhaps that is unnecessary.

He is called Alexander. I expect Great Aunt Elspeth will call him Sandy when she Comes Round. At present she is in Scotch Shock. I cringe in anticipation of her condolences.

"He's so fat!" wails Elaine complacently. "We call him Alexander the Great."

I think it would be more considerate to leave the classical

122

allusions to me, dear. That's all I've got left, these days. And to be honest, if you asked me which I'd rather have, Spouse back or A level Latin, I wouldn't hesitate for a moment.

Mustn't be too hard on Elaine. She has been looking after Henry and Harriet since September whilst I, for financial reasons, executed a brief tour of Canadian literary clubs. I suppose it was handy that she still hasn't managed to sell her house, despite the glistening perfection of her coved ceilings and dado.

Spouse commutes to Ealing. I am glad to see that renewed paternity of the most unrelenting kind has left him grey in tooth and claw. As for Elaine, she is quite frankly fat. For the first time in history I am *thinner than Elaine*!

"Welcome to the New Young Britain," sighs Spouse. Apparently this is Tony Blair's war cry. Sod that. Had enough of new young countries. Want to burrow back into the spongy timbers of the old, old Britain and spend the rest of my days in cosy mastication.

Enquire sweetly what I have missed on telly, whilst in the land of waffle ads.

"Oh *Pride and Prejudice* – you'd have loved it, Dulcie, it was so *you*!" gushes Elaine. A rogue memory strikes me. I turn to Spouse.

"Didn't Alice once say that you and I reminded her of Elizabeth Bennett and Darcy?"

He scowls, clearly convinced that though he himself is still fully in possession of his Darciliousness, I have unfortunately come to resemble Her Mother.

Once this awkward moment is behind us I observe that Spouse and Elaine are both looking decidedly shifty – as if they have something else to conceal, although after everything else they've concealed in the past it's hard to imagine what.

There is a brief, embarrassed silence. My bowels, sensing an impending crisis, rouse themselves and cry out "Worra – worra – worra – POOF!" My large intestine has been transformed into a Liverpudlian lager lout. When Spouse and I separated, it seems I was awarded custody of the irritable bowel. I wonder if he will want to come over at weekends and take it out for treats.

Spouse shifts uneasily in his chair and tweaks at the knees of his trousers.

"The thing is—" he falters and fails.

"You want a divorce?" I smile sweetly. He looks alarmed. "Well, no, I mean, of course, eventually, perhaps, but that wasn't it. The thing is, we – er we've sold the house."

"Oh, congratulations! Well done! And they say you can't buck the market. So you'll be off to Ealing soon then, I suppose?"

Elaine clears her throat and pulls down the hem of her skirt as if at a job interview.

"Not my house, Dulcie," she stammers. "Yours."

25 November

Awake from dream that I am living under railway bridge. Still, the railways had all been privatised so at least it was quiet. I do not dream about the Royal Family any more. And good riddance. The transatlantic drivel they excite is reason enough to jettison the Windsors. Let's have King Ian McKellen and Queen Judi Dench. What speeches! What larks! What elegant whirling of ceremonial frocks! The House of Luvvy. As for the Windsors, Let Them Make Documentaries. Or go to Hollywood. Farre as Deucalion offe!

And why do I dream I am living under a railway bridge? Because Spouse has, in my absence abroad, sold the house to the Assholes. Well, Mike and Jenny Hassell, to be exact, but my hearing is not as acute as it used to be and somehow, you know, I think it kinda suits them.

I stare at the ceiling. Soon it will be the Assholes' ceiling. I could be difficult about it, but why bother? I'm sick of 196 Cranford Gardens. It's full of Spouse's unwanted old possessions and I think I speak for us all when I say Enough.

"We could buy a little cottage Mummy!" cries Harriet, in an ecstasy of nesting. "With roses round the door and a swimming pool and stables and I could have a pony!"

But before I can begin the agonies of house-hunting we must tiptoe through the minefield of education. Harriet is ten, and Rusbridge Primary must be aching for her departure.

"I think we can discount St Archie's, for a start," says Spouse, tossing dog-eared prospectus aside.

"Oh, can we indeed?" I bawl. "Why? Because she's a girl?"

"I can't afford it, that's why," he snaps. He snaps earlier these days, like old elastic bands.

"Oh yeah!" I slam down my Boston tea-party cup. "You could afford it all right for the son and heir."

"I don't want to go to St Archie's!" yells Harriet. "They're all toffee-nosed gits!"

"I don't want you to go to St Archie's because you *want* to go!" I scream. "I want you to go because your father doesn't want you to go!"

"Don't be bloody silly, Mummy! Even Henry doesn't want to go there any more!"

"*I can't afford it!*" Spouse produces tired roar, like old lion metamorphosing into toffee bar.

"Where then?"

Well: there's Rusbridge Comprehensive (drugs, sex, rock'n-'roll, street art, performance art, agit prop, and National under 16 Champions at gobbing for charity). And on the leafier side of town, Lord William Wyman's Grammar School for Girls, set decorously fifteen yards away from Lord William Wyman's Grammar School for Boys. I think fifteen yards ought to be enough. Surely even girl whales would be safe at that distance.

We visit the schools. At RC, as it is known, there is a raucous mêlée of vibrant humanity, rather like one of Hogarth's paintings. I would have found it bracing, I'm sure, if I hadn't had a bit of a headache. Harriet ogles the bawling boys, many of whom seem ready to burst out of their blazers, kick down the peeling walls, and go forth to kill mammoth.

At Lord Willie's, as it is known, girls are doing Latin, also beneath peeling walls. There is an atmosphere of sly festering female wit, just like my own school. And here and there, an exquisite phenomenon steals over us. Silence. Yes! I remember now! Girls do better in single sex schools! I know I was confused by mine. I know I started out at eleven wishing I was Marlon Brando and ended up in the Sixth Form in love with dead homosexuals, but that could be seen as a cool alternative life-choice these days.

Diverted and reassured by the sight of some of Lord Willie's girls and boys snogging furtively outside the school gates afterwards.

"I like Willie's!" cries Harriet. "But I like RC too!"

"Latin!" I murmur dreamily. "I use it all the time."

"Say something in Latin then Mummy! Go on! Go on!"

"Er . . . Jam . . . aqua libra bovril spam ecover video."

"God! Cool! Did they have videos even in those days?"

And now for the house-hunting, perhaps the only blood sport available to the suburban middle classes.

2 December

I lie under a sheaf of estate agents' blurbs. My husband's left me, my bowel has gone irritable, my menopause is upon me, my house is sold, the grave yawns . . . Also cannot entirely forget Eric's parting threat to hunt me down and kneel imploringly on my doorstep until I relent. Wonder how long he would be detained by the false address I gave him.

That's another reason for moving, actually. Ring estate agents and ask to see Jasmine Cottage, which pouts tartily at me from beneath a heavy fringe of thatch.

Phone rings again immediately. It is Spouse enquiring about the house-hunting.

"And – er – there's something else. I think Henry wants to come to London with us. I can't afford St Archie's any more and there's a bigger choice of suitable schools there. He could come home to you at weekends, of course."

What, my baby? Leave Mamma? Although I am all too aware that Henry has already gone away into adolescence. The headphones have descended. He's stopped kissing me, too. Like father, like son.

Scarce have I put down the phone and shed a tear at Henry's premature fledging, than the doorbell rings. At the thought that it might be the dreaded Eric, my bowel cries "Horra horra horra!"

Under the circumstances it is almost a pleasure to see Bernard Twill from next door, who presents me with a carrier bag exuding green slime.

"My greengages were stupendous this year!" he brays. "I froze some for you so you could make jam!"

Confess that my last experience of jamming was fifteen years ago, with Bob Marley. Bernard insists he will be delighted to assist me. Suggest we do it tomorrow as I am rather busy today. Bernard bows quaintly and departs, saying he will go off and rustle me up some pectin.

Return exhausted to sofa, leaving the greengages to defrost all over the carpet. Well, who cares, I expect it's a fixture or fitting and therefore the more I can blight it before I am exiled from it, the better.

Doorbell rings again. Oh, what new torment? Nice young couple smiling at me.

"Hello!" beams the bloke. "We're Mike and Jenny Asshole."

Ah. The purchasers. They just happened to be calling and thought they'd drop by to say hello. No sooner are they over the threshold than her eyes are swarming all over my walls. She may be in love with my house but I think it's a bit distasteful of her to flirt with it under my nose.

"I'm thinking," she confides in ecstasy, "of rag-rolling this room."

Tempted to ask her if this means it will take spin, but refrain.

Beg them to range freely where they will whilst I work, and pretend to be writing something on a piece of paper. There is no food in the house and I am starving. Beans, bread, fruit, veg, chicken, flora, ketchup, and what was the other thing? Oh what?

"Thank you so much!" cries Jenny Asshole, folding up her tape measure. "Have you found anything yet?"

Assure her I am e'en about it.

"We'd hate to put pressure on you but our buyers are onto us all the time."

Wave them goodbye. "Worra plonker!" cries my bowel. Cannot but agree.

Pick up kids from school, and view Jasmine Cottage on the way home. Though it is charming on the outside, interior decor clearly perpetrated by Danny La Rue on acid.

"Oh Mummy!" breathes Harriet in the pink and puce bedroom with crystal chandeliers and flounced vanity unit, "could this be my room?"

"Perhaps, who knows?" I cry wildly, dragging her away. Henry stayed in the car and is unreachable within Walkman. Sensible chap, really.

When we get home, Harriet locks herself in the bathroom and five minutes later cries piteously "O Mum! There's no bogroll left!"

Ah. That was it. Tempted to instruct her to use the carpet. Am just tearing off suitable quantity of kitchen roll, when doorbell rings yet again. Open door to find a gigantic box – big enough, I realise with horror, to conceal a fifteen-stone lovelorn Canadian with a whacky sense of humour.

9 December

Large box on doorstep reveals not lovelorn Canadian but dishwasher. Printed card attached. "You may have lost a husband but you've gained a dishwasher." Dishwasher is placed in kitchen but not plumbed in. Have to send away delivery men as I have no idea where it can possibly go.

Gaze at it with the rapture which, when I was younger, would have been wasted on men. But how kind, nay, princely of dear Spouse! Ring to acknowledge. Baby bawling and Elaine shrieking in background.

"Thank you so much for the dishwasher, Gordon."

"What? Eh? What the hell are you on about?"

Ah. Not him then. Anonymous gift! Head spins, and for stupid moment name TOM flashes unbidden into my mind. The only person ever to leave anonymous salutations at my door.

But where, how, nay who is Tom these days? Stalinist stone-mason Sabrina has been chipping away at him for almost two years. No doubt by now she has sculpted him into a husband.

Realise have perfect excuse to ring his old Anarchist Buddhist plumbing collective: dishwasher to be plumbed in. Girl answering phone has never heard of Tom and offers instead Hilary, whom I remember. The company, incidentally is now called Plumbing to Die For. Feel that undertakers are missing a vital opportunity to make death sound sexy. Jones and Thomson, Funeral Directors to Die For.

Hilary arrives – more gigantic than ever and accompanied by Carl, a youth loitering palely on work experience. Hilary thinks Tom and Sabrina have gone to live in Italy. Recall Tom urged me to elope thither with kids. Sunk in bitter reflection, watch Hilary and Carl relocate washing machine upstairs in bathroom and plumb in dishwasher in the gap left in the kitchen.

128

"I give it six months," observes Hilary on departing. Not sure if she is referring to dishwasher or Tom's marriage.

Urge children towards epic food binge so we can dirty as many dishes as possible. They are halfway through Potato shaped like Endangered Species with Fried Egg when doorbell rings. It is Bernard Twill carrying preserving sugar and warm, clean jars. I had forgotten promise to make jam with him, or as it must now be known, by order of Conservative Government in a jam, conserve.

"I shall be honoured," breathes Bernard, standing too close, "to be appointed Chief Stirrer." Suspect that now I am Lone Female I shall receive impertinent geriatric advances.

Escape briefly upstairs to activate washing machine, and return to find children slinking off. Insist they stay and do their homework cosily upon kitchen table.

"We've reached boiling point, Dulcie!" cries Bernard. Wonder idly what Bernard would be like in bed. If I ever recruit new lover it would be prudent to avoid coronary patients. Recall films in which elderly gentlemen (Marlon Brando, Burt Lancaster, Jeremy Irons, etc.) pleasure young women, often without bothering to remove their trousers. Why is it that in films sexual coupling can be achieved within 3 seconds whereas in real life 3 minutes would be good going? Shoes, tights, knickers, and then down a bit, back a bit . . . worse than parking.

"We've reached setting point!" cries Bernard in triumph. "It's wrinkling!"

"Mummy!" roars Harriet. "It's raining!"

"Well, darling, it *is* winter."

"But it's raining *indoors!*"

There is a moment of stillness, of *conservus interruptus*. Water is falling from the ceiling upon the kitchen table.

"The washing machine!" I cry in terror, and hurtle upstairs. Bernard falters. Upstairs, for him, could result in sticky end.

Carpet squelches, but washing machine winks at me as if butter wouldn't melt in its mouth. It appears empty. I open the door, and a tidal wave of clean hot water gushes out all over my feet.

"Mummeeee!" from below. "Stop it! It's pouring now! You've drowned my maths book!"

Must do some more house-hunting as matter of urgency. Must find new billet before I render this one totally uninhabitable.

Phone rings. Seize it and identify myself with enraged grunt.

"Oh, hi Dulcie, this is Alice. Has the dishwasher arrived OK? We just wanted to give you the one thing that we knew would make your life a bit easier."

16 December

Right. Serious house-hunting now. Mike and Jenny Asshole are desperate to move in here.

"We mustn't lose them!" Spouse panics. "We could find you somewhere nice to rent, then you'd have escaped the chain, you'd be a Highly Desirable Buyer."

"I'd have to move house twice, though," I observe tartly. I used to observe things tartily. I think of this as progress, Spouse perhaps not.

"Well, *I'll* have to move house twice!" he retorts, allowing himself to slip for a fatal moment into martyrdom.

"Nobody would have had to move at all if you hadn't started knocking off Elaine!" I bawl.

All the same, I househunt. It keeps my mind off Christmas.

Today it's Jasmine Cottage, in the village of Carpworth. I don't know why, I'm inclining to the pastoral at the moment.

"There's still a bit to do on it," the Estate Agent warns me sweetly, "but it's got bags of potential. Mr Jenkins is expecting you at twelve-thirty."

Drive to Carpworth imagining a life drenched in the scent of Jasmine. Church bells. Village shops. I've got the hang of this jam-making now. I could bottle. I could crochet. I could gossip. I could solve murders! I could become Miss Marple.

Walks in the woods . . . Wait a minute. Somehow after Miss Marple, walks in the woods sound a bit dangerous. Is Mr Jenkins waiting for me alone? No mention of Mrs Jenkins. Decide if cottage is too remote, will drive straight past. But it is right on village street, and Mr Jenkins, standing by gate, flags me down with welcoming, and perhaps murderous leer.

One look at Jasmine Cottage, alas, is enough to inform me that any further glances will be unnecessary. The Jasmine has been replaced with concrete, as has half the garden. Mr Jenkins bids me admire his extension, adorned with festoons of mysterious cable. I keep my car keys concealed in my hand. One false move on his part and I shall smash them into his jaw.

What must once have been a pleasant sitting room has been partitioned with teak and bottle glass and a bar installed ritzily across one corner. A quaint mullioned window has been walled up. Perhaps I shouldn't wait for his false move. Perhaps I should smash his face in anyway.

He boasts of his plastic double glazing, which I affect to admire. No point in honesty. The endless bedrooms with their vanitory units are all stifling.

"And the master bedroom has an ong sweet," beams Mr Jenkins, revealing a gold-plated bathroom secreted within a wardrobe. An invisible miasma of toxins coalesce from the carpet, the curtains, the walls. I break out in prickly heat and feel faint. Attempt to remove coat stealthily, but I notice Mr Jenkins noticing it with alarm. He fears I am a female exhibitionist about to force my tapiocan menopausal nakedness upon him in the privacy of his own ong sweet. And so effective is his insulation, nobody will hear him call for help.

For my part, I no longer fear he will murder me. He is obviously only interested in murdering houses. Escape, return to car, drive to nearest pub and order stiff ginger beer and lasagne. Limp with horror not just at toxic house but at toxic waves of snobbery which threaten to suffocate me. Tell myself sternly there's nothing wrong with polypropethylene in the right place. Wonder where that might be. The Planet Zog perhaps.

Another house to see at 2 p.m. Apple Tree Cottage in Foxcombe. Shown round by Estate Agent as owners have already moved to Dulwich. No dreaded vanitory units here. Perfect taste. Victorian fireplaces reverently preserved etc. Nothing the matter with it. But yet . . . It did not turn me on. Something deadly dull about it. Apologise to Estate Agent for loss of libido, but she assures me kindly it doesn't matter, it happens to everybody at some time.

Arrive home and shriek with horror at postcard from Canada.

Dulcie, I've tracked you down, you cruel tormentor! Flying to London on 20 Dec, hope to persuade you to share wondrous firelit Christmas. Your devoted Eric.

Wonder if I can move house in four days.

131

23 December

"Alice? You've got to stay with me for Christmas! The dreaded Eric is coming over! I need a chaperone! And it's all your fault I went to bloody Canada in the first place!"

"We're just leaving for Zanzibar," Alice informs me serenely. "And if you can't fight off an over-amorous Mountie after everything you've been through, it's a pretty poor show."

Don't like the word Mountie. Conjures up image of palaeolithic courtship.

Although perhaps that would be preferable to Eric's particular form of poedry. Yes, Eric is a poed. Interesded in hisdory. 'Hisdory is mah passion – apard from you, Dulcie.' Oh well. Prepare chaste bed for him in Harriet's room and inform her she can come into my bed, news she receives with rapture.

"And you are never -- *never*, do you hear, darling – to leave me alone with Eric."

"Why? Is he a sex maniac?"

"Certainly not."

"Mummy – what *is* a sex maniac?"

Not now, darling.

We are performing last-minute anguished shopping trip in Tesco, before viewing three more cottages in vain attempt to avoid Eric by moving house before nightfall. Select sprouts.

"Sproutz meanz fartz," comments Henry too loudly from within his Walkman, like an old lady under the hairdrier.

"Mummy's got to fart a lot this Christmas!" yells Harriet into his earpiece. "To keep Eric's mind off sex!"

Hurriedly complete purchases and depart to butcher's, where I proudly collect my free-range 12 lb turkey.

"Mummy," Harriet's suspicious liberalism awakens. "Does the fact that the turkey's so small mean that it was a baby turkey?"

"No, no! Heaven forbid! I wouldn't dream of eating a baby turkey! No, it's a very old, small turkey. Like – er – Miss Marple."

"Oh no! I *love* Miss Marple! I'm not eating it! Never!"

View cottages. Occupants clearly mystified by this unseasonal interest in their accommodation, but seem to regard it as portentous. 'Fear not, for behold! A woman shall come unto thee, and she will bring forth her firstborn son, and her secondborn daughter, and their Walkmans and Hamsters, and they, will buy thy house, and it shall be called Duncohabitin.'

A guiding star might have been helpful in locating Sunnyside. Would never have thought of looking for it actually under the bypass. Ah well. Bank Cottage had mushrooms growing on the walls and smelt of cats' piss – one of my favourites, but not quite up to Mitsouko. Davera, a twee houselet owned by Dave and Vera, was so small they could hardly show us round without resorting to sexual intercourse.

Drive home in despair, which deepens when I find I have mislaid the front door key. Spouse and Elaine have gone off to her parents for the festivities, bearing their babe The Fat Bastard. (A descriptive term merely.) Bernard and Audrey Twill have gone to Kettering.

"You fool, Mummy! It's freezing! Find the keys! Find the bloody keys!"

"Oh God, oh God, oh God!" Forage, shivering, in handbag. Locksmiths surely all tucked up for fortnight of Christmas. Lose nerve, start to shake, teeth chatter: terrible attack of Kettering. Wonder if we could spend Christmas in the car.

Taxi arrives and disgorges large person who looms up path in the dark.

"Dulcie! Sweedheard! Here I am, fr Gahd's sake! And this must be Henry! And Harried! Gahd! A momend to dreasure! Hi kids!"

Acquaint Eric with our dilemma. He places his shoulder to the door and applies 15 stone of prime Canadian pork to the lock, which splinters. "Don' worry, I'll fix id fr yah!" He puts down his bags in the sidding room. "Whad a beaudiful home! The logs, the holly. It cheers the heard of the weary draveller! Bearing gifds I dravel afar!"

"He rescued us!" whispers Harriet, her beady eye already on the bag of gifds. "And he looks like Meatloaf! I don't mind if you marry him Mummy!"

For her Christmas, Mary was visited by Wise Men from the East. We have a Dickhead from the West. Still, at least he provided us with that underrated commodity: indoors. All

I have to do now is stuff Miss Marple, and avoid the same fate myself.

30 December

"Mummy! You've got to make an EFFORT! Grow your hair long again and wear contact lenses and earrings and skirts and high heels and try and be a bit more FEMININE!"

"Go to hell, darling."

"You bastard, Mummy! You're always losing your temper and swearing at me! And I'm only trying to help! And you're always swearing and shouting at people when you're driving! Like a horrible man or something!"

Yes, folks. I'm too shirty for my sex.

She may have a point, actually. I have let myself go, rather. The arrival of my Canadian admirer has cramped my style somewhat, but as soon as he rolls off back to Big Jaw I fully intend to resume my cussin' an' swearin', hard drinkin', nose pickin', finger lickin', fallin' into bed with mah spurs still jinglin', devil may care, Thelma and Louisiana.

Although I may have picked my nose a bit hard recently. I have developed a danged painful inner nasal canal. A stab of agony every time I flare my nostrils. Good job I'm not Juliet Stevenson.

I have made a New Year's Resolution, though. I'm going to find a south-facing, immaculate little cottage, cosily tucked among others, with GCH, UPVC WNDWS, FLLY FTTD KIT, DPC, WDWRM GRNTEE, STRPPD PN WD FLRS and BRGLR ALRM. In other words, the sort of cottage that doesn't have to be wrapped: you can wear it now. I don't even want to TCH a PNTBRSH.

"Hey, Dulcie! What say we go for a liddle toodle?"

I have got into the habit of driving Eric around the country-side. It's a strategy. The idea is, he'll fall in love with it instead of me. Well, it's ancient, lumpy, overgrown, and in areas of set-aside, forlorn and neglected. "Ah need mah ration of mediaeval archidecdure."

Announce to children that we are going off on another little

134

tootle. They give me to understand they will tolerate excursion if at some stage they can Buy Something.

"After all, Mum, we've got our Christmas money from Aunt Elspeth and we haven't spent it yet. And how can we write our thank you letters till we've spent it?"

Henry might, I suspect, enjoy job satisfaction as double-glazing salesman.

Soon we are trundling through winter landscape. Eric erupts into poedry.

"This is the year's midnighd . . . er, how's it go on, sweedheard?"

In the back seat, Henry is rapping along with his Walkman.

"Henry!" cries Harriet. "Your voice is going croaky! Stop the car, Mummy! I think Henry's voice is BREAKING!"

"It broke last week," Henry informs her airily.

"What happened?"

"Oh, I sort of, like, coughed, and a handful of sick came up, and that was it."

"GROSS! A handful of sick! What colour was it?"

"*Hey! Sweedheard! Look! Sdop the car! Getta load of thad!*"

For once Eric's interpolation is welcome. I stop the car and look where he points . . . and ZING!

That was the strings of my heart, folks. There, tucked away up a steep track, crouching woefully on the cold side of a hill, totally isolated and fringed by dripping woods, dark, dank, rotting, glowering, fraying at the edges, unbrushed, unkempt, abandoned, nay, untouched for centuries, its nostrils clogged with scabs, stands Chervil Cottage. For Sale. Apply Goatley and Cross, Estate Agents.

"Chervil Coddage! Whad kinda a name is thad?"

"Trendy, that's what," I snap, trying to fight off my horrible infatuation. "You might as well call it Salsa Cottage, or Clafouti Cottage, or Hummus Sweet Hummus."

The huge unmanageable garden seems, in the absence of an owner, to have run amok, rampaged onto the roof and kept on going.

It seems a suitable place for Henry to grow his beard, Harriet to embark on years of tireless squeezing and plucking, and yours truly to go quietly – or what the hell, noisily – to seed.

We drive fast back to Rusbridge in search of Goatley and Cross. I know the surveyor's report will be damning, but I don't care. I am deeply smitten. I, who was vacant, am now possessed.

Dammit, dammit, dammit.

6 January 1996

Desperate desire to view Chervil Cottage. Cannot wait till Eric goes back to Canada and besides, to be fair, he found it. (Bang goes New Year's Resolution: not to be fair.) Must wait until children are back at school, however, as they would only introduce irrelevances. Oh Mummy! Look! There's a toad in the airing cupboard! How sweet! Et cetera.

Must expect toads and decay as Chervil Cottage has been vacant since long before the birth of the Estate Agent who gave us the keys – a charming lad of approximately twelve years of age, who later informed us that he was the father of two children. The child is father of the child these days.

Heart beats giddily as we corkscrew down the lane beneath the beechwoods. Inform myself sternly there is to be no foolishness. At the first hint of rot we shall retreat. Lo! There it is! Beautiful, alone, and swathed in ivy. The Greta Garbo of cottages.

First hint of rot proves to be the garden gate, which disintegrates into a heap of dust and mushrooms at the touch of Eric's hand. Well, you would, wouldn't you?

"Oh Gahd! Whadda heapa shit!" He kicks the debris. Never mind. He returns to Big Jaw on Thursday.

"Demolition is not required, Eric."

"Sure, sweedheard. Hey! Talk aboud picduresque! I could come back in the summer and do id up for yah. An' maybe by then you'll be over this posd-draumadic maridal breakup frigidity syndrome." He leers hopefully. I am becoming attached to my frigidity, however. I doubt if I shall ever bother to look at a man again. Especially Eric.

We go in. At first I think the walls have been rag-rolled in tasteful sage green and dove grey, but it's only mould.

"Raid! I'll survey the dimber for yah!" Eric goes off, sticking his keys into the hapless windowsills. I tiptoe into two little downstairs rooms. Plaster is flaking off the walls. In the back kitchen is a butler's sink where I suspect the toad (Antony Hopkins) resides. 'The back walls of the ground floor are dry-lined,' the particulars inform me. Not all that dry-lined, actually, sonny.

I venture upstairs. Creak creak. Sweet little voice of housie. Stop it! Dear little bedroom with surpassing view of valley. Sweetie ickle peeping window under eaves. Open window. It falls out, but not, alas, upon Eric. Other bedroom has rosy wallpaper and tiny sampler, dark with grime and age, in which the words HOME SWEET HOME can dimly be discerned.

Burst into tears. Dear little house! Must have! Even an upstairs bathroom. Not to mention tiny attic for Henry's weekend visits. Back in bathroom, try tap. Must be practical. Tap gasps rustily. Become brisk and purposeful. March downstairs, locate stopcock under sink, and turn on. Hammering, groaning, sighing, shuddering, the house stirs, Lazarus-like, from its rigor. Eric remarks that I shall need a plumber. This observation upsets me for a moment.

Alarming noise upstairs. Rush up and find tap, which I had left on, spouting like Bergman's Virgin Spring. Water bouncing off washbasin and cascading onto floor. An inch deep already. Turn off, tear down ancient grimy curtains and mop. Cry from kitchen below indicates that water is falling on Eric's head. Well, it's a start. I'll work my way up to masonry in due course.

He turns off the stopcock and we depart before we can do any more damage.

"Well, I guess cute isn'd everything," sighs Eric, clunk-clicking as I rev up. "They should've called id Vile Cottage."

Do not tell him I am secretly in love with Vile Cottage, nay, preparing to flee to its beams the moment he leaves for Heathrow.

But hell! Volvo refuses to reverse. Comes to juddering halt. Eric says it's the brakes, and offers to walk to telephone box we passed two miles back and summon RAC. Accept his kind offer and settle back to stare deeply into house's eyes.

"Alone at last, darling!" I whisper. "I thought he'd never go."

137

13 January

Brave New World, here I come: 196 Cranford Gardens is sold, bar the signing. I am packing. Elaine, home for the weekend from Ealing, is helping me. The fat bastard dozes in his basket nearby.

"God, Dulcie, we're so broke!" she laments. It is true that the lion's share of 196's equity is coming to me, but then, I have no regular income, and Vile Cottage requires extensive repairs, perhaps even demolition. Besides, the equity from the sale of her house will all go to her – if she ever sells it. She's not really broke, only cracked. But with me it's dust and ashes.

"I'm even looking for work in London," she goes on. "But then, I'd need a full-time nanny so the first hundred quid would disappear straight away."

Acknowledge that it is exceedingly grasping of nannies not to work for nothing.

"Mind you, it's only money, Dulcie," Elaine always very good at dodging the unbecoming. "Having Alexander has made me much more aware of the spiritual dimension."

"Well, maybe you could get that kind of work," I suggest helpfully. "How about spiritual Ealing?"

The fat bastard awakes and bawls. Elaine thinks perhaps she ought to take him back home as she fears he has pooed.

Sigh with relief at her departure, and at the fact that my own are well past pooing in their pants. Though during attacks of financial vertigo, I cannot be so confident about myself. Harriet and I are moving into a small flat off the High Street until Vile Cottage is habitable. Henry, at school in Fulham, will join us at weekends. Elaine has started calling him Harry, possibly to make it all seem even more royal.

"We could pretend we're flatmates, Mummy!" cries Harriet breathlessly. She is even more enchanted with the flat than the cottage. From her bedroom window she will be able to see several real shops! Sod sheep and cows – this is really living! Point out that flatmates would share the cooking, cleaning and washing up. "Oh Mummy!" she cries in frustration. "Why do you always spoil everything?"

Switch on oven and prepare to spoil my last *Poulet Jardinière au Cranford*. We have turned against eating the four-legged, what with mad beef and Babe and Lucinda Lambton. As for chicken – I give it till Easter. Chicken's weight is 2.3 kg – whatever that means. Pounds and ounces have been hurled into the shredder, along with farthings, Montgomeryshire, Stork and Vim. Alas for the Wizard of Oz. It's the Wizard of Gram or nothing.

Mustn't give in to nostalgia for the shilling, the crown, the florin. Embrace your euro, or as the British always shorten everything, the uro. The small change can be genitals. Take care of the genitals and the uros will take care of themselves. How true!

But why stop at weights and measures and currency? Why not dismantle the whole archaic apparatus of minutes, hours, days and weeks? A minute could become one hundred hours, thus making sense of Harriet's periodic promise, "I'll tidy my room up in a minute." A Month could become one hundred New Minutes, i.e. about nineteen Old Months. Hey! That does away with tedious old Years as well! Terrific!

All we need now is to change the names. Minutes can become Instants, and Months can be named after the moon goddess, Diana. 'Happy New Diana.' Yes. A distinct improvement. And calculated in New Dianas we'd all be younger, too. Those of us at present, say, pushing fifty, would suddenly find ourselves just over thirty instead.

What is the first symptom of mad cow disease, by the way?

"Dulcie – I've got it!" Spouse bursts in waving the actual contract. Poor Spouse: so desperate to get us and this house off his hands, he couldn't even permit himself a sneer about Vile Cottage. He may have gained a pretty young mistress and a fat new baby but he has had to give up all his favourite hobbies.

"Contracts aren't what they were," laments Spouse, waving thin sheet of paper. "Where's the thick crackly old parchment? The sealing wax? That Gothic print? Vandals!"

Tempted to make cruel dig about thick crackly old wives, but refrain. Besides, though all around is ashes, I can feel the Phoenix feathers begin to sprout. My shoulder blades have gone all prickly.

20 January

Separated woman, forties, in advanced stage of decay, sks builder, GSOH, solvent, reliable, to shore up disintegrating old structures and render waterproof.

Actually it's only Vile Cottage I'm worried about. I'm through with love, I rumty-rumty-tum. Though I have three blind dates this morning the strings of my heart only go zing at the sight of real estate. I'm cottaging now.

"Mummy! I don't like the cottage. I want to go back to Cranford Gardens. It was lovely there, Mummy. I want our old house back!"

"We can't have it, darling. It's Mike and Jenny Hassells' house now."

"I hate them! Assholes!"

"Ssssh! Don't say that!"

"You call them that! Anyway, nobody can hear me."

We are miles from civilisation, i.e. parked outside Vile Cottage, awaiting the second of three builders coming to give estimates. The first never materialised. The cottage is unendurable even in scarves and mittens, so we sit in the car sipping Earl Grey from a flask and reading magazines. I read *Period House* and *Period Living* which exist to fan the first sparks of cottage love into blazing infatuation. Yes, I am becoming a Period Pain.

Harriet is wrapped in blankets, plugged into her Walkman and reading something called *Shout*. When not reviling me for ruining her life, she is singing along with Boyzone. 'It's not time to make a change/Relax, take it easy . . . etc.' Alas, the change is made. The die is cast. And I shall sing to my own tune: sing along with *Period House*.

'Rip that flex! Get a bit of rhythm! Sand those boards! Strip that beam!' Did I notice a bit of lino in the cottage kitchen? Well, rip it up! – no, wait, rip it back down, 'cos lino's *back in*! Forward to Antiquity.

My découpage quivers in anticipation of all that hacking

140

off, shoring up, stripping off, oiling, waxing and sponging. DIY was unsafe long before sex. Probably the reason men like DIY so much is they don't have to make sure the house is enjoying it.

"It was wonderful at Cranford Gardens, Mummy, wasn't it? You and Daddy were in love, weren't you? And it was the most beautiful house in the world."

We are interrupted in our respective pursuits of a mythical Golden Age by the arrival of a golden boy.

Jason Copstick, Builder, appears right on cue in transit van, which baulks at ascent of drive. Jason jumps out, peers up at the house, and says, "Christ!" He is a bit like Shane Warne – sort of Pigling Blond.

"God, Mum, he's gorgeous! He looks just like Ronan from Boyzone!" whispers Harriet, tearing off her Walkman and preparing to mate.

We go over whole house and agree that every room requires extensive repair. Fight off sinking feeling as Jason flashes his rigid rule about.

"Lovely old place!" he grins. "Only needs a bit of TLC." He leers outrageously. "Soon have you nice and cosy!"

Wonder which of us he is planning to have nice and cosy. Fight off familiar weakness for a bit of rough, which Harriet seems to have inherited.

"There, you see, darling," I beam at her. "The past is past. Fix your eyes on the future."

"And Jason!" salivates Harriet as he drives off. Don't blame her. Something very simpatico about him. Lovely boy. No need for any more estimates. Waste of time. Jason's the one.

Range Rover purrs up North Face towards me. Who now? Local lord of the manor introducing himself, prior to sweeping me orf my feet and installing me on Persian carpet by his baronial hearth? Posh-looking cove gets out.

"Mrs Domum?"

"Er . . . ?"

"Keith Carter." For a moment my mind goes blank. I know that name. Wait! He's the other builder. The one due now. Oh well. Have to go through the motions I suppose. We shake hands. Coldly. Jason's hands were hot. Keith Carter smiles enigmatically.

"It's none of my business, of course, but I couldn't help

noticing Jason Copstick driving away just now. I suppose you know he's bankrupt?"

Somehow this only makes me like him more.

27 January

What is it about Vile Cottage that turns all these builders off? They come, they see, they scarper. Poor Vile Cottage deteriorates daily. And our temporary pied-à-terre – the little flat just off the High Street – is losing its charm, if it ever had any. The fat woman in the flat opposite has gone miles off her trolley. She has taken to loitering on the landing in her peach candlewick dressing gown at 2 a.m. and singing in a powerful voice, 'Che sera, sera, Whatever will be, will be.'

"Oh well," says Alice, ringing for post-holiday gloat, "at least it's a song of philosophical resignation. You should suggest she gets counselling."

Suspect Mrs Diorama would respond more enthusiastically to Karaoke than counselling. Enquire whether Zanzibar was satisfactory.

"Exquisite. We'll show you the slides when we come. How about next week?"

"Oh God! I'm sorry -- this flat is more like a cupboard, and I'm afraid the cottage is totally uninhabitable."

"Nonsense, Dulcie," snaps Alice. "We don't understand the concept of uninhabitable. You should see where we slept in Kizimkazi. It's got a hearth, I suppose? Get a sweep in, buy a load of logs, and we'll be warm as toast. You and Harriet stay in the flat -- we'll camp out in the cottage and do all your decorating for you. You'll want the Dead Flat effect presumably. The National Trust's Mouse's Back is very attractive."

Appalled at her effrontery at annexing my cottage till I remember that she recently gave me a dishwasher.

"No, listen, Alice, the cottage is full of builders. Horrible leering macho types. Plumbers' bums up to their collars. Girlie mags in their toolboxes."

"Ugh! How gross. Let us know when they've gone." She

rings off in medium dudgeon, and I am left stimulated and sustained, as usual, by my conversation with supportive friend.

"Che sera . . . Whatever will be, will be . . ." Mrs Diorama has started up early this evening.

Suddenly seized by mad impulse, I rush out onto landing and prepare to counsel.

"Good evenin', Missis Doner, darlin'!" This is as near as she can get to my name. There is something awfully Harry Enfield about her at times. "Col' wevver, innit? 'Swhy I got my candawick robe on all day, keep de draughts out, eh? How your little cottage comin' on, darlin'?"

Something about her – perhaps her obvious derangement – invites confidences.

"To be honest, I'm desperate for a decent builder. Nobody seems to want work these days. I've had seven chaps round – seven! – and I've only had one estimate so far, and that was enough to rebuild Windsor Castle."

Mrs D. seizes my arm, her Levantine eyes liquid with pity and terror.

"Listen, darlin', you need my son-in-law Torpid, 'e's a lovely fella, he kin do buildin', heatin', 'lectric, the lot. Wait!" Paralysed with alarm, I watch her produce mobile phone from the depths of her dressing gown and engage someone in torrential intercourse. Eventually she rings off in triumph.

"He comin' round to see you Saturday mornin'!" she brays. "Do you lovely job, buildin', double glazin', I tell 'im, you give Missus Doner good price, she nice lady, OK?"

"Mummeeee!" Harriet screams from depths of flat.

"Must go," I twitch, backing away. "Thanks so much!"

Mrs Diorama nods, beams, closes her eyes, embraces the radiator and bursts into song.

"Mummy! Where were you? I was scared! I thought you'd gone away and left me!" Harriet fastens herself venomously to me like a brook lamprey to an incautious fisherman's heel. Since her Papa and Henry moved to London, she will not let me out of her sight except during *Neighbours*.

"I thought I told you to tidy your room! You've been playing with those Sindies again. Stupid bimbos!"

"They're not bimbos!" Severely. "They're Marine Biologists!"

Torpid Tarantino (I may have got his name wrong) appears

on Saturday and offers to resuscitate cottage for five thousand quid, starting immediately. This can only mean incompetence of the most ingenious kind, but I am too tired to argue. Some of us don't need National Trust paints for the Dead Flat effect.

3 February

I can't afford proper builders. But Torpid Tarantino, my black-market, cash-in-hand, nod's-as-good-as-a-wink man-who-can-do, has restored water and electricity to Vile Cottage and is now fiddling on the roof. The roof lends itself to bracing walks. You can step straight onto it from the back garden. Indeed so deeply has Vile Cottage been inserted into the hillside, it feels almost like a cave. I may be entering my Stone Age period.

I wonder if you can get Lascaux-style stencil kits of mammoth and fleeing antelope?

"Mummy, we want to spend a night at the cottage. Then it would seem more like ours."

Henry and Harriet look imploring. Poor chicks. Devastated by parental separation and arrival of fat cuckoo in Ealing.

"Well, why not, chaps? We could take our bedrolls and sleep in front of the fire."

"Hooray! You're *ace* Mummy!"

Pack bedrolls, sleeping bags, camping mugs, plates, cutlery . . . blankets, torch, candles, bogroll . . . washing-up-liquid, saucepans, food . . . ketchup to disguise the taste of the food . . . And all this in the first week of February. Still, I may have invented the next big thing in trendy winter holidays. Winter Squats.

And there is something delightfully *fin de siècle* about squatting in one's own house.

Luckily a sweep has already been with broom before to sweep the dust behind the door. All we need now is a large sack of logs, a small net of kindling, firelighters and several boxes of matches. On arrival at Vile Cottage it takes only twenty minutes to achieve blazing hearth. Unfortunately by the time we have unloaded the rest of the stuff from the car the blaze has dwindled to a smoky sulk.

"Henry, you're in charge of the fire. Harriet, come and help me cook the beans."

"Snot fair! Sexist! Why can't he cook the beans, the bastard?"

"All right, all right, we'll all cook the beans, and we'll all watch the fire."

"I don't mind cooking the beans," says Henry. "I quite like cooking actually."

Silenced by this astonishing revelation.

Henry goes into kitchen. Harriet and I sit by fire. FLASH-BANG-POP from kitchen. Henry, pale, rushes in.

"Mum the cooker plug's flashing!"

Hurtle to cupboard under stairs and switch off mains electricity.

"Stop it Mummy it's gone dark, you idiot!"

"Shut up Harriet, you nerd, she's got to switch it off or the house'll burn down!"

"I'm not a nerd, you bastard!"

"Shut up both of you and find the torch and the candles."

Investigate kitchen by torchlight and find discreet trickle of water running down wall adjacent to cooker socket. Turn off stopcock. Trickle peters out. Plumbing, then, not intrusion of weather. Not sure if this good or bad news. Return to sitting room and report no water.

"Oh, who cares?" cries Harriet. "I won't have to clean my teeth."

"Let's hope nobody gets diarrhoea," grins Henry.

"We won't be able to cook supper now," I sigh.

"Yes we will, Mum!" cries Henry. "We can cook it on the fire like at camp."

Camping indoors complete: beans on toast by firelight. The only thing missing is the irritating intrusion of insect life.

We doss down in the firelight without bothering to get undressed or washing. Quietness settles. The fire sinks. Harriet fidgets.

"I'm sorry, Mummy," she whispers urgently, "but I think I've got nits again."

"Never mind, darling," I whisper comfortingly. "You'll probably have Death Watch Beetle by morning."

Lie awake in icy draught reflecting that this has been an elemental experience. Disastrous conjunction of fire and water. Earth and air also seem a little too much in evidence.

We are after all supposed to be indoors. Uneasily aware that less than two miles away families are safely tucked up in proper beds enjoying all mod cons and wonder where I have gone wrong.

"I love you, Mummy!" whispers Harriet ecstatically. "Nobody else's Mummy would let them do this."

Wonder how long it will be before the children are taken into care.

10 February

"Mummy! Is there such a thing as heaven?"

"Er . . . I'm not sure, darling."

"Daddy says it's all codswallop."

"Well, Daddy says *Blind Date* is codswallop but it still exists."

"If there isn't a heaven," warns Harriet grimly, "I'm going to ask for my money back."

Not sure if the Almighty is aware of his responsibilities vis-à-vis consumer satisfaction. Money Back if Benighted.

Pondering uneasily where my next bit of consumerism is going to come from. Vile Cottage has gobbled up my meagre budget and is shrieking for more -- and we're still living in the grubby flat off the High Street. The builder Torpid has promised the cottage will be ready by March, in time for Harriet's birthday.

"Mummy, can I have a pony for my birth—"

"Certainly not!"

"You didn't even let me finish! You're always bloody well telling me off for that and you do it yourself!"

"Sorry. But you can't have a pony."

"Why not? There's that big field behind the cottage and it would be everso happy and I promise I'd look after it and give it food and water and everything and I'd spend all my pocket money on its hay oh please please please!"

"No."

Always enjoy the struggle about the pony. Only subject about which I can trust myself to be resolute. Cannot rise to horses. Too sleek, too gleaming, hooves and teeth too sharp somehow. Prefer my animals bald and crumply. Toads, elephants, Dr Johnson. No: cannot face horse. Would prefer a Yahoo. Living with Harriet has accustomed me to being crapped on from a great height.

"I hate you!" SLAM! She flounces out to her room. Although here in the flat she is denied her cadenzas of indignation. Her room is only four inches away and you can't really get up a good flounce in less than three yards.

Relax and enjoy solitude, although financial worries, like nits, soon resume their irritation. If only one could get a pestilential shampoo to banish those niggling little fears that eat away at your serenity: bankruptcy, writer's block, death, fainting in Tesco's . . .

I ought really to start work on another Bonkbuster, but I have lost interest in bonks and busts. Money is of course sexier than sex, I realise, now I have none of either. I lie awake longing for liquidity. Cupidity beats Cupid hands down.

Perhaps I should write a steamy no-holds-barred financial saga. The Bankbuster. Instead, however, my attention strays fatally towards recently ordered catalogue of roses. I would be neglecting my duty towards cliché if Vile Cottage did not have roses round its door, although at present just a door would be awfully nice. '*Rosa x richardii*. A rose of great historic interest, known as the "Holy Rose of Abyssinia", where it has been planted from ancient times in the courtyards of Christian sanctuaries.'

Somehow at these few words, all my anxieties evaporate. The Holy Rose! Sanctuaries! Of course there's a heaven. How could I have doubted it for a moment? Am beaming beatifically when Harriet comes back in.

"Mummy . . . you did say once you liked donkeys."

"Indeed I do, darling. I adore them."

I have always had a weakness for a shapely ass. Fur like old doormat, modest demeanour, bizarre bray like rusty machinery.

"Well can I have a donkey then?"

"Perhaps . . . one day."

"Oh yippee Mummy thank you thank you!"

Am embraced, then Harriet sets about her maths homework without being told, in ecstatic anticipation of her donkey. I

147

dream of the Holy Rose of Abyssinia entwined voluptuously about my ancient porch.

"Mummy, I can't help it – I adore Michael Jackson. He is nice, Mummy, isn't he? He is wonderful. We can call the donkey after him."

"Yes. Michael Jackass."

Have a horrid feeling that he might eat my Holy Rose of Abyssinia before it has a chance to climb up to my eaves.

Some time later I discover that the Holy Rose is only three feet high. Oh well. It'll just have to entwine voluptuously about my ancient knees.

17 February

Summoned to London by publisher. Constant turnover of ambitious young things means my editor is now somebody called Aileen O'Shaughnessy. As I drive to station, ponder on charms of Celtic fringe. O that I could have been an O'Shaughnessy. Or even an O'clock. Irish is very glamorous now. Even Belfast – especially since the rise of the sink.

Aileen. How much nearer can you get to mourning and keening without actually bursting into tears? Not that Aileen's communications have been lachrymose, so far. Quite the contrary. Indeed, she has inclined to the brisk. She rang to enquire about the progress of my latest book, and was too polite to mention the advance they had paid: an amoebic fragment of microscopic life devoured by Tyrannosaurus Cottage.

My builder thinks the staircase might be about to collapse. Perhaps this symbolises my repeated failure to aspire to higher things. I must however stop thinking about the cottage and spend the train journey feverishly conjuring up some convincing details of a literary work in progress.

"I don't really like talking about what I'm working on: it seems to put a jinx on it."

Aileen will have heard that one before. I need a piping-hot free-range hero, pronto.

A young man of gigantic aspect inserts himself with difficulty into the seat opposite. Are there growth hormones in the meat? And elegance hormones too. He is arrayed in pinstripe suit and huge black shiny shoes like limousines. In my day young men dressed sensibly in shoulder-length hair, garlands of flowers and panne velvet loons.

I need a hero, but this is not he. Can't get excited about politicians any more either. As for cricketers – whilst admiring corkscrew spin-bowling of the young South African Adams recently, realised that, given a fair amount of sexual precocity, I was old enough to be his grandmother. Anyway, my mind keeps wandering back to staircases. Staircases beat men hands down. At least they get you somewhere.

O where shall I find a hero to place my tin wreath upon? Fragments of poem gleam like graffiti upon the ancient wall of my brain. 'The tea rose, tea gown, etc., supplants the mousseline of Cos . . .' Ezra Pound lamenting the good old days when gods were priapic and religions rude and rampant. In his day, of course, the tea rose and tea gown were vulgar and modern. To me they resonate with antiquity.

If I live to see another summer, I shall find myself a tea-rose tea gown in the Oxfam shop. And perhaps a mousseline scarf to tie about my dear old hat. I want to be Gertrude Jekyll. I have, after all, an acre of brambles to play with. How can I think of men at a time like this?

Alice would be pleased. Oh God! She's coming next week, so she can see something of 'Henrietta' during half-term.

"You'd think she'd know my bloody name by now," sneered Harriet at this news. "I am nearly eleven."

"Hush! And be tolerant. She's your fairy godmother."

"If she's a fairy godmother why does she hate princes?"

Gaze out at the South of England, which some tactful deity has veiled in 20-denier fog.

Henrietta Jekyll threw up the sash window and felt the celtic zephyrs fondle the folds of her muslin chemise. Far below, labouring in the knot garden, was the sturdy figure of Ezra O'Hooligan.

Oh no! Dammit! It's a Badedas ad!

Perhaps I should try biography. But who's left to do, apart from God? And you'd never get his friends to talk. Ay me! Family life and DIY saps your creativity, as God was the first to discover.

"I don't want to go into details," I grin treacherously at poor Aileen, an hour later in the restaurant, "but I'm enjoying it more than anything else I've ever written and I'm thirty thousand words in already."

"Oh thank God!" cries Aileen with desperate relief. "All my other authors have got a terrible case of writer's block."

24 February

Half-term. Henry has arrived from London full of anxiety.

"Mum . . . ? Elaine says I'm not much like Dad. She says Alexander is a lot more like Dad than me."

Tempted to point out that the stepmother's baby is indeed bald, taciturn and greedy, but refrain. Assure Henry instead that he combines in his fair person the best qualities of both parents.

"What have I inherited from you, then?" he enquires with evident alarm. Privately suspect it's my horrible ability to bottle up guilt and anger and soldier on without complaining, but suggest instead he might have inherited my toes. Pretty safe bet as they are usually hidden and miles away from any naughty areas. Doesn't seem to reassure him, though. He retires with a sigh to the boxroom and plugs himself into BLUR.

"Mummy?" Harriet this time. "Are Alice and Saskia lesbians?"

"Well, as a matter of fact, yes. But lesbians often have better relationships than heterosexual women. They're more sensitive, better at talking things over, share all the housework as a matter of course: there's absolutely nothing wrong with being a lesbian."

"Well, who said there was?" Harriet looks astonished.

I'm exhausted already and it's only 9 a.m. An hour later Mrs Body arrives to give the flat a quick once-over, as Alice and Saskia are due any minute, and though most lesbians share all the housework as a matter of course, Alice and Saskia are honourable exceptions.

When they arrive, point out that they will have to manage

150

with Harriet's single bed, whilst Harriet shares with me and Henry is folded up in the box room.

"Oh, how sweet!" cries Alice. "It'll be just like college." Except that nowadays one is more interested in sleep, and being obliged to lie directly upon, or worse, beneath one's beloved is marginally less enchanting.

"So, Harriet. Where are you going to school?" enquires Alice, wasting no time in addressing The Big One.

"Lord Willie's Grammar School for Girls."

"Oh, well done, dear!" bellows Mrs Body. "I knew she would, look 'cos she's so bright, I would've liked our Trace to go there but she never managed to pass the test."

"Good God! Selection! How could you?" yells Saskia, releasing first socialist Scud.

Refrain from mentioning Latin and silence, and scrabble guiltily for trump card.

"Er – girls do better in single-sex schools." Cringing.

"Quite right!" agrees Alice. "Why should Harriet sacrifice her potential just to civilise bloody men?"

"It's not about sexual politics, it's about social divisiveness!" cries Saskia. "Are you a socialist, Dulcie, or not?"

"Dulcie's always been more of an anarchist," says Alice.

"I've never called myself a socialist," I bleat, cringing guiltily as if falling short of some majestic requirement. "But if I did, it's the public schools that'd get my goat."

"What goat?" asks Harriet, scenting the possibility of a pet.

"You paid for Henry to go to St Whatsit's!"

"His father paid. I wouldn't have sent him there if it had been up to me. Anyway, he's left now." Mega-cringe.

"St Archie's is a lovely school, dear!" Mrs Body is buffing up the candlesticks as eagerly as if they were scholarship boys. "I wish I could've afforded to send my Darren there."

"But that's exactly what's wrong with the system, Mrs Body!" brays Saskia. "You can't call it giving parents a choice if most of them can't afford it."

"Ah, but I'd like to think it was there, in case I ever could afford it, dear." At this riposte from the sacred proletariat, we all fall silent for a moment.

"Mummy," pipes up Harriet, who has been told to wait for a silence before making any remark, "Can I watch the video of *Blind Date*?"

Henry puts his head round the door, receives rapturous

lesbian salutations and cringes visibly. Ah. I knew there was something of mine he'd inherited.

In bed that night, Harriet whispers, "I don't want to be a lesbian, Mummy. I don't think I'd pass the exams."

2 March

Alice and Saskia admire the cottage. Harriet and I trail resentfully in their wake.

"What on earth is the point of that window?" sighs Alice, glaring at an inoffensive little back kitchen casement opening onto the adjoining hillside eighteen inches away.

"You might as well take this whole horrible back bit of roof off," suggests Saskia briskly, "and glass it in nicely. Get more light. Sort of conservatory feeling."

"I'll kill them in a minute!" whispers Harriet. "Dear old roof! I love it! It Must Always Be There!"

Begin to feel my cottage is not really my cottage at all.

From the dear old bedroom we survey the glorious valley. At least I don't have to be ashamed of the view. It may not compare with Zanzibar and St Lucia, but surely they will acknowledge its claims to the picturesque.

"Oh dear," Alice shakes her head with foreboding. "Awfully isolated, aren't you?"

Uneasily aware the same thought had occurred to me, often, but that I have always hastily swept it away.

"If I was on my own," muses Saskia, "I'd get a little flat in Bath or somewhere."

"Yeah," Alice nods. "You want to be at least within shouting distance of the neighbours, really. Where *are* the nearest neighbours, Dulcie?"

"Er -- I think there's a farm down there behind that wood."

"Hm," remarks Alice. "It's a long way to crawl."

Eventually Alice and Saskia leave me to my doom and depart for Taormina, where they will spend a bit more of Alice's father's fortune, cheerfully reviling men the while.

Next day Harriet is safely reinserted into Rusbridge Primary. I should be getting stuck into epoch or at least money-making oeuvre, but instead, after an early lunch, I slink back down the deserted lanes to Vile Cottage. Go round the back, outside, to inspect the horrid bit of roof, and ponder Saskia's suggestion of putting up some glass there instead – an idea I can't help finding rather attractive, despite every effort to repudiate it.

Claw my way up steep bank through brambles, and eventually gain some level ground from which to gaze down on roof. Step to one side and . . . aaaaaAGH! Foot, expecting ground, encounters vacancy, and plunges me down into yawning pit concealed by thorns. Left knee cracks inwards nastily on edge, en passant, like a stick across a masculine thigh. Agony, etc. Shriek sickeningly for five minutes.

Once resting from shriek, sober realisation dawns that I am stuck down five-foot deep hole. Impossible to climb out even if knee not comprehensively buggered. Curse – not Fate, cottage, Saskia or even self, but rather healthily, I feel, Spouse. Had he not gone off with Elaine I wouldn't be here, alone, dying in remote pit. I'd be basking in the safe, suburban comfort of 196 Cranford Gardens. In fact, I'd be having a last cup of tea before collecting Harriet from school.

Sacred Norah! The horror of dying in remote pit etc. nothing compared to the horror of little Harriet waiting alone in darkening playground, trying unsuccessfully to fight off tears. Shed a few myself, before sensibly calling for help for ten minutes. No answer, so enquire robustly of the Almighty if this is not the perfect moment to show his hand. Rescue me, O Lord, I beg, and I'll never be a naughty girl again. I'll even vote Conservative.

Listen. Silence. Nothing but bleeding birds and blasted lambs. Mind you, I bet you could call for hours in vain in bloody Bath, too. Builder's day off, soddim. Hatred of Spouse returns with gusto. Heap execrations on his head. Adorn him with gynaecological and scatological sobriquets. Cast aspersions on his legitimacy, manhood, sanity.

"You'll be sorry, you bastard, and about time too! You've never bloody cared. May all the birds in Ealing crap on your head and may the dogs defile the stones beneath your feet!"

Suddenly a face appears in the sky. It is a round, red face I have not seen before, and wearing a tweed cap.

"Ar," it says. "I wasn't sure whether to interrupt, like, in case you was a courtin' couple."

153

9 March

I've strained my lateral and collateral knee ligaments. Beat
that, chaps. I can't shop. I can't cook. I can't drive. It's what
I've been longing for all my life. I recline upon the sofa and am
waited on. I am spared the daily ordeal of Torpid Tarantino's
assaults upon my cottage and amuse myself by leafing through
Dulux's colour card. Diverted to find a blush-pink tone called
'Mistress'. Wonder if there is also a mousey grey called
'Ex-Wife'.

Mrs Body hoovers, shops, cooks, etc. most obligingly. She
has even sanitised the phone to assist my recovery. It rings –
fragrantly.

"Dulcie?" It is Elaine, who has relieved me of my husband
and my house and is still not satisfied. "How's your poor
knee?" God help us, surely she's not after *that*.

No. Instead she offers to help out by mistress-minding
Harriet's birthday party. She will take them skating whilst my
husband minds the baby. (Theirs.) Accept with gratitude. Mrs
Body offers to buy Harriet a present for me. I think perhaps I
will lie on the sofa forever.

Unfortunately, knee soon feels a bit better, though kneeling
and squatting still painful. Sacraments and excrements therefore neglected, but suspect shopping will be a possibility soon,
at which my heart sinks.

"Mummy . . . ? Can I have a hamster for my birthday oh
please please please I'll look after it I promise I'll love it
always and you'll never have to clean its cage out per-
leaze!"

"No."

Daughter runs off howling. Mrs Body enters with secret
parcel.

"I couldn't find that book you was on about, look, so I got
her a cuddly toy. I hope that's all right." Am afforded brief
glimpse of pink rabbit. Express rapture.

Get up and limp about a bit. We cannot all hope to be
whisked off our sofas by Robert Browning. Discover I can

drive. Visit Waitrose, and exhibit economy by buying only three sorts of sorbet.

"Mummy . . . ? If you can drive, you could drive to the ice rink as well and I could take two extra friends . . ."

"OK. *If . . .* hamsters are never mentioned again."

Spirit quails at thought of trying to navigate through unknown provincial city in search of Mecca Entertainments.

The day dawns: children are delivered and distributed between our two cars.

"Follow me!" suggests Elaine gaily. Stupidly insist that I will find it easily on my own, though I know I won't. Can't bear to Follow Her. Elaine disappears at speed, and our dear old Volvo lumbers off in roughly the same direction (a concession but briefly yielded).

The twenty-five miles of open country between us and the city are easily negotiated, though I would never have thought three little girls could have made so much noise. Shrieking with ecstasy – at present, only the non-chemical variety.

Soon, however, we enter the city's ghastly maw, and immediately I am lost, hurtling and swooping around underpasses, overbites and contraflows, and always in the wrong lane. Break out in cold sweat. Twenty minutes late already.

"Look for Mecca! Look for Mecca!" I cry, abandoning all pretence at composure. The girls have delighted hysterics.

"We've been here before!" cries Emily, recognising a malodorous underpass.

"It's like a bad dream!" shrieks Harriet. Eventually I see a car park, bolt inside it and announce "We're walking."

Enquire of youth whereabouts of ice rink. He looks doubtful and asks if we have a car. Insist not. Receive byzantine directions. Turn encouragingly to girls, cry "We're nearly there! It's only round the corner!" and collide briskly with unsuspected parking meter.

I am later informed by Harriet that this was considered the best moment of the whole day.

Facial injuries (invisible but agonizing: the worst sort) distract me from pain of knee. Ice Rink eventually attained. Elaine's party arrived hours ago. Whole place tacky and dismal: the damned circling aimlessly in the gloom, to hideous muzac. Dante's Inferno on Ice. Elaine is wearing a silly little skating skirt, lipstick of the Mistress shade, and looks completely at home.

This thought is a great comfort to me for days afterwards.

16 March

I know I said that strained ligaments were what I'd been waiting for all my life. But I was wrong. I suppose it would be easier for them to heal if I wasn't trying to move house. Or if I was moving house sensibly and expensively, with professional packers and heavers. But we do it bit by bit and on the cheap. A chest of drawers at a time in the back of the Volvo. This gives maximum opportunity both for new personal injury, and the revival of old favourites.

Ow! There it goes again. Drop drawers, seize knee and howl.

"Mummy! Be quiet! People are looking!"

"Let them sodding look!"

"And stop swearing! It's embarrassing!"

Henry picks up the dropped drawers and puts them in the car, too riled to speak.

"All right then." Once in the car, a peace process. "I'll stop swearing if you stop swearing."

It's going to be hard, though. Even the Archers are swearing now. Posh Caroline Bone said Simon was behaving like an absolute shit. It's clever editing, to put the obscenities into the mouths of the posh. Even better, the posh and elderly. My money's on 'Jack's a complete tosser sometimes' (Peggy) and 'I'm afraid Eddie Grundy is a cussed awkward sonofabitch' (Mrs Antrobus).

Determined not to swear any more, though. Not in front of the children, anyway. And not in public. Unbecoming in the elderly. Like jeans. Engage reverse gear with serene smile and prepare to extricate Volvo from High Street.

Then – crunch! Not a big crunch, nor a particularly loud crunch, but a crunch.

"Holy shit! We've run over something!"

Something small. A dog? A cat? Blood runs cold. Sweat runs hot. Dread swamps me. Must not drive off, though. Although – why not? Cannot face blooded corpse. Cast furtive glance in rear-view mirror. One or two people on pavement, but no ghoulish goggling. Not a fatality, then. Probably just an old cardboard box.

Drive off in a fit of irresponsibility. Cannot stand the sight of crushed cardboard.

"Mummy! You said we'd run over something!"

"I was wrong."

"I felt it." Henry has a way of sighing ominously that comes straight down the Domum line. Hope Spouse is doing a lot of ominous sighing in Ealing. Expect request for divorce any day now.

First, though, must bestow chest of drawers on Vile Cottage. Sun shines, etc. Catkins dangle. Lambs gambol.

"Oh, isn't the countryside marvellous in spring!"

"Mummy . . . Did Jesus go to the lavatory?"

Attain Vile Cottage, park, and ease ligaments out of car whilst pondering theological conundra.

Relieved to find nobody has burned down Vile Cottage in my absence – though would perhaps be even more relieved if they had. Sunshine is now pouring in through a side window, so Alice's surly remarks about the cold side of a hill completely unjustified. Henry helps to unload chest of drawers, then goes straight to his attic and shuts the door, suggesting he is in for an intense fit of hormonal brooding.

"Mummy! I want to paint this room purple. We can, can't we? Can't we Mummy Oh Please!"

"Er – well, I'm not sure if purple paint is actually available . . ."

"I could mix some up!"

Look for colour card. Where is handbag? Not in cottage. Limp out to car. Handbag not in car. Handbag . . . *gone*! Female equivalent of castration. Fly into complete panic.

Assemble indignant children and insist we must go straight back to flat to look for handbag. Arrive, park, rush upstairs, throw open door and find card on mat.

'You ran over your handbag. It's safe in my shop opposite J. Perkins Greengrocer'

Oh, J. Perkins, I love you! I forgive you your Coxs' Pippin's Apple's! Alice would say that handbag is a womb and a burden and that in running it over I am symbolically rejecting the traditional female role. Not sure if that's how J.Perkins will see it, though. Seem to recall he is rather handsome, and wonder

157

if, in rescuing my damaged womb-symbol, he is sent to make life fruitful again. My Green Man!

Perhaps in time I shall be able to caress his roguish apostrophes into a proper alignment.

24 March

J. Perkins, Greengrocer, who rescued my handbag when I ran it over, is not handsome. It is his assistant Dave Thanatos who broods, god-like, over the broccoli. J. Perkins is middle-aged and chirpy, and seems to believe he has been sent to organise my life. When we rush into his shop at 8.30 a.m. to furnish Harriet's lunchbox, he gives a hideous wink.

"Just look what I've got for you, dear!" he grins. It is an electronic keyring which, when you whistle, answers cheerily 'Widdly widdly widdly!' I am charmed. I shall never lose my car keys again. I thank J. Perkins fervently, and depart clutching today's other free gift: a pineapple which, when young, went five rounds with Mike Tyson.

We drive to Rusbridge Primary, whilst Harriet performs last-minute boot-cleaning operation with Mango Body Butter. Too buttery for my body but works a treat on her more supple and youthful boot leather.

"Ugh!" she wails, "My boots smell of fruit!" 'Widdly widdly widdly!' cries the keyring.

I switch on the *Today* programme. John Major is declaring that something or other will never happen: not today, not yesterday, not tomorrow, not nohow. 'Widdly widdly widdly!' cries the keyring. Cannot but agree.

"We're halfway to school now! Radio One!" screams Harriet in her trades union mode. (Outmoded, now, unfortunately.) At the sound of Chris Evans going widdly the keyring launches into a continuous aria.

"Oh shut up, you bastard!" cries Harriet hurling it backwards into the far depths of the Volvo's fundament.

Drop her at school and switch off radio. Silence, except for the pineapple's emissions which are becoming distinctly audible. Should go back to the flat and write, but cannot resist slinking off to Vile Cottage. Admire a new staircase which Torpid has just finished, then pore over paint recipe book. Find picture of a wall decorated with scumble, burnt umber and sand. Reminds me of the lurid but beauteous skies of J.M.W. Turner's *The Wreck Buoy*. Wonder how to share this thought with Torpid.

"Have you ever distressed plaster, Torpid?"

"Ngorongoro?"

We are still having slight failures of communication.

Torpid, who had been hovering in hope of PG Tips à la Tarmacadam, discovers I have forgotten to bring any fresh milk, and drives off in disgust. He promises however to get his friend Gravid to ring me. He knows about Rubbing off on Wood and Ageing.

Eat pineapple and admire the view. Pineapple tastes alcoholic, but that's fine by me. Alone with my house I open front door, sit on my new staircase and gaze out rapturously at the lambs gambolling. Wonder if my knee will ever get better. Who would have thought the old knee had so much ligaments in it? Mustn't curse it, though. Must heal myself through Caring. Stroke knee affectionately, which it enjoys. The ligaments of gratified desire.

At last, after several hours of dreaming and gazing, realise it is time to collect Harriet. Have wasted whole day. Thanks courteous knee. Rise from new staircase, to discover my arse is liberally coated with Herb and Resin Oil which Penetrates and Revives. Alarmed at the thought that my bottom is now highly inflammable. The slightest spark could result in conflagration. And this especially worrying since I begin to feel that the pineapple has gone critical and is hurtling downwards through my hapless guts like a demented depth charge.

Lurch to lav in alarm, at which sudden violent movement my knee ligaments are Torn Again. Whilst enthroned I realise a) we have run out of loo paper b) I have lost my car keys.

Forced to tear off convenient bit of old wallpaper with plaster still adhering. Arse is now lime-washed as well as a fire risk, and knee is going to need kneehole surgery. I'm not clinging to the wreckage – I am the wreckage. All I need now is a Wreck Buoy, although presumably nowadays the grandeur of J.M.W. Turner's version has been replaced by something that goes widdly widdly widdly. I should have listened to the pineapple.

1 April

Dream I am Tony Blair's friend and we are on the stump together. He seems to have annexed the place in my subconscious formerly occupied by HRH The Prince of Wales. This is probably because Charles is having such a bad heir day. Long time since I have dreamt about a Labour politician. This used to be a duty – now it has become a pleasure.

But we have no time to devote to such frivolities as democracy, the constitution or the crown. Nor can I give my mind to the genesis of the great book which, this time, has got to catapult me straight into the best-seller lists or the Booker prize. Enough of this total obscurity. By the time I'm fifty I've got to be fabulous. A millionaire by the millenium.

But for the time being, liquidity would make obscurity more bearable. How am I going to pay the decorator? He is called David and is preceded by an enormous paunch. We call him Gravid David. He is bolshie, racist and chauvinist. These are a few of my favourite things.

"What you want, love, is a nice spongeable vinyl, so you can, like, sponge the walls down easy."

But David – this is a study for God's sake. What sort of books does he think I write? Portnoy's Complaint? Pulp Fiction? Twenty Tremendous Soups? He wants to turn my study into a kitchen because that's where he thinks I should be.

Sod cookery, though. Bookery for me from now on. And for Harriet – eleven going on thirty – Hookery. Bravely I square up to David.

"No. I don't want a spongeable vinyl. It's a study. I want a nice flat matt brown."

"Brown?"

David looks puzzled. Attempt to explain the concept of brown.

But which brown, for my brown study? A sort of tawny, ochrey, Thirties teddy bear, nicotiney, Alan Bennetty brown? Or a deep mahogany, brooding, mysterious, shadowy . . . Gordon Brown! That's what I want!

"Nah, you don't want it dark. That'll make it look even smaller, see? You want a nice magnolia in a soft sheen type style, love. Get more light in, be able to admire yerself in the mirror, eh?" He leers. Well, of course, when not cooking or sponging down nice vinyl, women would be preening, wouldn't they. Stupid bastard. Tempted to knee him in the groin but alas, ligaments still a bit stiff. Also David's groin not visible beneath paunch. Inform him instead that I will supply brown paint and he must bear with me as it's one of my silly little feminine foibles and I'll probably change my mind within a week, fluffy little scatterbrain that I am.

David departs, leaving me to kick off my mules, perch on a pouffe and do my nails. Study colour charts for what I hope will be the last time for a decade. Drawn by darkness. Lux sucks. Locate Gordon Brown eventually on woodstain chart, between old American Mahogany and Dark Jacobean Oak.

Cannot forget what Gordon Brown said on *Desert Island Discs* recently: that he had expected to get married, but it just hadn't happened. O divine negligence! Would I had been blest with it myself. But he also said that 'though it hadn't happened yet, it still might'. Well, Spouse has requested a divorce. And since I've already been married to one Scots Gordon I have got the relevant work experience.

Come, Gordon, come: emerge from your penumbra
Stick that rose between your teeth and honey, hey!
Let's rumba!

On the other hand, with marriage going the way it is, perhaps Mr Brown is to be congratulated, nay venerated for his judicious omission.

Brain still busy with the idea of Treasury and lechery long after it should have been snoring in its basket. Let's get fiscal etc. Eventually fall into uneasy sleep at 3 a.m., hoping to dream of Jimmy White. At least it would rationalise my decor.

6 April

Spouse returns to Rusbridge to help with the move. Moving can be made even worse by the observation of a few simple rules. Move from the town to the country just at the moment when your children become teenagers. Move from a first floor flat when the lift's broken. Have half your things in store, and far too much stuff for the tiny cottage you're moving into. Above all have your ex-husband present to hurt himself, damage things, and claim the only desirable objects as his own, even though he would never even have remembered their existence otherwise.

"I think the Beethoven's *Quartets* are mine, aren't they?"

"No they're sodding not!" I snarl. "They're Beethoven's!"

"Mummy, don't swear at Daddy! He's only trying to help!"

"Sorry, yes, now I come to think of it, they are yours."

And now I come to think of it, they're scratched.

Harriet traps me in the kitchen where I am sellotaping up the top of the porridge box.

"Mummy!" she whispers, "I think Daddy is still in love with you! Let's have him back! You do still love him, don't you?"

Sellotape somehow gets wound round my fingers. Tear it off, together with favourite bits of epidermis, and hurl onto floor. Abandon attempt to seal porridge box and cram it into carton marked Food. Henry has gone into customs-officer mode and is labelling everything in silver felt tip.

"Harriet, be realistic. It's lovely of Daddy to come back and help us, yes. But Elaine and Alexander are waiting for him back in Ealing. Daddy has two families now. And they need him more than we do."

"They don't! Elaine is rich and we're poor. And she's young and you've got a bad knee and the menopause."

The phone rings.

"Hello, Dulcie, this is Penelope. How's the book going?"

"Er, fine. Terrific." Must start it soon. "Got about fifty thousand words in. Just moving house today, little hitch, nothing to worry about, I'll have a draft to you by the end of May, no trouble."

"Ah, well, that's what I wanted to talk to you about. The thing is — I'm leaving the company at the end of April."

"What! No! Oh God! This is awful! etc."

"I'm so sorry. I'm going to miss you all terribly. But I've decided I want to travel."

"To travel?"

"Yes. Get rid of my possessions and live out of rucksack for a year or two. I'm going to India. Might get a job or something. Get to know the people."

Fight off desperate urge to go with her. Offer congratulations and regrets.

"A chap called Oliver is taking all my clients over. I know you'll love him. He'll be giving you a ring."

Part, telephonically, from my beloved agent, with much lamentation. After we hang up, though, I realise it gets me off the hook of my invisible fifty thousand words – the emperor's new prose.

Spouse picks up magazine advocating Shaker style: gingham and pegs. Nostalgia for schooldays, perhaps.

"This Shaker thing is bizarre," he says. "We went to dinner with one of Elaine's posh friends in Primrose Hill and they had a Shaker kitchen, and she wants one, now – even though we've got a perfectly good kitchen already. The Haute Bourgeoisie all want to be Nouveau Pauvre. The Shakers must be turning in their graves."

"Or Shaking."

A cheap Transit van arrives and cheap Transit type removal men burst out of it like a pack of fat voles out of a hole. Their removal technique is of the hurly-burly school. At the height of the excitement, phone rings.

"Oh, hello, is that Dulcie? My name's Oliver Sackville. I'm taking over from Penny. I hear you're moving into a cottage and I'm sure you won't have time to come up to town but maybe I could come to you? Penny tells me you're more than halfway through your next book. Terrific!"

Much later in the day, as I am offering a high new shelf to the porridge packet, it leaps off and empties itself onto my head. Not sure whether effect is of bad dandruff, Shaker-style confetti or just good old dust and ashes.

13 April

"Mummy . . . ? Why does Easter keep moving about?"

Er . . . why does Easter keep moving about? It's one of those things I keep meaning to understand. Perhaps to do with Lent. Or Epiphany. Or th'inconstant moon. "Why can't it just always be on the tenth of April or something?" Harriet doesn't like inconstancy. Her father's moved to Ealing. Her brother's moved to Ealing half the time. She and I have moved to Vile Cottage, leaving the flat in town which she adored. "Why can't we go back to our old house in Cranford Gardens! Waaaaagh!"

Dry tears and offer treat, at which my daughter's greedy little eyes light up.

"What? A video?"

"No, don't be silly, darling, videos are for weekends. If then. Besides, it's seven miles to the video shop."

"I hate this cottage! It's miles to anywhere!"

"Why don't we ring up and ask if Poppy can come to play?"

"Oooh can we can we Mummy? Oh thank you!"

Ring and issue invitation, received with rapture. However Poppy's mother regrets her car is in for its MOT. This means a round trip of eighteen miles, since Poppy lives on the other side of Rusbridge.

"Mummy . . . ? We'll be passing the video shop on the way back—"

"NO! You've got a friend coming for God's sake! You don't need a video! Besides, we've already got masses of videos! I never had videos when I was your age! I never even had a telly till I was fifteen!"

Drive to Rusbridge with clenched teeth. Tendency of country lanes to reel and roll beginning to irritate me. A nice straight motorway would be the thing. Get to Rusbridge in five minutes. Also, although the situation of Vile Cottage is of beauteous seclusion, one would quite like a Waitrose just out of sight below the wood. Presumably one can confidently expect such improvements as various Euro-policies transform the whole of southern England into a tasteful patchwork of malls and bypasses.

There could always be a little nature reserve somewhere with an acre or two of woodland for the tree people.

Succumb in the end to the lure of the video, but not for them -- for me. Need cheering up, and must think of convincing scenario for new book. Watch three episodes of *Absolutely Fabulous* and emerge wishing I had written it, but also suffering from dyspepsia. Notice that Harriet and Poppy are re-enacting scenes from Ab Fab with their Sindies, including alcoholism and frequent references to buggery and bollocks. Suspect Harriet will not be asked back to play with Poppy.

Lurch to 'study' – a cupboard painted brown. Sit at desk, sharpen pencils, align paper with edge of desk. Must conjure up convincing details of work in progress, as new agent Oliver descends on me next Tuesday. Rifle through history in search of picturesque location for my next oeuvre. Regency done to death, although whether mankind will ever tire of cleavages debatable.

Recall that Minoan priestesses wore gowns revealing their breasts, and wrestled with snakes. Perhaps C of E could consider this for all parishes with women priests. Could rename churches Mass Parlours. Well, nobody's queueing up to watch Easter being moved about.

"O woe!" cried the High Priestess Shutuppet, as the multitude assembled in the opalescent edifice beside the glistening Nile, "I have over-whirled my best serpent and it hath snapped! The service begins in five minutes and I haven't even got time to gild my tits!"

"Chill out, babe," drawled Cerebos, the dog-headed god, sucking a lapis lazuli ice lolly on his crocodile-skin couch. "Why don'tcha wear a T-shirt for once and give 'em a real thrill."

"I've got a confession to make, Oliver," I smile artfully, three days later in The Fleece at Udderbury. "I decided what I'd written was complete crap so I burned it."

Oliver goes pale, which only adds to his beauty. He is a cross between Hugh Grant and Apollo. But the awful thing is – I just don't care. The only thing that could get me going now would be a dog-headed god. Or possibly a dog-headed dog.

20 April

"Mum . . . ? I hope you don't mind my saying this, but when you're not actually smiling, you look like the Grim Reaper."

Of course I am pleased that she has heard of the Grim Reaper. It shows some rudimentary familiarity with the tradition of Judaeo-Christian iconography. But I can't help feeling just a tiny little tremor of disappointment that I have started to resemble the old boy before I'm even properly out of my forties.

Oh well. Decide to do the only sensible thing: leap astride my skeletal horse and gallop off hollowly to the Body Shop. A day in Bath should raise the spirits. This is a place which has always welcomed the old, sick and ugly. After ten minutes' sauntering among the beguiling window displays I remember that it was the old, sick, ugly and rich Bath was interested in.

At the moment I am not only grim but skint. Oliver Sackville, my elegant new young agent, was sympathetic to my confession that, vis à vis writing, I have Bonker's Block. He suggested instead a variant on Home Alone.

"Look, Dulcie, you've, y'know, got your finger on the pulse of the culture with this return to single living thing. Not to mention this cottage in the country thing. Nobody buys fashion and passion magazines any more. Everybody's into stencilling their lintels."

I had noticed an increasingly desperate tendency amongst the fash'n'pashion mags: 'My husband has sex with a cauliflower.' etc.

"So, er . . ." this was Oliver at his most dynamic, "maybe you could, just, well, kind of live it for all of us, erm, y'know?"

"Sorry?"

"The Country Diary of an Edwardian . . . Divorcee?"

Am pondering the possibilities when Harriet pounces on Hawthorn Hand Cream.

"Here you are, Mum -- this is for mature skin. And I'll have this and this and this and this."

"Stop! Don't go mad! Remember we've only got ten quid!"

"But I'm right out of mascara!"

And this at eleven years of age. I steer her into a tea shop, where I covertly apply Hawthorn Hand Cream under the covers to make my hands look slightly less ghoulish and crepuscular. Order tea and teacake, trusting there is no bovine by-product therein. Suddenly endure qualm about the hand cream but dismiss it as hysteria. Take comfort in the wise words of our government: we are acting upon the advice of our scientists and anyway, there's a risk attached to everything. Especially voting Conservative.

If I was the Grim Reaper I know who I'd reap first. However, first further shopping must be avoided. Inform Harriet sternly we are to admire exquisite Georgian theatre, Costume Museum, and stunning architectural vistas.

"Sod that!" she cries. "I want to go to the Disney shop!" Deposit her at Disney and rush off to buy stencils for lintel.

Return to Vile Cottage spent and exhausted by our refreshing day in Bath. Am forced to stop off in Sodbury on the way home to buy Solpadeine from local chemists. "Solpadeine!" cries the girl to the Great Dispenser who lurks, veiled in mystery in his inner sanctum. Why do they do that? Might he one day cry "No! That woman is not to have it! She's so near the edge she might be reaped by nightfall!"

Brace ourselves for another night of darkness and strange noises. Harriet has not yet dared to spend a whole night in her own little room, and frankly I'm quite relieved, as I'm not sure I could quite manage a whole night alone in mine. Her snoring blots out the sounds of animals killing each other, out in the night.

Awoken at 3 a.m. by stealthy noise *in the room*. Rustle. Peer stealthily out from under duvet. Locate rustling in Body Shop carrier bag three feet from bed. Freeze in horror. Mouse leaps out and hurtles off into the blackness beneath the wardrobe. I expect it was looking for cheese and chocolate fur conditioner.

Drift back off to sleep wondering whether I should get a trap or a cat. Trouble is, I'm so tender-hearted, I couldn't reap a fly.

27 April

Have been encouraged by agent to write a country diary but keep being distracted by nature. Stare out of the window upon scene of beauteous burgeoning brambles. A pair of flirty birds go flickering through the trees. Find bird book, locate and identify. At last I have something to say to Aunt Elspeth. Seize phone.

"Aunt Elspeth! I've got a pair of long-tailed tits!"

"Och, guid, dear. But how are you coping with The Change, in general?"

Hang up in state of apprehensive transition.

Rush to mirror. Moustache clearly visible in late spring light. Always a mistake to hang mirror on wall sideways on to window. Seize Lancome *Primordiale Soin Rajeunissant Visible* and apply generously. It was a barbed Christmas present from Elaine. Do not observe much visible *rajeunissement* but still, it's early days.

The Change. So who am I changing into? Grey hair, moustache . . . Albert Schweitzer perhaps? Halo appears behind my head. Perhaps I shall be required to become a saint. Not many about these days. Except Nelson Mandela. Poor old bugger. A lifetime in prison, then he comes out, and everybody in the world wants to give him a cuddle, except . . . Ain't that just like life.

Realise halo is migraine aura. Panic. Have never had migraine whilst living in the country and suspect it will cause administrative complications.

Boy, does it. Taxi necessary to take Harriet to school next day, pick up Mrs Body and bring her back here for some high decibel housework. Then taxi summoned again to take Mrs Body back, pick up Harriet and bring her back here. Urgent need to develop relationship with taxi driver but not tonight, dear, I've got a headache.

Lie in bed tormented by my inability to remember the name of the man who shot Kennedy.

Mrs Body had left Harriet a nice little lasagne in the oven but I'm so convinced my tall, capable daughter will burn herself taking it out that I lurch downstairs, eyes firmly closed against the horrid glare of daylight, throw open oven, seize plate and burn myself instead.

Rush outdoors and vomit over brambles. Must do something about the garden one day. Country matters have me by the throat.

4 May

Some swallows have set up home under my deep eaves.
"Look, Harriet! The swallows are nesting!"
"Just a minute . . ."
Harriet's generation has no eyes for the swallow. She is busy trying to minimise her skirt by rolling it over at the top. Feel irritated. Recall also feeling irritated aeons ago when I did the same and my mother was irritated.

Henry condescends to mow the tiny lawn. Man and machine in perfect harmony. I run out and admire his work, strength, etc. trying not to notice that he has mowed the budding cranesbills as well. The sun shines. In the field nearby lambs are gambolling.
"Look! Darling! The lambs!"
"Is it supposed to do that?" frowns Henry at the buccaneering creature. He would feel more at ease with a lottery ticket. *Non* gambolling, *sed* gambling. My children are pig-ignorant of country matters. Elaine doesn't help, the cow. Always taking them off shopping in the West End.

Restlessly peruse pamphlets picked up in Info. Centre and come across 'Lackham Country Attractions: a Great Day Out for Everyone'. Agricultural Museum, rural crafts, dairying and cheesemaking . . . lovely old pigs lying hock-deep in muck . . . That'll do nicely.
"Come on!" I cry. "We're going to Lackham Country Park!"
"A Theme Park!" cries Harriet. "Hurrah!"
Uneasily aware that children think they are heading towards big dippers, ferris wheels and hurtling death rides. Perhaps one day this is what agricultural history will have come to. Giant carnival heads of Turnip Townsend and Mad Cow walking about in Day-Glo smocks and crying Hoe Hoe Hoe! Experience the 19th century thrashing machine as if you were an ear of

corn! Give birth under a hawthorn hedge! Marvel as thousands die of famine after the deadly attack of Captain Blight!

But first we must penetrate Chippenham, for my fledglings are screaming at me with open craws.

"Starving! Must have chips! Chips! Chips!"

We enter Chippenham. It must have been a fine old town once. Now it has undergone bypass surgery. Locate car park. Step out into puddle. Feel twinge of foreboding. Pedestrian route to town centre leads along edge of road down which cars zoom. Chip shop appears immediately. Perhaps Chippenham is all right after all. Guzzle guzzle. Burp.

Out into the rain. Have sudden rogue impulse to buy Harriet a pair of plimsolls.

"Don't want stupid plimsolls! Trainers oh please Mum trainers!"

"Not until your feet have stopped growing."

"Henry's got trainers and he's still growing!"

"Elaine bought him those. Plimsolls are a tenth of the price!" (because Made In India . . . possibly by children? Horrid qualm.)

Kindly woman in shoe shop measures Harriet's feet and as usual expresses incredulity that they could be so narrow. She inherits them from me. It is annoying that the only reliably slim part of my body is the bit nobody ever sees. I blame Chippenham.

Harriet resigns herself to being bought beautiful white classical plimsolls as worn in days of British Raj. On the way back to the car we have a tantrum. They demand Woolworths. I am intent on Tamworths. Aware that Country Attractions last admissions at 4 p.m. Must see hog in mud before sun sets.

Leave car park and creep through town centre desperately seeking Last Exit from Chippenham. No signs. Follow instinct and end up in hideous cul-de-sac offering two superstores, Holistic Health Centre and gridlocked traffic jam. "Therapy and stress management," reads Harriet. For people trying to escape from Chippenham, presumably.

After ten minutes I do the decent thing and settle down holistically to enjoy the quality of the traffic jam. By the time we get to Lackham Country Attractions it is closed and I am bursting for a pee. Loudly and embarrassingly (no doubt) persuade man to let me in for one.

"Where are the rides?" grumbles Henry.

"Never mind rides!" I cry. "Look at those lovely old barns!
We'll come another day!"

"Drive home fast!" demands Harriet, back in the car. "There's
a Keanu Reeves film on at six!"

Notice a songthrush as we drive home, but decide not to
mention it.

11 May

The knee is deemed worth a visit to the Orthopaedic Department at Frenchay Hospital. I thought I knew the way but a new
road has been hacked across country and us old peasants what
navigate by our country seats, by the feeling in our waters, us
be confused thereby and us goes a-hurtlin' off down suburbs
entirely unvisited before. Lost! Agh! Am going to be late.

Arrive at Frenchay from direction never before attempted
and fail to recognise it. Execute seventeen-point turn in cul-
de-sac. Arrive at hospital and seek parking place. Something
friendly about post-war prefab appearance of buildings. Realise
they remind me of my fifties primary school. Park'n'run
towards Orthopaedic Department, thus demonstrating that knee
is hardly buggered at all and this appointment is a waste of NHS
time, a concession to middle-aged hypochondria.

Orthopaedic Department full of people on crutches, in
plaster, etc. Apologise to clerk because I am five mins late,
then see sign warning that patients are being seen within two
hours of their appointment. Don't know whether to be grateful
or outraged. Limp ostentatiously to dark corner and launch
myself into serious *Hello!*-reading orgy. I am seated next to
the plaster room, into which the hobbling are summoned in
turn. There is the sound of an electric saw, and they hobble
out again a few minutes later without plaster. Like some kind
of antechamber to the afterlife. Cast off your earthly shards
and be free.

In order to feel less guilty about wasting NHS time when I
am surrounded by the so obviously really injured, I retrieve
notebook from handbag and scribble next bit of bonkbuster.

"Mrs Domum?" A jolly nurse invites me into the sanctum.

171

Everybody seems jolly in the Orthopaedic Department. Perhaps because they're not struggling with nasty internal illness, but are just folks to whom accidents have happened.

I am seen by beautiful doctor aged approximately eighteen. If I were a consultant and he was a nurse I could ask him for a date. Prepare to apologise for wasting NHS time.

"The thing is," he sighs, bravely wrestling with my cellulite, "these ligaments are worse than broken bones, really. They never get properly better . . . etc. . . . Perhaps some physiotherapy at Rusbridge Hospital . . . etc."

Realise with horror knee will be with me forever, like the poor. But even though I'm not wasting NHS time after all, I am really, because there's nothing they can do.

"I just want to discuss your case with Mr Blahbury," he says, and whisks off for a few words with the consultant. I overhear only tantalising syllables.

"There's this woman . . . fifty years old . . ."

Wait a minute, sonny! Not fifty years old! Not quite yet for God's sake! Forty-nine and a bleeding half, if you don't mind!

I don't actually shout it out loud, though. I'm saving up shouting in public for when I'm over fifty and beyond repair.

18 May

Julian Rainge-Roughver is coming over to spend the day with Henry. "I think I fancy Julian, Mum!" whispers Harriet in an ecstasy of panic. "Shall I put on the kiwi lip gloss or the strawberry?" Wonder how long till smoky bacon.

Greeted at The Laurels by Julian's Dad who admires my old Volvo and informs me that his has done 160,000. Annoyed to be thus trumped by a measly 10,000 miles, whilst aware that this is just another game men play.

"Can I bring *Robotcop*?" asks Julian, exhibiting video. "It's an eighteen and over."

Look enquiringly at Julian's Dad, who shrugs and says it's up to me, his cousin gave him it. Embarrassed. Agree uneasily, though would prefer *Robotcop* on someone else's

TV, or preferably planet. Who Killed Cock Robin too violent for me.

Lydia greets me in frantic style from upper window and demands I return her book, lent two years previously. Apologise in horror and assure her I will bring it back with Julian at 8 p.m. Drive home in frenzy attempting to recall title and appearance of Lydia's book. Remember only that it was out of print and of great sentimental value.

Arrive at cottage and shoo children out to experience nature. Sheep in field. Lambo not Rambo. Ransack bookshelves in search of I know not what. Close eyes and demand that mind comes up with name of Lydia's book. Mind prefers to admire the way John Major says 'wunt' and advises me that if this practice were to become more widespread, we could rejoice in Bungers and Mush.

Harriet runs in looking outraged. "Mummy! The boys are throwing stones at the sheep!"

Run out and deliver lecture on male violence and the sanctity of life, especially the woolly. Wait! – Stones . . . Ah! The Stones of Trewhatsit. Cornish saga by posh woman. Ransack other piles of books: under bed, all down side of stairs, in pantry, etc. Wonder if Spouse has taken The Stones of Trewhatsit to Ealing and if so, whether he has thrown it out already. Also wonder if he has got custody of the Rolling Stones records and if so, why the hell.

Children come in to watch *Robotcop*. Peep timidly at screen for a moment. Observe man being pulverised.

"That's the only violent bit!" cries Julian placatingly. "And it's a really good story!"

Leave the room and start to look for Rolling Stones records, then realise I should be looking for Lydia's book. Or even, ha ha, perish the thought, working.

Haunted by thought that I ought to forbid children to watch *Robotocop*. Shouldn't they be exchanging lavatorial jokes at their age? Plop Fiction . . . I don't wunt Rubutcup. Sounds like fetishistic brassiere. Why are all bras too tight, too loose or itchy round the back? Run upstairs and rip mine off. Burning a fire risk so throw it unnecessarily roughly in the waste paper basket. Only twenty years late.

Film ends. Set large tea before children, but their appetites strangely muted. Offer to play Consequences and Charades in futile attempt to antidote malevolent influence of celluloid culture. Boys sneer and withdraw to attic, Harriet hugs me and says she will play Consequences and Charades with me and I was right, the film was crap, boys are sub-human and she would not marry Julian if he was the last one left on the planet.

Drive Julian home. Lydia greets me with guilty look and hopes *Robotcop* wasn't too awful. Realise she is as guilty about that as I am about The Stones of Trewhatsit. Declare piously that *Robotocop* was vile, but I'm not in favour of censorship. Whilst she is cringing, slip in quick admission that I lent The Stones of Trewhatsit to Elaine. Lydia sighs. Assure her it will be back in her hands immediately, i.e. as soon as I've had time to ransack Hay-on-Wye. For the rest of the evening Harriet and Henry follow me in post-*Robotocop* angst from room to room, which would be irritating even in large echoing Edwardian spaces we used to enjoy at 196 Cranford Gardens. In confinement of cottage the family that stays together can sustain serious injury.

25 May

Harriet is obsessed by our bodily inadequacies. Her sap is rising, mine is sinking.

"I hate my nose!" she howls. "It's like a flaky lump of dough covered with zits!"

"A bit like an Eccles cake, then?" I enquire from my bath. She gazes at my half-submerged torso with frank dismay.

"Mummy! Your tummy's a cottage loaf and your neck is like a dead chicken!"

"Perhaps it would be kindest to drown me immediately."

"I don't know . . . what's liposuction?"

The pernicious influence of *Absolutely Fabulous* again.

"I think the surgeon makes a sort of slit and sucks the fat out with a vacuum cleaner."

"Ugh! Shut up Mum you're GROSS!"

She runs out and slams the door. Three quaint flakes of plaster float gracefully down into the bath. Perhaps I could improvise a sort of face-pack therefrom.

As for Henry, I despair. Harriet is rude, raunchy, aggressive and bolshy – a sort of loutess – whereas he becomes more and more secretive and demure. He tidies his room fanatically. He saves his money. I suspect he may prove to be a junior Rotarian or Mason. A Roti or Masonette. Despite exhaustive searches I can find no trace of dirty magazines. And he never listens to the Rolling Stones cassette I gave him for Christmas.

Haven't the Stones aged well? They look like toads that have had liposuction.

Still, at least when we're in private he still calls me Mummy. There's a paint in the Fired Earth V & A traditional range called Mummy. It's a sort of tired old pink. Quite appropriate really. Gaze up at the ceiling and wish I hadn't run out of money and energy before fixing the tired old bathroom ceiling. It really needs a facelift or a tummy tuck or something.

Get out of bath and contemplate myself naked in the cruel light of midsummer. It's a shame there isn't a use for cellulite. The Government should get a working party together and come up with some ideas. Maybe it could replace the mad bovine tallow in cosmetics. We could make lipstick out of it. Lipostick. What would cellulite actually look like? Rattle belly speculatively. One thinks of wallpaper paste somehow. Wallpaper the bathroom ceiling with your own cellulite.

But cosmetics and interior decoration are a bit frivolous really – I've got it! Insulation! Free to all OAPs with cavity walls. Send the lipo-tanker round . . . in fact, that's what we can use for fuel when the oil runs out. The car that runs on cellulite. The Fat Uno. Feel I am at the cutting edge of bio-recycling theory, and expect the phone call inviting me to join Professor Porritt's think-tank any minute.

1 June

Half-term. The children whizz off to London dying to see their Dad, and let's face it, their beautiful young obliging stepmother who cooks like an angel. Although what evidence do we have that angels cook at all, let alone like angels? 'And lo! An angel appeared unto them, and he said, "Just a sizzle of garlic, a squeeze of lemon juice, and a handful of chopped coriander, and bingo!"'

At this time of year one does see the wok of the Almighty everywhere. I stand enraptured and gaze over valley. I cannot understand why Henry and Harriet would rather watch *Neighbours*. At their age I was already writing tedious poems describing sunsets. But then, I was going to be a writer whereas it's clear that Henry is going to be a mercenary and Harriet is going to be mercenary. She despises my penury. I should be scribbling away at my Bimbuster instead of lying in bed gazing up at the beams and wondering about angels.

Leap decisively up, make cup of coffee in mug still dirty from yesterday, pull on hideous old tracksuit and fail to clean teeth. Ah, the solitary joys of sluthood! Thank goodness I haven't got a man coming round. I can revert to my true nature. In some previous existence I'm sure I was a vile old bachelor.

Suddenly notice that the desk is covered with what looks like mouse droppings, and notes are smudged with tears. Curious. Much against tender feelings, set trap. Wish had cat. But the trouble with cats is they kill swallows, such a crime one can only hope that the swallows come back as dogs.

Halfway through lunch (mushy peas out of tin, on toast) a knock on the door. Freeze in horror. Person from Porlock? Shattering my concentration just as I have launched into heavenly lunch? Solitary nutter with shotgun and grudge against middle-aged women in tracksuits? Run upstairs and look out through bedroom window upon balding head of man in anorak carrying map.

"Hello," he says in posh voice. "I'm terribly sorry to disturb you, but I'm afraid I'm lost." Enquire where he's heading for.

"I'm looking for Tom Tit's Bottom," he confesses.

Hello . . . think I'll stay up here somehow. Could be the equivalent of one of those funny phone calls. Inform him there is a farm beyond the wood and they're bound to know. He departs. Wonder if he could have been the love of my middle age, and if so, good riddance. You know who's going to be the love of my middle age? Moi.

Eventually it gets dark. Barricade doors and windows but leave bedroom window open for air. After five minutes bat flutters in, circles round bed, then flies off into study and does not return. Intrigued. Get up and creep after it in the dark. Observe it hanging from a beam above my desk, peeing and pooing merrily on my latest chapter. Obviously former literary critic. Proof of reincarnation! Hurrah!

8 June

Tongue informs me that a hole has appeared in a back tooth where previously there was a flawless wall of mercury or whatever they make amalgam out of. Alice rings and orders me to tell the dentist to remove all my amalgam fillings whilst he's about it, and replace them with something more neurologically friendly.

Distract her by enquiring if she is going off to anywhere exotic and she replies only bleeding Tuscany I'm broke. Wonder anew what it must be like to be the feminist heiress of an arms manufacturer. At least, I suspect he was an arms manufacturer. She always says he was an engineer but you would, wouldn't you?

Express sympathy that she is to endure Only Siena. Although suspect the concepts of Only and Siena are irreconcilable. Were the whole world to turn to coal, if Siena was spared I would think there was some justice in heaven. At this point Alice snaps, "Oh, spare me the martyred act, Dulcie!" and rings off with a slam. Fear I shall not receive postcard of the Palio this year. Dear old Palio, Jolly old Palio. Wish I was there, although not with Alice.

Harry Harriet to the dentist. In the waiting room she reads *TV Hits* and I read *World of Interiors*. Alarmed to discover that design-wise, we have reached the Age of Steel, although alas a little too late for David. Boggle at glamorous photos of chests of drawers, chairs, even a *lit bateau* made of steel, complete with tinfoil bedclothes. Fear this might make one feel even more of a turkey than usual. Although I've always wanted a *lit bateau*. Suspect it might lead to diverting wet dreams.

Harriet has No Cavities despite a diet of unrelieved Pop-Tarts and Coca Cola. This apparently is the Triumph of Fluoride. Mention Alice's views on amalgam and wonder

177

if it might be feasible to replace fillings with something more benign, such as eighteenth-century French cherrywood or quattrocento Sienese sun-burned brick. Dentist, normally a quiet and gentle soul, suggests Alice, and all other mischievous slanderers of amalgam, should be hung, drawn and quartered.

Harriet glares. I am being even more embarrassing than usual. Head full of metal and have irritated dentist – saintly chap who never hurts. Dentistry an intriguing skill. Polly Pocket version of engineering.

"You had chewing gum on the bottom of your shoe!" hisses Harriet afterwards in mortification. "I don't want to go back to school! I feel ill! Let's get a Brad Pitt video and go home!"

Ignore this plea as I am looking forward to an hour of exquisite solitude at the cottage before I have to rush back and pick her up again. Sunlight, Lapsang Souchong, perhaps even larks . . .

Volvo – appropriate use of steel – carries me ponderously along twisting lanes until I regain the face of my beloved, i.e. shy peeping cottage. Promise never to insert metal furniture into it no matter how chic. Sunlight and Lapsang Souchong mysteriously unavailable but enjoy PG Tips and rain with no less rapture. A sacred moment because spared the company of males and children.

Phone rings. It is Spouse wanting to grumble about life with vibrant young Elaine.

"She always wants to do things!" he whinges. "And she's never heard of Eccles and Bluebottle!"

Spouse evidently suffering from POW syndrome. Prince of Wales, Prisoner of War, what's the difference? Ring off without bothering to conceal my indifference and triumph.

Have hardly had time to regain my smug mug of Tips when phone rings again.

"Hi, Dulcie, this is Tom!" Heart gives tame little fillip. More in memory of past lurches than anything serious in its own right. "Long time no see. I hear you've got a fantastic cottage with an acre of wild garden? Listen – I've decided to live in a teepee this summer and I was wondering if you could get your head round the idea of having it at the bottom of your garden?"

Wonder what has happened to Sabrina, but fear she must have gone the way of all river goddesses. Also wonder – rather more urgently – if steel knickers are available, preferably fitted with mortise lock.

15 June

"Mummy? Why is Tom coming to live in our garden in a tent?"

"Because he's not getting on very well with his wife."

"Why can't I live in a tent then?"

"I've said no twenty times! – oh, all right, you can camp out once or twice at weekends—"

"Can I? Oh BRILLIANT Mum! Starting now?"

"No! Go away! I must SLEEP!"

Insomnia, perhaps caused by the light evenings and piercing mornings, the blasted dawn chorus, the anxiety about my divorce, the possibility of intruders, the certainty of bankruptcy, the new epidemics sweeping through the land . . . I catnap, now, at four o'clock, as soon as I get back from the school run.

4.20 p.m., roused from delicious dream about Courtney Walsh by phone call from Alice.

"Dulcie? Look, I'm ringing from Siena, so I'll be brief. I just wanted to apologise. I was a bit short with you when I rang last week, and we're sitting here on this lovely terrace – been putting back the Orvieto Secco for hours . . . what was I saying?"

"Apologising."

"Ah yes! Well, listen, forgive me. I'm not having a very easy menopause. I've got very low zinc. But enough of me. How are you? And the lovely female solitude in the dear little cottage?"

Unwisely confide the dire news that Tom and his teepee are daily expected.

"What? You fool, Dulcie! The first little shower and he'll have his legs under your table! I despair of you sometimes! – You're not sleeping with him again, are you?"

"Certainly not!"

"I should bloody well hope not. Well, don't offer him any home comforts. Let the bastard crap in a trench."

She rings off. No doubt the modulation from apology to

179

indignation and contempt was particularly gratifying. Return to bed hoping to find Courtney Walsh still waiting for me at the beach bar, but instead have horrible dream in which I accidentally kill a hedgehog.

"Mummy! Wake up, you've been asleep for hours! Tom's here and his friend Dog. He's weird!"

Drag myself out of bed. Cannot help feeling the perpendicular has been overrated. Wretched Goths obsessed with the vertical. If I'd been a twelfth-century architect I'd have laid out Salisbury Cathedral as a sprawling ranch-style bungalow.

Tom's and Dog's legs already under the table.

"We're making you a cup of tea," grins Tom. "Hey! You're looking great! I like your new hairstyle!"

"This is not a hairstyle," I inform him. "This is post-traumatic follicle disorder."

Cannot help noticing Tom looks handsomer than ever. I don't suppose he's even thirty-five yet. Dog, however, is showing signs of wear. His dreadlocks are now about a yard long. Indeed one of them is creeping towards the butter dish with every appearance of appetite.

"Hey, Dulcie, this wilderness of yours is cool," he growls, rolling his first Old Holborn. "It's a real nature reserve. Wouldn't be surprised if it got designated an SSI."

It emerges during the conversation that Dog is also planning an erection in my purlieus. He too has a teepee, and they are both terribly grateful for my enlightened hospitality.

"Mummy!" whispers Harriet, "are they gay?"

"No, darling. Be quiet and do some drawings." Harriet embarks on series of pictures of naked men.

"We'll dig a latrine and everything," Tom assures me. "We don't want to intrude. Although a bath now and then would be nice – we'd pay, of course. And incoming calls only." My fierce resentment at the thought of their intrusion into my bathroom is mitigated by an urgent desire to bath them both immediately.

"Mummy!" whispers Harriet, "what do gay men actually do with their willies?"

"Hang daisy-chains on them, darling."

"Sometime this summer," Dog informs me darkly, "the Third Great Antichrist is going to appear."

Just as long as he poos in the trench with the others.

The male members of our company go out to look for a flat piece of land whilst I survey the ruins of my quiet.

"Mum! Can I have Radio One?"

Gaze morosely at diary. Terrifying appointment looms next week: to escort Harriet's class round local church. Part of local history project. After that, dealing with the Antichrist should be a picnic.

22 June

Local History project at Harriet's school. They are to interview the oldest person they know. Then, on Thursday, I am to escort her class round St Hilary's Church. Must therefore bone up on St Hilary's. At present I am not even sure which sex, if any, St Hilary espoused.

"Mummy! Can I interview Great Aunt Elspeth?"

"No! We can't afford the phone bill!"

"I'll pay with my pocket money oh per-lease! I've got to interview someone old and you're not old enough!"

Strangely grateful for this thought, and give in as usual. Ought to phone Ex-Great-Aunt-in-Law anyway to assure her of my continuing esteem.

"Och, Dulcie, I've been thinking of you so much, dearr. Your wee cottage sounds terribly rrremote. I rreally can't forrgive Gorrrrrrdon for abandoning you like this!"

Although she cannot forgive him, I happen to know that she has wasted no time in winging her way down to Ealing to be taken to West End Shows and to admire young Alexander. Assure her I am perfectly happy living on my own in deepest rural seclusion. Do not mention the Temazepam and newly-installed bolts as thick as chipolatas on all doors.

"I'd feel much happierr, dearr, if you had a man about the place. I don't suppose you've got a New Friend yet . . . ?"

Impertinent old cow. What the hell does she mean by that? Does she think nobody will ever fancy me again?

"As a matter of fact, Auntie, I've got two strapping young men living in teepees in my garden."

Aunt flummoxed. She probably confuses teepees and tapas.

"Not . . . those New Age Travellers, is it, dearr? I'd be careful if I were you. If worrd gets about you could find yourself inundated."

Assure aunt this is unlikely in tone of voice suggesting she is an imbecile, although the same fear hovers in my own imagination.

"Mummy!" Harriet whispers. "Let me talk to her!"

Warn Aunt she is about to be interviewed, and hand her over with relief.

Whilst Harriet is failing to think of any questions, I pick up my favourite Pevsner, wander out onto the front doorstep, and look up St Hilary's. "Inside the porch a lively lierne-star vault with figured bosses . . ." AAAAh! That's better. Why do I always feel I've come home at last reading Pevsner, when I don't understand a single word? The same with cricket.

Lozenge, abaci, queenposts, piscina,
Silly mid-off and right-arm seamer,
Off-break, leg-break, flipper, and bosie,
Strapwork and stoup, Early Perp., Dec., and ogee,
Cusped and sub-cusped, out of the wood,
Collapse of middle order: something understood.

Find reference to plate, particularly Paten 'with lamb in a lobed depression'. Wonder if I am too.

Then recall Harriet's teacher of two years ago, Chris Lamb, and hope he will accompany us on our pilgrimage. Quite fancied him, indeed still do, though he is certainly not a candidate for the post of New Friend.

Harriet appears at my side. Sigh, and wonder how many years it will be before we can share an intoxicating bewilderment at Pevsner.

"Mummy – what's an orgasm?"

Startled at the possibility that aunt may have mentioned shortage of above commodity in pre-war Scotland. Explain without flinching (only thing to be said for my generation) nature of aforementioned sensation.

"Oh, that!" With throwaway indifference. "I get that watching Michael Jackson."

Staggered at this revelation. Did not experience anything approaching even flushwork panelling on my buttresses until I was twenty.

182

"How did the interview go?"

"Oh, fine. She couldn't remember anything, though. Do you think she's got Old-Timer's Disease?"

Much later realise this must have been reference to Alzheimer's.

Feel I am sitting wrecked on some beach like Lear, waiting for Gloucester. Debris of languages. Beckett-like.

The sound of young male footsteps breaks upon my quiet, and Tom and Dog appear, tossing away their dog-ends upon my hapless brambles.

"Er – Dulcie – any chance we could watch the cricket?"

Uneasily aware that I have just given Harriet permission to watch MTV, pop music TV prog on satellite. Oh all right, I admit it. I've got custody of the dish. It's the only way I could persuade the children to live in the country.

6 July

Is it safe to listen to Government announcements? Or do they, as I suspect, contain brain-rotting bullshit? Why have governments anyway? Why not, just, y'know, like, all live in teepees and have pow-wows. We wouldn't need a defence policy. We could bore our enemies to death.

"You haven't lived," Tom assures me, "till you've smelt the dew gathering in your eyebrows."

"Mum? Can I live in a tent in the garden too when I've broken up? Dad says it's all right by him."

I bet it's all right. With Dad being a hundred miles away in Ealing. Divorce has stalled. Spouse thinks the new law means he'll have to endure counselling. He'd rather have his toenails pulled off one by one and an outboard motor installed in his rectum.

"Mummy! Can I live in a tent too?"

"Y'know, Dulcie," Tom gazes up at my pitted beams, "I think you might have a bit of woodworm there."

Wonder if I shall ever get a moment of peace in which to peruse catalogue for forthcoming country auction. Need less furniture, not more, but am beguiled by the thought of 'A

183

Marx Merrymakers tin plate clockwork mouse band with 4 mice musicians seated at a piano (working order)'. Wish I could elope with them.

"Mummy! Can we have popcorn?"

"Well, there's nothing else left to eat."

Tom stirs uneasily -- his fifth mug this morning.

"Er -- my turn to go shopping, yeah, sorry about that. Dog and I got the munchies this morning. You seem to get a hell of an appetite sleeping in the open air."

He says this with the synthetic radiance of a nineteenth-century field labourer after twelve hours' toil. Doubt if said labourer would have broken into his landlord's house at dawn and eaten a whole loaf of bread, most of the Flora and several thousand milligrams of cheese. Not without being hung, flogged or deported anyway. Ah! The good old days.

Children make popcorn, though the sound of microwave pinging and sporadic popcorn fire hardly appropriate to an idyllic cottage. Hungry. Wonder if popcorn is genetically engineered. Don't even trust candlelight now I know about tallow. Oh, where can we flee? Back to the womb? Mind the fibroids.

What can I eat? Find only small green organic apple and bruised pear, rejected even by ravening Teepersons. They do say every pear eventually reaches a day of perfection on which it ought to be eaten. This pear's day must have been about a fortnight ago. Eat it, not without misgivings.

"If you guys want to get back in my good books, dig me a vegetable patch."

"It's too late for veg," Dog informs us, returning from the loo where he has spent the last half-hour. Needless to say, they have not dug even so much as a latrine trench. Sigh and look sour.

"Did I ever tell you how Sabrina and I split up?" asks Tom in tone of voice dripping with soft soap, suggesting that If Only Sabrina Had Been Me etc.

"No," I reply briskly, "Thank God."

Get up and walk out, carrying sale catalogue and apple. Harriet follows.

"Mummy . . . ?"

"Shut up I'm trying to read this."

'A small 19th century tambour fronted box containing various treen items . . .' Wait! Treen? Is that a misprint?

Weren't the Treens those blokes who hung out with the Mekon in *Eagle* magazine back in the Fifties? The Green Party would do much better if it had a Mekon.

"Mummy why does Eddie Izzard dress up like a woman?"

"Never mind Eddie – why the hell do I?"

Bring back the Treens, hanging, clockwork mouse bands, etc.

"Mummy! Can I have that apple?"

Wearily hand it over. Harriet takes enormous bite, then roars: "Ugh! Worm-'ole in it! Yeaugh! Orrible!"

She flings it fifty feet away into the nettles, and spits rest out. Ah well. At least it was a form of infestation Blake would have understood.

Henry joins us in the shadow of the brambles. The hops have romped right up the roof and there are jackdaws nesting in the chimney.

"Mum! When I leave school I want to join the Paras."

"What's that, darling?" I enquire sweetly. "Paratroopers or Parasites?"

13 July

Saturday. Must drive into Rusbridge for interview on local radio. Tom asks if he may have a bath whilst I'm out. Agree with sigh. Harriet insists she wants to stay in and watch *Baywatch*. Tom and Dog offer to babysit, or perhaps Babywatch. Harriet floats in that no man's land between baby and babe. At least, I damn well hope it's a no man's land.

"Mummy," she whispers just before I go. "If you like tits does it mean you're a lesbian?"

No darling I reply, just a human being.

Rouse Volvo and potter quaintly along country lanes, being dive-bombed by yellowhammers. A little bit of bread and no cheeeese. Must remember shopping.

Suddenly in rear-view mirror, huge Transit van appears, flashing. Ugly louts inside gesturing. Panic and pull over to let them pass. Van roars by. Yob leans out giving finger salute and howling "Gerroffarode yer stoopidfarkin' Caaaaoww!"

185

Feel surge of murderous adrenalin. Only weapons handy are a Mars bar, a pair of girl's gym knickers and some embroidery thread. Although Mars the God of War, not sure if even he could despatch two louts with chocolate, gym knickers and silk. And if he could, I bet a Tory MP's already booked him.

Due at Rusbridge local radio station in less than half an hour. Step on gas a bit, and come up behind sweet little blue Ford Popular. Aaaah! Nostalgia! Bless it! Pootling along. Even slower than me. Grateful. Dear little pram-wheels.

To attain Rusbridge, however, we must climb the Umpkin, quaintly named hill up which road zig-zags, then down the other side, affording splendid view of the Vale of Russ. Ford Popular engages second gear and splutters gamely up at five miles per hour. I'm not much of an overtaker. It's not cowardice, it's political principle.

The Umpkin steepens. The Ford Popular creepens. Getting very late for my live local radio version of *Desert Island Discs*. Sawn-off-version: only allowed three pieces of music. Seems particularly unfair that Bob Marley, Freddie Mercury and Wolfie Mozart should be dead whilst the road rage yobs enjoy rude health.

On the other hand . . . bleedin' tin box on wheels! Why can't it pull over? Ford Unpopular at the moment, mate. Gerroffaroad!

With a supreme effort, we reach the Ump of the Umpkin, and the Ford Popular pulls over into an Intensive Care lay-by to enjoy the view. We all hurtle past and then scream down the other side too fast, to show off our superior horse-power, importance of our schedules, etc.

Arrive five minutes early at radio station. Not really enough time to begin embroidering Harriet's name on her gym knickers for next year – eccentric request from Lord Willie's Grammar School for Girls. Name must also be embroidered on T-shirt. Serve me right for selecting a selective school.

Apparently it's so the PE staff can get to know the girls' names. Tempted to embroider OI YOU or perhaps even SILLY TART. Glad I resisted temptation to call my daughter Martina-Charlotte de Las Palmas de Santa Cruz.

Am interviewed by engaging woman who asks some astute questions about Elaine and Spouse. Assure her that transfer of Spouse to woman across road was just what I'd always wanted.

Return home so emotionally exhausted that forget to do shopping. Arrive to find Tom has made lovely lunch of falafel and salad and is serving it to Harriet under a tree outside the tents. Am invited to join them, awarded mug of tea, etc., and can't help feeling charmed and grateful.

Recount insult from van yobs though not own rage at Ford Popular. Tom insists he never exceeds forty miles an hour even downhill, though credit for this really due to antiquity of his vehicle.

Reveal frustration at embroidery project and Dog volunteers to do it. Amazed and incredulous. Dog assures me he learnt to sew at a Men's Lib Weekend where they baked cakes, sewed, and wept at sad movies. Just hope he can spell Harriet.

In bed that night, wonder how political conviction against overtaking relates to selective schools. Also wonder if the tee-pee dwellers will up sticks in the autumn. Almost hope not.

21 July

The end-of-term school fete (2.30 p.m.) coincides most perversely with the birthday party of Emma Rainge-Roughver (barbecue at 5 p.m.), the arrival from London of Henry's train (4 p.m.), the outbreak of typhoid in the teepees (continuous) and rain in all areas.

"Mummmagh!" cries Harriet at breakfast, "I forgot I'm supposed to be running a stall! It's lucky dip! I need a barrel of sawdust and hundreds of little presents all wrapped up!"

"Sod that," I reply helpfully. "How about Guess the Weight of the Mummy instead?"

"No! No EMBARRASSING! I must have a barrel!"

Lateral thinking required here. OK then, if you scrub out one of our dustbins and then find thirty old toys you don't want and wrap them in that wrapping paper Mrs Body's been saving every Christmas . . .

"Can't have Christmas paper! Embarrassing!"

Meanwhile I'll just drive to Rusbridge, buy sawdust, hundreds of little packs of sweets, usual weekend shopping, plus present for Emma, drive back, assemble Lucky Dip, prepare lunch, minister to ill hippies, nothing to it, all in a morning's work.

Phone rings. Harriet answers it as it's usually for her these days.

"It's Alice!" she hisses indignantly. "She called me Henrietta again!"

"Dulcie! Saskia's left me. For good this time. She's run off with a Gambian beach bum – can you believe it? I saw you through your dark night of the soul when Gordon left you – now you're going to have to see me through mine! I'm ringing from the airport – I'll be with you in a couple of hours." She rings off.

"Quick!" I cry to Harriet. "Tidy up your room! Alice is coming."

"What about the dustbin?"

"She can't sleep there."

"Why does she have to have my room? Tight!"

"Don't you want to share Mummy's bed?"

"Yeah! But don't mention it to anybody ever! And can we have choc ices in bed?"

"Oh all right – but don't tell Daddy! And go and tidy your room!"

Run out and scrub dustbin, which I seem to remember Shirley Conran suggested we should do every week in *Superwoman*. Once a lifetime's too often in my view. Especially as I fear the typhoid may have started there. Try to remember my dark night of the soul, and Alice seeing me through it, but in vain.

Leave Harriet in charge as Tom and Dog are still shivering in the sleeping bags and drive badly to Rusbridge. Buy huge bale of sawdust – can always scatter it on floor of teepees afterwards – and several thousand tiny presents, plus Disneyesque toilet water contained in plastic effigy of Arabian princess for Emma Rainge-Roughver. Free-range chicken to help Alice through dark night of soul, though doubt if experience will do same for chicken.

Drive badly home. Halfway down narrowest lane encounter stationary lorry. Part of the lorry's front has fallen off and driver is attempting to tie it back on with rope. Whilst he does this his trousers are slowly falling down. Somehow this seems to me, in my jeering pinko way, to symbolise England.

Eventually escape but two bends further on encounter middle-aged woman failing to control restless horse. Somehow this seems to me to symbolise – well, me, actually. Park and turn engine off to be especially considerate. This only seems to enrage horse more. Try and imagine what sort of life would have room in it for sitting on animals, and think if mine had room, would prefer to sit on amiable walrus.

Arrive home to find Harriet has not even begun to tidy room and is watching mind-rotting US soap. Scream abuse at her (returned with interest) till eventually something goes ping in my tonsils and can scream no more. Nasty taste. Blood? Harriet runs off in floods of tears. Blood, tears – all we need now is toil and sweat.

Unpack shopping with malevolent energy. What would they all do if I wasn't here to buy the goddam chicken for Sunday lunch? Eh? Eh? Eh? Suddenly recall Alice is a vegan. Oh well. Let her eat sawdust.

Hear her car draw up outside – unless it's Harriet sobbing or Tom retching. Uneasily aware that this morning's been a picnic compared to the way it's going to be this afternoon.

28 July

Alice has arrived with a broken heart, and left the bits all over the kitchen table.

"Can you believe it, Dulcie – a Gambian beach bum?"

"What was he doing in Siena?"

"Ditched by his last Sugar-Mommy. And Saskia's his next. How could she?"

I am trying to watch the cricket.

Alice despises cricket as a neocolonial patriarchal ritual of attrition. She despises football as a choreography symbolic of rape in all its brutality and cunning. She hates motor racing as the quintessence of macho swagger and environmental irresponsibility. Badminton's all right – although she's a bit worried about where they get the feathers for the shuttlecocks.

"Isn't she rather young for a Gambian beach bum? I thought most of them went for women in their sixties."

189

"Stop being facetious, Dulcie. It's not a joke! It's my life for Chrissake going down the PAN!"

Another salvo of tears, another ten yards of loo roll, another frantic scrabble for the cigarette pack.

At least she's driven Tom and Dog off the sofa. They're out in the garden, smoking rollups. Typhoid has been shrugged off with all the nonchalance of the young and sinewy.

Harriet hovers, consumed with jealousy. Alice has monopolised me for a whole week.

"Mummy!" a whisper. "Please can Gabrielle come over?"

Sigh. Gabrielle lives ten miles away. But wait! Escape!

"Sorry, Alice. I've just got to nip over to Rusbridge to collect a little friend."

"Fine," Alice blows her nose with a final Beethovian flourish and immediately lights up. "A little trip would do me good."

Harriet quivers in indignation.

"Er – would you mind not smoking in the car?"

Alice looks amazed and mortally offended.

"What is this Dulcie? Alphaville?"

"Look – you don't eat meat: we don't inhale smoke."

Alice stubs out her cigarette with vicious energy in my best saucer.

Tom and Dog enter the room covered in smell of smoke. Tom puts kettle on and Dog searches expertly for the chocolate biscuits. He knows all my hiding places. Henry also appears, though there is scarcely room for him to cross the kitchen without physical contact with another person – something he dreads.

"The Third Antichrist is due any day now," observes Dog to Alice, offering her one of my hard-earned Jaffa cakes.

Phone rings.

"Dulcie? This is Elspeth, dearr. How are you? I'm so worried about you stuck out there in the country, all on your own. You must be so tairrebly lonely. D'you think you could cope with a wee visitor next week? Only I thought I'd take my annual trip south a little early this year."

Eagerly anticipate her visit. Begin to suspect aunt may be Third Great Antichrist.

After ringing off, escape mêlée for five minutes of blissful solitude in loo. Bliss evaporates when I discover there's no loo paper left – and I bought six rolls on Tuesday. Wipe bum on wallpaper. Tearing bit off wall first, of course. Not total Yahoo. Go downstairs in blinding rage and burst into convivial kitchen.

"Why the hell is it always me who has to buy the bogrolls?" I screech. "You come here, you pee, poo, sneeze, cry your bloody eyes out, but do you ever buy a bogroll? Do you buggery!"

Everybody looks astonished, and kitchen miraculously empties. Harriet slings herself round my waist, rather like bum bag, morosely fingering her spots.

"Go on then," I sigh. "Tell me I was embarrassing."

"Oh no, Mum!" Harriet assures me. "You were brilliant! I think Alice's really selfish and thoughtless."

That's Harriet's job, of course.

Off to collect Gabrielle. On way to car, observe Tom and Dog digging whilst Alice weeds and Henry watches.

"Look!" cries Tom placatingly. "We're digging you a cabbage patch!"

Have never liked cabbage, and suspect they may in fact be planning my interment.

Sigh at thought of aunt's little treats – massive Dundee cake with specific gravity of planet Saturn, plus several dozen scones of stone. Not so much a good plain cook, more an arms manufacturer. Where's she going to sleep, anyway? With me? Shudder at thought. Who's going to rescue me from all this? Hey! Third Great Antichrist! What's keeping you?

3 August

Society is all but rude – To this delicious Solitude, as Marvell remarked. He didn't have two pubertal kids, two New Age teepees at the bottom of his garden, a broken-hearted lesbian all over his kitchen table and an ancient granite Caledonian aunt installed in his very own bedroom. I am sleeping under my writing desk, like a Dickensian clerk only without the youthful elasticity.

Every time I uncurl my spine I can feel the cogs clogging.

Still in two minds about HRT. Sometimes I think if I had it I would unfold gracefully like a Japanese paper flower in water. And sometimes I think I would die of inappropriately youthful delightfulness.

Great Aunt Elspeth however is convinced I am going to be murdered. The only thing that frightens her more is the possibility that she might be murdered. I'm also a bit worried that she might be murdered – by me. I assure her that serial killers do not target households quite as convivial as ours. But within twenty-four hours of her arrival the aunt has sown the seeds of the solitude she dreads.

She insists on cooking supper. "Cheaper cuts dearr": the bits of meat which the animals might have chosen to have removed whilst they were still alive, had cosmetic surgery been available to them. These excrescences were simmered for four hours with a handful of pearl barley and served with dumplings of pure cellulite.

Next morning Tom and Dog announce that they are going off for a few days to a World Music Festival.

"Will you hearr any grand auld Celtic music, I wonder?" ponders the aunt. "I used to love Andy Stewart."

Alice begins to looks shifty.

"I think I might tag along with the boys actually," she confesses. Amazing what Aunt E has achieved with only one stew. I shall cherish forever the memory of vegan Alice picking out the bits of pearl barley. "There's this Romanian band I want to hear. Vlad and the Impalers."

"Take care, Dulcie," Dog warns me solemnly as they prepare to cut and run. "Watch out for the Third Great Auntiechrist." At least I think that's what he said.

We wave them off. Their teepees remain. They are going to share a yurt with Bonzo, Planet and Angel from Brighton.

"Och, I do hope they'll be safe!" agonizes Aunt Elspeth. "D'ye think Alice might find herself a nice young man and settle down one day?"

Lydia Rainge-Roughver rings to invite Henry and Harriet to an overnight barbecue party. Sensing the invitation, Harriet scribbles 'I hate Emma she is a piosernous cow' but I ignore these graceful protests and assure Lydia I will deliver the children immediately, and with gratitude. Ask Elspeth if she would like to come for a spin but she says she would prefer to disconnect her hearing aid and have a nice little ziz.

192

Drive children to the Rainge-Roughvers', with all the para-
phernalia of a sleepover: bedbugs and bodybags and Swiss
Army Rolls &c.

"I hate Emma," spits Harriet, "and I won't speak to her and
I'll fart as hard as I can in her tent."

"I hope they've got a big bottle of Lambrusco again," says
Henry darkly.

Arrive back at Vile Cottage to find I, and other potential
murderers, am locked out. Hammer on door but no reply.
Bedroom curtains drawn to assist ziz. Aunt evidently lost in
dreams of the sway of Andy Stewart's kilt. Windows also
all shut, so cannot contemplate climbing in. Sit on doorstep
and hammer on door from time to time. Two hours pass. Pee
behind hedge. Getting thirsty. Drink last of warm flat coke out
of can in car. Hope no drowned wasps therein.

Hammer on door again. No reply. Perhaps aunt already dead.
Recall she has died before, or nearly. Getting very tired, hungry
and pissed-off. Decide to walk down lane to phone box and
attempt to telephone her into consciousness. Halfway there the
monstrous inconveniences of my life get the better of me and
I burst into tears. Three seconds later a car draws up.

"Excuse me – oh, are you all right? Can I help?"

Pleasant masculine voice, but turn to look into mad staring
eyes of serial killer.

"What's wrong?" asks the man with the mad staring eyes.
I look nervously up and down the lonely lane.

"My aunt's locked me out and I've been trying to wake her
up for two hours and I thought I'd walk to the phone box and
try ringing."

"Would you like a lift? Hop in."

Back off shaking head, at which stranger groans in exas-
peration.

"Look, I know I look like a serial killer but I'm actually a
landscape gardener. Here's my card."

It says JAMES CAMPBELL and mentions a Chelsea medal,
not awarded for homicide. Nice thick card. No silly logos.

"My role model," he goes on, "is Vita Sackville-West. Not
Fred." He looks sympathetic but still villainous. "Anyway,
how do I know *you're* not going to murder *me*? You might
be deliberately walking up and down this lane to lure men
to their deaths. You and your aunt could be crazy feminist
taxidermists."

Enjoy brief glimpse of alternative, and charming, lifestyle.

"Anyway," he resumes, "I only stopped to ask you where Acorn Cottage is."

Acorn Cottage is our nearest neighbour, decently veiled by hawthorn and several hundred yards away. Indeed so deep is its seclusion I never suspected its existence for the first six months.

"Just tucked away along there, on the left. Are you on holiday then?" Fear I may have left it too late for small talk.

"Sort of."

"I've heard it's a bit basic."

"Yes, well, my ex-wife got the Tuscan farmhouse."

What a world of socio-economic information is revealed in that brief ejaculation. Unless of course he's joking.

I begin to notice he looks rather nice in a John Emburey sort of way. Picturesquely crumpled. Nice big hands. All the better to – no, no. That way madness lies. I must come to terms with the idea that he is probably more frightened of me than vice versa. And, despite his middle-aged settlement, younger.

"Some of my best friends would say what I really need is a landscape gardener."

"Well," he shrugs, looking up at me with a faint grin, "would you like to show me your garden? And if we can't wake your aunt up I could break in for you. I'm quite used to swinging about in mid-air. Used to be a tree surgeon."

Begin to think he must have a lovely woodside manner. Not sure what Aunt Elspeth would think if she awoke to see John Emburey with mad staring eyes swinging about outside her bedroom window, but confident she would rise to the occasion.

He parks in lay-by and we walk up my steep drive. Although I've decided to trust him, am secretly clutching pencil in readiness to stab. After all, literary critics have been doing it for years. At the first sight of my acre of brambles, James Campbell utters faint choking sound.

"Good God! And you think I'm a murderer."

Agitated Aunt bursts out of front door.

"Dulcie dearr! Wherre have you been? I was about to starrt rrringing the hospitals!"

Assure aunt I have not had a prang, nor yet been murdered, although the night's still young. In fact it's still afternoon.

194

"Well dearr – are you going to introduce me to your frriend?"

Aunt beams in unpleasant Pandarus mode.

"Sorry, yes – this is James Campbell. My Aunt Elspeth."

Aunt goes pale. Suddenly recall her mother was a MacDonald, and she was brought up with series of blood-curdling warnings that the Campbells are Coming. And now they've come.

"Tell you what," says James Campbell, turning with a shudder from the contemplation of my garden, "I could murder a cup of tea."

17 August

Landscape gardener with mad staring eyes becomes understandably comatose in the presence of my aged aunt. We give him tea, and she attempts to initiate conversation about Harrogate, as he has just driven down from Settle. His eyes stop staring madly and within minutes of aunt's first few arias about parkin I begin to fear he will nod off. Perhaps he was sleepless in Settle.

Aunt offers him another stony scone – something Biblical there – and sensing his stupor, attempts to revive him with a more engaging subject, i.e. myself. She has clearly decided that he might rescue me from my forlorn role of abandoned wife and therefore exacerbate the monstrous cruelty of her nephew, my ex-Spouse. However details of Spouse's elopement with our impregnated neighbour remain as yet decently veiled.

"Och! She's so clever, she won't like me saying this but she is, she's written children's books and things for rrradio as well as those saucy bodicebusters!"

James Campbell twitches awake and expresses incredulity and admiration.

Why do people's faces always glow with veneration when they learn you are a writer? I would feel much more awe, indeed religious ecstasy in the presence of a nurse. Nay, I would kiss the hem of nursie's garment, and not in any nasty Dennis Pottery way either.

195

"It's only work," I mutter uneasily. "You did a far more important job, Elspeth, driving ambulances in the war."

Wish at all costs to divert conversation from subject of my bodicebusters. Feverishly hope Aunt Elspeth has not read the scene in *Birches* where Peveril and Dmitri wrestle homoerotically in the sauna, dressed only in fetishistic animal masks and anointed, rather appropriately perhaps, with goose grease.

Wish I could get back to my bodicebuster in lovely solitude. Wish Aunt would depart taking James Campbell with her. She can have him. Since Time Hath Digged Deep Trenches in Her Brow he could try a row or two of celery.

"I'm sure Mr Campbell would like a copy of *Birches*, dear."

"Oh no, Elspeth. I wouldn't dream of thrusting my tiresome works on anybody."

"Not at all. I'll buy one," he says gallantly, already suppressing a yawn just at the thought of it.

"All right. I'll thrust a copy into your pocket if you promise to do me a five-minute garden plan on the back of an envelope one day. Tit for tat. A tenner for a tenner."

At all this promising talk of thrusting, tits, tats and tenners, Aunt tiptoes out, encouraged.

"Well, look," suddenly he gets to his feet. He seems very big, but so does everybody in this cottage. He looks rather pleasantly rumpled but tired. A bit of a heap, really. Santiago da Compostella.

"Sorry about my aunt," I whisper. "She's going home on Sunday."

He pauses for a moment.

"I think she's rather a dear," he murmurs, "but maybe we could have a drink or something after she's gone?"

How sweet of him to like my aunt. Realise I quite like her myself.

Do not wish to mention babysitters yet, so accept gladly. Wonder if he has children, or if the ex-wife has relieved him of those too, like the Tuscan farmhouse. As he says goodbye he shakes hands, a pleasing ceremony. His hands are large and enveloping. Suddenly realise it is several years since I touched a man with pleasure. However, being a confident woman enjoying her independence I immediately put this out of my mind.

24 August

Tom, Dog and Alice return from World Music Festival. Tom has had his bio-equilibrium restored by an ecomancer who gazed into a small bead of his spit, told him he was smoking too much and advised a diet of herbs presided over by the planet Mercury. For this he paid £8.50 – a snip, I think you'll agree.

Dog has had his dreadlocks fitted with a strange percussive set of beads, and Alice has had her navel pierced.

"Finally," she confessed with a portentous sigh, "I feel as though I've repudiated my mother. I just hope it doesn't go septic."

I remain sceptic.

"Mummy!" Harriet whispers, "Can I have my navel pierced?"

"No!"

"Alice—"

"Alice is fifty!"

"Can I have a rabbit then?"

"No! I can't afford it!"

Great Aunt Elspeth awards children small cash gift each (enough for a rabbit, alas), implores me to invite the charrming landscape garrrdener Mr Campbell to dinner, and departs for Kirkwhinnie in time to make bramble jelly.

Return from station to find Alice, Tom and Dog discussing a highlight of the Festival: Prozac's 'Miserere'. Alice informs me Prozac are a Polish band from Krakow.

"Mummy! Did she say Crap Off?"

Enquire if any of my houseguests will be prepared to babysit tonight as I have a date. Tom looks up in horror.

"Who with?"

"A landscape gardener. He's renting the cottage down the road."

"What!?" Tom is outraged. "I thought you were, like, into your freedom and stuff."

"Yes," I assure him gaily. "I'm free to go out and have a

drink whenever I like, without having to make excuses to any blasted man."

Tom looks crushed, reaches for his tobacco tin and stalks out. I fear the herbs of Mercury will not be equal to this crisis.

"Dog in the manger," observes Alice.

"I'll babysit for you, Dulcie," Dog assures me. "I like playing with those Sindies, yeah. Cool."

Have always thought Dog ought to get himself a girlfriend.

"So who's this date?" asks Alice. "What's his name?"

"James Campbell."

"Oh no! Not another bloody Scot!"

Assure her he manifests no unpleasant Caledonian qualities.

"How old is he?"

"Fiftyish."

"Good-looking?"

"Er – mad staring eyes." All I can remember.

"JC," says Dog. "Same initials as Jesus Christ."

"Could this be the Messiah?" enquires Alice archly.

Escape into long soaky bath, and ponder novelty of my situation. Have not had a date for years. Wonder if JC regards it as a date, or even whether he has noticed I'm a woman. My criteria for success are modest indeed. Try to remember who JC looks like. Seem to recall it was a cricketer although alas not Courtney Walsh.

In honour of the occasion, I shave legs, but cut shins so badly will have to wear jeans anyway, thus obscuring only decent feature. Suspect Henry has been using my razor as it is clogged with down.

Harriet approves my ensemble. Jeans and T-shirt, casual, cool. But she informs me sternly I must wear lipstick or there will be Grim Reapercussions. Apply generously, then think better of it and blot off. Wonder how extensive are JC's preparations. Suspect scanty.

"Mummy, what shall I call my rabbit when I get it? I want a lop-eared one."

"Anthony Flopkins."

That's who JC looks like! A kind of inflated version of Anthony Hopkins. Well, over-inflated and then slightly punctured.

Drive off towards The Goose and Bucket in nearby scenic

198

village of Much Hislop. Tempted to pull into lay-by and reapply lipstick. Otherwise date could turn into Grim Reaper meets Hannibal Lecter.

30 August

Enter pub. No sign of big amiable crumpled landscape gardener with whom I have tryst. Damn it. Hate arriving first. Escape to Ladies loo and contemplate face in mirror. Wish it was somebody else's. In fact – it is somebody else's. Realise with remorse that twenty years ago when I thought I looked dreadful, I really looked fabulous. Stupid cow! Now I really look dreadful. Serves me right.

Emerge encouraged and cheered by these reflections. Still nobody in pub except barman who is fat and bald but no doubt still thinks he looks fabulous. Order first white wine, making private resolution not to exceed three.

"Cheer up!" exhorts barman, who is wearing a Hawaiian shirt – perhaps to conceal his own suicidal gloom. "It may never happen!"

Assure him that it already has.

"Tell you what," he says, grinning, "did you know you've got a double in Walthamstow? Lady doctor there, dead ringer for you, love. Lovely bedside manner an' all." He winks. Express interest, though confess that I can't stand the sight of blood.

"My wife can't stand the sight of hair," he declares, slapping his pate with brio. "I'm not a natural baldie, I shaves it orf twice a week. Ha ha!"

Begin to feel I shall not be allowed to brood over my solitary white wine. Cannot conceal hopeful look towards door.

"Meetin' somebody are yer?"

"Oh, just a friend – said he might drop in – probably won't make it – very busy – landscape gardener."

"Tell you what, love," he drops his voice. "If it's a patio you're after, me and my friend Tone'll do you a lovely job, a fraction of the price and throw you in a nice little fibreglass pond for no extra charge."

Express gratitude, though not sure being thrown in a nice little fibreglass pond would do much for my hairstyle.

"Ha ha! You're a one entcha? Tell you what. I seen you around with your kiddies. You live up that old cottage just past the wood on the B1212. You're that writer lady, entcha? You ever met that Jilly Cooper? Bet she's a goer. My name's Ron by the way. Pleased to meetchoo."

Reveal nomenclature and shake hands. After all, although Ron is fat, bald, vulgar and irritating, he is at least here and prepared to serve me -- though not, I trust, in any equestrian sense. Whereas James Campbell had obviously never been awarded a Chelsea medal for punctuality. Come to think of it, he didn't look all that much like Anthony Hopkins.

Manage to escape from pub after entrance of blonde girl in miniskirt distracts Ron from his plans for my patio. Drive home cursing Campbell, and resolving never to arrange to meet a man anywhere ever again. Lurch malevolently into kitchen to discover James Campbell sitting drinking white wine with Alice.

"Dulcie!" Campbell staggers to his feet apologetically. "My car broke down in Boggart Louche -- had to walk all the way back -- thought I'd call in here to see if you'd given up on me and come home -- and Alice was kind enough to offer me a glass of Muscadet—"

My Muscadet. Hardly enough left to hurl over an irritating landscape gardener or ex-best friend.

"Jim was just telling me," cries Alice, "about how he's going to transform your garden, Dulcie."

Jim, eh? How dare she call him Jim before me? Boggart it, I'll never call him Jim now. Not even if he begs me.

Lurch towards cupboard, hurl open door and claw pack of coffee out onto floor.

"Give me a quote for transforming my garden, you mean," I reply with synthetic gaiety. "I've just spent a pleasant evening with another chap who's also coming to give me a quote."

At this rebuke James Campbell blanches. I know they're only after my money these days but the joke's on them. No good looks and no big bucks either. Phone rings.

"Hello, love. This is Ron down the pub. Would tomorrow morning be convenient for coming to see about that patio job?"

Agree uneasily. Don't even want a blasted patio.

"Oh damn," says Campbell, "I was hoping you could come and have a look at this house I saw today. I'd like your opinion."

"Never mind, Jim," says Alice. "I'll come instead. Poor Dulcie's so busy, she never has time to enjoy herself."

My problem is, I can't quite work out whether it serves me right, or not. That's me, folks. The last bastion of old-fashioned liberalism.

6 September

The teepee dwellers' woodsmoke takes on an autumnal whiff.

"I suppose I'll have to find somewhere to live this winter. God knows where," laments Tom soulfully. "Ironical, huh? Five or six years ago we'd have given anything to be free to live together. Now we are and . . ." He shrugs piteously, gazing into my houseowner's eyes. "I was hoping that when Sabrina chucked me out, and you agreed to me living here in my teepee, who knows . . . ? You're still really, like, special, Dulcie. More than you'll ever know."

He sighs. The awful thing is, I don't want to be, like, special.

"Look, Tom, maybe we'll never go a-roaming again together but what the hell, we can still share a cup of tea."

"But since this landscape gardener bloke came on the scene . . ." Tom shakes his head with jealous foreboding.

"What do you mean, came on the scene? All he's done is give me a price for redesigning my garden. And I can't afford it. So that's that."

"I've noticed the way he looks at you."

"For God's sake Tom, don't talk such utter crap!"

I am more irritated than I admit. Not just with Tom's morbid jealousy. The trouble is, James Campbell doesn't look at me at all, let alone in A Way. He comes when he wants a bit of local knowledge, and having extracted it from me, departs without reluctance.

I have started inventing local knowledge in revenge. How dare he not even fancy me a little tiny bit? He's no oil painting himself. But all he seems to fancy is cottages. He's got house-hunter's syndrome. He got all excited about an old mill down past Lower Badinage, so I told him it was haunted by a man who died after being dared to eat a live goose in 1785. I was tempted to add that it was haunted by the goose as well, but I didn't want to blow my cover.

Wonder if I shall ever be goosed again. Might have to take a last nostalgic trip to Italy. There it's a matter of honour to goose even mustachioed old lesbians.

Still, count my blessings. At least Alice has departed, leaving a couple of weeks before the swallows. She has gone to Sicily, professing not to understand why I was unable to accompany her. She knows in some theoretical way that I have children, but expresses only impatience when I remind her that they have to be educated, fed etc.

"The female turtle manages it better," she observed. "Lay the eggs in the sand and then bugger off, I say."

Tempted to remind her that elderly lesbian turtles are not, so far as I am aware, brought meals on wheels etc. by other turtles' children.

"You're so stressed out, Dulcie," Tom accuses me. "Why don't you book an aromatherapy session with my friend Aggie? She's brilliant at releasing blocked channels."

"All right then."

Tom looks astonished. Clever move on my part, eh? Accept aromatherapy from his friend instead of a-roaming with him.

Aggie is summoned and arrives next day. Somehow I had expected a ragged New Aggie person with a glittering stud in her nose. Instead I behold an immaculate young woman in a quasi-nurse's uniform with a spotless batterie de therapy including a couch which unfolds, and upon which I sit coyly whilst she asks me about my life and health.

Assure her I am perfectly well apart from menopausal delusions, headaches, backache, irritable bowel, bad knee, and general debility. She invites me to prostrate myself on her couch, naked except for a pair of ragged Sloggis. Slaggis really. Aggie informs me that fennel and jasmine should get things moving. Close my eyes as her hands swish up my back and foam about my shoulders like the sea caressing lonely old rocks. Wonder who James Campbell really fancies, and decide not to care.

Am just drifting into peaceful sleep when I hear a step

in the open doorway and a masculine voice saying "Oh
– sorry."

Jolt up in panic and endure the fateful moment when James
Campbell discovers that my bosom resembles a couple of tired
teabags.

"Oh hello!" I gasp in horror. "Would you – like a cup
of tea?"

13 September

Alone at last. Well, by my standards. The visitors have gone,
the kids are back at school, even the teepee dwellers are pulling
up sticks. Tom and Dog have been invited by a local rock star
to caretake his converted mill in Much Kidding, in return for
total replumbing. I am pleased for them and might even miss
them a little bit if there's a job requiring manly strength. On
the other hand . . . here I am at last alone with James Campbell
in The Frog and Bucket, the first fire o'the autumn crackling
at our side.

"Let's make a pact," he says suddenly. "Let's not mention
our marriages."

"I know! Let's sum the whole thing up in a sentence and
then never mention them again."

He sinks in silence for several minutes. Realise I have
imposed word games on a man whose talents are horticultural.
Wonder what manner of window box might symbolise his
marriage.

"Well . . ." he begins, "Francesca was Ophelia, you know.
Mad as a hatter. Nicknamed God's creatures. Froggy, Owly,
Pussy, Mousy . . ."

Express distaste, though guiltily aware have oft done same.
Frustrated by the constraints of a mere sentence, James
Campbell launches into a two-hour lament for the wife he
has left in Yorkshire, and I am mortified to discover she is
a rare beauty, wilful, proud, stubborn, etc., all the picturesque
things women are supposed to be. Find myself sagging even
more boringly than usual, and at end of evening, hear myself
disastrously offering cocoa.

"What a nice idea," he smiles, looking at me properly for the first time. "Francesca would never have said a thing like that."

Hey! Could it be, folks, that I am heading for Camillahood?

We drive in convoy back to Vile Cottage. Harriet is overnighting with new friend Victoria, so coast is clear for cocoa followed by perhaps a little middle-aged ogling. Mustn't rush it. As we get out of our cars, a charming moth flies past.

"Ah!" exclaims JC, "A Burnished Brass! I love moths. They have such lovely names. Mother Shipton, Silver Y, Garden Tiger, Sallow Kitten," he pauses. Love his moths already. "There's even a moth," he goes on, "called Blair's Shoulder Knot."

Figure appears in the porch of the cottage. Effing Tom.

"Er – sorry, Dulcie. Dog got too many mushrooms into him and went apeshit. Completely out of order. Can I sleep on your sofa? It's only for tonight."

20 September

James Campbell stares morosely into his cocoa and I into my Passion Fruit'n'Vanilla herb tea, whilst Tom, evidently under the influence of something a little stronger, rants about Life, The Universe and Everything. As soon as he can decently escape, Campbell disappears into the night.

"Well, thanks for ruining my date," I throw a couple of old blankets onto the sofa as if Tom were a smelly old dog, not a still divinely handsome thirtysomething.

"Dulcie!" he fixes me with reproachful old-dog gaze. "How can you treat me like this? How can you be interested in that guy? He's just a mess. I can't believe it. I just can't believe you don't fancy me any more. Not even a tiny little bit."

I can't believe it either. But it's true.

"I mean, what do you see in him?"

"I haven't had a chance to see anything in him yet."

"Well, look – just for old time's sake—" Tom grabs me as I totter past with dirty mugs destined for the sink, and attempts with some awkwardness to manoeuvre me onto his knee. "Just one last stand for old time's sake, eh? Nothing heavy. Just a cuddle. That's all I need."

"Get off, Tom!"

Reluctant to hit him over the head with favourite National Trust mug. Typical female reaction. Grabbed without compunction, hesitate to defend myself in case I hurt the aggressor or damage the weapon.

"I can't sleep on the effing sofa, anyway, for God's sake – it's almost a yard too short."

"You may be bloody marvellous, Tom, but I don't think you're quite eight feet tall."

"Hey! Where's like this sarcasm coming from, huh?"

"Oh, all right – you can have Henry's bed. Up in the attic."

With much sulking, he goes, complaining that he can't move about in the attic except on his knees, but that's what I want anyway. Retire to bed more than usually fatigued. Wonder what James Campbell makes of it all.

Harriet needs new school shoes. The old summer shoes have had it. Now it has to be Doc Marten's sensible lace-ups, which luckily are also dead cool. We walk through Rusbridge.

"Don't put your arm around me, Mummy! For God's sake, never do that again!"

"Sorry, darling."

"Don't call me darling!"

"Sorry. Oh look, they've got some Hunchback of Notre Dame dolls in there."

Such a relief after the cosmetic Sindies. But we can't really think of it as progress until a woman who looks like the Hunchback of Notre Dame is reading the News on TV.

"Mummy! Never, never, mention dolls in public again!"

"Oh, sorry."

Reach out in apology but my horrible clinging hand is shrugged off.

"I think I need a bra too," Harriet marches into M & S. Steer her away from the black lace padded platform models and towards something a little more white and meek. She observes, not without accuracy, that though barely visible, her bosom is almost as big as mine.

On the pavement afterwards we argue about something, and

she stomps off ahead of me. I notice that every single middle-aged man walking towards us – including chaps encumbered with wives and kids – every single bloke ogles her in passing. Blood runs cold. Think of Thailand. Or perhaps Bradford.

Alice rings to offer a Mediterranean perspective on my troubles, although her verdict on the Tom harassment situation is the usual I Told You So. Halfway through our conversation, Harriet appears before me in her lingerie. Am ambushed by ridiculous impulse.

"Oh, you'll never guess, Alice!" I gush. "Harriet's wearing her first—" Horrified signals from Harriet. Realise I am being awful, and stall. Alice hostile to bras in any case since she burned hers in 1968.

"Her first what?" demands Alice, irritated at my hiatus.

"Her first – her first – good conduct badge from school. How geriatric, Alice – I'd forgotten the words 'good conduct'."

"Well," sighs Alice, "I suppose it's a start."

27 September

We've been watching the repeats of *Father Ted*. This makes me want to go to Ireland.

"Mum! I think Father Dougal's sexy don't you?"

"A bit young for me, dear. I prefer Father Ted." The awful truth is I'm starting to fancy Father Jack.

The nice thing about Father Ted is that it's a family which isn't blood-related.

"Oh God, Mum – I'm getting your feet!" Harriet stares in horror at her toes like cauliflower florets. "Still, at least I've got Dad's hands." She admires her long thin fingers.

"Yes, you certainly have," I observe waspishly. "Their aversion to exertion."

"What does that mean?" she roars suspiciously.

I switch on Radio One to distract her. I have to admit I'm developing a partiality for Chris Evans. When she leaves the house, Harriet pityingly switches Radio One off and says Torment over Mum. But actually . . . when she's gone I often *switch it back on again.*

206

She catches the bus to Rusbridge now. It's half a mile to the bus stop, and the walk home includes two hundred yards of secluded footpath. She forbids me to meet the bus, though.

"I'm grown up now, Mum. I can be independent! Where are my socks?" Locate same. "Mum . . . ? Is Camilla Parker Bowles Prince Charles's . . . girlfriend?"

"Er . . . yes."

"Does anyone mind?" The young brow grows dark with concern, nay, panic. "*Does Diana know?*"

Wave her off. Heart in mouth. Horrid deserted countryside. Robin sings his autumn song. Cobwebs like looking glasses. But what use is that? If only robins were six feet tall, and could be trained to escort one's children to school. ('Whadjer lookin' at, jerk? Wanna peck?') And apart from the loneliness of the landscape, so loved by Wordsworth but now so damned menacing, the bus hasn't got seatbelts. And rioting and swearing are apparently de rigeur. But of course one must use the bus. Public transport. Use it or lose it.

Sink into armchair, sip China Tea and try to stop worrying for long enough to contemplate work. James Campbell has gone up to settle something in Settle. I daresay his glamorous pouting ex-wife will tempestuously tempt him back to a life of exciting torture. And we never even so much as shared a solitary cup of cocoa together. First it was Aunt Elspeth, then Alice, and Tom and Dog of course, and the children.

"You seem to have a very gregarious lifestyle," he observed once. This remark has lodged in my memory like a splinter. First of all, the word 'lifestyle' is somehow gratuitously offensive. I'd assumed I was above 'having a lifestyle'. That was what wallies and yuppies aspired to. Secondly, like any person of refined sensibility, I hate everybody. (With one or two exceptions.) Gregarious? I'd rather clean out Princess Anne's stables with a toothbrush than go to a party.

I am by inclination a hermit. It's just that I can't stand living alone in a cottage in the country. Creeeek – slam! There it goes again. The attic door slams *by itself when there isn't a single window open* and *it only does it when I'm here alone.* I'm not gregarious, just scared stiff.

Seize book to distract. Literary Guide to British Isles. Discover that D.H. Lawrence was drummed out of Zennor during the First World War for having a beard and a German wife. I suppose that was Zennorphobia.

Footsteps without. Hair stands on end. Too soon for postman.
Footsteps hesitate. Evidently trying to decide which window to
break. Stand up, still holding Literary Guide to British Isles,
but now in weapon mode. Wish it was The Reader's Digest
Book of What to do in an Emergency, because heavier. A
shadow crosses the window. Bulky figure. Run upstairs, open
bedroom window and look down on hideous youth of gigantic
aspect. Wish bedroom contained vat of boiling oil. Wonder if
I'd get planning permission for a chip shop up here.

"Can I help you?" I enquire sweetly. He looks up, scowling.
Prepare to hurl literature at his head. Suspect it will be his first
contact with it.

"I'm looking for my father," he mutters. "Mr Campbell. The
farmer says he comes here sometimes."

5 October

"Mummy . . . I think I fancy Gus." Gus is the son of James
Campbell, elusive landscape gardener, at present negotiating
a divorce settlement in Settle. Gus has been travelling, flew
in from Sydney and fetched up at his Dad's cottage without
warning. Nobody there, so he turned up on my doorstep.
Pausing only to eat everything in the fridge, he instantly
crashed out in Henry's bed in the attic, where he has been
for two days.

"Mummy . . . ? Can I go and wake him up? I could take
him tea and sandwiches."

"No! Let him sleep! If you want to be really useful, how
about getting me tea and sandwiches?"

"Er -- I'll just watch *Eastenders*."

I eavesdropped on a bit of it recently, and it seemed a young
woman was pregnant by her brother, or possibly the chap she
was living with, or then again possibly the bald but sexy bloke.
She was distressed because she'd seen one of them kissing her
brother – or perhaps her brother was kissing himself, which is
at least safe sex.

It reminded me somewhat of the relentlessly histrionic
Neighbours. "Oy noy, Shane's in a coyma," only without

208

the kookaburras. You know you're desperate for a holiday when you feel a flash of excitement at a glimpse of sub-tropical suburbia on TV. When Gus finally emerges from my attic I'm going to cross-question him not about his father but his travel.

If only my generation had had Travel! All we had was French penfriends, and an Italian course whilst at University. 'You are very beeeeautifoool!' I expect Florence is now a World Heritage Site. I expect they've got a plastic replica of the Piazza della Signoria so we won't wear the real one out. I wouldn't mind a week even in a polystyrene Piazza.

I sit sipping *una camomila*, surrounded by brochures. Faraway names drift idly through my imagination. Watamu, Kanifinolhu, Luxulyan – I might make it to Luxulyan as it's only in Cornwall. I also have a perverse desire to penetrate Staffordshire, but literature's to blame for that. At least Luxulyan sounds as if it might have palm trees and kookaburras.

"Mummy, is Gus going to live next door always?"

"Why?"

"I think I want to marry him."

"Don't rush into anything. You're only eleven after all."

In the middle of the night I hear Gus foraging for food. I have placed sliced white bread and baked beans in a prominent position and hidden the taramasalata, the olives, the parma ham and mangoes as they might be the nearest I ever come to a holiday. In the morning we discover he has found everything, eaten it all and left the debris all over the table. Swear softly.

"He can't help it, Mum! He's got jet lag for Chrissake!"

"Well, I've got life lag."

Wonder when James Campbell will return from Yorkshire. I expect the divorce negotiations are punctuated by frenzied bouts of sado-masochistic double-digging and mulching, perhaps even pricking out or dead-heading.

Today I am driving Harriet to school as I have a radio interview in Rusbridge. Not book promotion any more, just talking about migraine. I am now no longer a novelist, merely a person with a malady.

"Don't kiss me Mummy!" hisses Harriet, sidling out of the car. "And smile! Not that much! Don't show your horrible old teeth!"

She flees from my deformities, and I drive on cheerfully to radio date. Dear radio! It just doesn't care how bad you look.

Time for treat first: cup of tea in cosy café. Sun on shoulders. Taking time out. Sunbeams slant through steam. Faint scent of rose geranium from my old hippie scarf, long and trailing in bright confident reds, and tipped with tiny, sweet Bengali bells. Wish I was in Bengal.

Quick trip to loo before leaving. Encounter difficulty, as so often. Loo seat will not stay up, and door will not stay shut. Perform necessary act with one arm extended forward and one back – in yogic or tantric posture perhaps, who knows? Hampered by these difficulties I discover that instead of wiping my bottom in the usual manner I have somehow got in a tangle with my trailing hippie scarf and inserted several sweet little Bengali bells into my colon. Wish again I was in Bengal, and not vice versa.

19 October

Get out of bed: spine crunches. Hobble to bathroom: knee twangs. Scowl into mirror: another 300 grey ones. Have had PMT for six weeks. Hurl toothbrush into bath. Suffering from age rage.

Hate this time of year because it reflects own decrepitude. Decay everywhere. James Campbell returns from Yorkshire looking ten years older, his divorce negotiations concluded.

"No more house-hunting for a while," he sighs grimly. "Must draw in my horns. I've got to stay in Acorn Cottage all winter and lump it."

Acorn Cottage is twice the size of mine and much more luxuriously appointed. Spoilt bastard. Still, glad he is to remain next door, though no sign of pleasurable anticipation on his part. Even now he is yawning, despite my best efforts with Body Shop Activist oil. I may be politically inert but at least I smell radical.

Not disheartened, however. TV soaps suggest that anyone living next door to anyone else is bound to end up in bed with them sooner or later. However, I expect he'll manage to recruit a lissom bimbo. Crumpled and fifty is still sexy for men. I bet he won't draw in his damned horns for long.

Not that I have the slightest interest in James Campbell, or indeed anybody of that – what was the word? Sex. Menopause has completely removed my libido and replaced it with that thing Keats liked so much. Mellow forgetfulness. Lethe. Murmuring of innumerable hormones.

"Mum! Wake up! It's seven o'clock!"

"Oh Soddit!"

Shoot from bed like greyhound from trap, cellulite billowing in wake. Another disadvantage of country life. One has to rise before dawn to get anywhere where anything is happening, and then leave immediately in order to get back again.

"Mum! Where are my tights?"

"I don't know! You should keep things tidy instead of just hurling them on the floor!"

"Well you hurl yours on the floor!"

Bend down to remove heap of my dirty clothes from floor. Recall letting them drop like autumn leaves last night, in a mood of mellow fruitfulness. As I bend down, an unfortunate blast of air escapes from my person.

"Mum! You're disgusting!"

"Sorry. It was all those lovely English apples."

Bra falls to bits in my hand. Close bosom-friend. Seek safety pin. Wonder what crop top would be like. Would all be safely gathered in quite securely enough? Nothing for breakfast.

"Yuk! These plums are sour!" Harriet spits stone across room. Have been meaning to make jam with them. Must do it today. They're already thinking about mouldering.

Have missed bus, so must drive her all the way.

"Waaaaaaarp!"

"Oh God!" screams Harriet. "The car's farting now!"

Elderly Volvo's exhaust has been exhausted for some time. Now something has definitely gone. Waaaaaarp past Acorn Cottage, where drawn curtains show that James Campbell and his somnambulist son are sunk in stereo slumber.

"Don't take me all the way to school!" implores Harriet. "Drop me off round the corner. It's so embarrassing!"

After discharging Harriet, drive straight into car clinic where Volvo is installed on ramp and cranked up, revealing its underside in auto-gynaecological frankness.

"It's snapped," says mechanic with autumnal sigh. Heart

sinks. Wonder if HRT might be necessary also for car. Mechanic invites me to go shopping for an hour whilst he fixes it. Would rather watch him stripping it down than endure dreaded shopping – mundane female destiny.

Slouch reluctantly to lingerie dept. Nobody sells knickers any more, only thongs à la Baywatch. Not so much underwear as colonic irritation. Examine bras, and select cheap £3.99 model plus Wonderbra to try on just for fun. Amazing! Wonderbra cranks me up rather like ramp in car clinic did for Volvo. I now have teenage tits. Only problem is, when I take the bra off, they hit my shoes.

In middle age, gravity bestows gravitas on the scrotum, but bosom acquires only pendulous redundancy. Men ripen, women rot.

Collect car, and drive home to discover my marrows have dried out and I can't get my jam to go stiff. Recall one of Harriet's toddler friends referred to this month as 'knocktover'. Now I understand why.

26 October

Receive letter from bank enquiring indignantly why my overdraft has gone over limit. Woman overboard. Scrabble through statements with sinking feeling. Discover standing orders amount to more than income. Panic. Cannot believe, sometimes, that I was born under parsimonious sign of Virgo. Splurgo, more like.

"Mum! Can we get a video out? *Clueless*? It's brilliant!"

"No we can't! I'm bankrupt!"

"Aw! Tight!"

Half the standing orders appear to be insurance premiums. I'll be fine if I die or become disabled. But if somehow I manage to stagger on in reasonable nick I'm really buggered. Thoughts turn to winning the lottery – a sign of absolute desperation. The number 26 comes into my head. Is this a Sign? Or is it just the date?

I am now too old, and have always been too ugly, to be a rich man's bimbo. If only I were in a position to ask questions for cash, perform insider dealing or duchess counselling. No, let's get real – perhaps I could manage another children's book. A ghost story. The Vanishing Dosh. Ring my agent and ask if extra contract possible. He thinks I must first deliver something for adults – "You know, a sexual triangle or something, set in say, 1990's New York and put a lot of shopping in it? Kind of The Shopping News."

Assure him I will consider idea, though aware that shopping may have to become a distant memory, rather like sex. Ring off in deep despondency. Wonder if I could start new career as, say, token crone TV newsreader. Fear however that I would be sacked in first week for weeping.

Dash off letter to Bank Manager promising strictest economy, and cringing little card to Spouse asking for once-in-a-lifetime loan. Take solemn vow never to go into Waitrose and load up with their tropical fruit salad again, even though it's Harriet's only source of vitamins. Gaze morosely out of window at dying vegetation, and realise I must learn the art of making dying vegetation soup.

"Mum! I've got three pounds of my own money! Can I rent Clueless?"

"What's it about?"

"It's about this girl, she's beautiful, like a Sindy doll, and rich and she loves shopping and clothes and—"

"It sounds vile. Pass me that onion." Must conjure up soup of sunlit peasant past. Delicious smells drifting down garden paths past hollyhocks, sheepdogs, poultry, rose-cheeked babes. Pastoral Soup.

Wait! Recall I have old copy of Mrs Beeton, complete with adverts for Bumstead's Pure Royal British Salt. Wonder if Bumsteads also produced politically correct salt for suffragettes.

Locate soup section and peruse. 'Sheep's Head Broth'? How ghastly. I can't face food that actually looks at you. I wish they would take the heads off whitebait. And gingerbread men. 'Turtle Soup, Cow Heel Soup, Giblet Soup, Eel Soup, Kidney Soup, Bone Soup'. Nostalgia for pastoral soup vanishes. Suppress attack of fastidious fin-de-siècle retching.

Set lentils to cook – always a sign of crisis. Sorely tempted to set fire to wretched cottage and live in garage, as recommended by Shirley Conran. Might be quite pastoral in the summer.

213

Phone agent again and enquire what publishers really want. He says a big blockbusting modern novel that takes the lid off state of the nation.

Ring off, feel faint and lie down on sofa. Form unconvincing plan to write book in rough Rusbridgean dialect about street kids drugging, fighting, puking, etc. Feel fainter. Place head between knees. Revived by smell of burning. Hope it is the house, but alas! It is only the lentils.

"Mum! Oh pleeease can we rent *Clueless*? It's based on Jane Austen."

"What?"

"It's based on Jane Austen's Emma. She tries to—" Drive to Rusbridge. Purchase two bags of chips and rent *Clueless*. Zoom home and wallow on sofa in flawless vision of California where everyone is beautiful, wealthy, witty and wise. Survival of The Pastoral. I knew it must have holed up somewhere.

2 November

Invited to Cleveland to give a talk. James Campbell surprisingly offers hospitality to Harriet for two nights. Harriet desperately excited at the possibility of confirming her engagement to Gus before my return. Remind her that she is eleven and he is twenty, and am reviled.

"In Ancient Egypt," she cries, "I'd have been married long ago!"

"Yes," I reply crisply. "To your brother." She runs off screaming.

Arrive in Durham after dark. Determined to enjoy myself for thirty-six hours and return to Rusbridge with some notes still in my purse. Taxi whisks me up and down dark switch-back roads towards my B&B. Taxi radio crackles: "Wha tha fook's he dooin' theeah?" Woman taxi driver sighs and turns volume down. Realise I am in the Kingdom of Gazza, more or less.

B&B v. pleasant, though bedroom burdened with redundant Lloyd Loom chair. Chair blocks way to loo. Relocate it, but now it blocks way to bed. V. hungry, but not sure I could manage to eat whole Lloyd Loom chair. Not without ketchup, anyway.

Venture out and admire castle and cathedral floodlit against flying clouds. Find agreeable Balti restaurant and order Chicken Tikka. All other customers University students. Initial impressions of Durham suggest Cambridge before it was ironed.

Wonder how exactly Gazza related to Bamber Gascoigne, and whether Gazza could have inherited the *University Challenge* mantle.

"An' now, Corpus, yeer star'a fer ten – wheeah the fook is tha neerest Balti?"

I love Tandoori, sure, but I love Balti more.

Next morning explore Cathedral, which looms out of golden morning light like great ship. Extraordinary monument to irrational belief. Nice blank arcades. In the south they would be crowded with funerary monuments. Visit tomb of St Cuthbert, a charming chap who spent whole nights in the sea, singing and praising God. Whereas in Barbados this would be a chic combination of nightlife and watersports, in Northumberland it smacks of sanctity. Sea otters kept his feet warm. This detail alone is enough to rekindle my flagging faith, and when I read above Bede's tomb that 'Christ is the Morning Star' I almost hurl myself face-down on the flagstones, weeping and begging forgiveness.

Or perhaps it's just PMT. Although I seem to have had Premenstrual Tension, now, for weeks and weeks. Perhaps it's Post-Menstrual Tension setting in for the next two decades. Depressed by this idea, visit Cathedral shop and cafe, where I buy four postcards reduced to 5p each and consume a meek cup of cheap tea. Notes still unused in purse. Feel I am doing really well. Won't even buy a lottery ticket this week. Cuthbert would've been proud.

Walking through the town afterwards, I am seized by a beautiful gypsy.

"Your man's gone!" she cries – rather unnecessarily loudly, I feel. "But don' fret, love. You're better off without him. He's gone off wi' a younger woman, hasn't he? Her name's something like . . . Eileen?"

"Elaine."

"You should never have trusted her, love, she's a trouble-maker. But don't fret. You're strong and brave, and you've

215

got to be strong for your children – you've got two children, haven't you?"

Nod dumbly. Tears course down cheeks because somebody's told me I'm strong and brave. No tissue in bag, and no sea otter to wipe my eyes with. Not even small helpful mouse.

"I see a cottage," she cries, staring into my eyes. "You've been decoratin' it!" Later I notice there is a smudge of white emulsion on my coat. But even so, you have to admit it's impressive. "I see writin'!" she goes on. "Are you writin' something? It's a book!" Acquiesce. "It's going to be a success!" she cries. "I can see you going to London because of this book!" Try to hide horror at this news. "An' your daughter's going to work in America! And you're going to have lots of grandchildren!"

At this point the power grows weak, and she somehow persuades me to trust in God and give her all my money.

Walk on downhill shaken, stirred and terrifically broke until I realise I have to walk back uphill again, to visit the cashpoint. Still, what the hell. No wonder they built a cathedral here.

7 November

Grab bull by the horns and ask James Campbell over to dinner. Also have, as requested by him, videoed a couple of the Rosemary Verey garden programmes which he had to miss. Bribe Harriet and Henry to go to bed early. Henry immures himself in attic, turns up his sound system and, I suspect, gets out girlie mags. Pulsating attic; in Harriet's room, on first floor, Sindies discuss latest drugs deals, rapes and custody battles in transatlantic twang. Feel that my own social life on the ground floor v. mediocre.

Have decided to cook noisettes of lamb as recommended in magazine. Have never even bought noisettes before. Wonder which part of lamb they represent. Recall that noisettes is French for nuts. Hope not. Also recall French butter called *Noisy* butter. Nutty butter . . . buttery nuts. Recall *Last Tango in Paris* and conclude that though James Campbell is equal to the Marlon Brando part, I am several decades too old for Maria Schneider, and fall far short of what is required in the balcony department.

Fry noisettes fast to seal, as directed. Several of them pop out of their containing rubber bands and reveal their true identities, i.e. insignificant little scraps of flesh. Cannot persuade them back into circular shape, and wonder why anyone bothered to invent the principle of noisettes in the first place. Begin to feel that sour tide of resentment which always sweeps over me whenever cuisine is attempted. Wonder if I should chop up noisettes and make simple lamb stew instead, but decide to soldier on. Peel, chop and boil swede. Even I can do that.

"What's that horrible smell, Mummy?" Harriet pokes her head round the door to offer encouragement.

"Go away! I've paid you to stay upstairs!"

"Put some lipstick on. You look grim. And mascara."

"I don't want bloody mascara! Go to bed!"

"Are you going to seduce him Mummy?"

"Certainly not! We're just going to have supper and doze in front of the telly. A boring middle-aged date."

Harriet expresses disgust and withdraws.

Put spuds in oven, aware that I should have done this first. Ten minutes later, decide they will never be done in time, fish them out again, burn fingers, chop them up and boil them (spuds not fingers – but only just). Mash with swede, butter, salt and black pepper. Delicious, though would have been even more delicious if somebody else had cooked it.

Campbell arrives, looking tired and self-pitying as usual and launches into a blow-by-blow account of the week's disasters. Hardly bothers to ask how I am. Transparently not interested. Devours my noisettes and mashed root vegetables with eagerness and looks round for a pudding. Clearly disappointed by mere fruit and cheese. Also drinking hard – brought two bottles of Beaujolais.

Slump in front of TV. Have come to love Rosemary Verey's high, clear, melancholy voice and her sweet paw-like feet, but she is not at her best with Prince Charles. But then, who is? Video tape not in the first flush of youth, and distorts Prince Charles's remarks almost maliciously.

"And how many varieties of thyme do you have here?" enquires Rosemary.

"Fifteen," replies the royal sage.

"And how many of these did you plant yourself?"

"The whole buggering lot."

"Did he say buggering then?" I ask Campbell, more in hope than expectation.

"Blithering."

Dear fogeyish Prince! Clearly believes also in the conservation of conversation.

Next he shows us something tender, which, he complains, at the first sign of frost, "just goes fucked". James Campbell, clearly getting rattled, informs me it was not 'fucked' but 'phut'. Amuse myself with fantasy tour of Highgrove with HRH and Rosemary Fing and Blinding all around the border. Gardening could do with an injection of sex and violence, I feel. Charles II would have pulled her down behind the fuchsias.

At end of programme, turn expectantly to James Campbell, but he has fallen asleep. Realise my Prince Charming is a couch potato. Also seems likely that I am, for him, an Object Unrelated to Desire. Tiptoe away to do the washing-up. Quite relieved actually. Halfway through the dirty saucepans a pair of arms steals round my waist, but it is only Harriet.

16 November

"Go to Trebah," says James Campbell on hearing I'm off to Cornwall. He offers hospitality to Harriet but she prefers to stay with Mrs Body.

"She gives us chicken nuggets and chips every day, and when I stayed with James he forgot to buy any food at all!" she confides. Glad I am to travel alone, avoiding male improvidence, boozing, prejudice, etc.

Insanity soon sets in. Only a few miles beyond Exeter the Volvo starts to talk to me, in the accents of Max von Sydow. "I kan't stand nineteenth-century musik," he announces. "It's all either lugubrious or hideously hearty." Switch off Classic FM. It's a bit much when your car becomes an intellectual snob.

There's something about a woman travelling on her own

which makes people nervous. Stop for lunch and enter restaurant, where my arrival clearly seen as inauspicious. "A woman on her own! Quick! Kill the fatted tennis racket. Stir fry with small stones and garnish with chopped garden string." Devour the lot unflinchingly, just to spite them, and utter strange gravelly burp.

Unfurl Ordnance Survey map of Cornwall. Names of villages sound like a couple of Staffordshire bull terriers quarrelling over a tennis ball. Harrowbarrow! Pencarrow! Perranarworthal! Locate also Trebah. A garden of note, apparently. Sounds like a Mississippi floosie. Resume journey in howling gale. November is so bracing.

Arrive at length – and Cornwall goes on longer than Beethoven – in pretty little harbour town of Mennawpawes. Collect key to cottage on Marine Parade i.e. ten feet away from crashing surf. Throw open bedroom window, breathe deeply, and enjoy prospect of a shag on the rocks. Wave breaks, shag flies off, and several gallons of spray hit me in the face. Close window smiling as if I'd planned it like that.

Night creeps up. At home, maternal responsibilities prevent worst excesses of cowardice, but here I can let rip. Something goes ping out in the kitchen. Will I be pinged to death? Oh well. Could be worse. Could be ponged. Notice stealthy rustling sound behind me, but realise eventually it's the sound of my own neck against the back of the sofa.

Retire to bedroom and shove wardrobe up against the door. This saves the mystery intruder the tedious chore of strangling me as I can be conveniently crushed by the falling wardrobe as he bursts in. Secrete beneath bed strange vase in which, if unavoidable, I shall pee. Hope not, as vase is tall, thin and tippy and carpet new. If I was a man, could pee out of window. Although west wind would probably cast it back in my face.

Wish I could have got Volvo up the stairs and into bed with me. Although he'd probably have snored, or got auto-erotic. The gale blows all night, which is lucky as it drowns the crash tinkle tinkle pad-pad-pad of my own palpitating organism,

Next day drive to Trebah, to humour James Campbell. Gardeners so damned evangelical. Will give it five minutes and then find pub. Notice at entrance says it's a twenty-five acre sub-tropical ravine. OK, will give it ten minutes.

Enter and am dumbstruck. Towering palms, primaeval tree ferns, clouds of rhododendrons, a frothing lake of hydrangeas.

Expect at any moment to meet dinosaur or perhaps Adam and Eve. Wander alone and enchanted through rainforest smell. Small river drops in series of cascades and pools down to private beach. Great leaves as big as dining tables. Mists, shafts of light, calls of birds. Parrots, hummingbirds – no, sorry, got a bit carried away there. But certainly buzzards and wrens.

Sit on bench, contemplate this paradise and feel dizzy with joy. Wonder if I could reproduce the effect in a window box. Want to stay here forever. Apparently Trebah is open every day of the year. Wish I lived next door. After two hours, drag myself away and attempt to explain rapture to Volvo.

"I thought you'd never come back," he grumbles. "Let's vind a villing station. I veel like getting tanked up."

Typical man – I mean, car. I've been on my own too long. Drive off dreaming of warm palms and gently steaming ferns. Exit pursued by an angel.

21 November

"Dulcie? Are you taking Bowel Flora? Have you had a coffee enema? You really must get into detoxification."

Alice is in the hands of a food therapist. As usual at such times, I close my ears. Have no wish to experience margarine suppositories however polyunsaturated. And in my humble experience coffee is best experienced in a cup.

Promise, however, to take magnesium, calcium and something else, possibly Paestum, to stave off the need for HRT. Ring off and count blessings. Not a food therapist for a start. Have particular aversion to enemas since I suffered one at the age of two and they gave it to me in the sitting room to minimise the trauma and the nurse played the piano and sang 'Who Killed Cock Robin' the while.

When I told that to the kindly psychotherapist at Cambridge her eyes lit up. "How interesting!" she scribbled it all down. "Rape, theft and iconoclasm." No wonder I'm so screwed up. I'm not sure about the iconoclasm. Perhaps it was ectoplasm. I can't remember words these days.

"Mum! My knickers are too tight! I need new ones!"

"I can't afford it!"

"I'll borrow some of yours then!"

Harriet completes debriefing and ransacks my drawers.

"Hey! Mum! I didn't know you had things like this!" she flourishes ancient scarlet and black lace numbers. "Can I borrow them?"

"No! They're silly. Pantomime pants. Burlesque."

"What does burlesque mean?"

Demystification. Harriet tries them on and flounces around, every inch the pubescent. I lie on the bed and stare. Maybe I do need HRT. Maybe I am toxed as well as foxed. Count blessing: not poxed.

My daughter is an eleven-year-old courtesan: I have become a born again virgin. There are as many sorts of virgin as there are supermarket cheese: the mild virgin, the Cathedral City virgin, the extra mature virgin, and the vintage virgin. Like those middle-aged nymphs who serve in National Trust tearooms, all wrinkles and floral pinafores.

Amongst the blessed ranks of the latter I am now enrolled, emeritus. I qualify because it's more than three years since Spouse attempted dalliance with me, and after three years I think you lose your previous status, as with penalty points on your driving licence. If John Donne were alive now he'd get done, all right. He'd get more than three pips on his Roving Hands Licence.

Stare at portrait of John Donne. Dashing, dark, curling moustache, feather in hat. If vicars looked like that nowadays the churches would be full. Perhaps Tony Blair should cultivate the Donne look. Tempted to read one of his sermons, but can't find the book, so pick up E. Annie Proulx's *The Shipping News.* Brilliant, terrific, but I have a bit of trouble occasionally with the Newfoundlanguage. '. . . the rattle of wash-ball rocks in hissing wave, turrs, the crackery taste of brewis . . .'

Doorbell rings. Harriet rushes shrieking into wardrobe. Don't answer it Mummy! I don't want anyone to see me like this! Lean out of bedroom window and discern in the gloom the familiar figure of James Campbell dripping by my porch. He looks up, a middle-aged Romeo.

"Sorry to bother you, Dulcie, but I was feeling a bit . . . lonely over there, and I saw your light was on."

"I'll be right down." Lonely, eh? His son Gus has gone to

221

stay with a friend in Norfolk, leaving his father awfully flat and, I suspect, frightened of the dark.

"Get into bed Harriet, I'll kiss you goodnight later," I hiss, diving into my Italian shoes. I'm still all right by artificial light from the calves down.

"Don't let him snog you!" whispers Harriet in horror, hurtling off to hide in her room.

Go downstairs with ominous feeling, as if I am about to be de-Floraed. Open door to find James Campbell almost in tears.

"I'm sorry," he says, clutching at my sleeve. "I always get a bit wobbly in the autumn. It's S.A.D."

So it's not me he's after, it's my wattage. Switch on all the lights, put the kettle on and prepare to banish melancholy with the radiance of my chastity.

30 November

It is Sunday afternoon. The omnibus edition of *Eastenders* has left us longing for a bald ex-gangster with olde-worlde chivalry.

"Mum . . . ? Why's it called the Omnibus Edition? What's an omnibus?"

"It's er . . . Latin."

"Latin for what?"

"Er . . . something to do with all. All the episodes."

Harriet goes pale.

"Oh Christ!" she cries. "I've left my History homework at Emily's."

"What! And you haven't done it yet? You said you had."

"I *had* done my English and Maths. I just *forgot* about History. I'm only human for Chrissake Mum. C'mon! We've gotta get it."

My Sunday afternoon surfing the sofa disappears. And I was so looking forward to that menopausal climax: the *Antiques Roadshow*. The important teapot. The slipware owl staring unblinking at us from the seventeenth century. The well-oiled fowling piece.

"You can video it Mum!"

"I can't! I don't know how to set the clock!"

"Oh never mind! We could even go in a real antiques shop! And I won't grumble I promise! It's a lovely Sunday afternoon trip!"

And so we stumble out into the murk.

Emily, with whom Harriet overnighted last Friday, lives beyond Rusbridge in the quaint mazey hill-village of Pussage. Exactly where in Pussage is uncertain as Emily's mum collected Harriet from school on Friday and delivered her to Gabrielle's on Saturday morning. Harriet was only prevented from serial overnighting at Gabrielle's on Saturday by the urge to collect her pocket money, which required her endurance of my eccentricities for the rest of the weekend. We never had overnighting in my day. It was straight home, spam sandwiches by the electric fire and the Cold War on the wireless. Ah, happy days.

I did try to phone Emily's first but it was permanently engaged. Still, now (twelve miles later) we are approaching Pussage. Walls loom out of the darkening fog. "Was that it?" "I dunno!" "Well you were here on Friday." "Snot my fault! It was dark!" "It wasn't dark on Saturday morning!" "Well, I didn't *notice*! How did I know you were going to *ask* me where Emily lived?"

"How am I supposed to know otherwise? I don't know Emily. I've never even met her mother."

"Well I didn't *know* you didn't know her mother!"

"OK, it's my fault. I should have known you didn't know I didn't know her."

"You're spoiling our lovely Sunday afternoon trip!"

"Listen Harriet, you should be bloody grateful I'm prepared to drive twenty-five miles to fetch something you left behind. Or shall I turn round and go home again?"

"I was only *joking*!"

This is the all-purpose evasion of responsibility. I recommend it to governments. When we said it was safe to eat beef, we were only joking.

"I'm going to stop and ask at that house."

"No! *Embarrassing*!"

"You can stay in the car."

"No! It's dark now!"

With some effort, we recall that Emily's surname is Waters,

223

and receive directions to her house, which is only a hundred yards up the road. Unfortunately the surname Waters precipitates a dying-for-a-pee crisis. Drive with crossed legs through thick fog, missing Cotswold walls by a hair, and eventually, after another three miles' aimless meandering, locate Owl Cottage.

Collect homework, thank and depart. Could not ask for pee as daughter would've died of shame. Still, darkness and fog assist my feral inclinations.

"Wait! I'm bursting! I'm going to pee behind that wall!"

"Mum!" Horrified hiss. "You're peeing in somebody's garden! Stop it!"

Flee to car and drive recklessly home. After ten minutes recall that I had invited James Campbell round to obliterate the *Antiques Roadshow* with one of his self-pitying monologues. So at least we've been spared that. He doesn't like antiques because you can't take cuttings from a Chippendale.

"So what's your homework, darling?" I enquire as we gain the brief respite of Rusbridge bypass.

"The Fall of the Roman Empire."

Ah. Life was so simple then. All they had to worry about was the barbarians. My problem is, I am one.

7 December

Serve me right for peeing outdoors in the murky November night. Piles have descended majestically from my fundament. Riled by way my bum keeps following me about, making foul remarks and misbehaving. Rather like rowdy teenager. Needs sitting on, hard.

Intense irritation. Recall disgusting sight of dogs scooting around on their backsides and feel pang of sympathy. Visit chemist's, as I have several other embarrassing purchases to make. Seven weeks of PMT have finally given way. Also we have lost the nit-comb.

Annoyed by uncompromising names of haemorroid remedies. Anusol for example. Sounds foul. One might as well call it Arseoleoil. Why not Outback Cream, as it goes down under? Preparation H hardly any better. Horrible coy Fifties euphemism, like Dr White's. Need something really positive, really bouffant, really *now*. Blairol? Sounds emollient.

Hide pile ointment and panty-liners under unnecessary face flannel to minimise shame. Six people are queuing in silence at the till, which has broken down. The sales assistant has to write everything down laboriously by hand, out loud. Out very loud. Tempted to drop, basket and flee. One dreads the intrusive 'Is it for yourself?' Wish I was from another planet where parasites unknown and orifices unnecessary.

Recall, whilst queuing, other word ending in oid: asteroid. Count blessing. At least haemorroid seven miles across is not hurtling towards us through hyperspace. Another blessing: lifestyle in which purchase of condoms unnecessary.

Eventually escape, vowing never to go in that shop again. Collect Harriet from school and drive home fast through darkening lanes, desperate to repair lower regions of infernal fire. Flee to bathroom and am poised in anusolean musing when the phone rings.

"Harriet! Answer it!"

"Awwww! I'm watching *TFI Friday*!"

Brief pause. Harriet bawls up stairs: "It's James Campbell on the phone!" The man has a perfect genius for mistiming.

Hobble downstairs and acquiesce in his plan to come over tonight bringing Indian takeaway, although beg for something very mild as fear Vindaloo would cause dismay in the outback.

Bribe Harriet to go to bed early. Not that I want to be alone with him. I just want to be spared the ordeal of him observing her behaviour. Rake nits, taking grim satisfaction in the certainty that, five or ten years ago, I would be lying in a bath with a face pack on, perhaps even (God forbid) shaving my legs and conditioning my follicles in his honour. Some progress anyway. Must remember to tell Alice.

"Mum! Can I shave my legs?" The girl's psychic.

"No! You'll ruin them! It'll grow back all stubbly and twice as thick!"

"But I look like an effing monkey!"

"Less of the effing please Harriet!"

Shoo her into her room, assuring her of the perfection of her limbs.

James Campbell's Indian takeaway proves delicious, and

afterwards, under the influence of a few beers, he even looks me in the eye and asks me how I am. Reply splendid. (Heroically.)

"I wish I could've come with you to Trebah."

Suppress burp (tiresome intrusion of etiquette) and assure him I wish he could've, too — although secretly convinced it would have spoiled it for me. Never visit a magical garden with a gardener.

"You're such good company, Dulcie. You're an angel for putting up with me. I'm such an arsehole. You've been incredibly patient. You're adoreable. Come on, give me a cuddle."

Whoa! Steady on, there! At the very moment when I have ceased to fancy him, and decided he is a self-obsessed bore, at the very moment, moreover, when my bodily disasters disincline me to any kind of intimacy, James Campbell leans forward, takes me in his arms and kisses me on the lips. And I haven't even shaved my legs.

Wonder if he really fancies me, or whether he's just trying to get warm. Man's a complete enigma. Wish he hadn't referred to himself as an arsehole moments before the invitation to kiss. Society is getting so foul-mouthed. Even guilty myself occasionally. Just hope that somewhere deep in hyperspace, travelling towards our planet at the speed of light, is seven-mile-wide asterisk.

14 December

Smooching on sofa with crumpled middle-aged landscape gardener. He evidently feels vintage sap rising but I am myself disturbingly distrait. Find myself wondering if something's burning out in the kitchen, and whether Spouse will visit Great Aunt Elspeth at Hogmanay this year complete with his old and new families, leaving me exquisite solitude for several days in which to . . . well, smooch on the sofa with James Campbell. If only I can remember how to do it.

Urgent need to awaken my libido. Try thinking of James as Antony Hopkins as Mr Knightley and myself as Tina Turner as

Emma but this is too tiring to sustain for long. Perhaps it would be better to leave libido slumbering and curtail smooch whilst it is still safely confined to areas remote from my piles.

Phone rings. Leap from his arms to answer it, though aware I ought to ignore it.

"Dulcie? This is Alice. I've discovered this marvellous book. It says cancer is caused by a parasite, a sort of fluke thingie and you can stop it before it starts by zapping it with some black walnut tincture stuff and then have all your metal fillings replaced with plastic. Have you still got metal fillings?"

"Mum!" Harriet bawls upstairs. Tell Alice I will ring tomorrow, but wish her luck zapping her flukes. "Muuuum!"

James Campbell sighs and slouches off to the kitchen muttering about putting the kettle on. Not sure if I'm grateful smooch was interrupted or not.

"Mummy! I can't get to sleep! I keep thinking about Keanu Reeves and getting sexy feelings!"

So that's where I left my libido. It's wasted on the young. Their hormones drive them mercilessly towards copulation just at the age when they should be mastering the subjunctive.

Tuck her up, kiss, and whisper story about Humpty Dumpty in attempt to turn back the clock.

"Shut up about Humpty Dumpty Mum! I'm eleven years old for Chrissake! Get in bed with me!"

Am more tempted to get into bed with Harriet than with James, to be honest, but insist I must depart and she must sleep.

Descend stairs with feeling of foreboding and find my swain making a cup of tea.

"I was talking to the farmer today," he says briskly, for all the world as if we weren't locked in each other's arms five minutes ago, "and he was pissed off because he's just had to send six cattle for slaughter. They've caught TB off the badgers. And because of the public outcry nobody will do anything about the badgers. And it's not doing the healthy badgers any favours either, letting the infected ones multiply and spread."

"How do they know it's the badgers that's giving the cattle TB?" I enquire, charmed to discover that agricultural conversation does not require a libido.

"You'd soon change your tune if Harriet caught TB."

Wasn't aware I had a tune, but never mind. Not really

227

concentrating. Even though I was not entirely enraptured to find myself being kissed by him, I don't like the way he appears to be ignoring it now. It's all right for me to be in two minds about it, but he should be panting and growling by now, and telling me I'm gorgeous.

We drink tea, discussing diseases. Perhaps each of us is wondering about the other's HIV status. No wonder the smooch has cooled. Now he's stopped kissing me, though, I find I would quite like a bit more. My libido stirs, stretches, shakes itself and climbs gingerly out of its basket like an arthritic old cat. However, Harriet comes down suffering acute insomnia. This is enough to forbid any further caresses. James goes home without even a meaningful look.

Awoken at 3 a.m. by panting and growling under window. James Campbell, returned, steaming with lust that will not be denied? Peer out of window and discern in moonlight wheezy old badger foraging for nuts under my bird table. Admire its charm briefly, then close window, and go and close Harriet's. Not sure how TB is caught but suspect that we'll be all right as long as we can persuade badgers not to piss in the fridge.

21 December

Vile Cottage slumbers under a mean moon. I lie awake wondering whether I can get away with ignoring Christmas. The overdraft goes down further than horseradish. Of course there will be a present each for Henry and Harriet, but as for the rest, I am losing my nerve.

I have also so far ignored Saskia's latest exhibition in London. Dust and Ashpans it's called. Aware that last day is tomorrow, and I ought at the very least to appear in the visitors' book applauding her artistic dexterity and comparing her favourably with Donatello.

Have just resolved to stay beneath duvet for the next week, when small stone goes crack against my bedroom window. Panic. It's got to be James Campbell, who has not appeared since our tentative middle-aged snog. Has he recovered his nerve? Hope not, as am wearing thick black woolly leggings which transform my lower half to bear's legs. Grab old camel dressing gown of Spouse's – another passion-killer – and run to window. Sure enough it's Campbell.

"Dulcie! I'm fo forry. Have you got any painkillerf?"

Enquire why he is talking like a feventeenth-century book and he reveals he haf toothache of a particularly favage fort.

Run downstairs, let him in, and ransack medical cupboard whilst he sits on the sofa groaning and berating himself for ignoring his ex-wife's entreaties to visit the dentist at least once in the past ten years. Wonder if my own dear ex-spouse is ever racked with similar torments. Certainly hope so.

Administer two painkillers of the anti-inflammatory sort with name like anagram of Oprah Winfrey. Offer him ice cream to slurp, which might numb the inflamed nerves.

"Bleff you!" he cries, showering me with fragments of Viennetta. "You're fuch a phriend. I'm fo forry to difturb you. What more can I fay?"

As little as possible, I reckon. I light the fire and attempt to initiate conversation about my hellebores. But James can only lament the inflammation of his facial nerve. The brufens prove useless and I am moved eventually to ring the doctor, even though it is 2 a.m. James Campbell assures the doc he is in fevere pain and is questioned about his size and weight. "Big," he admits. "Clofe on fixteen ftone."

The doc instructs him to double his dose, and take four codeines as a kind of chaser. James obeys, and promptly falls asleep on my sofa. Charmed by his sudden descent into filence, I cover him with a blanket and return to my bed, confident there will be no feventeenth-century rompf tonight.

Next day I drive him to the dentist, drop Harriet off at Mrs Body's for an out-with-the-Bodys experience in Rusbridge Mall, and drive James back to my place, minus one of his back molars. On the way we stop at the embarrassing chemist's where I buy half a hundredweight of codeine, paracetamol and brufen, assuring the chemist I am not contemplating suicide – yet.

Dose the patient up with drugs, offer him spittoon, conjure up for him a mouthwash of brine which smells slightly of the North Sea, only without the sewage, and place him on the sofa with the TV remote control. He thanks me feebly in Pepyspeak and begs me to name the favour I would like in return. Tempted to ask for ten thousand quid.

Should I now rush off to London to catch last day of Saskia's exhibition? Could do a bit of last-minute Christmas shopping if I lose my nerve. Saved from this prospect by phone call from Alice informing me that the exhibition is going to Swindon in January and I can catch it there.

"It's marvellous what she does with dusters and curtain rings," raves Alice. "It's kind of politically correct bondage. And they're selling earrings made out of curtain rings. It could be the next big fashion statement."

Ring off relieved, and even stirred. Suddenly realise I don't have to risk universal opprobrium by ignoring Christmas. The men can have dusters and the women can have curtain earrings. Cheap, cheerful, and politically impeccable.

"Dulfie," enquires James piteously, "If there any chanfe of fome ife-cream?"

He's got a nerve.

28 December

"Mum," Harriet informs me, "I'm going out with Gary Barnwell."

"Really? Where exactly are you going? And when?"

A girl's love life begins, these days, After Eight.

"I'm not really like, going out with him, Mum. It's just you ask somebody if they'll go out with you and if they say Yes, then you're going out with them. You don't actually go out with them really."

Charmed by this metaphysical arrangement. If only we'd had it in our day. I could have had a virtual reality marriage for a start. Spouse, and more importantly, his socks and shirts and dirty cups, could have disappeared whenever I took the goggles off. Instead I had to wait for an obliging neighbour to come along and covet him.

The delightfulness of this transition has been very evident for the past week. Spouse, as I still think of him, has been railroaded by Elaine into a Country Christmas. Instead of staying put in perfectly adequate Ealing, Elaine wanted to rent a twee cottage in the woods hereabouts. Spouse has had to struggle with potties, cots, bibs, high chairs, hot-water bottles, tree, decorations, logs, firelighters, turkey . . . Ho ho ho!

I am torn between a kind of retrospective rage that he never did half these things for me, and a triumphant glee that he is having to do them now for her. I could never fancy a man who let me enslave him. Except a bank manager perhaps.

Tonight James Campbell is invited over, as are Spouse and Elaine. Great Aunt Elspeth will be babysitting for young Alexander in the twee rented cottage. Elaine is attempting to potty-train him. Too early, of course. Another charming sensation: I can draw on my extensive prior experience and matronise her.

"There won't be any more babies, I can promise you, Dulcie," she groans, half-asleep in a deep armchair. I am preoccupied by the awareness that James Campbell is late. Nothing is more galling than being stood up in front of your ex and his new improved wifelet.

"What's he like, this new man of yours Dulcie?"

"He's not my new man."

"Oh come on! I bet he's a demon lover." She's dying to pair me off with somebody, to legitimise her theft of my husband.

"Well at the moment he's just a neighbour. And rather a boring old fart."

At this very moment James Campbell arrives. Pleased to find he looks as if he's made an effort. Nice lovat green cords and faded tweeds. More hair than Spouse, too. Elaine sits up and prepares to flirt, but he almost ignores her and instead, kisses me on the cheek. Perhaps I am 'going out with him' in the eleven-year-old sense.

Spouse embarks on a series of feverish jokes as if to prove that though he has less hair, he has more wit.

My nervousness is exacerbated by a growing conviction that somebody has stepped in some dogshit. Go out to kitchen and examine soles of shoes. Pristine. Return and offer guests bowls of peanuts'n'crisps, glancing surreptitiously at their footwear. Hope it's Elaine. Dread lest it be James. I don't want them to think he's a dog's doo-doo dude.

Who could bear to own a dog in town, these days? Who could bear to pick up articles with one's hand in a plastic bag? Metaphysical, virtual dog the only option. Return to kitchen and attempt to turn thoughts from excrement to nourishment.

Baste the sea bass, cool the coulis and am terrified by the terrine. Am planning later to provide sound effects of instant coffee manufacture to cover the noise of my toxic cafetière.

Exhausted by cuisine. What we really need is the virtual reality dinner party. Re-enter sitting room with bottle of chilled Chardonnay and suddenly notice Harriet's shoe lying beside sofa. This is the source of pong. Seize with fire-tongs and hurl it out of window.

"Typical of Dulcie's problem-solving," remarks Spouse acidly. He paid for the shoe in question.

"Don't worry," says James Campbell consolingly. "I'll sort it out for you later."

Good God. He must really love me after all.

11 January 1997

Am massively broke, and Volvo is celebrating the onset of its MOT by developing an extensive repertoire of unusual sounds. Chaka chaka chaka wheeeeeee BOOMBOOMBOOOM. Not so much a car, more a Latin American dance band.

The Bank Manager is as stonily impassive as an Aztec god. I fear human sacrifice may be necessary. Restlessly revolve ideas for increasing income or further reducing expenditure. Vile Cottage is, alas, too small to accommodate a lodger – unless I move out altogether and sleep in the tumbledown Cotswold privy.

"Cheer up, Dulcie! Something'll turn up."

This is James Micawber Campbell. Very chipper now that the days are drawing out again. Also he has landed a big contract with a film director who has bought a Cotswold Manor House. It's Dag Zitzone, who directed *Last Tango in Lapland*, about lap dancing and table tapping or whatever it's called. He's ordered an old-fashioned English garden with quaint mazes and a very wanton green.

The bill in box hedging alone will be in the hundreds, James tells me. Feel box hedging is what my garden needs, too. Alas, I can't afford box. Except possibly cardboard box outside Waterloo. Clearly James will be doing very well out of Zitzone. Wished I had tried a bit harder when he kissed me last month. If only Harriet hadn't woken up.

He hasn't attempted any dalliance since, but then, there hasn't been a promising moment. I have been dogged by children, and when they went to their Dad's, James was with his ex in Yorkshire. Now he's cheerful and busy and it's the time for structural work and planting trees etc., he has other ways of keeping warm. Even now he is rising from my kitchen table and putting on his coat. OK, Harriet's doing her homework in the next room but all the same . . . not a look, not a peck.

"Dulcie!" Alice rings from London. "Disaster! The money's all gone."

Et tu, Alice? The heiress of the arms manufacturer? Express astonishment, whilst managing to hide nasty irresistible sense of triumph.

"Yes. It's terrible. The investments all went wrong." She launches into a financial saga about how the peseta imploded all over her Malaysian portfolio and how she'd be sacking her broker except he's been arrested.

"God, it's awful, Dulcie! We're living in Edmonton."

Establish that this is the untrendy part of North London, not somewhere in Canada – which of course would be even worse in Alice's eyes. Remind her that Edmonton featured in John Gilpin and therefore must be full of olde coaching inns, turnpikes, wigs, bosoms, etc. She instructs me to get real and invites me up to see the Howard Hodgkin exhibition.

"Slabs of vibrant colour!" she shrieks. "A dynamic fusion of passion and suction!" At least I think that's what she said. Or it may have been another reference to her finances.

Buy ticket for London, and wonder if it would be cheaper if I disguised myself as a bicycle and travelled in the – suddenly realise with grief and outrage that guards' vans have been quietly phased out whilst I wasn't looking, along with farthings and honour. And, I realise once installed on train, old people. There are only young people now. I am the oldest person in the compartment. The other wrinklies are all at home in bed with woolly hats on, but I still foolishly attempt to cultivate a lifestyle.

Purchase tube ticket for £3, valid for Zones 1 and 2, whatever they are. Alphaville looms. Meet Alice and Saskia as instructed at Mandeer, subterranean Indian Vegetarian Restaurant just behind Tottenham Court Road in Zone 1. Buy enormous plateful of delicious Ayur Vedic veg and rice for £3.

"We keep coming here every time we get hungry," says Alice. "The only real expense is the cattle truck back to Edmonton. It's perfectly possible to survive in London for £25 a day if you don't buy anything." Inform her that, train fares to London apart, it is my hope now to survive on £25 a week.

Wonder if Vile Cottage could set up as a rustic cabaret. Although the ceilings are too low for table-dancing, the rooms are so small that lap-dancing is almost unavoidable.

18 January

Venerable Volvo's MOT due. Drive it with caution to garage in purlieus of Rusbridge, accompanied by soprano duet and Latin-American rhythm section which has recently replaced sound of engine. Fearful lest the old beauty should fail its test. Sense of fellow-feeling also. Am myself so choked up with detritus, suspect that carbon dating is the only sort of dating I can hope for now.

Hire car for the three days it will take to complete old Volvo's facelift. Now I must face something called a Renault, which I soon discover is Gallic revenge for years of Anglo-Saxon attitude.

Without power steering, and adorned with a handbrake which requires two-fisted yanking up to shoulder level, it sulks as determinedly as a Paris waiter. Ten minutes pass before I can get it off the slightly-sloping forecourt. Harriet sinks deep into her balaclava.

"Stop it, Mum! Embarrassing!"

"Stop it? I can't start the sodding thing! Bloody French rubbish! Papa! Nicole! Gitanes! Johnny Hallyday!"

"Shut up! Stop swearing! It was your New Year's Resolution!"

"Have you ever tried watching French TV news? Can you

take it seriously? How can you respect a nation that can't play cricket?"

Brief struggle with car has pushed my political position ·vis-à-vis Europe into extreme xenophobia. Convinced that the only thing to be said for the French is the usefulness of their bons mots, vis-à-vis among them.

Eventually we lurch off down the High Street in search of a series of bends mild enough for the Renault to get round in one shoulder-wrenching swoop. God knows what will happen when we arrive at the mountainous hairpins of home.

"Mum, are you in love with James Campbell?"

"Certainly not!"

"Good! Because I want you and Dad to get together again."

Of all the things Harriet ever says, this more than anything has the power to sap my emotional energies. Remind her briskly that her father lives with another, more desirable woman who has a child by him, and that even now the divorce papers are strewn across my desk awaiting signature. This means two sets of Christmas and birthday presents, and declare that Elaine is a generous and exotic shopper. At this thought Harriet's tears dry, and she consoles herself by ransacking Waitrose for a wide range of junk food.

Eventually we arrive back in our own icy lane, and point the Renault at the sheer cliff face which is our drive. Renault dithers, slithers, and plunges off sideways.

"You fool, Mum!"

I become aware that one of the car's back wheels is sticking up in the air, rather like a dog peeing against a lamp-post, and for the first time in eighteen months I am glad the cottage I bought is secluded. We get out and survey the full ghastliness. I am aware the car's nose has come to rest against a bit of old wall, and think fondly of the hundred pounds deposit which was not even mine to bestow in the first place.

Carrying the shopping up the cliff face is no joke either. I am beginning to wish I had at least some auto-immunity to draw on at moments of crisis. There is a message on the answerphone from the garage. "Mrs Domum? I'm afraid your steering rack's gone."

"Oh Mum!" Harriet wails. "What if old Volvie fails his MOT? We won't sell him, will we? We'll keep him for ever! Even if he's not allowed on the road we'll keep him and I'll live in him in the summer."

Volvo evidently father-symbol. Promise to keep Volvo in retirement, like Chekhovian nanny, and assure her I will never consult Ford Escort Agency.

Ring garage and report difficulties. Eventually two chaps arrive in a Transit van. Trevor Bailey and Sting. They drag Renault off the rocks with something called a D-clamp, and are kind enough to refrain from any jocular remarks in my presence. I wave them off, then walk back into the house. The wind grabs the door, which slams behind me, dislodging the wok from its hook on a beam. It misses my head by inches. The Wok of Damocles. If cars don't get you, cookery will.

25 January

The Volvo passed its MOT, though it had to be awarded a new steering rack, and the mechanic informed me that the parker-bowles were quite worn out. I wasn't surprised. Paying his bill is a problem. I eye Harriet's Building Society book at times, aware that this is as low as anyone could sink.

"I'll pay for it, Mummy! Take all my money, please!"

She has not inherited her father's Caledonian instincts in financial matters. My own reckless, feckless housekeeping is but a poor example.

A few moments later she enquires whether she may take a couple of friends to Centerparcs for her birthday "just for the weekend."

"Look, Harriet, I've just told you I can't even pay the man who did the car. How the hell do you expect---"

"Don't shout! Snot fair! I only asked!"

She stomps off to her room with slam and élan for the incredible sulk.

Sigh deeply and contemplate overdraft, which is now so big it blots out the sun. I have become convinced that everyone I pass in the street must be aware of it. When letters from the bank arrive I scream and throw them on the fire, unopened.

Pick up old copy of *Country Homes and Interiors* and even though my penury is now registering on the seismographs in Uppsala, I cannot help coveting a door knocker shaped like a pineapple, such as Georgian sea captains would instal when safely returned from the still-vexed Bermoothes. I have no door knocker. This will fox the bailiffs.

Notice ad for wood antiquator. Wonder if I could rent out my children as antiquators of houses. Their hormonal slamming and stomping would turn your post-war semi into a frail, disintegrating seventeenth century cottage in no time.

Pity the poor child. Recall the Menarche as a lamentable occasion. Crime and Punishment in one red droplet, like the anti-Labour posters. As for the Menopause, it seems to involve the period of a dormouse preceded by the PMT of Tyrannosaurus Rex. Or rather, Regina.

O my God! Mention of dinosaurs reminds me that my commuting son is due to arrive in Rusbridge by bus in fifteen minutes – about half the time it will take me to drive there.

"Harriet! Come on! We've got to collect Henry! Now!" Dive into two extra sweaters, bodywarmer and anorak.

"Well snot my fault!"

Sulkily she comes downstairs, wearing satin mini-skirt and sparkly sawn-off sweater. Her navel winks roguishly at me in the gap between them (like a cat's arse). That is a sight Tyrannosaurus never had to endure.

"Put your coat on! It's *winter*, Harriet!" Sulkily she concedes a thin synthetic jacket. "And a hat, darling!"

"A *Hat*? No chance."

The Volvo sulks also. Won't start. Snigger-snigger-snigger. It's laughing at me.

"Start, you bastard! You had a bleeding MOT only last week!"

"Don't shout at him, Mummy! It's not his fault! He's only cold!"

Ask Volvo politely to start. It obliges.

As we drive past James Campbell's house he appears, gesturing in a quasi-urgent way which suggests that the moment has arrived for him to declare his undying devotion, perhaps even to marry me and share his considerable fortune.

I drive on past, expressing in one frantic wave the impossibility of stopping, the humanitarian urgency of my mission, the fact that I will, be what is frivolously known hereabouts as 'straight back', and that I find him more attractive than I have ever shown – perhaps not quite up to the standards of a Georgian sea captain, but the nearest thing available locally.

Helen Mirren would've been proud. Hope he will not miss any of these subtleties, feel I have jilted him, and sulk.

We are twenty minutes late picking up Henry, who does not deign to speak to me for thirty hours. Now, that's what I call a sulk. Their father's sacred inheritance, in spades. Since I've learnt to ignore it, I find it quite restful. If only it was an Olympic event. I've often thought the Domums could sulk for England.

1 February

"Mummy, I still haven't spent my Christmas money. Please can I have a cat? I'll look after it and everything I promise!"

"NO! I can't even pay the electricity bill! They'll probably cut us off next week! Then the only way you'll be able to keep warm is with a hot-water bottle."

"A cat would keep me warm. Anyway, if the electricity gets cut off the kettle won't work."

Sickened by this idea. Cups of tea are my only luxury now. I have about fifty a day. Wonder if the cesspit can cope.

Attempt to soothe Harriet by stroking her hair. Crackle, flash.

"Bloody hell, Mum! What was that?"

"Er – static electricity."

"What's that?"

Am I from outer space? Am I, in fact, Supercrone? Complete with knee-length knickers worn outside legwarmers? Harriet fingers my fingers in fascination.

"Your hands are so rough, Mum – like sandpaper."

Hastily grab old tube of hand cream. Don't like this finger-shockin' business. Would prefer it if my digits went back to being acoustic.

I concede a day in Bath. Drive there and immediately feel better. One can float in the atmosphere, soak up the street life. We lunch in synthetic Italian restaurant overlooking the Post Office junction. Lovely banana split, marvellous views of other people's toddlers having tantrums. Make secret plan to retire here, although would need to win lottery first. Might also essay timid elderly love affair. In fact – I could run an introduction agency for the elderly. Fogeys and Crones. Forget all this slim attractive with GSOH stuff. 'Stiff old bastard with bunions (70ish) seeks shapeless sixtyish slapper for scrabble twice weekly.'

"Mum . . . Can we go to the Disney shop?"

There she could buy a Sindian doll shaped like a character in a film. Wouldn't mind a nine-inch Antony Hopkins as the Butler Stevens in *The Remains of the Day*. Especially if you could wind him up and get him to make the tea. Don't fancy nine-inch Hannibal Lecter though. A bit like a Jack Russell. You could wind it up to drive off intruders.

Bow to the inevitable and endure the Disney store, muttering occasional asides about the superiority of books and hand-carved wooden toys from Omsk. Harriet inspects every item minutely, and then astonishes me by leaving the store without making a purchase. Wonder if she is ill.

Reclaim car and as we are driving out of town she embarks on a litany of regret that her twenty quid is still unspent, and ignores my congratulations on the subject. Suddenly notice we are passing delightful toyshop full of wooden hand-carved stuff from Omsk. Turn abruptly into side street and park recklessly.

Wallow for ten minutes in attractive mélange of toys, few requiring electricity or containing plastic. Kits with which to research the Pharaohs or recreate the Industrial Revolution. Teddy Bears with such gravitas, they look like the Pre-War Cabinet. Harriet seizes a wonderfully lifelike cat, £19.99 and will never need feeding or injections.

Return to find car has been awarded a parking ticket. Leap in and drive like hell out of town.

"I'm going to call her Felina," announces Harriet. Suggest she could call it Felina Fcott. Harriet mystified.

When we get home, half the lights are not working and the time-clock on the central heating stands at ten to three although it is five past six. Fiddle futilely with lightbulbs. Notice my hands smell electric. Wonder if by some osmotic process I am soaking up the electricity supply, and whether it is a by-product of the menopause.

Harriet plays happily with her cat whilst I reapply hand cream, then notice it's the hand cream that smells of electricity. One of the ingredients is glycerine. Nitroglycerine?

Bomb-making equipment? Convinced that one day I shall be arrested as IRA suspect. Might be quite restful in prison actually. Somebody else could worry about the electricity.

"Mum? I hate Tony Blair now he's said we've all got to have more homework."

How to alienate a generation at a stroke. Still, I expect he's just trying to prove he's grown up.

8 February

Windmill is erected on brow of nearby hill, causing terrific stink among the locals. A debate rages in the sedate pages of the *Rusbridge Gazette*. The Nimbys complain that it spoils their enjoyment of the trees, etc. The Greens retort that the trees would probably vote for wind rather than acid rain or clouds of invisible fallout from the ageing Magnox reactors nearby, of which we have a matching pair – always makes them more desirable, as they say on the *Antiques Roadshow*.

I can see the windmill from my attic, and feeling a sudden surge of eco-political fervour, rush up there to offer admiration. Must stand up and be counted. Although ran up stairs too fast, so must first sink down onto Henry's bed, tidily made but with faint subterranean crackle suggesting hidden girlie magazines. Not very PC, but hope the poor boy does have some kind of fun. Life not fair – to him or me.

Drift off to sleep even though it is 11 a.m., and dream that erotic funfair has been established on brow of nearby hill, complete with Arousal Carousel, Windmill Girls and unusually explicit Big Dipper. Cruelly awakened by phone.

"Dulcie? It's Alice. Listen – the Maharishi has just sent out this bumf about the orientation of houses. Yours faces west, right?" Refuse to commit myself as I sense an approaching Vedic insult. "Well I'm sorry Dulcie but it's bad news. Houses facing west mean poverty, lack of creativity and vitality."

Briskly repudiate verdict, terminate phone call and slump dully onto the piles of unpaid bills.

Wonder if house could be screwed round on its axis to face a more prosperous direction, or if I should brick up the front door and burrow upwards through the hillside at the back, like a meercat. Wish I was a meercat sometimes. Free childcare for a start. And dicing with scorpions wouldn't be much worse than my customary attempts at cuisine.

Re-examine idea of erotic funfair. Seems an attractive commercial concept. Unfortunately I lack the millions necessary to nurture it, and not enough room in garden even for quite small Ghost Train, or rather Harem Scare'em. Must get real and have idea which will rescue me from the dreadful consequences of my house facing west. If only attic contained unexpected Rembrandt or garden a Saxon burial hoard. If only I had a matching pair of something desirable.

Peruse *Rusbridge Gazette*. Only jobs advertised are for cleaners, cooks and childminders – work for which extensive experience has left me totally unqualified. Recall I am supposed to be a writer. Must turn my back on historical bonkbusters and plunge into up-to-date shopulating and copulating oeuvre.

"Horn o'mead, please, Hrothgar, and 'ave one yerself," Wulfric slapped down a couple of groats and ogled Hrothgar's daughter Hotskerta who was salting the knobs of kebabed wolf. She would be ripe for a bit of Sax'n'Vileness come maypole time, thought Wulfric. Something glittered on her neck. "What kind of torque is that?" enquired Wulfric.

But Hotskerta looked past him, to where a cold gust of air ushered in a stranger. He was tall, shaven-headed and dark-eyed.

"Bonsoir," he bowed slightly. "I am Guillaume de la Marinade, your new Lord of ze Manoir. Give me a glass of Mouton Cadet '61, containing 250 fl. mml. Nozink more or less. And away wiz zoze wolf-chips, zey contravene Euro health-et-sauvetage regles numero 22156/4bis. As ze sardine observed to ze mad cow, we are all existentialiste now, hein?"

Nothing for lunch except last choc ice in freezer. Consume it thoughtfully. Wonder if you could make ice lollies shaped like Bill Clinton's not-private-enough parts. Is this the business idea which will make my fortune? Gaze out into sodden garden.

Could I get a euro-grant to grow organic coriander there? Not sodden likely.

BBC not likely to ask for 12-part series based on Norman Conquest either. Or if they did, it would be Andrew Davies they asked. Wonder if, when Normans arrived, there were still a few Romans around running pizza parlours. Also wonder what it must have been like to have a king called Harold Godwin. Although I think we've got an inkling of that.

15 February

Parcel arrives from Kirkwhinnie: large, heavy, exciting parcel. Eagerly we unwrap it, Harriet fantasising about Game Boy, myself dreading Aunt Elspeth's Dundee cake. Several pieces of wood fall out onto the floor.

"Wha' the bloody ell's tha'?" demands Harriet. She's been watching too many episodes of *Eastenders* – twice.

"It's a—" puzzled myself for a moment, but locate helpful diagram. "A bird table! How kind of Auntie!"

Harriet drifts off, less than enchanted, to lament the fact that it's Friday, and there's no *Eastenders* now till the Sunday omnibus.

"I ha' Gra'," she grumbles. (This being translated means I hate Grant. Grant, for those who have not yet heard the call, is a bald publican with a Byzantine private life.) "He's really, li', 'orrible to Tiffany. An' I ha' L'raine too. She's a selfish cow just like Tiffany said."

Tiffany is not a lampshade, except on the *Antiques Roadshow*. I love the *Antiques Roadshow* because as you get older you think objects can never let you down. Then as you get even older you realise that they can, too. What you fondly thought was an exquisite little eighteenth century side table was cleverly botched together in Coventry in 1955. Indeed, what Aunt Elspeth has sent us may well turn out to be a do-it-yourself Louis XIV secretaire kit.

Once you realise objects are just as treacherous as lovers, then you turn to *Songs of Praise*. Harry Secombe. If I get really old I shall follow him. Nearer, my Goon, to thee.

Seizing the hammer from its sleep of ages in the airing

cupboard, I boldly go out to erect the bird table. Harriet declines to assist me.

"Don't you care," I rebuke her feelingly, "about the poor little blue tits?"

"Mum," she groans, "'s freezing! If I go aht I'll get poor little blue tits meself!"

Nobody cool wears a coat. Of course it is an act of eccentric cruelty on my part to suggest one.

I struggle alone with the bird table for twenty minutes, swearing with gusto and what Aunt Elspeth might regard as ingratitude. Eventually I have to prop the bird table up with a number of large rocks, two of which inflict injury upon me. Adorn bird table with the peanuts, seeds, etc., which Elspeth had the foresight to include, then go indoors and prepare to twitch.

Birds ignore bird table but indulge in mating rituals on the nearby wall.

"Mum! What're they doing?"

"Mating. The birds pair up, traditionally, on the Fourteenth of February."

"What! Have birds got willies, then?"

Hesitate. Am, ornithologically speaking, in deep water. Also emotionally 14th February a difficult subject. Neither of us got a Valentine, and though I have extemporised briskly on the joys of independence and the miseries of love-gone-wrong, I am up against biology. A relentless pre-Palaeolithic impulse is driving my daughter towards her fifteen pregnancies in the cave followed by death of old age at thirty-one.

"Do the birds have one partner or do they, like, do it with everybody?" At last I've managed to get her interested in birds, though not sure they provide a better moral model than *Eastenders*.

"One partner, er, usually. I'm not sure about sparrows."

"And do birds stick with one partner for ever? Or do they, like, sleep around?"

"Well . . . turtle doves pair off for life."

"So if you and Daddy were turtle doves you'd still be married?"

"Unless Daddy had been grabbed by a sparrowhawk." (Let's look on the bright side.)

Some time later Harriet returns with strange expression which rouses my suspicions.

"Mum . . . Emily's got a virtual reality cat. It's, like, on her computer, and it purrs and you can play with it only it never needs feeding or vets' bills. And it's only—"

"NO!"

"But it wouldn't chase the birds!"

"It would chase the virtual birds."

Peruse Authors' Licensing and Collecting Society Newsletter. They are trying to contact John Murray, involved in *Thunderbirds* (Gaelic version). What next? Celtic Daleks? Jones the Pod?

Notice windmill not moving today. Worried. Want to help. Fart in an easterly direction all day, but doesn't seem to do any good.

22 February

"Mum? Can my friend Sam come and stay the night on Saturday? She's everso pretty and clever and nice and she hasn't got a single spot." Declare I shall be honoured to entertain such a paragon.

Shortly afterwards am seized with a longing to be somewhere far away. Seize Michelin Guide and am transported to Viviers in the Rhone Valley. Here some Bishops enjoyed a cushy number in the thirteenth century and acted as hosts to St Louis when he was travelling south to the Seventh Crusade.

"Can we have pizza Mum because that's Sam's favourite? She came top in maths she's a genius." Hope Sam will not develop stigmata all over the sofa.

James Campbell rings to ask if I would like to go out to lunch on Saturday. Presumably wants to unload his latest cargo of self-pity. Explain that Harriet is having a friend to stay. Boldly he suggests he should come over and lunch at Vile Cottage instead. Pushy bastard.

Saturday arrives. I have decided to offer pizza and chips to everybody. If my personal eccentricities have failed to arouse the fellow's interest my culinary arts certainly won't.

"Promise you won't do any snogging, Mum! Ugh!"

Assure her I have not the slightest desire for even a peck on the cheek from Mr Campbell, and I'm sure he finds me quite vile.

We drive many miles to pick up Sam, who preserves a Sphinx-like decorum. On arrival at Vile Cottage they disappear to beautify themselves. I peel spuds for real chips, unwrap pizza and read the paper. So indifferent have I grown to the idea of James Campbell that I don't even bother to sniff my armpits in his honour.

When he arrives, however, he envelops me in an embrace and kisses me on the lips with sudden fervour. His skin smells so unexpectedly delightful it takes my breath away. Pheromone thingies. Has his sap finally started to rise?

"How are you, Dulcie?" he asks, with tender concern.

At this promising moment Harriet and Sam clatter downstairs decked out like courtesans at carnival, hoping to pick up a couple of bishops for the weekend. James lets go of me, with strange reluctant air at which my poor old menopausal ducts summon up their energy for one last crusade.

"Pizza and chips!" he salivates at my pizza whereas he toyed limply, weeks ago, with my coulis. So bloody there Delia! "What a wonderful woman you are!"

Astonished by this praise. Despite the obvious attractions of the pubescent courtesans, he still seems to be looking at me quite a lot, and without repulsion or even his habitual indifference.

I offer Sam more pizza, salad, coke, chocolate cake afterwards, etc., which she condescends to accept without acknowledgement. Harriet follows me into the kitchen and hisses, "Why doesn't she say please and thank you, the cow! I hate her now! And she said I had acne! I don't want to go upstairs with her afterwards I want to stay here with you!"

"You can't! You said you liked her!"

"Well I don't! And you said you didn't like him!"

"Well I've changed my mind!"

Shoo girls upstairs and just as I turn to face James, the phone rings. It is Aunt Elspeth enquiring after my social life. Extensive reassurance seems unavoidable, and whilst I am about it, he does all the washing up.

Just as I ring off, a blast of TV noise bursts from the sitting room. I find Sam drooping picturesquely on the sofa. Enquire where Harriet is. Sam shrugs. I run upstairs and attempt unsuccessfully to bribe Harriet to be nice to her. Harriet refuses, declares she has a headache, insists I drive Sam home, and dives under her duvet. Descend and acquaint James with the situation at which he offers to scrub the algae off my old path with his stiff broom while I am away. Whatever next?

Apologise to Sam for Harriet's sudden indisposition and drive her home.

"Thank you very much for having me," she says with synthetic delight, under her ma's eagle eye. Wonder if I shall ever be able to say the same to James.

1 March

On the way home I encounter the farmer's Landrover in a narrow part of the lane, and stop to ask how he is. He replies hopping mad and ready for murder. It appears six of his cattle have just been returned from the slaughterhouse because they were 'too muddy' and a consignment of lambs because they were 'too wet'.

He identifies the problem as a Euro-vet of German origin installed at the abattoir who vetoed his sturdy British cattle on spurious EEC grounds. "A little bit o'mud?" he roars, "what do they ******* expect? They're cattle ent they? I don't keep them on ******* Axminster."

He declares that the Referendum Party offers the only hope and I do not dare to disagree, only affirming that I voted to stay out in '74. This used to be a useful boost to one's credentials, but is increasingly nowadays only a way of showing one's age. We deplore all foreigners, bullfights, etc., and part exhilarated.

As I drive the last mile, I wonder how long it will be before it becomes a kilometre and a bit. Then cricket teams will have to be reduced to ten members and silly mid-off renamed something less patronising. Grind my teeth at the thought of the Eurocrass, although wishing with some fervour that I was in Assisi, Tavira, Cadiz, or St Maximin-de-la-Sainte-Baume, though not sure about Baden-Baden.

I hope they keep their bland, sterilised Euro mitts off our currency – the only one to feature a tennis player. Take two ten-pound notes, fold one in half to expose only the brow of Charles Dickens, superimpose it upon the bottom half of the Queen's face, and what do you have? John McEnroe. I expect you could be thrown in the Tower for suggesting such a thing four hundred years ago.

Arrive at Vile Cottage to find James Campbell playing Scrabble with Harriet, and losing gallantly.

"James lets me use rude words!" she cries in ecstasy.

"I've got all that algae off your path," he smiles, "and I'm hatching a plan to transform your garden into a little orchard. Sit down, I'll make you a cup of tea . . . if you like?"

Slump gratefully onto kitchen chair, and inform him I am too broke to afford landscape gardening.

"Oh, I wouldn't dream of charging for it," he beams. "You've been very good to me, you know. It'll be a labour of love. You're sitting on an acre of exquisite possibility, Dulcie." This is the nicest thing anyone has ever said about my arse.

Wonder if 'you've been very good to me' is Campbell speak for I fancy you. And wonder if the love he'd be labouring with would be directed at myself or my acre of wilderness. Remark that he seems in good spirits and wonder if the arrival of March has dispelled his SAD.

"Well, it's that or the Prozac," he grins.

Harriet sips her milk with paralysing slowness, watching us avidly for any signs of middle-aged foreplay. James's organic corduroys creak restlessly. His strange moss-coloured eyes range freely over my crow's feet. Our dalliance, if that's what it is, could well qualify for the Soil Association symbol.

"Mummy," Harriet remembers a grudge, "why can't I go to Majorca with Daddy and Elaine at Easter? Snot fair!" They have issued invitation to Henry only, assuring Harriet it will be her turn next time. Diverted at the thought of Spouse going to Majorca – one of the many places at which, in the past, he has sneered. Suggest that Harriet might find consolation in the video of *Sense and Sensibility*, at which she runs off salivating at the thought of Willoughby.

James Campbell's more of a Colonel Brandon. Big, well-used hands, too marked with toil for the EEC.

"I was wondering," he murmurs, "if you'd like to—" The phone rings. It is my agent, informing me that the Germans have bought the rights to one of my books, and this means an extra £1,500 or so within a month or two. Darling old Germans! I take it all back. Sod the pound! Give me the mark. I expect we can have just as much fun with their banknotes. With Beethoven's scowl and bad hair and Kohl's jowls you could make -- well, yours truly, to be honest.

8 March

"Dulcie? This is Alice. Look, you must be bored to death out there in the country. Saskia and I were wondering if you'd like to do a house-swap with us at Easter."

Wonder why she never suggested this when she was renting villas in Capri, St Lucia, etc., only now her accommodation has dwindled to a semi in Enfield. Express gratitude and promise to consider offer, though privately convinced the best thing about Enfield is Harry.

It's not that I don't fancy a break. I'm gasping for it. Jealous up to here of Spouse's trip to Majorca. Aunt Elspeth rings from Kirkwhinnie, on a bad line.

"Och, Dulcie, it's a bitterr wind cszak!" she cries. "I'm so worried about you! Now listen, dearr: I was going to leave you a little csakcsakcsak no point in waiting till I csakcsak might as well have it now. My sister Mairi's got a daughter-in-law Lesley and she's got a little house on the West Coast csakcsaxckxaxakka book you and Harriet in csakazzakka vacancy in the gap before Eastercsakka."

Understand dimly that the aunt is offering me a free holiday on the west coast. Remember Oban, with a shiver. Still, it'll be somewhere else: a different, more exotic shade of grey. It'll make a change, being buffeted by sea spray instead of our usual pesticide-laden zephyrs. Express gratitude. Aunt promises she will send the details.

Ring off and look out of window. James Campbell is imposing himself, stone-age style, on my brambles. He is making me an orchard all of my own. Feel tender and put on kettle. He comes in, throws off his suede gauntlets and accepts a steaming mug of tea. Violent exercise has given his manly features a glow and raised his pheromone level to Cartland danger point. Any minute now his profile will go chiselled.

Thank him for his efforts, and remark that spring has brought a sparkle to his eye.

"I'm always hopeless in the winter," he admits, "and this has been the worst few months of my life. You've been my port in a storm, Dulcie." Assure him he can drop anchor in my bay any time. Heart begins to quiver strangely. He has not kissed me since a half-hearted smooch in mid-December and I'd assumed he'd thought the better of it.

"I'm no use with women," he declares suddenly. "I suppose what I'm trying to say is I like you a lot. The trouble is, Dulcie, you scare me stiff." He makes a helpless little shrugging gesture which somehow pierces my heart. Suddenly I realise it's my profile that has gone chiselled. He's the one awed by my authority, my macho swagger and *that's the way he likes it*. Bloody Nora! Stride over and insert myself masterfully into his big, scared arms.

A Beethoven kiss ensues. It goes on forever, and all the sweeter for not being adulterous. At least, not all that adulterous by my standards.

"Go on," he murmurs when we finally surface, "you've got to take me in hand and do what you want with me."

Since it's two hours before Harriet arrives back from school, I oblige him in his tree-surgeon's thornproof gear.

Afterwards he reveals that he's rented a little cottage on Tresco and wants nothing more than to spend a fortnight in it with me. Alas, I am committed to Oban.

"But it'll be bloody freezing there!" he cries in dismay.

Agree that it seems a crying shame to have to take separate holidays so soon after coming to an understanding upon the kitchen table.

"Never mind," he says, kissing me on even my deepest wrinkles, "parting makes the heart grow fonder."

Harriet comes home; James departs. I pace about throbbing faintly, cursing aunt's rogue generosity and cringing at the thought of a fortnight Mulling things over on the Firth of Lorne.

Next day details arrive and I discover that I was deceived by the bad line and that Aunt Elspeth is not sending us to the West Coast of Scotland, but the West Coast of Barbados. Oh all right then, auntie: twist my arm.